Until the
Darkness
Comes

Kevin Brooks was born in Exeter, Devon, in 1959. He studied psychology and philosophy in Birmingham and cultural studies in London. He spent much of his early life writing and recording music, and later turned to painting and sculpting. He worked as a civil servant, a crematorium handyman, a hotdog vendor at London Zoo, a post office counter clerk, a petrol station attendant, and a call centre operator.

Since 2002 he has written eleven novels for teenagers and has won several awards, including the Canongate Prize for New Writing, the Branford Boase Award, the North East Book Award, and the Angus Book Award. In Germany, his books have twice won the prestigious Jugendliteraturpreis and he has also been awarded the Buxtehude Bulle and the Golden Bookworm.

A Dance of Ghosts, his first novel for adults, was published in 2011. He lives in North Yorkshire with his wife Susan.

Also by Kevin Brooks

A Dance of Ghosts

Kevin Brooks

Until the Darkness Comes

arrow books

Published by Arrow Books 2012

2 4 6 8 10 9 7 5 3 1

First published in Great Britain in 2012 by
Arrow Books
Random House, 20 Vauxhall Bridge Road,
London SW1V 2SA

www.randomhouse.co.uk

Addresses for companies within The Random House Group Limited can be found
at: www.randomhouse.co.uk/offices.htm

The Random House Group Limited Reg. No. 954009

A CIP catalogue record for this book
is available from the British Library

ISBN 9780099553823

The Random House Group Limited supports The Forest Stewardship Council
(FSC®), the leading international forest certification organisation. Our books
carrying the FSC label are printed on FSC® certified paper. FSC is the only
forest certification scheme endorsed by the leading environmental organisations,
including Greenpeace. Our paper procurement policy can be found at
www.randomhouse.co.uk/environment

MIX
Paper from
responsible sources
FSC® C016897

Typeset in Stempel Garamond by Palimpsest Book Production Limited
Falkirk, Stirlingshire
Printed and bound by CPI Group (UK) Ltd, Croydon, CR0 4YY

For Jess, our beloved friend and saviour.
Your head will always rest in our laps.

Until the Darkness Comes

1

They came out of the house together, mother and daughter. The mother was thirty-seven years old, the daughter eighteen. They were arguing. I couldn't hear what they were saying because I was sitting in a bus shelter about forty yards up the street, and a cold hard wind was blowing in from the sea, drowning out the sounds of their voices. But as the mother glanced impatiently at her watch and opened the door of an old Ford Escort parked outside the house, and the daughter stayed on the doorstep angrily pulling up the hood of her coat, it wasn't hard to guess what the argument was about.

I don't have time to give you a lift, OK?

It'll only take five minutes.

I haven't got five minutes.

Fuck's sake, Mum. I'm going to be late—

And whose fault is that?

They both looked older than they were, tired and worn out before their time – tired of the same old arguments, tired of each other, tired of everything. It was too hard, this life. It ground you down, day after day . . .

It turned your heart to stone.

The mother paused for a moment, looking back at her daughter – *why does it always have to be like this?* – but

1

the daughter was blanking her now, avoiding her gaze, staring hard-eyed at nothing.

The mother shook her head, got in the car, and drove off up the street.

Her name was Serina Mayo.

As the Escort approached the bus shelter – the engine coughing, blue-grey exhaust fumes billowing in the wind – I instinctively lowered my eyes and pretended to read the newspaper in my lap, but then, almost immediately, remembering where I was and what I was doing, I raised my eyes again and gazed quite openly at the car. I didn't have to worry about my cover being blown. I didn't *have* a cover. Not today. I didn't need one. Even if Serina did notice me watching her – which, given the faraway look in her eyes, was highly unlikely – she wouldn't think anything of it. She didn't know who I was. She'd never seen me before. She'd have no reason to suspect that I was watching her. All she'd see was a somewhat dishevelled forty-year-old man, with a week's growth of beard and a bandaged hand, sitting in a bus shelter watching the cars pass by.

I watched her car pass by.

I watched her.

Serina Mayo.

She had dyed black hair, pulled back tight and tied in a ponytail. Her lips were thin, her eyes heavily made-up, her mouth set hard in a permanent scowl. It was a harsh face, dark and brittle, the skin lined and cracked like the varnish

2

on a dusty old portrait. It was the face of a once beautiful woman who'd suffered too much, too young.

The car passed by, taking Serina with it.

I watched it go, coughing on the exhaust fumes. It slowed down at the end of the street, backfired once, then turned left and disappeared round a corner.

I lit a cigarette.

Serina Mayo . . .

The mother . . .

In 1991, at the age of eighteen, Serina had an affair with my father. My father was forty-seven years old at the time. In February 1992, he locked himself in his office at home, drank most of a full bottle of whisky, and shot himself in the head.

The daughter . . .

Her name was Robyn.

She was walking away down the street now, struggling against the wind. Her hooded head was bowed down, her arms crossed over her midriff, keeping her zipperless coat closed.

I got to my feet, lit a cigarette, and followed her.

It was around ten o'clock in the morning and the streets were quiet. Working people had gone to work, the postman had been and gone, the school run was over. In a place like this, nothing much would happen now until lunchtime.

As I approached the Mayos' house, I crossed the road for a closer look. It was a small terraced house, the pale-yellow paintwork faded and flaking, the windowsills rotten and cracked. There was no front garden, not even a yard. The front door opened directly onto the pavement. Which meant that as I walked past the house, all I had to do was turn my head and gaze through the downstairs window, and I could see directly into the sitting room. There wasn't a lot to see – settee, armchair, TV, bookshelves . . . framed seascapes hung on the walls. It was just a sitting room.

I carried on walking.

Robyn had reached the end of the street now and was crossing over a junction and heading off to the left. I wasn't familiar with the streets round here, and I didn't know where she was going, so I picked up my pace and hurried after her. When I got to the junction, I was just in time to see her turning right off another terraced street into a narrow lane that, as far as I could tell, would lead her across to the caravan park.

I paused for a moment, thinking things through.

The caravan park would be almost deserted at this time of year. Even in the height of summer, it wouldn't be all that busy. But now, at the tail end of October, any tourists would be long gone, and the only people left in the park would be . . .

Who?

Locals?

Islanders?

Why would *any*one want to stay in a caravan at this time of year?

I didn't know.

All I knew was that I could only see part of the caravan park from here, so if I stayed where I was I might lose

4

sight of Robyn. But if I went after her, there was a fairly good chance that she'd see me – a stranger, a lone man, following her into the park – and I didn't want to give her any cause for alarm. She might even decide to confront me, and I didn't want that either.

Not yet anyway.

I gazed over at the caravan park again. It was set back about four hundred yards from the beach, its southern edge bordered by a narrow strip of scrubland and ditches. Between the caravan park and the beach, a small public car park gave access to an open area known as the country park, which was basically just a sloping field with hedged pathways on either side, a covered bandstand in the middle, and a steep flight of wooden steps at the end that led down to the beach. In the summer months, the country park was the place for picnics and kite-flying and occasional brass-band performances, but now it was just another windswept emptiness.

An emptiness that offered an unblocked view of the caravan park.

Robyn was entering the park now. She still had her head bowed down, and it was clear from the way she was threading confidently through the caravans and trailers that she knew exactly where she was going.

I watched her for a moment or two, still unsure what to do.

Stay here and hope that I didn't lose sight of her?

Or cut down the little track to my right that led to the country park?

Whatever I did, it didn't really matter.

I didn't know what I was doing anyway.

I crossed the road and headed down the track.

Hale Island lies just off the coast of Essex, about ten miles south of Hey. It's only a small place, about four miles long and two miles wide at its broadest point, and it's joined to the mainland by a short causeway known as the Stand, a narrow road that bridges the Blackdown estuary. Most of the time you wouldn't know it's a causeway, and you wouldn't know it's an island either, because most of the time the estuary is just a vast stretch of reeds and brown ooze. But when there's a flood tide and the estuary rises a yard or so above the road, and nothing can pass until the tide goes out again . . . then you know it's an island.

The track led me out into the potholed car park at the top of the sloping field, and as I crossed the car park, scanning the rows of caravans and trailers up ahead, I couldn't see any sign of Robyn. A fine rain had begun to fall, a thin silver drizzle that drifted in the wind like spider silk, and the predominantly white roofs of the caravans were shining dully in the sinking light.

I shielded my eyes and gazed around the caravan park again.

Nothing.

No movement, no sign of life.

I looked over my shoulder. Apart from a lone Volvo estate with blankets and a dog basket in the back, the car park was empty.

No movement, no sign of life.

Nothing.

I turned back to the caravan park, lit another cigarette, and waited.

Waiting, watching . . .

I'm good at it.

It's what I do.

I wait and I watch.

It's not much of a life . . .

But it's what I do.

I closed my eyes for a second or two and went back to the moment when Robyn had come out of the house with Serina. It was the first time I'd seen her – the first time I'd seen either of them – and since then Robyn had been walking away from me, with the hood of her coat pulled up, so all I really had to go on was that very first glimpse of her coming out of the house.

But that was enough.

I studied the picture of her in my mind. On the surface, she looked like the young girl she was – fashionably tattooed and pierced, underdressed in a thin white parka over a tight white vest and low-slung track pants . . . blonde hair, white teeth, red lips, smoky eyes. But just below the surface, beneath the veneer of the ordinary young girl, Robyn was something else. Hollow-eyed and gaunt, her dyed-blonde hair dull and brittle, her pretty face cast with the same harsh beauty as her mother's . . .

She was a junky.

She looked like a junky, she walked like a junky. The bowed head, the tightly crossed arms, the blind determination to get where she was going . . .

7

Junky.

I was sure of it.

I could have been wrong, of course – it wouldn't have been the first time – and I really hoped that I was, but as I opened my eyes and saw Robyn coming out of a dirty white caravan at the lower end of the park, I knew straight away that I wasn't. She'd changed. She wasn't all tensed up and tight any more, she was loose and relaxed . . . kind of floaty and sleepy-looking. And she was smiling too. Smiling to herself, smiling at the world, smiling dopily at the bare-chested man who was standing in the doorway of the caravan. Tall and muscled, with long greasy hair and biker tattoos, he was in his mid- to late twenties. He smiled at Robyn as she turned and waved goodbye to him, but as she did a little pirouette and began walking away, his smile disappeared like a light going out. He watched her for a moment, his eyes cold and empty, then he wiped his nose with the back of his hand, spat on the ground, and closed the caravan door.

I turned my attention back to Robyn.

She was heading in my direction now, slowly making her way towards a narrow pathway that crossed the scrubland and led up to the car park. I waited a moment, idly looking around, then I casually put my hands in my pockets and wandered off down the field.

I was nothing, nobody.

I wasn't worth noticing.

I was just a lonely middle-aged man, wandering around on his own, looking at stuff, idly passing the time of day . . .

That's all I was.

Nothing to worry about.

Nothing to fear.

Not that Robyn would be particularly afraid or worried about *any*thing just now. Not if I was right, and she'd just had a hit of something. She'd be lost in her own little bubble, disconnected from the rest of the world, safe and warm and happy. And I knew that I had no right to feel anything about that. Whatever Robyn did to herself, whatever life or non-life she chose, it was nothing to do with me. And even if it was . . .

It wasn't.

And who the fuck was I to talk anyway? I wasn't exactly—

Shut up, John, the voice in my heart said. *Just concentrate on what you're doing.*

'I don't *know* what I'm doing,' I muttered.

Well, there's *a surprise*.

I'd reached the bandstand in the middle of the field now, and so far I'd resisted the temptation to look back and see where Robyn was going. I guessed it was probably OK to look now, but I took my time anyway, just in case – stopping at the bandstand, taking out my cigarettes, pausing to gaze out at the sea. The tide was out, the grey sands of the beach merging into the slick brown ooze of mudflats. Flocks of waders were stalking in the mud – long-legged birds, poking and searching, scything their beaks through the mud – and just off the shore a fishing boat was puttering along through the rain. Further out, I could just make out the low black outline of a container ship inching silently across the horizon. Heading for Harwich, I guessed.

I lit my cigarette and slowly turned round.

I couldn't see Robyn at first, and for a moment I thought I'd lost her. But then, as I carried on looking around, gradually widening my search, I saw a flash of white over to my right, at the edge of the field – a slim hooded figure ducking through a gap in a hedge. She disappeared for a moment, dipping down out of sight, and then she reappeared about ten yards further on. I was pretty sure now that she was heading for a raised dirt pathway that followed a little creek all the way along to the easternmost end of the island. I carried on watching her for a while, just to make sure, but when I saw her climbing some wooden steps set into the bank of the pathway, I knew I was right. I still didn't know where she was going – or why it mattered, or what I was doing – but I knew that the pathway ran parallel to the beach . . .

And, again, that was good enough for me.

I turned round and made my way down to the beach.

The pathway and the beach are separated by a broad spread of saltmarshes, a thick green carpet of ground-hugging plants dotted with countless boggy pools fringed with reeds and rushes, so although I was plainly visible to Robyn as I walked along the beach, there was enough of a barrier between us for her to happily ignore me. And besides, she wasn't really paying attention to anything anyway, just dawdling along the pathway, lost in her own timeless world.

It hadn't taken long for me to draw level with her, pass her by, and then gradually slow down so that I was matching her pace but deliberately keeping in front of her.

So even if she did happen to notice me, she wouldn't think I was following her.

Way up ahead of me I could see two coated figures and a golden retriever ambling along the shore – a middle-aged couple, I guessed, they probably owned the Volvo in the car park – but, apart from that, the beach was deserted. All I could see as I looked into the distance was a long stretch of sand and shingle, the glimmering ooze of the mudflats, and the silent grey emptiness of the sea. And all I could hear was the moaning wind and the ever-present voice in my heart.

Are you all right, John?

'Not really,' I said quietly.

It'll be OK. You just need to get some rest.

'Yeah . . .'

I glanced over at Robyn. She'd stopped to light a cigarette, turning her back to the wind, lowering her head, cupping the lighter in her hands . . . *click, click, click*. I watched her for a moment, waiting for her to lift her head and blow out a cloud of smoke, then I pulled up my coat collar and walked on.

I used to visit Hale Island with my parents when I was a kid. Sunday afternoons, we'd drive down from Hey, park in the car park, and then spend an hour or two just strolling along the beach – Mum and Dad walking together, talking quietly to each other, while I went off on my own, scuffing along the strandline, kicking up junk, looking for jewels – tropical beans, cuttlefish bones, mermaid's purses . . .

I was happy then.

And now . . . ?

There didn't seem to be any jewels any more. No tropical beans, no cuttlefish bones, no mermaid's purses . . . just plastic bottles, bits of polystyrene, food wrappers, carrier bags. Nothing worth picking up. Not for me, anyway. Maybe if I was a kid now, *these* things would be my jewels. Plastic jewels, jewels of rubber and polythene . . . polystyrene pearls.

Or maybe I was just remembering stuff that never happened anyway.

Maybe there never were any jewels on the beach . . .

And I was never happy.

By the time I was nearing the end of the beach, and Robyn was approaching the end of the pathway, I began to wonder what I was going to do if she just kept on going and then cut down to the beach and started walking back in my direction. What would I do when we passed? Would I say anything to her? Would I stop and talk to her? Or would I just smile and nod my head, as I had with the Volvo couple and their dog a few minutes earlier? Smile, nod, and walk on by.

I didn't know.

I couldn't decide.

In the end, though, I didn't have to.

Because just as I reached the old stone pillbox that, for me, had always been the signal that the end of the beach was near, I glanced over and saw Robyn disappearing off the pathway and heading down to a little wooden bridge that spanned the creek. As her hooded head bobbed out of sight, I tried to think where she could be going. What was on the other side of the creek? Not much, I vaguely remembered. A few remote houses, a small farm or two, maybe a church. This was the east of the island, the wilder side. Visitors and tourists generally keep to the west side, the village side, where the sand is soft and the streets and the shops are never too far away. But down here the only people you're likely to see are locals, fishermen, dog walkers . . . the occasional anorak with a metal detector. And kids sometimes, at night, doing their stuff in the dunes . . . sex, drugs, whatever.

I couldn't see Robyn now.

She'd gone.

I didn't know where.

And there was no point in trying to find out. If I wanted to follow her now, I'd either have to cut across the salt-marshes or run along to the end of the beach and then double back along the path to the point where she'd disappeared. I knew there *were* tracks across the saltmarshes, but I also knew that unless you know exactly where the tracks are, there's a good chance you'll end up getting stuck in the mud. Or worse. And as for running along to the end of the island . . . well, I really didn't feel like running just then.

I was too tired.

Too lifeless.

And it didn't matter anyway.

I'd done what I'd set out to do. I'd seen Serina and Robyn. I knew what they looked like. And I had a *sense* of them now – who they were, what they were, what kinds of lives they were living . . .

I lit a cigarette and looked out over the beach. At the end of the island, shrouded in a mist of rain, I could just make out the Point, a slim finger of shingle that juts out from the beach and is bounded by the sea on one side and ancient mudflats on the other. Beyond the mudflats, in the mouth of the estuary, the fishing boat I'd seen earlier was skirting a small wooded island about half a mile from shore.

A young woman was standing at the end of the Point, looking out over the mudflats. She didn't seem to be doing anything, she was just standing there, gazing in silence, the wind ruffling her hair . . .

I wondered if she might know where Robyn had gone. I could try asking her, couldn't I? She probably wouldn't mind. I could just walk up to her and say, 'Excuse me, I'm sorry to bother you, but—'

No, John, Stacy said to me. *Just leave her.*

'Why?'

She's sad. She doesn't want to talk to anyone. Just leave her.

'OK . . .'

It doesn't matter where Robyn has gone anyway, does it?

'No.'

You've done what you set out to do. You've seen her. You know what she looks like.

'She looks a bit like Dad.'

She looks a bit like you.

'You think so?'

Yeah . . .

'Do you think she's Dad's daughter?'

14

Possibly.
'So she *could* be my sister?'
Half-sister.
'Half-sister.'
Yeah, she could be.
'Shit.'
You're tired, John. You need to go back to the hotel and get some rest.

I looked over at the Point again, looking for the sad young woman. But she wasn't there any more. She'd gone.

The wind was getting up.

The rain was turning cold.

I buttoned my coat and headed back to the hotel.

2

Stacy was my wife . . . Stacy Craine. She was my wife. Seventeen years ago, on 13 August 1993, she was raped and murdered by a man called Anton Viner. Two weeks later, I shot Viner in the head and disposed of his body in a crematorium furnace.

Stacy has never left me.

She's always in my heart.

She'd been there five days ago when DCI Mick Bishop had shown up at my office in Hey and suggested that I leave town for a while.

'How long's a while?' I'd asked him.

'Ten days . . . couple of weeks. Just until it all blows over.'

'It's all going to just "blow over", is it?'

'It will if you do what I tell you.'

I looked at him. 'So I just go away for a while, and when I come back . . . everything's just as it was?'

'That's right.'

'And you can live with that, can you?'

He smiled. 'It's not going to kill me.'

'What about the business?'

'What business?'

'My business.'

'What about it?'

'Well, if I go away for a couple of weeks—'

'Just shut it down, for fuck's sake. I mean, it's not as if the world's going to stop turning without your fucking private investigation business, is it?' He grinned at me. 'What's the worst that can happen? You lose a couple of insurance fraud cases? You miss out on the opportunity to catch another DVD pirate?'

'It pays the bills,' I said.

'You need money? I can let you have—'

'I don't need your money.'

'So what's your problem?'

'Nothing . . .' I'd sighed, shaking my head. 'Nothing at all.'

Just do it, Stacy had told me later that night. *You might as well. Just close down for a couple of weeks, go somewhere nice, and try to forget about everything. You never know . . . you might even enjoy it.*

I wasn't sure that I was going to *enjoy* being on Hale Island, and it probably wasn't the kind of place that Stacy had meant when she'd told me to 'go somewhere nice'. But I'd been thinking a lot about my father recently – his past, his history, his suicide – and when I'd got in touch with Cal Franks, my nephew-in-law and occasional colleague, and I'd asked him to find out what he could about Serina Mayo, and he'd found out that she lived on Hale Island, *and* that she had an eighteen-year-old daughter . . . well, I'd just thought to myself, why not?

17

Pack a bag, book a hotel, close down the business . . .
Jump on a bus . . .
Why not?
Just go.
Try to forget about everything.
Why not?
There was a lot to forget.

The hotel I was staying in was a rackety old place called Victoria Hall. It was the kind of hotel that in its day had probably been quite grand, but over the years, as its business had declined, its grandeur had gradually faded. It was still perfectly habitable, and from a distance it still looked fairly impressive, but up close you could tell straight away that its best days were long gone. The weather-beaten walls, the peeling paintwork, the creaking wooden floors, the doors that didn't shut properly, the stale and musty atmosphere . . .

It was hardly The Ritz.

But it was close to the village, and it backed onto the beach, and it was relatively cheap. And the rooms were spacious, with double windows that opened out onto a balcony, which meant that I could smoke. But the main reason I'd chosen to stay at Victoria Hall was that I remembered it from my childhood. We used to drive past it on the way home from our Sunday-afternoon trips to the beach, and there was always something about the place that fascinated me . . . I didn't know what it was. I didn't even know that it was a hotel at the time. I just liked looking at it – the big white house with the funny little windows, the tall brick chimneys, the crooked wooden balconies – and I always wondered what it would be like to live there.

And I know that bringing childhood wishes to life is rarely a good idea, because their reality is usually so drab and disappointing, but in this case . . . well, the way I saw it, I was feeling so shitty about everything anyway that a bit of disappointment probably wouldn't make much difference.

It was around 11.30 when I got back to the hotel that day. The white-haired old man who managed the place was sitting behind the reception desk idly reading a newspaper, and when I came in he looked up and smiled at me, his bright old eyes peering over the rims of his reading glasses.

'Good morning, Mr Chandler,' he said. 'Enjoying the weather?'

From the slight twinkle in his eyes, and the almost imperceptible emphasis he gave to the words 'Mr Chandler', I couldn't help thinking that he knew it wasn't my real name. He'd given me the same kind of look when I'd checked in as John Chandler the day before, the kind of look that's as good as a wink – *don't worry, John, your secret's safe with me.*

Or maybe I was just being paranoid.

Maybe I was seeing things that weren't there.

Not that it mattered. The only reason I'd checked in under a false name was that my real name, John Craine, had been in the news for the past week or so, and the whole point of being here was – in Mick Bishop's words – to let things blow over. But even if this old man *did* know who I was, and even if he *did* leak it to the press . . .

Well, so what?

All I'd have to do was pack up and go somewhere else.

'Excuse me,' I said to the old man, going over to the reception desk. 'You haven't got a map of the island, have you?'

He put down his newspaper, reached under the desk, and passed me a photocopied map.

'Thanks,' I said, studying it.

'Is there anything in particular you're looking for, Mr Chandler?'

'Just "John" is fine,' I told him, without looking up. '"Mr Chandler" makes me feel old.'

'Arthur Finch,' he smiled, standing up and offering his hand. 'I *am* old.'

I smiled back and shook his hand, then looked down at the map again, trying to locate the spot where Robyn had left the pathway. The pathway was marked with a dotted line, and as I followed it back from the Point and then scanned the area just north of the creek, the only thing I could see on the map – apart from saltmarshes and a few scattered farms – was a small black cross.

'Is that a church?' I asked Arthur Finch, indicating the symbol.

He angled his head to get a better look. 'Where?'

'There.'

'Ah, right.' He smiled. 'No, it used to be a church, but I'm afraid this map's a little out of date. It's actually a farm shop now.'

'A farm shop?'

He nodded. 'Hale Organics. They sell locally produced meat, home-made cheese, free-range eggs . . . that sort of thing.' He looked at me. 'I can find out their opening times, if you're interested.'

I shook my head. 'Is there anything else around there?'

'What are you looking for, exactly?'

'Nothing really . . .' I smiled at him. 'It's just that it could get a bit boring, you know . . . walking up to the end of the beach every day and then turning round and walking all the way back again.' I shrugged. 'I was just wondering if there was anywhere else I could go, that's all.'

'Well,' he said, turning his attention back to the map. 'You can cross over the creek here, and there's a little path that takes you to the farm shop. There's not a lot else to see around there – a few farms, a bit of woodland – but from the farm shop you could follow the East Road all the way along the coast back to the Stand, and then back along the Coast Road to the village.' He looked at me again. 'It's a fair old walk . . . probably a couple of hours or so. And I wouldn't recommend it unless the weather improves.'

'Right . . .'

'And, of course, there's a lot more to see if you head up towards the west of the island.'

'Yeah,' I said, picking up the map. 'I might just do that.'

'Is there anything else I can help you with?'

'Not just now, thanks.'

'Will you be dining here this evening?'

'I don't know.'

'Not to worry,' he said, smiling. 'I doubt if we're going to be fully booked.'

I nodded, suddenly feeling incredibly tired. Too tired to speak. Too tired to smile. Too tired to move.

'Well . . .' Arthur Finch said hesitantly. 'As I said, if you need anything else . . .'

I just nodded again, hoping that I didn't look as bad as I felt. I could tell from the way the old man was looking at me that he was beginning to suspect that something wasn't quite right, and I knew that if I didn't move now, or say something else, he was going to start asking himself some serious questions – *what's he doing? why's he just standing there? what the hell's the* matter *with him?*

So I took a deep breath, placing both hands on the edge of the desk to steady myself, and then – forcing the shape of a smile to my face – I mumbled something vague enough to mean anything, nodded again, and shoved myself off from the desk.

My head was gone now.

My legs weighed too much.

I'd forgotten how to walk.

But somehow my instincts, and the desire to avoid the embarrassment of falling over, kept me going – one step, another step . . . just keep moving – and by the time I was halfway across the lobby I'd almost got the hang of walking again, and I probably didn't look *too* much like a zombie. It was tempting to look back over my shoulder and smile casually at Arthur, just to show him how normal I was, but even the thought of it – walking *and* looking over my shoulder – made me feel dizzy. So I just carried on as I was – one step, another step . . . one step, another step . . .

You can do it.

Luckily my room was on the ground floor, so I didn't have to worry about stairs, all I had to do was keep going in a straight line – across the lobby, through the door at the end, past the staircase, along the corridor . . . one step, another step . . .

I could do it.

Just keep going . . .

As I reached the end of the lobby and pushed open the door, someone on the other side pulled it open, and I staggered through and bumped into a man in a red waterproof coat.

'Sorry,' I muttered, keeping my head down and stepping unsteadily to one side.

'No problem,' the man said. Then, 'Hey, are you OK?'

I felt his hand on my arm then, a helping hand, and I looked up at him. He had a beard, and glasses. A kindly face.

'You all right, buddy?' he said.

American.

'Yeah . . .' I mumbled. 'Yeah, thanks . . . I'm just . . . yeah, I'm fine.'

He let go of my arm and stepped back, looking genuinely concerned. A woman was standing beside him, also dressed in a red waterproof coat, and behind them both, watching me curiously from the foot of the staircase, was a gum-chewing teenage girl. Wife and daughter, I assumed.

'You need any help?' the man asked me.

23

'No . . . thanks.' I smiled at him. 'It's just a . . . a migraine . . .'

'Oh, yeah,' he said, nodding knowingly. 'They can be real bad.' He glanced at the woman next to him. 'Your sister suffers from migraines, doesn't she, honey?'

The woman nodded, looking at me. 'She has to lie down in a darkened room.'

'Yeah, me too . . .'

'OK,' the man said. 'Well, we won't keep you . . . you take it easy, OK?'

I nodded. 'Thanks . . .'

'See you later.'

'Yeah.'

As they headed off through the door into the lobby, the teenage girl glanced back at me and smiled. Dressed in a black puffa jacket over a big white hoody, and a short denim skirt over skinny black jeans, I guessed she was about fourteen or fifteen. She had earplugs in, the wires snaking out from under her hood, and as her still-smiling face disappeared through the door, I wondered what she was listening to . . .

Something new?

Something I wouldn't like?

Something I'd never heard of?

And I wondered how I'd feel if *I* was her father, and I didn't like the music she listened to . . . what would I do?

You wouldn't do anything.

'I'd feel old.'

You are *old.*

'She smiled at me, Stace. Did you see her?'

24

Yeah.

'She smiled at me.'

I know.

It wasn't a migraine . . . I've never had a migraine in my life. But it's easier to tell someone that you're suffering from a migraine than to tell them that you're sinking down into the black place. And that's all it was – the deadening fatigue, the weight of tiredness, the void in my head – it was the black place, the fog of depression that creeps up on me every now and then and drapes me in darkness for a day or two.

It had been stirring inside me for a while now, threatening to rise up and drag me down, and usually when I feel it coming I just go to bed, close my eyes, and let it happen. It's not a nice experience, and sometimes it can get really bad, but it's been with me for a long time now, and although it's not the kind of thing that you can ever really get used to, at least I know what it is. I know how it works. And because I know that it's not going to *kill* me, and that it's *not* going to last for ever, I don't normally bother trying to fight it.

But this time . . .

Well, this time, when I'd felt it coming on, it just hadn't been *convenient* to close my eyes and let it happen. The case I'd been working on had fucked me up. Bad stuff had happened. People I cared about had been hurt . . . and I'd had to deal with that hurt. Theirs, mine . . . I couldn't just close my eyes to it, I had to deal with it. And I can't deal with anything when I'm in the black place. I can't do

25

anything at all. So I'd had to keep it at bay. And that meant self-medication – alcohol, drugs, whatever it takes. Alcohol to drown it, smother it, numb it. Speed and cocaine to lift me above it. More alcohol to let me sleep, more speed to wake me up . . .

More of everything . . . just to keep going.

And the more you keep going, the worse it is when you stop.

So you don't stop, you just keep going.

You shuffle into your hotel room at 11.45 in the morning, you close the door, lock it, and shuffle over to the table by the wall. You uncap the bottle of whisky on the table and half-fill a glass tumbler, take a long drink, shudder, then top up the glass and head over to the double windows. You open the windows, step out onto the balcony, and light a cigarette. It's cold, you shiver. You drink more whisky. You're so tired, so weak, you can hardly stand up. You lean against the balcony rail and look out over the beach, the dull skies, the blue-grey sea . . . the emptiness. You hear the mournful cry of seabirds, the distant clink of rigging, the wind in the air . . .

You smoke.

You drink.

The black place is coming.

Let it come.

You're ready for it now.

You finish your cigarette, finish your drink, go back inside and pour yourself another. You go back out to the balcony and light another cigarette. Your hand hurts, the fractured bone throbbing dully in the cold. You think of Cal Franks – hospitalised with a broken leg, a broken arm. And Bridget Moran – a shattered mind, a broken heart . . . a long way from here. You raise your glass and drink to her, and then to Cal . . . and then to yourself.

You take it easy, OK?

The father's voice . . .

The father.

The daughter.

And now you close your eyes to the cold grey world and you see her face again, the daughter's face . . . smiling at you as she goes through the door. And you can see yourself too, standing there looking back at her, wondering what kind of music she's listening to, and whether her father likes it or not . . . but you know in your heart that what you're *really* wondering about is how things might have been . . . if Stacy hadn't died, if the child she was carrying hadn't died inside her . . . you could have been a father. You could have had a daughter. She could have grown up into a gum-chewing teenage girl who listened to music that you didn't like . . .

And that would have been fine.

It would have been . . .

Don't, John. Please . . . don't.

'I can't help it, Stace. I just—'

I know.

'It would have been so good.'

Yeah . . .

'You and me, our daughter—'

It might have been a boy.

'No . . .' I smiled. 'It was a girl. I can see her . . . she's pretty. Just like you.'

Go to bed, John. Finish your drink and go to bed.
'OK.'
You'll be all right.
'Yeah.'
Go on, off you go.
'I love you.'
I know.

I didn't go to bed straight away. I stayed out on the balcony for a while, drinking and smoking, thinking things through . . . good things, bad things, the things I'd done, the things I had to do.

I kept drinking until I couldn't drink any more.

And then I had one more . . .

A final cigarette.

A *final* final drink.

And then I shut the windows, closed the curtains, lay down on the bed, closed my eyes, and let the black place come.

3

I slept almost solidly for about twenty hours, only getting out of bed to use the toilet and smoke a cigarette, and when I finally woke up at around eight o'clock the next morning, I was surprised to find that the worst of the black place had gone. It usually stays with me for at least a couple of days, sometimes a lot longer, and although I was still a long way from feeling all right again – my head was throbbing, my muscles ached, my eyes were stiff with the weight of depression – I knew that I'd had it easy this time.

It was still there though, the black place.

I could feel it inside me.

It had only crawled halfway back into its hole.

It hadn't quite done with me yet.

But for now . . .

I showered and dressed, made myself a cup of coffee, and went out onto the balcony for a cigarette. The beach looked much the same as the day before – cold and grey, the skies clouded over, a gusting wind blowing in from the sea. The only difference today was that the tide wasn't quite so far out, and I could see the ripple of shallow waves lapping quietly over the shimmering ooze of the mudflats.

It was Saturday.

The beach was deserted.

No dog walkers, no fishermen, no one at all.

I finished my cigarette, put on my shoes, and went to get something to eat.

Breakfast was served in a small, dark-panelled room at the front of the hotel. Only three tables were occupied when I went in. A grungy-looking man in a baggy check shirt and ripped jeans was sipping coffee at a single table by the door, an elderly couple were hunched quietly over bowls of porridge in the corner, and the American family – father, mother, daughter – were sitting at the table nearest the window. The mother and father were drinking orange juice, while the daughter was busy with a mobile phone, her thumb skipping rapidly over the keys.

They all glanced up at me as I entered the room.

'Hey,' the father said, smiling. 'How are you feeling today?'

'Yeah, a lot better, thanks.'

'Well, that's good.'

I smiled at him, not sure if I should say anything else, or just sit down at a table. And if I *did* just sit down at a table, should I make an effort to be friendly and sit near the Americans, or should I do what I'd naturally do and sit as far away from them as possible? In the end though, the decision was made for me as a waitress appeared from the kitchen.

'Table for one?' she asked.

I nodded.

She indicated a table by the wall, and by the time I'd sat down and ordered – fried eggs, toast, coffee – and fetched a newspaper from a rack on the wall, the American family had forgotten all about me and were getting ready to leave their table. I sat back, pretending to read the newspaper, and watched them as they put on their coats and gathered their things together. They were all dressed very similarly to the day before – the parents in their red waterproof coats, the girl in her white hoody and puffa jacket – and from the amount of stuff they were putting into various pockets and bags, I guessed they were going out somewhere for the day. The mother was carrying a good-sized shoulder bag that looked fairly heavy, the father had a paperback book in his hand (*A Guide to British Coastal Birds*) and a very expensive-looking camera slung round his neck, and the girl was stuffing all kinds of gadgets into a small black rucksack – iPod, earplugs, headphones, some kind of games console . . . a Nintendo or something.

As they left the table and headed for the door, I looked up and smiled at them again.

'Do you think it's going to rain?' the father asked me.

'Probably,' I said, glancing out of the window.

'Typical English weather, huh?'

I nodded in agreement.

'Well,' he said, slipping the bird book into his pocket. 'If you visit England, I guess you know what you're in for. The weather's all part of the package.'

I nodded again. 'I suppose so . . .'

He looked up as the waitress appeared carrying a plate of fried eggs on toast. 'OK,' he said to me, stepping aside to make room for her. 'Well, we'll leave you to it then.'

'Thanks . . .'

'See you later.'

'Yeah.'

As the three of them trooped out, the waitress set down my plate. She was quite a serious-looking woman, in her late twenties, early thirties maybe. No make-up, mousy-brown hair, dressed in a plain white T-shirt and jeans.

'Careful,' she said. 'The plate's hot.'

'Thanks.'

'Did you want your room cleaned today?'

'Sorry?'

'I was going to do it yesterday afternoon, but your door was locked.'

'Oh, right, yeah . . . I was sleeping. Sorry.'

She shrugged. 'No need to apologise. You can sleep whenever you like.' She smiled then, which kind of surprised me, and the smile momentarily lightened her face. 'I'd sleep all day if I could.'

I realised then that in a hotel like this, particularly in the off season, she probably wasn't *just* a waitress, she was probably everything else too – receptionist, cleaner, administrator, chef . . .

'My room's all right, thanks,' I told her. 'You can leave it until tomorrow if you want.'

'Are you sure?'

'Yeah.'

'Are you OK for towels and stuff?'

'Yeah.'

'All right . . . but if you need anything, just let me know.'

'Thanks.'

'I'm Linda, by the way.'

'John,' I said.

She nodded. 'Enjoy your eggs, John.'

I watched her go back into the kitchen, wondering briefly why she worked here – why would *any*one want to work in a run-down old hotel in the middle of nowhere? – and then I remembered all the nothing jobs that I'd done over the years. I'd had my reasons for doing them, so I guessed that she probably had hers. Not that it was any of my business, of course. And to be perfectly honest, I didn't really care anyway. It was just a thought, that's all.

Just a thought . . .

Eat your breakfast.

There was no salt and pepper on my table. I got up, looked around the other tables, and finally spotted a cruet set on the table by the window. I went over and picked up the salt shaker, and that's when I saw the diary – a small pink notebook with flower stickers on the front and the words *My Diary* embossed in glittery gold lettering. It had been left on the table where the daughter had been sitting, half-hidden under a folded cotton napkin. I picked it up and looked out of the window, not really expecting to see the Americans, but there they were – the three of them standing at the end of the car park, the girl patting her pockets and searching anxiously through her rucksack. I saw her father say something to her, and then I saw her looking back at the hotel, and I raised my hand and waved her diary. She frowned at me for a moment, then her father pointed at me, spoke to her again, and she looked back at me, realising now what had happened. Her father gave her a reassuring smile and put his hand on her shoulder – *go on, run back and get it, we'll wait here for you.* And she set off, hurrying across the car park with a mixture of relief and embarrassment on her face.

I went out into the lobby to meet her.

While I waited at the front door, I noticed that she'd written her name on the front of the diary – *Chelsey Swalenski* – in black felt-tip. Her handwriting was surprisingly childish – the letters not joined up, a little heart symbol in place of the dot on the *i* – and I wondered if I'd overestimated her age. Maybe she wasn't fourteen or fifteen after all. Maybe she was only thirteen, or even younger. Or maybe she just wasn't very good at writing . . .

I looked up as she came through the door.

'Oh, thank you *so* much,' she said, slightly out of breath, glancing at the diary in my hand. 'I thought I'd lost it.'

I passed her the diary. 'You left it on the table.'

'Thank you,' she repeated, her eyes fixed on the notebook.

'It's all right,' I said, smiling. 'I didn't read any of it.'

It was meant to be a joke, but as soon as I'd said it, I wished I hadn't. Because Chelsey was blushing now, and she looked really uncomfortable, and I didn't blame her. If I was a teenage girl and a forty-year-old man had told me that he *hadn't* read my diary, I'd probably feel really uncomfortable too. Even if I didn't actually think that he *had* read it, I'd have the *idea* in my head that he had.

'Sorry,' I said to her. 'I didn't mean—'

'It's OK,' she said, still not looking at me.

'I'm an idiot,' I said.

She glanced up at me, a hint of amusement showing in her pale blue eyes.

'An English idiot,' I added.

She laughed.

I smiled. 'It's all part of the package.'

'What, being an idiot?'

'Yeah, the English are all idiots. We can't help it. It's a genetic thing.'

'Right . . . like a national characteristic?'

'Exactly.'

She wasn't blushing any more, and she looked reasonably comfortable.

'So,' I said, 'are you on holiday here?'

She nodded. 'Kind of . . . my dad's been trying to trace his roots, you know, his British ancestry.'

'What, here? On the island?'

'All over really. We've been to Scotland, Essex, Kent . . . this is our last stop though. Well, we're going to London on Monday, and then flying back on Wednesday.'

'Are you looking forward to going home?'

She shrugged. 'Sort of . . . I mean, I miss my friends and everything, but it's been pretty cool over here . . .' She glanced out through the door, waved at her parents, then turned back to me. 'I'd better get going.'

'Yeah, of course.'

I watched her go, hoping that she'd look over her shoulder at me . . . and she did. A quick wave, a smile, and then she was gone. And I was left standing there, wondering if I'd done the right thing. Maybe I shouldn't have talked to her? Maybe I should have just given her the diary and kept my mouth shut?

Why?

'She probably thinks I'm a creepy old man.'

You're not creepy.

'She doesn't know that, does she? And neither do her parents. I mean, look at me . . . I look like a fucking tramp.'

No, you don't—

'*And* they saw me yesterday when I was shuffling around like a zombie.'

John—

'I wouldn't like it if a zombie-tramp talked to *my* daughter.'

She likes you, John. They *like you.*

'Really?'

Yeah. Now shut up and go and eat your breakfast.

I had no idea how Serina Mayo would react when I told her who I was, and as I left the hotel later that morning and headed off towards her house, I promised myself that whatever she did, however she reacted, I'd accept it without question. If she told me to go away and never bother her again, that's what I'd do. If she pretended that she'd never known my father, I'd apologise for my mistake and leave it at that.

Whatever she wanted . . .

It was up to her.

It had to be.

And that went for Robyn too.

Robyn . . .

The idea that she might be my half-sister was so confusing that I hadn't really been able to think about it rationally . . . in fact, it was such an alien notion that I'd barely been able to think about it at all. Everything about it was simply too much. How would I feel if she really *was* my half-sister? How would I feel if she wasn't? How would she feel about me? It was all so hard to imagine that, up until now, something inside me had just kind of blocked it all out.

But now . . .

Well, now I was turning left into the street where Serina and Robyn lived . . . and I was walking slowly along the pavement towards their house . . . and any minute now I was going to be knocking on their door, or ringing their bell, and everything I'd been blocking out was going to be right there in front of me, and suddenly I wasn't at all sure that I could face it.

I stopped and lit a cigarette.

My hands were shaking.

It was starting to rain.

I stood there for a while, smoking and thinking, and for a moment or two I seriously considered turning round, going back to the hotel, and forgetting all about it. What was the point? What was I hoping to achieve? Serina Mayo was just a woman who'd once had an affair with my father. And her daughter . . . ?

Her daughter might be my father's daughter.

My half-sister.

My blood.

37

No . . . I couldn't just forget that.

I put out my cigarette and carried on down the street.

It took a lot of effort to reach up and knock on their door, but I knew that if I didn't do it now, I might never do it at all. *Just do it*, I told myself. *Don't think about it, just do it.*

I took a breath . . .

And did it.

Knock, knock.

Then I stepped back and waited.

You should have shaved, I found myself thinking. *Or at least combed your hair.*

I ran my fingers through the rain-soaked mess of my hair.

I put my hands in my pockets . . .

Took them out again.

I could hear footsteps inside the house now. Someone was coming.

Shit . . .

I was terrified.

I heard bolts being unlocked, a key turning in the door, and then it opened a few inches – as far as the security chain allowed – and Serina Mayo was peering out warily through the gap.

'Yes?'

'Serina?' I said, doing my best to look friendly.

'What do you want?'

'I'm John Craine,' I told her. 'I think you knew my father . . .'

*

It was obviously – and understandably – quite a shock for her, and for a while she was visibly shaken, but once I'd made it perfectly clear that she didn't have to talk to me if she didn't want to, and that if she wanted me to leave, I would, she gradually began to relax a little. She was still fairly wary as she invited me in and made me a cup of coffee, but I did my best to put her at ease.

'I'm sorry for just turning up unannounced like this,' I said, following her into the sitting room. 'I did think of phoning you first, or writing you a letter or something, but I just thought . . . well, it just felt a bit impersonal.'

'Please,' she said, indicating an armchair by the window. 'Sit down.'

I sat down.

She remained standing. 'I don't suppose there's much point in asking how you found me, is there?'

'What do you mean?'

'You're a private investigator, aren't you?'

'How do you know that?'

She smiled. 'You were on Sky News about a week ago, telling a reporter to fuck off. And there's been all that stuff in the newspapers about the missing girl you found and the man who killed her. I mean, I didn't know for *sure* that you were Jim's son until the police press conference, you know . . . when they started talking about your wife . . .'

'Right . . .'

Serina looked at me. 'And I remember, you know . . . when she was killed. It wasn't long after Jim died, was it?'

I nodded. 'About eighteen months.'

She sighed. 'I always wondered . . .'

39

'What?'

She sat down and took out a packet of cigarettes. 'Do you mind?'

'I'll join you,' I said, reaching for my cigarettes.

She offered me her packet. 'Have one of these.'

We both lit up, and Serina passed me a glass ashtray.

'Jim never liked me smoking,' she said, smiling. 'Sorry, I keep forgetting . . . I shouldn't be calling him Jim—'

'It's all right with me.'

'Are you sure?'

'Yeah.'

She took a long drag on her cigarette. 'God, this is all so weird . . . I mean, I always wondered if you'd show up one day, but I wasn't even sure if you knew about me. And even if you did . . .' She shrugged. 'Well, I suppose I just took it for granted that you'd hate me as much as your mother did—'

'I don't hate you.'

'Why not? I ruined everything—'

'He loved you, didn't he?'

'What makes you say that?'

'It's the truth, isn't it?'

'Well, yes . . . but—'

'It's the only thing that makes sense,' I said. 'I was never really that close to my dad, so I didn't know him all that well, but I know what kind of a man he was. And I know that he'd never have risked his marriage and career for someone who didn't mean anything to him. He just wouldn't . . .'

'He didn't,' Serina said quietly. 'Of course, we both knew

that it wasn't right, for so many different reasons, and we both tried hard to stop it happening, but it was just . . . it was impossible. We loved each other, and there was nothing we could do about it . . .' She shook her head. 'Nothing at all.' She lapsed into silence for a few moments then, just staring at the floor, deep in thought, and when she began speaking again, her voice was a broken whisper. 'It's so hard to explain . . . I mean, I know how it must look – a messed-up eighteen-year-old girl and a middle-aged married man – but it wasn't like that. It really wasn't. Jim didn't take advantage of me or anything, we just . . . we just really liked each other. He was the first person I'd ever met who treated me with respect. He treated me like a *person*. And he *believed* in me too. He was kind, caring . . . he was everything I'd never had. And we didn't do anything *wrong*. I mean, we didn't start seeing each other until after Symons' trial . . .' She paused and looked up at me. 'Do you know about Symons?'

I nodded. My father was a police officer, and he'd met Serina when he was heading up the investigation into a serial paedophile called Mark Symons. Back in the early 1980s, Symons had managed a youth club in Hey that was supposed to provide help for kids with 'problems' – drugs, alcohol, petty crime. The club was run in conjunction with the police and the local authorities, and it wasn't until almost a decade after it had been set up that the allegations against Symons began to emerge. By this time he'd moved up in the world – promoted to a senior management position in 1987, elected as a local councillor a few years later, and in early 1992, just before my father arrested him, he was selected as the prospective parliamentary candidate for Harwich.

Serina had been one of his victims.

I looked at her. 'How old were you at the time?'

'Twelve,' she said, stabbing out her cigarette and lighting another. 'I was twelve years old when that dirty bastard started fucking me . . .'

'Christ . . .'

She shook her head. 'It went on for ages, he fucked up dozens of kids . . . mostly girls, but quite a few boys too. He didn't give a shit. We were all too scared of him to do anything. Even after he was arrested, most of us were still too frightened to come forward. Symons had a lot of powerful friends – politicians, judges, policemen . . .' She looked at me. 'You know Mick Bishop, don't you?'

'Yeah, I know him.'

'He had some kind of connection with Symons. Your father knew about it, and he guessed that Bishop was passing on information about the investigation to Symons, but Jim could never prove it. And the trouble was, the only evidence he had against Symons was the testimonies of the kids he'd abused, and although we weren't kids any more, most of us were still pretty fucked up, so there was a pretty good chance that no one would believe us.'

'How did Dad persuade you to testify?'

She smiled. 'He was just really honest . . . with all of us. He said he couldn't promise us anything, he couldn't *guarantee* that he'd get Symons locked up, but he was confident that if we all stuck together and believed in what we were doing, the truth would come out in the end.' She took a

42

hard drag on her cigarette and breathed out a long stream of smoke. 'Anyway, like I said, me and Jim didn't start seeing each other until after the trial, and even then we didn't really *do* anything. We mostly just talked, you know? It was me that wanted to take it further. Jim kept saying no, he couldn't . . . you know . . . it wasn't right.' She sighed. 'We only ever slept together once.'

'Really?'

She nodded. 'It all went wrong after that. Symons' conviction was overturned by the Court of Appeal, and a retrial was ordered, so suddenly I was back to being a witness again, and Jim was back to being the Senior Investigating Officer, and we both knew that the retrial was a sham, that something dodgy was going . . . and that's when . . .' She sighed again. 'Well, I'm sure you know the rest.'

In January 1992, my father had come into possession of a video that showed Mick Bishop and two other police officers torturing a drug dealer and robbing him of five kilos of cocaine. After passing this video and other incriminating information to his immediate superior, DCI Frank Curtis, my father was subsequently accused of fabricating evidence and making false statements about a fellow officer in a deliberate attempt to ruin his career. Three weeks later, while suspended from duties pending a full investigation, £25,000 in cash and two kilos of cocaine were 'discovered' in my father's station locker, and conclusive evidence was produced of his inappropriate relationship with Serina.

Two days later, he killed himself.

I looked at Serina now, trying to imagine how she must have felt back then. It was almost impossible to comprehend, but I could tell from the look on her face – her lost eyes, her emptiness, her ingrained suffering – that she'd never got over it.

'Did he talk to you before he killed himself?' I asked her quietly.

She shook her head. 'Once the retrial was ordered, Jim said we couldn't see each other any more. The last time I spoke to him was about a month before he died.'

'How was he then?'

'What do you mean?'

'His state of mind. I mean, was there anything . . . was there any indication . . . ?'

'That he'd kill himself?'

'Yeah.'

She sighed. 'Not really. But it was always hard to tell with Jim. He suffered quite badly from depression, and some days it got so bad that he could barely even talk, but even then . . .' She shook her head. 'I don't know, there was just something about him, a strength, an inner belief . . . he just never struck me as the kind of man who'd kill himself.' She looked at me. 'But I was wrong, wasn't I?'

'You didn't see him for a month,' I said. 'A lot can change in a month.'

'Maybe . . .'

'Did you know that he'd been suspended?'

'I didn't know *any*thing. I didn't even know that he was dead until I read about it in the newspaper. The rest of it – his suspension, the corruption charges, the fact that someone had been *spying* on us . . . it was weeks, *months*, before I knew about any of that.'

'You know he denied everything, don't you?'

'Everything?'

'Well, almost everything. He didn't deny his relationship with you, but everything else – the drugs and the cash they found in his locker, the claims that he fabricated evidence against Bishop—'

'Bishop framed him.'

'How do you know that?'

She shrugged. 'Bishop was bent . . . still is. Jim was on to him. Bishop had to bring Jim down. Simple as that.' She lit a cigarette. 'And with Jim out of the way, Symons' retrial was fucked too. Which I'm sure Bishop has never let Symons forget.'

'There was no retrial?'

She shook her head again. 'My evidence was no good any more because I'd slept with Jim. Jim was dead, his reputation ruined. And most of the other witnesses had suddenly decided they didn't want to testify after all, so it all just fell apart.'

'Symons walked?'

'Yeah.' She smiled coldly. 'Last I heard, he was working for the European Commission in Brussels . . . doing very well for himself, apparently.'

'And what about you?' I asked her.

'Me?'

'Yeah. What happened to you?'

'After Jim died?'

'Yeah.'

'Nothing . . . nothing happened to me. I was just . . . I was back where I'd started from. I was nothing again. Just a fucked-up little nothing.'

I lit a cigarette. 'When did you find out you were pregnant?'

She looked at me, her eyes guarded, and for a moment or two I thought she was going to lie to me, or tell me that it was none of my business, or maybe just tell me to fuck off. But as I took a long drag on my cigarette and tapped ash into the ashtray, I saw the wariness disappear from her eyes, and I knew that she'd decided to be honest with me. As she leaned forward in her chair and began to speak, I could feel a sudden tension in my heart.

'It was about three or four weeks after Jim died,' she said quietly. 'I really had no idea, you know . . . we'd only slept together that once, and it never even occurred to me that anything might come of it. But then I missed my period, and I started feeling sick in the mornings, and I took a test . . . and, well . . . that was it. Positive. I was having a baby.' She shook her head, half-smiling to herself. 'I couldn't believe it.'

'And Dad . . . he was definitely the father?'

'Oh, yeah,' she said confidently. 'It couldn't have been anyone else . . . there *wasn't* anyone else.' She looked at me. 'I might not have known what I was going to do about the baby – whether or not I was going to have it, and if I did, how I was going to look after it – but the one thing I *did* know was that Jim was the father.'

'Did anyone else know?'

She shook her head. 'I've never told anyone.'

46

'Not even Robyn?'

She frowned at me. 'You know her name then?'

I nodded. 'Does she know who her father is?'

'It was difficult,' Serina said wearily, stubbing out her cigarette. 'Everything was difficult. I was young, confused, all on my own . . . I had no job, no money. I didn't know anything about being a mother. Social Services kept telling me that Robyn would be better off in care, but there was no way I was going to let that happen. So I really had to prove myself, you know . . . I had to fight all the fucking way. And I did my best, I really did. But by the time Robyn was old enough to be told about Jim – this would have been when she was around eleven or twelve – she was already too fucked-up to care. I mean, I still sat her down and told her as much as I thought she needed to know, but I might as well have been talking to the wall. She just sat there, staring right through me, and when I'd finished, all she had to say was, "Is that it? Can I go now?" And she's never mentioned it since.'

'Really?'

Serina nodded. 'She's a wonderful kid underneath it all – smart, thoughtful, funny, caring – and I love her more than anything, but she's always been pretty mixed-up. Just like me, I suppose. Always skiving off school, shop-lifting, fighting, drinking . . . and then, about two or three years ago, she started getting into drugs. It was just a bit of dope at first, which I wasn't *too* bothered about, but then she got into skunk, which fucked her up quite a bit, and pretty soon she was doing all kinds of shit . . .' Serina lit another cigarette. 'That was one of the reasons I decided to leave Hey and move down here. I thought it would help Robyn, you know, get her away from Hey, away from all the crap.'

'Did it work?'

'Fuck, no. If anything, this place is even worse. It's a junky's paradise down here.'

'Really? How come?'

'God knows . . .' She shook her head. 'All I know is that Robyn never has any trouble getting hold of what she wants, and she never has to go far to get it.'

'Where is she now?' I asked.

'Working,' Serina said, glancing at her watch. 'She's got a part-time job at the farm shop across the island. She does all sorts – shop assistant, waitress . . . they've got a little café there, you know? And she does a bit of driving for them sometimes too.'

It was hard to believe that a serious drug habit could be funded by a part-time job in a farm shop, but I didn't want to get into that now. All I wanted was . . .

What?

What *did* I want?

To go? To get out of this house?

To be on my own?

To think about things?

To have a drink?

Or maybe I just wished I'd never come here in the first place?

I really didn't know.

'Does she know about me?' I asked Serina.

'What do you mean?'

'Robyn . . . does she know she has a half-brother?'

Serina avoided my gaze. 'I was going to tell her,' she said quietly. 'I mean, when I told her about Jim, I meant to tell her then . . . but it just didn't feel right. You know, she wasn't listening anyway, she didn't seem to care . . . so I thought I'd just wait until the time was right.' Serina sighed. 'I'm still waiting.'

'So she doesn't know anything about me.'

'No. I'm sorry. I know I should have—'

'It's all right,' I said. 'I understand . . . I mean, there's no reason—'

'Yes, there is,' she said firmly. 'You're related, for God's sake. You both have the same father. You should at least have the right to decide if you want to know each other or not.'

'Yeah, but if Robyn doesn't *want* to know—'

'Robyn doesn't know what she wants. That's why she's such a fucking mess. All she ever wants to do is blank out the world and lose herself.'

Sounds familiar, I thought.

'Yeah, well,' I said. 'I don't want to make things any worse for you, and if you don't want to tell her about me, that's fine. I'll just . . . well, I'll just leave you alone. But if you think she might want to see me . . .' I took a business card out of my pocket and passed it to Serina. 'My mobile number's on there. If you can't get through for any reason, I'm staying at Victoria Hall—'

'You're staying here, on the island?'

I nodded. 'I'll probably be here for another week or so. I'll leave it up to you and Robyn if you want to get in

49

touch again. I mean, if I don't hear from you before I leave . . . well, it's up to you, OK?'

'Would you like to see her?'

'Yeah . . . yeah, I think I would. But if you think it's best to leave things as they are . . . well, like I said, it's up to you.'

She smiled at me. 'You remind me a lot of your father.'

'Yeah?'

'He was a thoughtful man. Too thoughtful, sometimes. If he'd cared about himself as much as he cared about other people . . . well, maybe things would have been different.'

I nodded, not knowing what to say. I didn't know if she was right about my father's thoughtfulness – I never knew him well enough to know – and I wasn't quite sure if she was saying that *I* cared too much about other people too, just like him. But I knew that if she *was* saying that, she was wrong.

She'd got to her feet now and was glancing at her watch. 'I'm really sorry,' she said, 'but if I don't get going in a couple of minutes I'm going to be late for work again.' She shook her head. 'I've already been late twice this week.'

I stood up. 'Where do you work?'

She shrugged. 'It's just a checkout job. There's a little Co-op in the High Street, you know . . . it's not much. Just a job.'

'A job's a job,' I said.

'I suppose.'

As I followed her out of the front room and along the hallway towards the front door, I could feel a sense of

50

emptiness in the air. The carpets were old and worn, the paintwork creamed with age, and although the house itself was relatively clean and tidy, the whole place was dulled with a palpable sense of neglect. It was a sorrowful house, a dead house. The air felt spent and unappetising, as if it had been breathed too many times, strained through the lungs of tired lives.

4

On the way back to the hotel, I stopped off for a drink in a pub called The Swan. It was a fairly big place, with a good-sized bar and a function room at the back, and it was furnished quite traditionally with dark wood panels, bare floorboards, and sturdy old tables and chairs. Stained-glass windows warmed the pale afternoon sunlight, bathing the dimly lit bar with a muted glow of dappled colours. The pub was situated just outside the village, about half a mile from the hotel, and it had the feeling of a place that didn't get too busy during the day but livened up quite a lot at night. There was a small stage at the far end of the function room, with a couple of microphone stands and some monitors stacked up at the back, and posters were dotted around the walls advertising various upcoming events – live bands, quiz nights, a local talent show.

Now, though, the bar was almost empty. No more than a handful of tables were occupied – a few couples talking quietly to each other, a solitary businessman staring at his mobile phone, a red-faced old drunk reading a newspaper – and there were three young men huddled around a quiz machine at the end of the bar, arguing noisily with each other about the answer to some stupid question. But that was about it. There was no queue at the bar, no one waiting to be served. The barman was a middle-aged man in an open-necked shirt, his tightly curled hair as stiff as a Brillo pad.

'What can I get you?' he said to me, wiping his hands on a cloth.

I asked him for a pint of Stella and a large whisky.

'Any whisky in particular?' he said. 'Bell's, Teacher's . . . we've got a really nice single malt—'

'Bell's is fine, thanks,' I told him.

'Ice?'

I shook my head, hoping he wasn't going to ask me any more questions. *Just get me the fucking drinks*, I thought, smiling at him. And as he smiled back, then picked up a glass and turned to the optics, I found myself wondering why everyone asks so many questions these days. Every time you buy something – cigarettes, food, a newspaper – you have to answer questions. *Do you need a lighter? Did you know these are two for the price of one? Do you want a half-price bar of chocolate with that?*

No, I fucking don't. I just want you to take my money, put my stuff in a bag (*Do you need a carrier bag today?*) and shut your fucking mouth.

She was right, wasn't she? Stacy said.

'Who?'

Serina. I mean, you really do *care about other people too much, don't you?*

I laughed.

'Did you say something?' the barman said.

I stopped laughing and looked at him. 'No, sorry . . . I was just . . . I just remembered something.'

53

He gave me a funny look, then nodded at the drinks on the bar. 'That's £5.40, please.'

'Thanks,' I said, giving him a twenty.

As he went to the till to get my change, I took a mouthful of lager, topped up the glass with the whisky, then took another long drink. It tasted good, just right, the clouded heat of the whisky tingling with the ice-cold snap of the beer. I could already feel the alcohol filtering into my heart and loosening the tightness under my skull.

When the barman brought me my change, I asked him if there was a smoking area.

'Out the back,' he said, indicating a door at the end of the bar. 'Through the door and down the corridor.'

'Thanks.'

He nodded, then turned suddenly as a loud shout rang out from one of the boys at the quiz machine. I looked over and saw that it was nothing, just one of them getting overexcited, waving his hands around and shouting his mouth off to one of the others. He was a tall and rangy kid, about eighteen or nineteen, with a long pockmarked face and cropped hair. The kid he was shouting at looked just like him, only not so tall, and maybe two or three years younger. His brother, I guessed. They were both wearing identical white tracksuits, the bottoms of the trousers grubby and wet from trailing on the ground.

The other kid with them looked like he had something wrong with him. Short and dumpy, his skin quite dark, he had a tousled mop of thick black hair, large staring eyes that didn't seem to blink, and – strangest of all – a torn strip of grubby white rag hanging from the corner of his mouth. As he stood there staring bug-eyed at me, he was chewing mindlessly on one end of the rag, like a cow chewing the cud, while at the same time wrapping the other end round his fingers and fiddling with it – twisting it, waggling it, tugging it up and down.

'Hey, Neil!' the older brother called out to the barman, swigging from a bottle of Budweiser. 'Who wrote *Mice of Men*?'

'Of *Mice and Men*,' his brother corrected him.

'What?'

'It's *Of Mice and Men*.'

'*What*?'

'Look,' the brother said patiently, pointing at the quiz-machine screen. 'See? The question is "Who wrote *Of Mice and Men*?" not "Who wrote *Mice of Men*?" *Mice of Men* doesn't make sense.'

'Neither does fucking *Of Mice's Men*.'

'All right, boys,' the barman said cautiously. 'Let's keep it down a bit, OK?'

It was meant to be a firm but friendly warning, but there was no confidence or authority in his voice, and when the older brother turned slowly and stared at him – his mouth tight, his eyes cold and hard – the barman couldn't even hold his gaze. He just looked down, fumbled for a glass, and pretended to concentrate on cleaning it.

I looked back at the brother.

He was smiling now, the vicious grin of a cruel little boy.

'What are your choices?' I said to him.

He turned to me, jutting his chin. 'You what?'

'The quiz question – "Who wrote *Of Mice and Men*?" What choices have you got for the answer?'

He tried his tough-guy stare on me, but I just smiled back at him, and after a moment or two he sniffed hard, hiked his shoulders, and turned to his brother.

'What's the choices, Kyle?' he said.

'I already told you the answer,' Kyle said. 'It's—'

'What's the fucking choices?'

Kyle sighed. 'A, J.K. Rowling, B, Ernest Hemingway, or C, John Steinbeck.'

His brother looked at me. 'What do you think?'

I looked at Kyle. 'Who do you think it is?'

'I *know* who it is – it's Steinbeck. I did it at school—'

'You never *go* to fucking school,' his brother said. 'You're just guessing, like you always do.'

'I'm *not*—'

'I lost twenty-five quid the last time I listened to you.'

'Yeah, but that was—'

'You think it's Steindick, yeah?'

'Stein*beck*.'

His brother looked at me again. 'Is he right?'

I shrugged. 'Well, it's not J.K. Rowling . . . and I suppose it *could* be Steinbeck, but . . .'

'But what?'

'I'm pretty sure it's Hemingway.'

'No!' Kyle snapped. 'It's not fucking Hemingway—'

'Shut up, Kyle,' his brother said, still looking at me. 'You're *pretty* sure?'

'Yeah.'

'I lose thirty quid if you're wrong.'

56

I didn't say anything, I just smiled at him.

He carried on looking at me for a while, his brow furrowed, trying to work out whether he should trust me or not, and then eventually, after a quick glance at Kyle, he turned back to the quiz machine, paused for a second, and hit a button. There was a moment's silence, then red lights started flashing and the machine went *WAH-WAH-WAH-WAAAH! YOU LOSE!*

'*Fuck!*' the brother spat, slapping the screen with the flat of his hand. 'Fuck it!'

'I *told* you,' Kyle said. 'I fucking told you it was—'

'Shut up!'

'Why'd you listen to him? I told you—'

'Shut the *fuck* up!' He turned angrily to me. 'Hemingway, shit . . . you fucking *wanker*. Thirty quid that cost me, thirty fucking *quid*.'

'Yeah, well,' I said, sipping my drink. 'That's the way it goes, isn't it? You win some, you lose some.' I turned back to the barman. 'I'll have another large Scotch, please. Bell's, no ice. And a bottle of a Budweiser. No glass.'

He shot a wary glance at the three boys, then nodded at me and went to fetch the drinks.

'Hey!' I heard the brother say.

I ignored him.

'Hey, fuckhead. I'm talking to you.'

I waited for the barman to bring the drinks, gave him a £10 note, took a mouthful of whisky, poured the rest in my beer glass, then turned back to the brother again. He hadn't moved, he was still standing over by the quiz machine, glaring hard at me. His face was glowing red – partly from anger, I guessed, and partly from embarrassment.

'You did that on purpose, didn't you?' he said.

I picked up my beer and the bottle of Bud and started walking over to him.

'You fucking knew, didn't you?' he said, stepping back a little. 'You fucking *knew* it was the wrong answer.'

I stopped in front of him and looked him up and down. There wasn't much to him, really. He looked hard enough, and I guessed he could probably get pretty nasty if he wanted to, but only if all the odds were stacked in his favour. He'd kick the shit out of you if you were on the ground, but he'd never be the one to actually put you on the ground.

'What's your name?' I said to him.

He frowned at me. '*What?*'

'What's your name?'

'Why the fuck—?'

I stepped closer to him. 'What's your name?'

'Lyle,' he said, trying to sneer, but not succeeding. 'Not that it's any of your—'

'All right, Lyle,' I said, smiling at him. 'I've got a question for you . . . you like questions, don't you?'

'Look,' he said, defensively. 'All I'm saying is—'

'You see this bottle of Budweiser?' I said, showing him the bottle.

'Yeah . . .'

'OK, here's the question. Are you listening, Lyle?'

'Yeah.'

'All right. The question is, What am I going to do with this bottle of Bud? Am I going to A, Drink it? B, Give it

58

to you? Or C, Smash it over your head and cut your fucking eyes out?' I smiled at him. 'Do you understand the question?'

His eyes blinked rapidly. 'No . . . I mean, yeah . . . I don't—'

'Do you want to hear the answers again?'

He shook his head. 'Why are you—?'

'I need an answer, Lyle.'

'I don't—'

'Quickly.'

'Drink it?' he stuttered.

'Guess again.'

'I don't *know*—'

'You've only got two choices left, Lyle. B, I'm going to give the bottle to you. Or C, I'm going to smash it over your head and cut your fucking eyes out. Which one are you going for?'

'B . . . ?' he muttered.

'Are you sure?'

'Yeah . . . yeah, I'm sure.'

I passed him the bottle. 'You win.'

He breathed out, blinked again, and hesitantly took the bottle from my hand.

'Drink it then,' I told him.

He took a shaky sip.

'All right?' I said.

'Yeah . . .'

'OK, I'm going outside for a cigarette now. I'll be about ten minutes. I don't want to see you when I come back, all right?'

He nodded.

I looked at him for a moment, seeing myself in his eyes, and then – with a cold vein of reflective hatred coiling in my guts – I turned round and walked away.

There was a heated parasol in the smoking area outside, but although the air was sharp and cold, and the lowering sky was misted with rain, I didn't want any shelter. I needed the cold air, the dampness, the open skies . . . I needed *something*. I moved across the small paved yard, stopped by the far wall, and lit a cigarette. I blew out the smoke and breathed in through my nose, trying to savour the freshness of the rain and the faint tang of salt in the air . . . but all I could smell was stale alcohol and cigarette smoke.

I took a long drink of whisky and beer, swallowed it down, then drank again.

'Fuck it,' I said.

A lone seagull squawked from a nearby rooftop.

I pulled up the collar of my coat.

What's going on, John? Stacy said.

'Nothing . . .'

Her voice in my heart went quiet, but I could feel her looking at me, her eyes repeating the question – *what's going on?*

'I don't know, Stace,' I sighed. 'That kid, Lyle . . . I don't know. He just really pissed me off.'

He's just a boy.

'He's a piece of shit.'

So what? The world's full of shit, you know that.

'Well, yeah . . .'

You see it every day.

'I know.'

You just accept it.

'Yeah, I *know*—'

So what's got into you? What was all that self-righteous crap about just now?

'It wasn't—'

Yeah, it was. Don't lie to yourself, John. You know it wasn't right.

I drank some more beer and looked up at the sky. The clouds were low and grey, the darkening layers shifting ponderously in the wind. I put out my cigarette and lit another.

Are you upset about Bridget?

'No.'

Just call her, John. Talk to her. It'll be all right.

'I'm not upset about Bridget.'

So what is it? What are you so angry about?

'I don't know.'

Is it your dad?

'No.'

Serina, Robyn . . . Mick Bishop?

I shook my head. 'I really don't know, Stace. I just feel . . . I don't know. Something's fucking me up, but I don't know what it is.'

Well, you need to sort it out, John. It's all right being fucked-up, that's part of what you are. But what you did just now . . . that's not you. And I can't be with you if you're not yourself. Do you understand?

'Yeah . . . I'm sorry.'

I know. It's all right. Her voice smiled sadly. *You'd better go back in now, you're getting wet.*

'OK.'

I'll see you later . . .

'Yeah.'

Lyle and Kyle and the rag-sucking kid had gone when I went back inside, and without them the pub felt a lot more relaxed. A couple of people nodded at me as I went up to the bar and ordered another beer, but I didn't acknowledge their gratitude – if that's what it was. I didn't want to be thanked for doing something stupid.

'Do you want another Bell's with that?' the barman asked me, placing a fresh beer on the bar. 'It's on the house.'

I looked at him. 'What?'

He smiled. 'You scared the shit out of Lyle Keane, *and* you got him to leave. That's worth a free drink in my book.'

'Yeah, well—'

'Mind you,' he added, pouring me a large whisky, 'I'd watch my back now, if I were you. Lyle's not one to forget something like that.' He put the glass of whisky on the bar. 'You're not local though, are you? I mean, you don't live on the island?'

I picked up the whisky and the glass of beer.

'What I mean is,' the barman went on, 'if you don't live here, there's nothing to worry about, is there?'

'Thanks for the drinks,' I said, nodding my head.

And I went back out into the rain.

*

62

Bridget Moran lived in the upstairs flat of my house in Hey. She'd been my tenant for more than ten years, and for most of that time we'd been friends without ever really knowing each other. We'd stop and talk now and then, maybe share the occasional cup of coffee together . . . but it had never gone any further than that.

In the last few weeks though, things had changed. Bridget had broken up with her boyfriend, we'd started seeing a lot more of each other, and eventually we'd ended up sharing a bed together. It was the first time I'd slept with anyone since Stacy had died, but – more than that – it was the first time I'd felt remotely close to anyone since Stacy had died, and for a short while afterwards I'd begun to feel the faint stirrings of some kind of contentment again. It was by no means a perfect contentment – and despite Stacy's heartfelt approval of Bridget, I couldn't help feeling that I'd betrayed my wife's love, and that there was nothing I could ever do to change that – but at least, for a time, Bridget had taken away my constant need to be someone else, some*thing* else, anything but me . . .

For the first time in years, I was close to finding happiness.

And maybe if I'd done things differently, maybe if I'd been more careful . . . maybe Bridget might not have been hurt. Maybe, or maybe not . . . I don't know. But I don't suppose it matters now. It happened. She was with me, I was working a case, bad stuff happened. She was attacked, she was beaten, she was almost killed. And worse . . . the love of her life *was* killed, and she came very close to taking a life herself.

63

And all because of me.

I'd brought death and violence into her life. And while I knew that her physical injuries would heal, I also knew that she'd never fully recover from the damage to her heart. The pain she'd been through that night would haunt her for the rest of her life. It would become part of her. It would change her.

It already had.

When I'd gone to see her in hospital the day after it had all happened, I could tell from her eyes, the way she spoke to me, the way she looked . . . deep down inside, she was already a different person.

'Are they keeping you in for a while?' I'd asked her.

She nodded. 'Another day or so. It's routine for a serious concussion, apparently. They want to take some more scans, you know, just to make sure . . .'

'Right.'

'How's your hand?'

I smiled. 'It hurts.'

'Is it broken?'

'Just a bit . . . hairline fracture.'

She smiled weakly and looked away.

'I'm really sorry, Bridget,' I started to say. 'I just wish—'

'It's not your fault, John. He did it, not you.'

'I know—'

'And there's no point *wishing* anything. It happened, didn't it?'

'Yeah.'

'It fucking happened . . .'

Neither of us said anything for a while then. Bridget just

64

lay there on the hospital bed – her eyes closed, her battered face void of emotion – while I sat beside her, not knowing what to do. What could I do? Say sorry again? Pretend that everything was going to be all right? No, there was nothing I could do.

So I just sat there, waiting.

I looked at the floor, I looked at my hands, I looked at a nurse walking past. The nurse smiled at me, I smiled back. I looked at Bridget. She was so still and quiet, her breathing so steady, that I thought she'd gone to sleep, and I wondered if she was simply exhausted, or if she was under the influence of sedatives. But then, without opening her eyes, she said quietly, 'I'm not coming back to the house, John.'

'What?'

She opened her eyes and looked at me. 'When I get out of here, I'm going to stay with my sister. She's got a little cottage in Dorset . . . she keeps pigs and stuff. I'm going to stay with her.'

'OK . . .' I said.

'I need to get away from everything.'

'Yeah, of course. I understand.'

'Sarah can look after the shop . . . and I'll just . . .' She closed her eyes again. 'I need to get away . . . I'm tired . . . I'm not coming back . . . I can't . . .'

'What do you mean?' I said. 'You're not coming back at *all*?'

She didn't answer.

'Bridget?'

I didn't know if she was asleep again or just pretending

to be asleep so that she didn't have to talk to me. Either way, I didn't see much point in staying any longer. I briefly took hold of her hand, gave it a squeeze, then got to my feet, leaned over, and kissed her lightly on the forehead.

'I'll call you, OK?' I said.

But she didn't reply.

And later that day, when I went to see her again, she'd gone. Checked herself out, I was told. Gone to stay with her sister, in a little cottage in Dorset . . .

With pigs and stuff.

Shit.

I knew that Stacy was probably right, and that I ought to just call Bridget and talk to her, and maybe it *would* be all right . . . maybe she hadn't changed all that much after all. I *wanted* to call her, I'd been wanting to call her ever since she'd left, but that afternoon, as I sat outside the pub in the rain, drinking, drinking . . . trying to stop thinking, I *really* wanted to talk to her. I *needed* it. I wanted to find out how she was, to let her know where I was, and what I was doing. I wanted to tell her about Serina and Robyn, and how it felt to find out that Robyn was my half-sister . . .

I just needed someone to talk to.

Someone I cared about, someone who meant something to me . . .

Someone who wasn't dead.

Maybe that's it, Stacy's voice said. *Maybe that's what's fucking you up so much.*

'What?'

Me.

'No—'

I'm dead, John. I've been dead for seventeen years. You need to let go of me.

'I can't—'

You have to. I'm not real, you know that. I'm not Stacy. Stacy doesn't exist any more. She's gone. I'm not even her voice. I'm just . . .

'What? You're just what?'

Nothing. I'm nothing. And that's what angers you – sharing your life with nothing. That's why you wanted to hurt that boy, Lyle Keane, and that's why you're sitting out here in the rain, drinking yourself stupid.

I drained my glass and lit a cigarette.

John?

'I'm not talking to nothing.'

Call Bridget. Right now. Just call her, for God's sake.

I looked down at the mobile in my hand, keyed in Bridget's number . . . and then, just as I knew I would, I hit the END button and put the phone back in my pocket.

I'd call her later.

Right now, I needed another drink.

I was fairly drunk when I got back to the hotel, but it wasn't the kind of drunkenness I was looking for, the kind that empties your mind and dulls you into a dreamless sleep, instead it was the kind that keeps hammering away inside your skull, demanding more, like a beaten-up old fighter who won't stay down and take the count no matter how many times he gets hit.

As far as I can recall, it must have been around three o'clock when I entered the hotel lobby. Arthur Finch was just on his way out, walking three lurcher dogs on leads, and there was an elderly woman at the reception desk. I mumbled something to Arthur, nodded at the woman, and headed off to my room. There was no one else around, the corridor was empty, and because the whole place was so hushed and still – and because I was so stupidly drunk – I found myself tiptoeing along the corridor, trying to be as quiet as possible, not wanting to disturb the afternoon silence . . . but the more I tiptoed, the more the rainwater squelched in my shoes, and by the time I reached my room, I realised that I was making more noise on tiptoe than I would if I was walking normally. I was squelching along the corridor with all the finesse of a loose-booted giant crossing a swamp. At least, that's what it sounded like to me. But I was drunk, my senses distorted, and the truth was that I couldn't have been making that much noise, because when I swiped my keycard and opened the door, and I saw the woman crouched down on the floor, frantically zipping up my holdall, it was quite clear that she hadn't heard me coming.

5

As the woman quickly stood up and turned towards me, her eyes momentarily wide with surprise, I realised that it was Linda, the waitress I'd met that morning.

'What are you doing?' I said, glancing down at my holdall.

'God,' she gasped quietly. 'You really gave me a shock—'

'What are you doing?' I repeated, glaring at her.

'Sorry,' she said. 'I was just finishing up in here. I know you said not to bother cleaning your room, but—'

'What were you doing with my bag?'

'What?'

'My holdall . . . what were you doing with it?'

'Nothing,' she said, frowning at me. 'I was just tidying it away.'

I stared hard at her, convinced she was lying, but I couldn't see any trace of guilt in her eyes. In fact, if anything, she seemed genuinely upset and offended by my questioning. I gazed quickly round the room, noticing the freshly made bed, the hoovered carpet, the cleaning trolley over by the window, the vacuum cleaner beside the bed, still plugged in . . . and the feeling began to grow that I'd just made an idiot of myself. I *was* drunk, my senses *were* distorted, and when I'd opened the door and seen Linda crouched down in front of my holdall . . .

'Why were you zipping it up?' I asked her.

'What?'

'Why were you zipping up my holdall?'

'I just *told* you,' she sighed. 'I was tidying it away.' She shook her head, weary now of my accusations. 'Look, if you don't *want* me to come in here, if you don't *want* me to touch anything—'

'I'm sorry,' I said. 'I just thought—'

'Well, you were wrong, weren't you?' She shook her head again. 'Christ . . . I'm just trying to do my job, that's all. I mean, it's bad enough as it is, cleaning up other people's shit all day . . . making their beds, tidying up their fucking clothes.' She glared at me. 'And now I've got to put up with you calling me a thief—'

'I didn't say that.'

'You *thought* it.'

'I'm sorry,' I said. 'Really . . . I just made a mistake, OK? I'm really sorry.'

'Yeah, well . . .'

'It was probably just the door . . .'

'The door?'

'Well, it was closed, locked, you know . . . so I wasn't *expecting* anyone to be in here. It just gave me a bit of a shock, I suppose. I wasn't thinking straight.'

'Oh, right . . .' she said, nodding slowly and glancing at the door. 'I didn't realise . . . I usually leave the door open when I'm cleaning a room, but I had to shut it when I was hoovering, and I must have forgotten to open it again.' She smiled warily at me. 'I'll make sure I leave it open next time.'

I smiled back. 'And I'll try to make sure I don't say anything stupid.'

She grinned. 'Fair enough.'

'Does that mean I'm forgiven?'

She looked at me. 'I suppose so . . .'

'You're not going to get your own back by spitting in my breakfast, are you?'

'No,' she said, laughing. 'No, I'd never do that.'

'Really?'

She grinned again. 'Do I *look* like someone who'd spit in your food?'

I didn't answer that, I just smiled and stepped out of the way as she started gathering up all her cleaning stuff, but as I watched her unplug the vacuum cleaner and wind up the cable, and I studied the sternness that had returned to her face, I thought to myself – *well, actually*, yes . . . *you do look like someone who'd spit in my food*. And I also reminded myself that just because someone doesn't look as if they're lying, that doesn't mean they're not.

'Right,' she said, looking round the room. 'I think that's everything.' She started pushing the cleaning trolley towards the door. 'I'll get out of your way now.'

I followed her out into the corridor, wheeling out the vacuum cleaner.

'Thanks,' she said.

'No problem. And again, I'm sorry about—'

'It's all right,' she said, waving away my apology. 'Forget it.'

'Right, well . . . I'll probably see you later then.'

She nodded, smiled, and headed off down the corridor.

I went back into my room, closed the door, locked it, then put my eye up to the peephole in the door. After a moment or two, I saw Linda coming back along the corridor. She loomed up close to the door, her face distorted in the fisheye lens, then she collected the vacuum cleaner and disappeared back down the corridor again. I waited for a while, watching the warped tunnel of the corridor for any sign of movement, and then – seeing nothing – I turned round, picked up my holdall and took it over to the bed.

There wasn't much in it – a few clothes, a half-bottle of whisky, cigarettes, a paperback book . . . nothing of any great value. And when I unzipped the bag and had a quick look through it, nothing seemed to be missing. I pulled out some of the clothes and dug down into a small inner pocket that was fastened with a Velcro flap. I opened it up, took out a folded envelope, and carefully checked inside. Again, as far as I could tell, nothing seemed to have been touched. When I'd left the hotel that morning, the envelope had contained two grams of amphetamine sulphate, a wrap of cocaine, and a small lump of cannabis resin.

It was all still there.

I took a wrap of speed from the envelope, put the rest back in the holdall, then went over to the table by the wall and poured myself a whisky. I didn't *want* to be drunk any more, but I didn't want to be in that fuzzy no-man's-land between drunk and sober either. All I wanted was . . .

I didn't know what I wanted.

I opened the wrap of speed, tapped out a ragged line, and snorted it through a rolled-up business card. The sulphate burned, sour and satisfying, in the back of my throat. I sniffed hard, washed down the bitter snot with a mouthful of whisky, and lit a cigarette.

'Shit,' I said to the empty room. 'Fuck it.'

The rain had stopped when I opened up the double doors and went out onto the balcony. It was late afternoon now, and the daylight was just beginning to fade. The sun was hidden behind a canopy of thick grey clouds, and all I could see was a pale orange glow spreading over the horizon and a dappled luminescence rippling across the sea. It looked timeless, primeval, untouched . . .

Unknowable.

I sipped whisky and smoked a cigarette, feeling the rush of speed in my blood, and I wondered what I was doing. But there was no answering voice in my heart now, no dead love to help me out.

Stacy had gone.

I'm nothing . . .

I was on my own.

I closed my eyes and tried to think, but I couldn't seem to get hold of anything. Nothing would stay still. Whatever thoughts I had were tumbling around inside my head, flitting in and out of focus like the shadow shapes of bats in the grey light, and all I could make out were bits of things – faces, voices, names, feelings – none of which made any sense. Everything was broken, disordered, out of place.

I opened my eyes and gazed out across the empty beach. The sun was low in the sky, the tide was in, and the mirrored sea was eternally dark and still. In the windless calm I imagined the sweet drift of a siren song, calling me out into the twilight . . . a song of past and future, a song of life and death.

I couldn't hear it.

It wasn't there.

Just like everything else.

It was nothing.

But that didn't seem to matter any more.

I went back inside and put on my coat. I took the half-bottle of whisky from my holdall and stuffed it in my pocket, snorted some more speed, then went back out onto the balcony and closed the double doors behind me. The balcony backed directly onto the beach, and although there was no gate or anything, all I had to do was clamber up over the wooden railing, drop down the other side, and there I was, on the beach.

I waited for my head to stop spinning, then started walking.

6

It's quite possible that the act of suicide was on my mind as I walked the beach that evening. I may well have been thinking about my father's death, and the reasons behind it, and Serina's conviction that – despite his depression – he wasn't the kind of man who'd kill himself. And there's a good chance that these thoughts might have developed into the familiar consideration of my own life and death, especially given the circumstances – the drink, the drugs, the emptiness . . . the beckoning hush of the sea. It's not hard to imagine myself standing on the shoreline, gazing out over the heavy black water, wondering how it would feel to sink down into the depths and simply disappear. It wouldn't have been the first time I'd considered it. And I'm fairly sure that, having given it a reasonable amount of thought, I would have come to the same conclusion I always come to – that killing yourself is certainly an option, and possibly the only real life choice any of us truly have, but it can only take you so far. It can't go back in time and render you non-existent, it can't remove the stain of life. All it really has to offer is an early retirement. Which is fine, if that's what you want.

But it's never been enough for me.

Of course, it's equally likely that I *wasn't* thinking about suicide as I walked the beach that evening. Perhaps I had other things on my mind. Perhaps I was wondering about the sad young woman I'd seen at the Point the day before . . . what had she been doing there, just looking out over the mudflats, gazing in silence, the wind ruffling her hair? And why was she sad? And perhaps I was thinking that she might be there again, and that if she was, maybe I could try talking to her this time . . .

Or then again . . .

I could have been hoping to come across Robyn. I had no idea when the farm shop closed, or what time she finished work, and there was no guarantee that she'd come back along the pathway by the creek when she did finish work. But I could have been thinking that this might be *around* the time that a farm shop might close on a cold wet Saturday at the end of October, and that it wasn't impossible that Robyn might walk back along the pathway at the end of her day . . .

I could have been thinking about any or all of these things as I walked the beach that evening, or I could have been thinking about none of them at all. The truth is, I really don't remember. I was drunk, mindless, out in the cold, a passenger in my own body. I could feel the sulphate racing in my blood, my heart, my head, lifting me up through the numbing cloud of alcohol, and to me it felt like paradise. A somewhat pathetic paradise, perhaps . . . but paradise nonetheless.

All I can really remember, until I got to the pillbox, are one or two vague sensations, a handful of disconnected moments, like blurred snapshots of a forgotten journey. The feel of wet sand beneath my feet as I walked the west side of the beach . . . stumbling over a lump of driftwood half-buried in the sand, cursing it, then laughing at myself, then crouching down and grabbing hold of the driftwood and pulling it out of the sand, looking at it, studying it, wondering where it had come from – a boat, perhaps? a wooden dinghy? a fishing boat? – then sitting down in the sodden sand, with the weather-worn lump of wood in my hand, sipping from the half-bottle of whisky and smoking a cigarette . . . and then, some time later . . . crossing over to the east side of the beach, below the country park, where the sand turns to shingle that crunches satisfyingly beneath my feet . . . and I'm wondering *why* it's shingle here and not sand – is it something to do with the tides, or with the age or the lie of the land? – and it's then that I hear a voice . . .

'All right?'

. . . and for a moment I think it's a voice in my heart, or in my head, but it's a male voice, and I don't recognise it, and when I slow down and turn to my left, I see a man sitting on the wooden steps that lead down from the park to the beach. He's tall and muscled, with long greasy hair and biker tattoos . . . the man I saw Robyn with at the caravan. He's wearing a heavy black coat and motorcycle boots, and he's smoking a cigarette and staring at me.

'You going somewhere?' he says.

I don't reply, I just look at him for a moment, noticing the mobile phone in his hand, and the black light of drugs in his eyes, and then I turn away and carry on walking. And almost immediately he's gone from my mind, forgotten . . . and all I'm doing is walking, walking, heading vaguely

77

for the Point . . . and it's started to rain again now, and the wind's blowing hard, and it's getting dark . . . and the tide seems further in on this side of the island, the sea further up the beach, so I edge up towards the higher ground near the saltmarshes . . .

And the next thing I remember is a brief flash of light, out at sea, just off the Point . . . out in the gloom . . . a wink of white light . . . and at the same time I think I hear something, a low puttering sound in the distance, but when I stop walking and listen again, all I can hear is the wind and the rain and the stirring of the sea. The tide is turning, going out, the wind is whipping up waves . . .

The stillness has gone.

And so has the distant light.

It was probably nothing . . .

I was drunk, mindless, out in the cold . . .

I was probably just seeing things.

When I got to the pillbox, I suddenly remembered something that I wished I'd remembered the day before. It was one of those long-forgotten memories that often only come back to you when you're intoxicated, looming up through the unguarded depths of your mindless mind, taking you by surprise. And when these lost memories do come back to you, they can sometimes seem so fresh, so vivid, so vital, that it's hard to believe they've been hidden away in a dusty old box in the basement of your mind for so long. They're not just idle memories, they *mean* something.

And that was it . . .

The pillbox meant something to me.

Like most of the World War Two defence posts dotted along the Essex coast, it was a squat, circular building, about ten feet across, with thick concrete walls and a solid flat roof. My father once told me that it had been built on the ruins of an 18th-century lookout tower, and that when he was a child you could still sometimes find remnants of the ancient stone building scattered around in the sand. But although I'd often looked for these old stones, digging around in the sand, I'd never found any.

The pillbox would originally have been about seven or eight feet high, but over the years it had gradually been half-buried by the shifting sands, and now – from the outside at least – the roof was only about four feet off the ground, the perfect height for sitting on. And when I was a kid, every time I came down here, I'd always hoist myself up and sit on the roof, dangling my feet over the edge . . . I just couldn't resist it. And after a while it became one of those things for me, the kind of thing you just *have* to do. A personal superstition, I suppose. If I didn't sit on the pillbox, something bad would happen to me. Of course, even then, I knew that this was totally irrational – how could there *possibly* be any causal connection between sitting on a pillbox and something bad happening to me? – but that didn't make any difference.

I still had to do it.

And now, all these years later, nothing had changed. As I stood there by the pillbox that evening, swaying gently in the rain, I knew that it didn't matter that I *hadn't* sat on the roof when I'd been down here the day before. I knew how ridiculous it was to even *consider* the consequences of breaking a long-forgotten childhood superstition . . .

But even so . . .

There was no point in breaking it again, was there?

And besides, I asked myself, stepping up to the pillbox. *What harm can it do?*

With my back to the wall, I put my hands on the edge of the roof and clumsily hoisted myself up.

It felt good, just sitting there in the rain, looking out to sea. I smoked a cigarette, drank some whisky, let my mind wander. I found myself trying to remember how it had felt up here when I was a kid, and at first the only thing I could really identify was a distant sense of being alone. I would never have actually been on my own, of course – my parents would always have been somewhere close by – but I think I probably liked to imagine that I was alone. There was just me, sitting on my pillbox, and no one knew where I was, or what I was doing . . . and as I thought about that now, I felt something else from back then – a faint flicker of illicit excitement. Which, for a few moments, didn't make any sense. I was just a kid back then, a young boy, and all I would have been doing was sitting on the roof of a pillbox – where was the illicit excitement in that?

But then, almost immediately, it came back to me. I didn't just sit on the pillbox, did I? I went inside it too. There was an entrance at the back, an opening in the wall at the bottom of a short flight of concrete steps. It was half-buried in the sand, like the rest of the building, but there was just enough room for a young boy to squeeze through. I'd slide in feet first, I remembered, my heart pounding as I dropped down into the dim and dank interior. It always smelled of urine in there, and sometimes of shit too, and I was always careful not to step in anything as I started poking around. I don't know if I really understood what other people got up to in there, all I knew was that I wasn't supposed to know about it. And that's partly why it was exciting. Quite often, all that was in there were a few empty beer cans, or maybe an empty Clan Dew bottle. But there was always the graffiti to look at, the dirty words and crudely scrawled pictures, and sometimes there might be a scrap of clothing that someone had left behind – a sock, a scrunched-up pair of pants – and very occasionally I'd come across the ripped-up remains of a pornographic magazine. They were always ripped up, I remembered, the pages torn into pieces, and if you wanted to see the naked women you had to fit all the pieces back together again, like a pornographic jigsaw, and somehow that made the whole thing feel even more shameful.

But I still did it.

I was a boy.

What else was I going to do?

I was a boy . . .

Jumping down off the pillbox now, stumbling in the sand, almost falling over . . . I was drunk. A drunk boy. I was timeless, ageless. It was dark. I took my penlight from my pocket and moved round to the back of the pillbox. I knew that I probably wouldn't be able to get inside – it had been a fairly tight squeeze when I was a kid, and I was thirty-odd years older now, thirty years bigger, and after thirty years' build-up of wind-blown sand, the entrance had probably shrunk quite a bit too – but even if I couldn't physically get through the opening, I still needed to see it, to remember it, to relive the feeling of sliding in feet first, my young heart pounding . . .

When I clicked on my penlight and shone the beam at the steps leading down to the entrance, I was surprised to find that I was both right and wrong about the opening. It wasn't any smaller than I remembered – in fact, it was bigger. The accumulated sand had been dug away, right down to the foot of the steps, so the entrance was no longer buried at all. But it was no longer just an opening in the wall either – it had been fitted with a door. A solid, black, cast-iron door. A health and safety measure, I guessed. To keep out the sinners – the teenage drinkers, the vandals, the lovers . . . the curious ten-year-old boys.

I was pretty sure that the door was locked. It had a sturdy-looking keyhole, and it would have been odd if it wasn't locked, and it certainly looked as if it was locked . . . but I cautiously made my way down the steps anyway, just to make sure. One step at a time, keeping my hand against the wall, shining the torch at my feet . . . I could smell it now. The dank air, the stench of urine . . . the smell of the pillbox. At least, I *thought* I could smell it. It could have been just a sense memory.

The door, as I'd guessed, was locked tight. It had no handle, nothing to get hold of . . . and when I shone the penlight into the keyhole, I could tell that there was no point in trying to pick the lock. A reasonably proficient lock picker could probably open it, but even if I'd been stone-cold sober, it still would have been way beyond me.

I turned round and went back up the steps.

The rain was falling quite heavily now, and the wind was getting stronger all the time, and I knew that I ought to start making my way back. But I was determined to at least get a look inside the pillbox before I left, just to see . . .

I don't know what.

Just to see, I suppose.

I went round to the front, where I knew there was a gun slit cut into the wall. It was a few feet across, and no more than six inches deep, and it was situated quite low down in the wall, which made it fairly awkward to see through. But once I'd crouched down and leaned forward a little, it wasn't too bad. The first thing I saw in the beam of my penlight was another health and safety measure – a strong metal grill fixed into the slit. I couldn't quite see what purpose it served, as the slit was too small for anyone to squeeze through anyway, and I wondered for a moment if it was meant instead to keep people from using the pillbox as a rubbish dump . . . but then, as I leaned in closer and shone the penlight through the grill, I suddenly stopped thinking altogether.

There was something in there . . .

Something . . . some*one* . . .

Lying on the floor.

I wiped rain from my face, rubbing at my eyes, wanting to believe that I was seeing things – I was drunk, speeding . . . hallucinating . . . my mind mixed up with twisted memories – but I knew, without question, that this was no illusion. The figure I could see, lying in the darkness on the cold stone floor, was all too real.

It was a girl, a young girl. She was lying awkwardly, half on her side, half on her back, with her head bent back at an unnatural angle to her body. There was an ugly red swelling on the side of her face, and heavy bruising around her throat. Her pale blue eyes were open, staring lifelessly to one side, and she was wearing the same clothes she'd been wearing that morning – a black puffa jacket over a big white hoody, a short denim skirt, skinny black jeans.

It was the American girl, Chelsey Swalenski.

I don't know how long I stayed there, shocked and motion-less, just staring in disbelief at her poor broken body . . . the sight of it emptied me of everything. Every thought, every feeling, every sense . . . everything died in me. I couldn't think, couldn't breathe, couldn't make a sound. All I could do was gaze down into that lonely darkness, staring into those dead blue eyes, remembering how *alive* she'd been the last time I'd seen her – walking across the hotel car park, glancing over her shoulder at me, giving me a quick wave and a smile . . .

And now . . . ?

Now she was nothing.

There was no doubt in my mind that she was dead, almost certainly from a broken neck, but as I rubbed my eyes again, this time wiping away tears, I knew that I had to make absolutely sure. I took a deep breath, paused for a moment to brace myself, then I leaned in close to the grill again and positioned the penlight so the beam held steady on her face. It was almost unbearable – staring at her empty eyes, her pained mouth, her rigid white skin

– and I could feel the tears streaming down my face, but I didn't turn away. I kept looking for any sign of life – a breath, a twitch, a heartbeat, anything – but there was nothing there, no movement at all. I gave it a minute, then another . . . and then another, just to make sure. And then, with a heavy sigh, I turned off the penlight, moved away from the pillbox, took out my mobile and dialled 999.

7

The reality of drunkenness bears little relation to its romance, and one of the many differences between the two is that if you experience a sudden shock when you're drunk in the real world, you *don't* suddenly sober up. It'd be nice if you did, but you don't. No matter how traumatic the experience is, no matter how devastating – physically or emotionally – and no matter how much you wish that you *were* suddenly sober, it just doesn't happen.

It can't, simple as that.

It's physically not possible.

When you're drunk, you're drunk.

And whatever happens, you have to deal with it drunk.

And sometimes the best way of doing that is to do as little as possible.

So after I'd spoken to the 999 operator, giving her as much information as I could – and answering her questions as lucidly as I could – I just lit a cigarette, headed off down the beach, and sat down on a bank of shingle about twenty yards from the pillbox. The operator had told me that the police were on their way, and that in the meantime I should just stay where I was and not touch anything.

And that was fine with me.

I could do that.

I could just sit here and wait.

It was raining really hard now, great solid sheets angling down through the darkness, and the wind was roaring in off the sea, moaning and howling all around me, but I was drunk, and this was the real world, and I didn't really care . . .

I just sat there in the darkness, smoking and waiting . . . trying to ignore the instinctive questions that were already beginning to ask themselves – who? how? why? when? I didn't *want* to think about them. I didn't want to think *detectively* about Chelsey Swalenski at all, I just wanted to feel whatever I felt. Sadness, sickness, anger . . . helplessness. I just wanted to *feel* for her, for her life, her death, her parents . . .

But the questions wouldn't go away. Who did it? Who killed Chelsey? And why? When did it happen? What was she doing out here anyway? And where were her parents? Did the long-haired biker have anything to do with it? Why had he asked me where I was going? And the flash of light I thought I'd seen earlier, and the distant puttering sound . . . could that have been a boat?

I lit another cigarette from the stub of the one I was smoking, then reached into my pocket, pulled out the half-bottle of whisky, and took a long shuddering drink. If I couldn't suddenly be sober, I thought, I might as well carry on being drunk.

The police arrived about twenty minutes later, two uniformed officers in a Land Rover. I saw the lights from a long way off – the flashing blue light, the full-beam headlights – and as they crept slowly along the beach towards me, bobbing up and down with the uneven ground, I got to my feet and made my way back up to the pillbox. The Land Rover was keeping to the higher ground to avoid getting bogged down in the shingle, and as it finally crunched to a halt about ten yards away from the pillbox, I crossed over to meet the two officers. They both had all the gear on – waterproof coats, stab vests, high-vis jackets, peaked hats, jangling belts – and they both looked as if they'd seen it all before. The one in the driving seat was a big barrel-chested man with a grizzled and heavyset face, who I guessed was in his late forties. The other one was younger, mid-twenties, trim and fit-looking.

'John Chandler?' the older one said, getting out of the car and shining a torch into my face.

'Yeah,' I said, shielding my eyes from the light.

'I'm Sergeant Boon,' he said, coming towards me, 'and this is PC Gorman,' he added, indicating his colleague. 'You reported finding a body?'

I nodded, reminding myself that at some point I'd have to admit that Chandler wasn't my real name. Boon had stopped in front of me now and was peering impassively into my eyes.

'Are you all right?' he asked.

'Not really, no.'

He nodded knowingly. 'Where is it then, this body?'

'In the pillbox.'

He glanced behind me at the pillbox, then raised his arm and scanned the surrounding area with his torchlight. 'Inside the pillbox, yeah?'

'That's right. I saw her through—'

'Are you on your own, Mr Chandler?'

I looked at him. 'Yes.'

'There's no one else with you?'

'No, I'm on my own.'

'Have you seen anyone else in the area?'

I shook my head.

'Right,' he said, looking briefly at Gorman. 'Let's take a look then, shall we?'

As the two of them moved off towards the pillbox, and I started to follow them, Boon turned round and said, 'You stay where you are, OK?'

He waited for me to stop before turning back and carrying on. I stood where I was and watched them approach the pillbox. They moved with the cautious confidence of police officers – walking side by side, sweeping the ground in front of them with their torches, their eyes on constant alert. When they reached the pillbox, Boon gave the beach another quick scan with his torch, then turned to Gorman and said, 'Check round the back, Phil.'

As Gorman moved round to the back of the pillbox, I watched Boon stoop down and shine his torch through the gun slit. I pictured the beam of the torch slicing down into the darkness, and the image I'd seen came back to me – Chelsey's broken body, lying on the cold stone floor . . . her lifeless eyes, her battered face, her stolen grace . . .

It wasn't right.

No one should have to die like that.

Not like that . . .

'Mr Chandler!'

I looked up at the sound of the voice and saw Boon beckoning me over to the pillbox. Gorman was standing beside him, and neither of them looked overly concerned about anything. If the sight of Chelsey's dead body had shocked them at all, they certainly weren't showing it. *Maybe they really* have *seen it all before*, I thought to myself as I headed over to the pillbox. But there was something about the way they were looking at me that told me there was more to it than that.

'Right then, Mr Chandler,' Boon said as I stopped in front of them. 'What's this all about?'

'What?'

'How much have you had to drink tonight?'

'What's that got to do with anything?'

'How *much*?'

'Quite a bit,' I admitted, wondering what was going on. 'But I still don't see—'

'Have you had anything else?'

'What do you mean?'

'You know what I mean.' He stared into my eyes. 'What is it? Coke, smack—?'

'What the fuck's the *matter* with you?' I said, suddenly losing my temper. 'There's a dead girl in there, for Christ's sake. A murdered girl. And you're standing here asking me stupid fucking questions—'

'What does she look like, this girl?'

'*What?*'

'Describe her.'

'You've just fucking *seen* her! You *know* what she looks like.'

'All right, John,' he said calmly, stepping closer to me. 'Let's just take it easy, OK? There's no need to get upset.'

'I'm not—'

'All right, that's enough,' he said firmly, taking hold of my arm and leaning forward to stare into my eyes. 'Now, for the last fucking time, what does she look like?'

I really didn't understand this at all, and for a moment or two I wondered, quite seriously, if I'd drunk so much that I'd passed out at some point and missed something, something that would make sense of what was happening. But it was just too confusing to think about, and – for now – all I could think of doing was to play along, do what I was told, and see what happened.

'She's about thirteen or fourteen,' I sighed. 'Light brown shoulder-length hair, blue eyes, quite slim, about five foot three. She's wearing a white hoody, a black jacket, denim skirt, black jeans. Her name's Chelsey Swalenski. She's American. She's staying with her parents at Victoria Hall.' I looked at Boon. 'All right? Is that enough for you?'

'More than enough. So you know her then?'

'No . . . I'm staying at the same hotel, that's all. She left her diary behind . . .'

'She what?'

'It doesn't matter.' I looked at him again. 'So are you going to *do* something now?'

'What would you like me to do?'

'Your *job*, for fuck's sake. Call it in, secure the area, just do what you're supposed to fucking do—'

'Come over here, John,' he said, leading me by the arm

towards the pillbox. He stopped by the gun slit in the wall. 'You saw her through here, is that right?'

'Yes.'

'It's pitch-black in there.'

'I've got a torch.'

'Really?'

I nodded. 'A penlight.'

'OK . . .' he said. 'So you had your penlight out, and you were looking in through this gap in the wall . . . is that correct?'

'Yes.'

'And you saw this girl, Chelsey Salinski—'

'Swalenski. Her name's Chelsey Swalenski.'

'Swalenski, right. You saw her inside the pillbox?'

I didn't say anything then, I just looked at him, not wanting to think what I was beginning to think, but I could see it in his eyes now, I could see what was coming. And as he crouched down by the gun slit, grabbing my arm and pulling me down with him, I already knew what I was going to see when Boon shone his torch through the gap. I didn't *want* to see it, because it wasn't possible, and the last thing I needed just now was to see the impossible.

'Well?' Boon said, his eyes fixed on me.

I turned slowly and gazed down into the pillbox.

There was nothing there.

No body, no dead girl, no Chelsey . . .

Nothing at all.

The pillbox was empty.

*

'She was there,' I said simply to Boon. 'She was dead. I saw her . . .'

'Really?'

I looked at him. 'I *saw* her.'

'So where is she now then?'

'Give me that,' I said, snatching the torch off him. I leaned in closer to the gun slit and shone the torch through the gap again. The beam was a lot more powerful than the beam of my penlight, flooding down into the pillbox and lighting up every inch of the concrete chamber, and no matter how long I carried on searching – moving the torch around, scanning the floor, shining it into every corner – I knew I was wasting my time. There was no body down there, just dust and sand, shallow puddles, dirt, beach debris . . . bits of nothing.

'She was down there,' I repeated, unable to think of anything else to say. 'I saw her.' I looked at Boon. 'You have to believe me . . .'

'All right,' he sighed, getting to his feet. 'Let's say, just for a minute, that you *did* see her. She's definitely not there any more, is she?'

I stood up. 'No, she's not.'

'So what's happened to her?'

'I don't know . . .'

'Are you sure she was dead?'

'Well, yeah . . . as sure as I can be.'

'She wasn't just asleep or something?'

'No . . . absolutely not.'

'Did you check for a pulse?'

I shook my head. 'I didn't go in . . . I couldn't, the door's locked.'

'The door at the back, you mean?'

'Yeah.'

'It was locked?'

'Yes.'

He looked at Gorman, who was standing off to one side, talking quietly into the radio clipped onto his jacket. 'Phil?' Boon said.

'Just a second,' Gorman said into the radio, turning to Boon. 'Yeah?'

'Did you check the door at the back?'

'Yeah.'

'Is it locked?'

'Yeah.'

Boon turned back to me. 'It doesn't make a lot of sense, does it, John? I mean, even if there was someone in there, dead or alive, how the hell could they have got out between the time you saw them and the time we arrived? You were right here all the time, weren't you?'

'Not *right* here . . . I waited over there.' I pointed down the beach to where I'd been sitting.

Boon looked down the beach, then back at me. 'So what are you saying? You think that while you were waiting, someone could have unlocked the door, removed the body, and taken it away? Without you *knowing*?'

I thought about it, trying to work out if it was possible. Had I fallen asleep at any point? Was I so drunk that I wouldn't have noticed someone removing a body from a pillbox twenty yards away from me?

'It's not *im*possible . . .' I muttered.

'What?'

I looked at Boon. 'I said, it's not impossible.'

He looked back at me, shaking his head in exasperation, then he took my arm again and led me round to the back of the pillbox. The ground here was mostly sand, firmly packed and dark with rain, and when Boon stopped a few yards away from the pillbox, shining his torch at the area around the steps leading down to the door, it was easy to make out the two sets of footprints in the sand.

'Those are PC Gorman's prints,' Boon said, lighting up one of the trails. 'And those . . .' He lit up the other set of prints, then shone the torch back at the trail I'd just made. 'Those are yours. Do you agree?'

'Yeah.'

He turned then, scanning the ground all around the back of the pillbox with his torch. 'Can you see any other footprints?' he asked me.

'No . . .'

'Any sign that anyone else has been here?'

I shook my head.

He looked at me. 'Do you think it's possible for someone to remove a dead body from the pillbox and not leave any tracks?'

'No,' I said quietly. 'No, it's not possible.'

'Right,' he said, heading over to the steps. 'Wait there.'

I watched him go down the steps to the cast-iron door. He stopped at the bottom and took a big old key from his coat pocket, unlocked the door, and swung it open. As it clanged heavily against the concrete wall, Boon stooped down, almost doubling over, and squeezed through the doorway into the pillbox.

Nothing happened for a few moments. I could see his torchlight sweeping around inside, and I guessed he was just double-checking, making absolutely sure that there wasn't anything in there, and then his head popped round the doorway and he called out to me to come down.

I went down the steps and joined him inside the pillbox.

'See?' Boon said, waving the torch around. 'Nothing. No dead body. Nothing at all.'

He was right, there was nothing in there at all. No body, no trace of a body, no sign that a body had ever been there . . . there weren't even any empty beer cans or bottles or torn-up porn magazines. There was just a damp concrete floor, moss-stained concrete walls, bits of patched-up brickwork here and there, and that was pretty much it.

'Satisfied now?' Boon said, looking at me.

I looked down at the floor, staring at the spot where I'd seen Chelsey's body. There was nothing there . . . nothing at all.

'John?' Boon said.

'What?'

He just looked at me then, and I guessed that he was waiting for me to admit that I must have been mistaken. But I knew what I'd seen. And I knew it was real. It wasn't my imagination. It wasn't an illusion or a hallucination. I *knew* what I'd seen.

'Sarge?'

It was Gorman's voice, calling down the steps from outside.

'Hold on,' Boon called back, ushering me towards the doorway. 'We're just coming.'

As I went back up the steps, I glanced over my shoulder and saw Boon relocking the cast-iron door and slipping the key back into his coat, and I wondered briefly where he'd got it from, and why he'd brought it with him . . . and, come to that, why he'd insisted on showing me inside the pillbox when we'd already seen all there was to see through the gun slit.

I didn't have time to come to any conclusions. I'd reached the top of the steps now, and Gorman was standing there with a mobile phone in his hand, and as Boon came up the steps behind me, Gorman said to him, 'I've just spoken to the manager at Victoria Hall.'

'Arthur Finch?' Boon said.

'Yeah.' Gorman glanced at me, then turned back to Boon. 'He said the Swalenskis *were* staying there, and they do have a fourteen-year-old daughter called Chelsey, but they checked out earlier today, around lunchtime.'

'Right,' Boon said, looking at me.

'No,' I said firmly, shaking my head. 'No, that's not right . . .'

'Come on, John,' Boon said, taking my arm. 'I think we'd better get you back—'

'No, hold on,' I said. 'They *weren't* checking out today. Chelsey told me. They were heading off to London on Monday and then flying back to the US on Wednesday—'

'She told you that, did she?'

'Yes—'

'Why?'

'Why *what*?'

'Why would a fourteen-year-old girl confide in you?'

'She wasn't *confiding* in me . . . we were just talking.'

Boon tightened his grip on my arm then, and – without saying another word – he began leading me off towards the Land Rover. I realised that there was no point in struggling or trying to make him listen to me any more. All that would do was make things worse. So as I stumbled along beside the big man, and Gorman trailed along behind us, I just kept my mouth shut and tried to think . . .

But it didn't do much good.

By the time we'd all got in the Land Rover – me in the back, Boon and Gorman up front – and Gorman had started the engine and begun driving us back along the beach, the only solid thought I'd come up with was – *what the* fuck *is going on here?*

8

No one spoke for a while. The Land Rover moved steadily across the beach, crunching through the shingle, bouncing up and down over the uneven ground, and I just sat there in the back, gazing out into the ocean darkness, listening to the sound of the rain hammering down hard on the roof of the car, and the hypnotic clack-clack of the windscreen wipers, and the unintelligible voices crackling away on the police radio . . .

I'd pretty much given up on trying to make sense of anything for the moment. There was nothing I could do until I had more information, and I wasn't going to be in a position to gain more information until Boon and Gorman had finished with me, and I had no idea what they were intending to do with me anyway. I guessed, if they wanted to, they could probably charge me with wasting police time, or making a hoax emergency call, or some kind of public order offence. But unless they had motives that I didn't know about, I really didn't think they'd bother. On the other hand, I got the feeling that they weren't going to just drop me back at the hotel, say good-night, and forget all about it either. In their eyes, I was a drunk outsider who'd dragged them out into the rain, strung them along with an outlandish story, and generally pissed them off. They'd want at least some reparation for that.

And until they'd taken it, there was nothing much I could do. So I just sat there in the back of the Land Rover, gazing out through the rain-streamed glass, waiting to see what happened.

The only vehicular access to the beach was a launch ramp at the boatyards on the west of the island, and as we drove up the ramp and turned right, heading up a steep hill back towards the village, I assumed that I was being taken to the police station. But after a few minutes, Boon muttered something to Gorman, who was driving, and Gorman flicked the indicator and pulled in at a bus stop at the side of the road. I looked around, wondering why we'd stopped. There was nothing here. Large detached houses were set back from the road behind high hedges and solid stone walls, and I could just make out a few turrets and chimney tops in the sterile glare of unseen security lights, but that was about all I could see. There was very little traffic on the road . . . no pedestrians, no passers-by.

'Right then, John,' I heard Boon say. He'd turned round in the passenger seat now and was looking directly at me. 'Before we go any further,' he continued, 'we need to get a few details straight. All right?'

I nodded.

He smiled.

And the questions began.

*

I decided it was best to come clean straight away about who I really was, so I told Boon my real name, and I explained why I was using an alias, which unfortunately meant letting him know that I was a private investigator. I would have preferred to have kept that to myself, but given the situation I couldn't see any way round it. And, besides, once they started checking my details, which they no doubt would, they'd find out what I did for a living anyway. So there was simply no point in lying. Not yet, anyway.

'Yeah, I thought I recognised you from somewhere,' Boon said, nodding his head. 'John Craine . . . yeah, of course . . . you were on the news a few weeks ago, weren't you?'

I nodded.

He grinned. 'I seem to remember you calling a reporter an annoying cunt on live TV.'

I shrugged.

Boon looked at me. 'It was the Anna Gerrish case, wasn't it?'

'Yeah.'

He paused for a moment then, deep in thought, and I just stared at him, keeping my face as blank as possible, letting him know that I'd told him as much as I was going to about my involvement in the Anna Gerrish case.

'Is Mick Bishop still running the investigation?' he asked me.

'As far as I know,' I said, shrugging again. 'It's nothing to do with me any more.'

'Really?'

'Call Bishop if you want,' I said, staring at Boon. 'I'm sure he'll be more than happy to answer your questions.'

I didn't know whether Boon knew Bishop personally or just by reputation, but either way I guessed he'd know that you don't just call up Mick Bishop and start asking him questions, especially about one of his cases, not if you know what's good for you anyway. And I could tell by the flash of caution I saw in Boon's eyes that I was right.

'So . . .' he said, slightly wary now. 'Your reason for being here, on the island . . . it's nothing to do with the Gerrish case?'

I shook my head. 'I'm not working on anything, I'm just taking a break from it all. Like I said, the only reason I'm not using my real name is to keep the press from bothering me.'

'All right,' he said, his confidence coming back. 'I suppose that's fair enough . . . but it doesn't actually *explain* anything, does it?'

'Like what?'

'Well, for a start, I wouldn't mind knowing what you thought you were doing this evening – wandering round the beach in the dark, in the pouring rain, pissed out of your head.' He raised his eyebrows at me, waiting for an answer.

'It's not a crime, is it?' I said.

'That depends.'

'On what?'

'Well, you haven't *just* been drinking, have you? I can

tell from your eyes that you're on something, coke or speed would be my guess, and I think you'll find that possession of a Class A drug is still against the law.'

I didn't think he'd appreciate me telling him that amphetamine is actually a Class B drug, so I didn't. I just kept quiet and looked at him.

'And what were you doing at the pillbox anyway?' he said.

'Nothing . . . I was just . . .'

'Just what?'

'Look,' I sighed, 'I wasn't *doing* anything, OK? I'd had a few drinks during the day, probably a few too many, and I just went for a walk on the beach to clear my head, that's all. When I got to the pillbox . . . well, I don't know, I was just a bit tired, I suppose. I stopped for a cigarette, and I was just kind of looking around, you know . . . just being nosy . . .'

'Right,' said Boon, without much conviction. 'And what about the dead body then? What was that all about?'

I shrugged. 'I really thought I saw it . . . honestly, I could have sworn it was real.'

'And what do you think now?'

'I don't know . . . I was pretty drunk, I suppose. And I was cold and wet, and tired . . .'

'Anything else?'

I hesitated for a moment, weighing up the pros and cons of admitting that I'd taken some speed, and I was fairly sure that if I did tell Boon the truth, he wouldn't do anything about it, but in the end I decided not to take the risk. 'I fractured a bone recently,' I said, showing him my bandaged hand. 'I've been taking prescription painkillers . . .' I shrugged again. 'I might have overdone it a bit.'

Boon nodded, but again I wasn't sure that he was totally convinced. 'So are you telling me now that you were so whacked out of your head on booze and painkillers that you thought you saw something that wasn't there?'

'I can't think of any other explanation.'

'And why do you think that what you saw, or what you *thought* you saw, was the dead body of a teenage girl who was staying in the same hotel as you?'

'I've no idea.'

'Is she pretty?'

'What?'

'This girl, Chelsey . . . a pretty little thing, is she?'

'Fuck you.'

Boon smiled. 'Well, she was obviously on your mind, John. You can't blame me for jumping to conclusions.'

'Is that it?' I said, staring at him. 'Are we finished now?'

Boon held my gaze for a few moments, then turned to Gorman. 'What do you think, Phil?' he said calmly. 'Are we finished yet?'

'I wouldn't have thought so,' Gorman replied.

They both smiled at me then.

And the questions continued.

I only had myself to blame. If I hadn't told Boon to fuck himself, they probably wouldn't have carried on questioning me for another twenty minutes or so, just to piss me off. Not that it really mattered. I was in no great rush to be anywhere else, and I knew they were just fucking me around, so all I had to do was sit there and answer their questions – what's your full name? date of birth? address? business address? contact telephone number? how long are you staying here? – and eventually they'd run out of things to ask, and that would be it.

And that's pretty much how it panned out.

Gorman made a point of calling in my details to check me out, but all he came up with was the fact that my car had been impounded a couple of weeks ago, towed away for parking in a pedestrianised area, and that I still hadn't paid the outstanding fine or made any effort to reclaim the car.

'You need to sort that out,' he told me.

'Yeah, I'm going to,' I lied.

He looked at Boon, asking him if there was anything else. Boon thought for a moment, then shook his head.

And that was it.

Gorman started the Land Rover, looked in the mirror, and pulled away.

It was around eight thirty when I finally got back to Victoria Hall. Gorman drove the Land Rover into the car park, pulling up in front of the hotel, and Boon got out and came round to open the back door for me. As I stepped out of the car, my right leg suddenly gave way and I stumbled sideways into Boon, almost knocking him over.

'Shit!' he said. 'What the fuck—?'

'Sorry!' I said, grabbing hold of him to keep my balance. 'It's my leg . . .'

'Fucking *hell*!'

'Sorry,' I said again, straightening up and rubbing the back of my thigh. 'It just went dead, you know . . .' I winced painfully. 'It's coming back to life now.'

'Fuck's sake,' he muttered, glaring at me. 'You're a fucking mess, Craine. You know that, don't you? A fucking mess.'

I rubbed the back of my thigh again, then reached into my pocket, took out my cigarettes, and lit one.

Boon carried on staring at me for a while, his eyes filled with disdain, and I just smoked my cigarette and looked back at him, waiting for him to deliver his parting shot, but eventually, somewhat to my surprise, he just sighed and shook his head, as if he simply couldn't be bothered with me any more, and without another word he turned round and got back into the Land Rover.

I watched it pull away, the tail lights hazing in the still-falling rain, and then I just stood there for a while, looking out across the car park, smoking and thinking . . . and I remembered looking out of the breakfast-room window that morning, just after I'd found Chelsey's diary . . . that small pink notebook with flower stickers on the front and *My Diary* embossed in glittery gold lettering . . . I'd picked it up off the table and looked out of the window, not really expecting to see the Americans, but there they were – the three of them standing at the end of the car park, Chelsey patting her pockets and searching anxiously through her rucksack . . . and I'd seen her father say something to her, and then I'd seen her looking back at the hotel, and I'd raised my hand and waved her diary . . . and she'd frowned at me for a moment, but then her father had pointed at me, and spoken to her again, and she'd looked back at me, realising now what had happened . . . and her father had smiled and put his hand on her shoulder – *go on, run back and get it, we'll wait for you here* . . . and she'd set off, hurrying up the driveway with a mixture of relief and embarrassment on her face . . .

And now, some twelve hours later, she was dead.

Murdered.

I still had no idea what had happened to her body. I couldn't even begin to understand it. But no matter how impossible it seemed, I knew that it had to be possible, because it had happened. Her body *had* been there, that was a fact.

I'd seen it, stared at it. I'd cried over it.

It was there.

I put my hand in my pocket and felt the cold steel of the key I'd just lifted from Boon's coat pocket when I'd stumbled into him getting out of the car. It was the key to the pillbox . . . the key, perhaps, to a young girl's death.

I put out my cigarette and went into the hotel.

It was my turn to start asking some questions.

A middle-aged couple dressed in rambling gear were talking to Arthur Finch as I approached the reception desk – chatting about the weather, laughing and joking, telling him their holiday plans. Arthur looked nervous when he saw me – fidgety, tense, forcing himself to smile – and as I got closer, I could see that his hands were shaking. He was more than just anxious, I realised, he was scared . . . not *of* me, I guessed, but *because* of me. And despite my conviction that he'd lied to PC Gorman about the Swalenskis checking out, I couldn't help feeling a little bit sorry for him. He was just an old man, a frail and frightened old man . . .

And Chelsey Swalenski is dead, I reminded myself.

I waited for the ramblers to leave, ignoring their cheery greetings, and then I stepped up to the reception desk.

'Evening, Arthur,' I said, looking him in the eye. 'What a night, eh?'

He glanced behind me, making sure that the ramblers had gone, then leaned towards me and spoke in a whisper. 'What on *earth* is going on, John? The police called earlier, asking questions about you and the Swalenskis, something to do with their daughter—'

'Yeah, sorry about that,' I said, smiling. 'It was my fault, just a stupid misunderstanding. It's all sorted out now.'

He frowned. 'But they said that you thought something had happened to her—'

'I got her mixed up with someone else, that's all.'

He shook his head, looking perplexed. 'I still don't understand . . .'

'Look,' I said, pretending to lose patience. 'I just made a mistake, OK? I saw this girl, and I thought she was in some kind of trouble, and she looked just like the American girl, so when I called the police to report it, I told them who I thought it was . . . but then it turned out that this girl *wasn't* the American girl after all, and not only that, she wasn't actually in trouble either.'

'I see . . .' Arthur said, nodding.

'It was all a bit embarrassing really.'

'Well, yes . . . I can imagine.'

His voice, and his eyes, had become quite distant now, and I got the feeling that he was weighing up what I'd just told him, trying to work out if the bare bones of my story made sense in view of what he knew . . . whatever that was. The trouble was, I was almost totally in the dark here, because I didn't *know* what he knew, which meant that I had no way of knowing if my story made sense or not. So all I could really do was keep playing for time, try to keep him off balance, and hope to get something out of him before he clammed up.

'I felt so stupid,' I said, laughing quietly. 'I mean, when the police told me that they'd called you, and that you'd told them the Swalenskis had checked out at lunchtime . . . I felt *such* an idiot. And what made it even worse was that I'd talked to Mr Swalenski at breakfast and he'd *told* me they were checking out today—'

'Really?' Arthur said suddenly, his eyes widening. 'He *said* that?'

I nodded casually. 'Is there any reason he shouldn't have?'

'No, no,' Arthur stuttered, trying to compose himself. 'No . . . it was just—'

'They *did* check out, didn't they?'

'Yes . . . yes, at lunchtime,' he said, nervously clearing his throat. 'They took a taxi to Hey. I believe they were going on to London for a few days before flying back to Dallas.' He looked at me. I stared back at him, saying nothing. 'That's where they're from,' he went on, looking away. 'From Dallas . . . he's a professional photographer, apparently, Bryan . . . Mr Swalenski. A wildlife

109

photographer, you know, he takes pictures for books and magazines . . .'

'Really?'

'Yes,' Arthur said, nodding overvigorously now. 'He specialises in birds, photographs of birds . . . I think that's partly why he brought his family down here, because of all the seabirds, you know . . . sort of a working holiday . . .' He paused then, smiling uncomfortably, and I think he'd suddenly realised that he was talking too much, over-compensating with the truth to cover up his lies. 'Well, anyway . . .' he muttered, turning his attention to a pile of papers on the desk. 'I'd better get on, if you don't mind . . . things to do, you know . . .'

'Of course,' I said. 'And I'm sorry again for causing you any trouble.' I smiled at him. 'It won't happen again, I promise.'

He nodded, avoiding eye contact.

I turned to go, then immediately turned back. 'Do you know which taxi driver took them to Hey?'

'Sorry?'

'The Swalenskis . . . you said they took a taxi to Hey.'

'Yes . . . that's right.'

'Who drove them?'

'Why? I mean, does it matter?'

I shrugged. 'Just wondering, that's all.'

He frowned at me.

'Don't worry about it,' I said, smiling again. 'I'll ask around. Maybe someone else—'

'It was Eric,' he said wearily. 'Eric Atherton. Island Cabs. He picked them up at twelve thirty and drove them to Hey.'

'Eric Atherton?'

'Yes.'

'Thank you.'

Arthur nodded, picking up the pile of papers. 'Now, if there's nothing else . . . ?'

'I'll leave you to it.'

9

Back in my room, I stripped off my wet clothes and took a long hot shower. The speed had lost its edge now, and although I was far from sober, my drunkenness was beginning to turn cloudy and stale. It's never a good feeling, coming down from being drunk, and under normal circumstances I probably would have just knocked myself out with another couple of drinks and then gone to bed to sleep it off.

But these weren't normal circumstances.

And, unlike Arthur, I really *did* have things to do.

So I stayed in the shower for a while, soaking up the steam, sweating out some of the cloudiness, and I thought about Arthur Finch, and Sergeant Boon . . . and the biker from the caravan who I'd seen on the steps at the beach . . . and I remembered the handwriting on a flowery pink diary – *Chelsey Swalenski* . . . the letters not joined-up, a little heart symbol in place of the dot on the *i* . . . and I heard again the sound of her voice . . . *we're going to London on Monday, and then flying back on Wednesday* . . .

Monday.

Not Saturday.

Monday.

I got out of the shower, put on some clean clothes, and called Cal Franks.

Cal was Stacy's nephew, and he's been working on and off for me for almost fifteen years. Even when he was a skinny little fourteen-year-old kid he could do things with a computer that literally left me speechless, and over the years he's developed his skills to such an extent that he now makes a very lucrative living from 'doing things with computers'. Whether these things are always strictly legal or not, I honestly couldn't say. I don't ask, and Cal doesn't tell. And that's the way we like it. Similarly, if I'm working on a case and I need Cal's help, whether it's something to do with computers or phone technology, surveillance equipment or security systems, it's entirely up to me how much I tell him. If I don't think he needs to know everything about the case, I don't tell him everything. And he's fine with that. And if, for any reason, he can't help me, or he doesn't want to, he just has to say so, and that's fine with me.

It's a perfect working relationship . . . and it has to be, because Cal is much more to me than *just* my nephew-in-law, or *just* someone I occasionally work with – he's one of the very few people I genuinely care about. And that's why, when I called him that night, I was half-hoping that he wouldn't answer. The last time I'd asked him to help me with a case – just a few weeks ago – he'd ended up getting beaten half to death. He was still in hospital now, recuperating from a broken leg, a broken arm, and some fairly serious head injuries. He's a young and reasonably healthy man, and I knew that his body would heal quite quickly, and I also knew that he didn't blame me for what had happened and that he was coping with everything in his usual carefree manner. As soon as he'd been moved from intensive care he'd transferred himself to the best private hospital in Hey, and when I'd last visited him, just before leaving for Hale, he was sitting up in bed, tapping away on a laptop, with one of his many mobile phones plugged into his ear, another one downloading one of his self-designed programs, and an iPad resting at the foot of his bed keeping him up to date with all the latest share prices.

So, yes, I knew that he was coping . . . but that didn't change the fact that he'd been badly hurt, and that it could have been a whole lot worse, and that none of it would have happened if I hadn't got in touch with him in the first place . . .

So I had my reservations about calling him again.

But I also had a promise to keep.

Just before I'd left the hospital, Cal had said to me, 'If you need anything else when you're away, John . . . I mean, if you need any more help with Serina Mayo or her daughter, or if you need any help with anything else at all . . .' He'd paused then, looking into my eyes. 'Don't even *think* about not calling me, OK? If you ever did that . . .' He shook his head. 'Well, I'd hate that more than anything. So, please . . . just, you know . . .'

'OK,' I'd told him.

'Promise?'

'Yeah, I promise.'

Of course, that didn't stop me from hoping that he wouldn't answer his phone, but as soon as the ringing tone kicked in, I kind of knew that he would. You can always tell, can't you? A ringing tone either sounds like it's going to be answered or it sounds like it's wasting your time. This one wasn't wasting my time.

'Hey, Uncle Johnny!' Cal said, answering after just two or three rings. 'How are you doing? You OK?'

I couldn't help smiling at the manic glee in his voice.

'Yeah, I'm fine,' I told him. 'How about you?'

'Yeah, pretty good . . . I'm getting a bit stir-crazy, you know, stuck in here all the time, but hopefully I'll be out in a couple of days.'

'Yeah?'

'Yeah, the leg and the arm are OK, they just want to make sure that there's nothing wrong with my head before they let me out.'

'Sounds to me like you could be in there for a long time then.'

He laughed. 'Yeah, you're a funny man, Nunc. Very *droll*.'

I heard a female voice in the background then, a quiet giggle, and then the sound of another voice, also female.

'I'm not interrupting anything, am I?' I said.

'What? Oh, no . . . it's all right, just some friends, you know.'

'I hope they're looking after you all right.'

'I'm not complaining.'

'I bet you're not.'

He laughed again. 'So, how's it going down in sunny Hale?'

'Not so sunny, to tell you the truth.'

115

'Have you seen Serina and Robyn?'

'I spoke to Serina this morning, but Robyn wasn't there.'

'And?'

'Well, Serina confirmed that Robyn is definitely my dad's daughter—'

'Really?'

'Yeah, it's a pretty weird feeling, Cal, suddenly finding out that you've got a half-sister you've never met.'

'Are you going to meet her?'

'I don't know . . . it's kind of complicated. Robyn doesn't know anything about me, and she's got a lot of problems in her life anyway . . . so I don't know if meeting up with her is a good idea or not. I've left it up to Serina to decide.'

'Right . . .'

'But, anyway, that's not really what I was calling about. I need you to do something for me, Cal.'

'About time. I'm getting bored stupid in here.'

'Yeah, well, it's not much. I just need you to get into a couple of systems for me.'

'No problem,' he said, and I heard him tapping keys. 'I'm ready when you are. Where do you want to go?'

'Victoria Hall, the hotel I'm staying at. Their reservation system.'

'Right.' *Tap tap tap.*

'What I need to know is the check-out date for a booking in the name of Swalenski. Two adults and a teenage daughter . . .' *Tap tap tap.* 'I don't know when they checked in. Their home address should be somewhere in Dallas.'

'Dallas, Texas?'

'Yeah.'

'OK . . . hold on a sec.'

I heard more tapping, and it wasn't hard to imagine Cal sitting up in bed, his fingers skipping over the keyboard, his eyes glued to the screen . . . and I could see his beautifully ravaged face in my mind, the rings in his ears, the eyebrow studs, the scarecrow mess of jet-black hair that had recently been partly shaved . . .

'How's your hair doing, Cal?' I said. 'Is it starting to grow back yet?'

'I don't want to talk about it,' he said sulkily. *Tap tap tap.* 'I'm going to have to wear a hat for fucking months when I get out of here.'

'You could always try shaving the rest of it off. You never know, it might suit you. You'd look like—'

'Swalenski,' he said suddenly. 'Here we go. Bryan Swalenski, his wife Ruth, and their daughter Chelsey.'

'Yeah, that's them.'

'Their home address is Fairview Vale, University Park, Dallas. They checked in on Monday 25 October—'

'What's the check-out date?'

'Hold on . . .'

I heard more tapping again, then a faint murmur of puzzlement, then more tapping.

'Cal?' I said.

'Yeah, sorry . . . I'm just double-checking something.' *Tap tap tap.* 'OK, I thought so . . .'

'What is it?'

'The check-out date's been changed. It comes up now as today, Saturday 30 October, but on the original

117

booking they weren't due to check out until Monday 1 November.'

'Can you tell when it was changed?'

'Today, 18.08.'

'Today?'

'Yep.'

Just gone six o'clock this evening . . . six hours *after* the Swalenskis were supposed to have checked out. It was also around the time that I was talking to Boon and Gorman at the pillbox.

'Is there any way of telling who changed the date?' I asked Cal.

'No, the system's password protected, so anyone who knows the password can get into it and make amendments to bookings.'

'What's the password.'

Tap tap.

'Honey.'

'Honey? As in bees?'

'Yeah.'

I thought about that for a moment, but it didn't seem to have any significance. 'What room were the Swalenskis in?' I asked Cal.

'Sixteen,' he said. 'One, six. It's a family room, apparently.'

'Did they leave a phone number?'

'Yeah, mobile and landline. The landline's a US number. Do you want me to text the numbers to you?'

'Yeah, please.'

'OK, what else?'

'Is there a facility on the system for assigning a blank keycard to a particular room?'

'Yeah, of course.'

'How does it work?'

It didn't take long for Cal to explain, and it all sounded fairly straightforward. I'd made some notes just in case I forgot anything, but there wasn't really much to forget.

'Anything else?' Cal asked me.

'Yeah, can you check the airlines, see if you can find the Swalenskis' flight back to Dallas. They're probably flying from Heathrow, and I'm almost certain they were due to fly out on Wednesday 3 November, but that might have been changed. Or cancelled. And it might *not* be Heathrow—'

'Don't worry,' Cal said. 'I'll get what you need. It might take a bit of time—'

'That's all right, there's no hurry. I just need to know . . .' I paused, realising that I didn't really know what I needed to know.

'John?' Cal said quietly. 'Are you all right?'

'Yeah . . .'

'What is it? I mean, what's going on down there?'

'I don't know, Cal,' I admitted. 'It's probably . . .'

Nothing, I was going to say. It's probably nothing. But that wasn't right. A girl had been killed, her body had disappeared, her parents were missing, and someone was trying to cover it all up. That was hardly nothing, was it?

'John?'

'Yeah, sorry, Cal . . . I was just thinking about something.'

119

'Are you sure you're OK?'

'Yeah, honestly. I'm fine.'

'You're not doing too much, are you?'

'What do you mean?'

'You know what I mean.'

I thought about the coke and speed in my bag, and I knew that I'd be taking more of it tonight, and probably tomorrow too . . .

'You just worry about yourself, Cal,' I told him, lighting another cigarette. 'I don't want you going home unless the doctors say it's OK, all right?'

'Yeah . . .'

'And in the meantime, don't overexert yourself.'

He laughed. 'What's *that* supposed to mean?'

'And don't forget to text me those phone numbers.'

'It's already done.'

'Oh, right . . .'

'I'll get back to you about the Dallas flight as soon as I've got something.'

'Thanks, Cal.'

'And John?'

'What?'

'Have you called Bridget yet?'

'Yeah,' I lied. 'Yeah, I spoke to her earlier. She's fine.'

'Really?'

'Well, no . . . I mean, she's not *fine*, obviously. But she's, you know . . . she's coping.'

'Is she still at her sister's?'

'Yeah.'

'When's she coming back?'

'Not for a while yet.'

'Right . . . and how was it? I mean, talking to her . . . was it OK?'

'Yeah, yeah . . . it was . . . you know . . . it was—'

'You haven't called her, have you?'

I sighed. 'I'm *going* to, OK?'

'When?'

'When I'm ready.'

'And when's that going to be?'

'I don't know . . . I just . . .'

'Just fucking *call* her, John, OK?' Cal said.

'Yeah, I know.'

'Just do it.'

'I will.'

'When?'

'Right now, as soon as you've gone.'

'Promise?'

'Yeah, I promise.'

'Right, well, I'm going then. I'll speak to you later.'

'Yeah, see you, Cal.'

As soon as he'd hung up, I uncrossed my fingers, opened the text Cal had sent me, and punched in Bryan Swalenski's mobile number. There was no ringing tone, no voicemail, nothing. Just the dull hum of a dead line. I tried his landline number. It took a while to connect, but eventually it started ringing, and after a few moments an answerphone message clicked in: *Hi, this is Bryan Swalenski, please leave a message after the tone.*

I didn't leave a message.

What could I say?

I lit a cigarette, sat there smoking for a while, and then I called Ada. Ada looks after the business side of my private investigation company in Hey – administration, finance, invoices, tax . . . she basically keeps everything organised, including me. I didn't actually *need* to speak to her – the business was temporarily closed down, so there wasn't really anything to discuss – but I knew Cal would be checking up on me, ringing my number to make sure that I'd called Bridget, as I'd promised him I would, and – knowing Cal – he wouldn't just call once to check that my number was engaged, he'd give it a few minutes and try again . . . and I didn't want to have to explain anything to him. I didn't want to admit that I was scared of calling Bridget, that I was frightened that she might tell me that she was never coming back . . . or maybe it was the other way round, and I was scared that she might tell me that she *was* coming back.

I didn't know . . . and I didn't want to think about it.

Not yet.

But I didn't call Ada *just* to make Cal think that I was talking to Bridget, I called her because I like her. She's a fat and grumpy old woman, and she doesn't care what anyone else thinks of her, and I always feel totally at ease in her company.

'Yes?' she said coldly when she answered.

'Hi, Ada. It's me.'

'John?'

'Yeah.'

'What's going on?'

'Nothing . . . I just thought I'd give you a call, you know, see how things are . . .'

'A *social* call?'

'There's no need to sound so surprised.'

'No? When was the last time you called me just to "see how things are"?'

'Yeah, well, maybe I'm turning over a new leaf, changing my ways—'

'Yeah, right,' she said, laughing. 'Of course you are.'

'I *could* change,' I said, smiling to myself. 'I mean, if I really wanted to—'

'John, you can't even change a fucking light bulb.'

It was around nine thirty when I got off the phone. Talking to Ada had helped take my mind off everything else for a while – I'd purposely avoided telling her anything about Chelsey – and as I lit a cigarette and went out onto the balcony, my head felt a little less cluttered. The rain had stopped now, and the night was cold and still. The sea was as black as the starless skies, a liquid shimmer on the horizon, and if I closed my eyes and listened hard, I could hear the sigh of the surf rolling gently over the shingle.

I stayed out on the balcony for a while, just smoking quietly and listening to the night, then I went back inside and redialled Bryan Swalenski's phone numbers. As I expected, nothing had changed – a dead line, an empty house.

Dead and empty.

I turned on the TV and flicked through the channels until I found a film that didn't look too bad, and then I set myself up on the bed with cigarettes, speed and whisky, and I settled down to wait.

10

It was three o'clock in the morning when I left my room and padded down the corridor towards reception. The hotel had been quiet for hours – no TV sounds, no distant voices, no sounds from anywhere at all – and I was as sure as I could be that no one else was around. Arthur Finch had told me when I'd first checked in that the reception desk was unstaffed between midnight and six in the morning. He'd also told me that if I did happen to need anything during the night, all I had to do was pick up the phone on the reception desk and it would automatically ring through to the private rooms at the back of the hotel where he lived. I didn't know exactly where these rooms were located, but there was a doorway marked PRIVATE just to the right of the reception desk, so I guessed they weren't too far away. Not that I was particularly worried. Arthur Finch was an old man, he'd had a stressful day, it was three o'clock in the morning . . . he was unlikely to be wide awake.

And even if he was . . . ?

Well, fuck him.

I'd reached the door at the end of the corridor now, and as I pushed it open and went through into the lobby, I could feel my heart pounding dully in my chest. The lobby was empty, the lights were on, and in the carpeted silence

I could hear a low humming sound in the air. It was a night sound – water pipes, heating, computer terminals – the kind of sound that's always there but is too quiet to be heard during the day. Or maybe it was just me, the hum of the blood in my veins . . . the hum of the machine beneath the skin.

I put it from my mind.

As I crossed over to the reception desk, I scanned the room for CCTV cameras. I couldn't remember seeing any in the hotel, and there were no public warning signs anywhere saying *CCTV IN OPERATION* or *SMILE! YOU'RE ON CCTV*, and by the time I'd reached the reception desk I was fairly satisfied that I wasn't being watched. I paused for a moment, looking around once more, then I carefully lifted the hinged flap at the end of the desk and stepped through into the other side.

The computer terminal was on, the password screen showing. I keyed in HONEY, pressed ENTER, and the menu screen came up. It took me a while to get the hang of it, but after a few false starts, I got into the reservation system and brought up the details for room 16. It was listed as AVAILABLE. I found a blank keycard – they were in a little cardboard box by the screen – and followed the instructions that Cal had given me earlier. It wasn't difficult – select ASSIGN KEYCARD, swipe the blank card through the reader on the desk, select KEYCARD CONFIRMED, and that was it.

There were eight rooms on the first floor, and room 16 was just over halfway along the corridor on the right. I held my breath for a moment as I swiped the keycard through the lock, half-expecting to see the little red light that would tell me the card wasn't working, but instead it flashed green straight away, and I quickly opened the door and went in.

The lights were off, the room pitch-black. I took out my penlight, held it up, and shone the beam around the room. It was the same basic design as my room, the same fixtures and fittings, everything set out in the same position. The only difference, as far as I could tell, was that this room was slightly bigger than mine, and it had two beds instead of just the one – a double in the middle of the room, and a single against the wall. Both the beds were made up. The curtains were closed, the air smelled of furniture polish, and the room was clean and tidy. It looked exactly as it was meant to look: like a hotel room whose occupants had recently checked out.

I moved away from the door and started wandering around, looking more closely at everything. I wasn't sure what I was looking for – and even if I found anything, I wasn't sure what it would tell me – but for now I was content just to look. I took my time, moving deliberately from place to place, trying not to make any noise. I checked every drawer, every inch of the floor. I looked in the wardrobe, under the beds . . . the bedside tables, the windowsill, behind the curtains . . .

There was nothing.

I went into the bathroom.

There was nothing in there either. Everything had been cleaned out, wiped down, tidied up. Fresh towels were folded on a rack, fresh toiletries were lined up next to the sink – unopened mini-bottles of shampoo, shower gel, body cream, soap . . .

No trace whatsoever of Bryan Swalenski, his wife, or his daughter.

Nothing.

At least, not that I could see. I had no doubt that a thorough forensic search would find plenty of evidence that the Swalenskis had been here, but that wasn't the point. There was no question that they *had* been here, the question was – when did they leave? And where were they now? And, in Chelsey's case, where was her body?

But I knew now that I wasn't going to find any answers in here, so I moved out of the bathroom, shone my penlight around the room once more, just in case I'd missed anything, and then I turned to leave.

I heard the muffled cough just as I was about to open the door. It came from the corridor outside – the sound of a half-stifled, hand-over-the-mouth cough – and although it startled me a little, and I instinctively switched off the penlight, I wasn't overly concerned. It was probably just a guest, I assumed, coming back from a late night out . . . and when I put my eye to the peephole in the door and saw who it was, my assumption seemed to be confirmed. The figure coming down the corridor was the man I'd seen in the breakfast room that morning, the grungy-looking man in the check shirt and jeans. He had a keycard in his hand, and he was glancing at the door numbers as he passed . . . there was nothing to worry about. Any second now

127

he'd find his room, open the door and go inside, and then all I'd have to do was wait for a while, just to make sure that he didn't come out again, and then I could safely slip out and go back to my room. No problem. Nothing to worry about . . .

Except that he was approaching room 16 now, and instead of just glancing at the door number and passing by, as I expected him to do, he seemed to be slowing down . . . he *was* slowing down. He was looking over his shoulder, looking back down the corridor . . . and now . . .

'Shit.'

He'd stopped, right outside the door. Right in front of me. And now he was reaching up, the keycard in his hand . . .

I didn't have time to think, I just moved as fast as I could – back into the room, sharp left, flat against the wall, fumbling in the darkness for a place to hide . . . and then the door opened, letting in light from the corridor, and just for a moment I could see where I was, and as the door closed, shutting out the light, I quickly stepped forward, lowered myself to the floor, and scrambled under the single bed.

I'd barely stopped moving when the beam of a torch began sweeping around the room. There was no sound of footsteps, no sense of movement, so I guessed the grungy man was staying close to the door for the moment, cautiously checking things out before he went any further. I took the opportunity to inch a little closer to the wall. There wasn't much room under the bed, certainly not enough to allow me to change position, so all I could do was lie there – face down on the floor, my head turned sideways – and try to make sense of what was happening.

The torchlight wasn't flashing around quite so much now, and I got the impression that Grungy Man was taking a closer look at things. The table by the wall, the curtains, the floor, the double bed . . . the torchlight moved deliberately over every part of the room. And then I felt, rather than heard, him moving. Soft vibrations in the floor, the *feel* of footsteps on the carpet, a faint stir of movement in the air . . . I held my breath. His feet appeared, a pair of Converse trainers, walking slowly in the shadowed light of the torch. I could hear him breathing, a slight phlegmy rattle in his throat. He moved past me, over to the table by the wall, round the double bed, and then he stopped by the window. I couldn't see what he was doing, but from the brief clink of curtain rings I guessed he was taking a look outside. Another quick clink as the curtains closed again, and now he was coming back towards me – back round the bed, back past the table, back to the middle of the room . . . where he stopped again. Nothing happened for a few seconds, he just stood there, perfectly still, the beam of the torch not moving . . . and my heart was beating so hard that I was sure he had to hear it. But then he sighed, a long heavy breath, almost a groan, and as his feet began moving again, heading back towards the door, I heard him muttering under his breath, 'What the *fuck* is going on here?' And for a weird little moment, I thought I was listening to myself. The illusion was quite vivid – the sound of the voice, the words . . . the sense of frustrated bewilderment. That wasn't Grungy Man out there, it was a somewhat dishevelled forty-year-old man with a week's growth of beard and a bandaged hand . . . a man in a dull black suit, his eyes glazed and bloodshot, wandering around the room with a torch in his hand, not sure what he's looking for, or why, not sure of anything at all . . .

An uncertain man.

I could hear myself going into the bathroom now, into the sterile white emptiness . . . there's nothing in there, everything has been cleaned out, wiped down, tidied up . . . fresh towels folded on a rack, fresh toiletries lined up next to the sink – unopened mini-bottles of shampoo, shower gel, body cream, soap . . . no trace whatsoever of Bryan Swalenski, his wife, or his daughter . . . and I know I'm not going to find any answers in here, so I move out of the bathroom, shine my torch all around the room once more, just in case I've missed anything, and then I turn round, open the door, and leave.

As the door thudded shut, the illusion broke, and I came back to myself again. I was here, not out there. It was Grungy Man who'd gone into the bathroom, not me. And now he'd left, and I was alone in the darkness, lying in the dust beneath a dead girl's bed, trying to make sense of what was happening.

Was Chelsey really dead?

Had I really seen her body in the pillbox?

Maybe I *had* been mistaken. Perhaps the lie I'd told Arthur Finch, that I'd got Chelsey mixed up with someone else . . . well, maybe, in a twisted kind of way, that wasn't so far from the truth. Maybe I *had* got Chelsey mixed up . . . mixed up with another teenage daughter, a daughter who'd never lived . . . never been born, never had a chance to die . . .

Was I really that fucked-up?

I knew it was possible. After all, if I could believe that another man was me, even if it was only for a few illusive moments, what faith could I have in anything else I believed? But faith is blind, I reminded myself as I crawled out from under the bed and slowly got to my feet. Faith has nothing to do with reason. And just because I'd imagined that Grungy Man was me – or, at least, some kind of echo of me – that didn't necessarily mean that I had to doubt everything else. The sense of illusion I'd experienced just now . . . well, that was understandable. I was tired, exhausted. It had been a long and confusing day, and the black place was still lurking around inside me, trying to drag me down . . . and I was whacked out of my head on whisky and speed . . .

I was tired, that's all it was.

Just tired.

I had no reason to doubt myself.

I sat down on the edge of Chelsey's bed, rubbed my eyes, and stared into the four o'clock darkness.

11

I woke up to the sound of my mobile ringing. For a second or two I wasn't sure where I was, and in a brief moment of panic I thought I'd fallen asleep on Chelsey's bed and was still in the Swalenskis' room.

'Shit,' I said, sitting up quickly and looking around.

I realised almost immediately that I wasn't in the Swalenskis' room, and a split second later it all came back to me – leaving their room last night, this morning, coming back to my own room, lying down on the bed . . .

I sighed with relief, leaned across to the bedside table and picked up my still-ringing mobile. The caller ID told me it was Cal.

'Hey,' I muttered, rubbing the sleep from my eyes.

'Happy Halloween, Nunc!' his cheery voice boomed.

'What?' I mumbled.

'Halloween . . . it's Halloween today, John. You know, ghosties and ghoulies, trick or treat—'

'What time is it?' I asked, squinting at the curtained light of the window.

'Just gone twelve . . . are you all right, John? You sound a bit fucked.'

'Yeah . . . no, I'm all right. Just . . . hold on a second.' I lit a cigarette, sucking down a lungful of smoke, and a rise of nausea welled up inside me. I closed my eyes and willed it back down, then took another drag. 'What time did you say it was?' I asked Cal, coughing.

'Five past twelve, just gone midday—'

'And what day is it?'

'Sunday. The last day of October, Halloween—'

'Fuck Halloween,' I said, coughing again. 'I hate Halloween.' I cleared my throat. 'Did you find out anything from the airlines?'

'Yeah, that's what I'm calling about. Do you want to hear it all now?'

'Yeah.'

'Are you sure? I mean, I can call back in a few minutes if you like, give you a bit of time to wake up and—'

'Just tell me what you've got, Cal.'

'OK . . . well, as you thought, the Swalenski family are booked on a flight from Heathrow to Dallas/Fort Worth International on Wednesday 3 November. It's a British Airways flight, leaving at 11.25, arriving at 15.25. The reservation's for three people: Bryan Swalenski, his wife Ruth, and their fourteen-year-old daughter Chelsey.'

'And it hasn't been cancelled?'

'No. I did some more checking and found out that they've got a room reserved at the Novotel Hotel in Paddington, checking in Monday, checking out Wednesday. And that's not been cancelled either.'

'That's great, Cal, thanks.'

'He's a freelance wildlife photographer,' Cal went on. 'And his wife's a teacher. According to her Facebook page, they've been in the UK for the last two weeks. Bryan's been working some of the time, photographing seabirds for a forthcoming book, and he's also been trying to trace his family history. From what I can gather, Ruth and Chelsey just seem to like being with him, whatever he's doing.'

'Yeah,' I said thoughtfully. 'I can understand that.'

'She seems like a pretty good kid.'

'Who?'

'The daughter, Chelsey. I mean, I'm only going on what I saw on *her* Facebook page—'

'Chelsey's on Facebook?'

'Yeah . . . she doesn't use it all that much. I mean, she doesn't write tons of drivel like most people—'

'Can you look at it now?' I asked.

'Yeah, hold on . . .' I heard him tapping keys. 'Are these people in some kind of trouble, John?'

'I don't know . . . I think so. I mean, it's looking that way . . . but I could be wrong.'

He was silent for a moment, just tap-tap-tapping, and then he said, 'OK, here it is . . . Chelsey Swalenski. Lives in University Park, Dallas. Comes from University Park, Dallas. Born on 28 April—'

'Can you tell when she last used Facebook?'

'She sent a message to a friend called Megan at 8.22 yesterday morning.'

'Nothing after that?'

'No.'

'What did the message say?'

'Not much really . . .' Cal started reading Chelsey's message. '*Hi Megan, I'm still on the island. The weather's*

134

crappy but it's kind of OK. The people here are nice, but a bit weird sometimes. And the hotel's a bit old and spooky. But it's all right. I'll text you some more pictures soon. See you next week! Love, Chelsey. And that's it.'

'Right . . . and she sent that yesterday morning.'

'Yeah, at 8.22.'

'How did she send it?'

'What do you mean?'

'There's no Wi-Fi here. The hotel doesn't have any Internet access, as far as I know.'

'She used her phone.'

I lit a cigarette. 'Is there any way you can track it?'

'Her mobile?'

'Yeah.'

'Have you got the number?'

'No.'

'All right, just let me see if I can find it . . .'

I heard him tapping keys again.

I said, 'What if she's not actually using her mobile at the moment? Can you still track it?'

'I just need a roaming signal,' he said, still tapping. 'She doesn't have to be making a call . . . OK, I've got her number. All I've got to do now is load the program . . .' *Tap tap tap.* 'Are there any other numbers you want checking while I'm at it? I mean, do you want me to try her parents' phones?'

'Yeah, that might be useful.'

'No problem. Let me call you back in five minutes, OK?'

*

135

It took him a bit longer than five minutes, and by the time he finally got back to me I'd showered, made coffee, changed the bandage on my hand, and smoked a couple of cigarettes. I was smoking another out on the balcony when Cal called back.

'Good news and bad news,' he said. 'Which do you want first?'

'The bad.'

'Right. Well, I couldn't get a current trace on the parents' phones, which either means they're both turned off or the batteries are dead. Bryan's phone was last active at 9.07 yesterday morning, and Ruth's hasn't been on since Friday night. They were both last used in roughly the same location, but it's impossible to get a precise positional trace because there aren't enough base stations around Hale to narrow it down.'

'But they were definitely on the island?'

'I'd say they were either on it, or fairly close by . . . within a five-mile radius.'

'What about Chelsey's phone?'

'Well, that's slightly better news. The problem with pinpointing the exact location is the same, but Chelsey's phone *is* still active. She hasn't used it for quite a while, but it's still giving out a signal.'

'When did she last use it?'

'Yesterday afternoon, 15.25. She sent a short text to someone called Keenan. It just said, *hey k, 6 days!!* followed by a smiley face.'

'Keenan . . .' I muttered. 'Is that a boy's name?'

'Yeah, I traced his number to an address in University

Park, Dallas, just a few streets away from where the Swalenskis live. He's probably just a friend of Chelsey's, a boyfriend maybe . . .'

I closed my eyes for a moment, remembering the first time I'd seen Chelsey – at the foot of the hotel stairs, chewing gum, listening to her iPod, the wires snaking out from under her hood . . . and I remembered wondering then how I'd feel if I was her father and I didn't like the music she listened to . . . and now I couldn't help wondering how I would feel if my fourteen-year-old daughter had a boyfriend . . . a boy called Keenan who lived a few streets away . . .

Would I be happy for her? Worried? Over-protective? Would I hate this Keenan kid no matter how nice he seemed, because boys are boys, and even the nice ones can't help wanting what they want . . . ?

'John?' I heard Cal say. 'Are you still there?'

'Yeah,' I said, opening my eyes. 'So . . . Chelsey's phone is still active, but you can't get an accurate fix on it, is that right?'

'I can narrow it down a little bit more than her parents' phones, but it's still not much to go on. I mean, I'm pretty sure the phone's on the island somewhere, but that's about as close as I can get.'

'Can you tell if it's moving or not?'

He hesitated for a moment. 'The signal's static. It hasn't moved since yesterday afternoon.'

'Right . . .'

'Does that make any sense? I mean, does it help at all?'

'Maybe . . . I don't know. To tell you the truth, nothing makes much sense at the moment.'

137

'Is there anything else I can do?'

'Yeah, there's a man staying here . . . I don't know his name. He's in his late twenties, early thirties, and I'm pretty sure he's on his own. Can you hack into the reservation system again and see if you can find him? There aren't that many people staying here, and as far as I know he's the only youngish man on his own, so it shouldn't be too difficult.'

'Yeah, no problem. What do you want to know about him?'

'His name, what room he's in . . . who he is, what he does, where he lives . . . anything you can find out really.'

'Consider it done.'

'Thanks, Cal.'

'Is that it?'

'Yeah, I think so.'

'Right. OK . . .' He sounded hesitant. 'So . . . are you going to let me know what's going on down there, John? I mean, you don't *have* to, of course, and it's perfectly OK if you don't . . . it's just . . . well, it's a lot easier for me to help you if I know what I'm helping you with.'

'Yeah, sorry,' I said. 'I'm not trying to hide anything from you, Cal . . . I just want to make sure of things before I go any further. Just give me a bit more time, OK?'

'Yeah, of course.'

'I'll explain everything soon, I promise.'

He laughed quietly. 'Is that a *real* promise this time?'

'What do you mean?'

'Well, you *promised* me you'd call Bridget last night, remember? But you didn't, did you? You called Ada instead.'

'I *knew* you'd check up on me.'

'Someone's got to.'

'Yeah, well—'

'You *promised* me, John.'

'I know, but—'

'You're the one who's always saying that a promise is a promise.'

'I had my fingers crossed.'

'What?'

'When I promised you I'd call Bridget . . . I had my fingers crossed.'

He laughed. 'You can't do that.'

'Why not?'

'We're not in the playground, you know,' he said, still laughing.

'Who says we're not?'

'I do.'

'Yeah?' I said, smiling. 'You and whose army?'

He was still laughing as I cut him off.

It was too late for breakfast in the hotel now, and although I didn't really feel like eating, I knew I ought to have something, so I decided to walk into the village and see what I could find.

There was no one at the reception desk as I entered the lobby, but just as I was passing the desk, the door to the right of it opened and Arthur Finch came out. He paused in the doorway for a moment when he saw me, not sure what to do, but then he suddenly looked down as one of his dogs loped out from the hallway behind him, squeezed past his legs, and trotted out into the lobby. It was a golden-coloured lurcher – smooth-haired, bright-eyed, kind of dopey-looking – and as it lolloped up to me, smiling its dog-smile and wagging its long whippy tail, it was impossible not to smile too.

'No, Honey,' Arthur called out softly, following her across the lobby. 'Come here, good girl . . . come on . . .'

Honey, I thought, letting the dog sniff my hand. *Honey*.

'Sorry, John,' Arthur said, coming up to me and gently taking Honey by the collar. 'She knows she's not supposed to come out here . . .' He leaned down and smiled at the dog. 'You *know* that, don't you?'

Honey sat down, lifted her head to him and thumped her tail on the floor.

'She's a beautiful dog,' I said.

Arthur looked at me, and when he saw that I'd meant what I said, a kindly smile spread across his face. It was a good smile, a true smile, and as I looked into his eyes, my gut feeling told me that I wasn't in the presence of an inherently wicked man. Misguided, perhaps. Frightened, ashamed, weak . . .

But not wicked.

'Come on, girl,' he said quietly to his dog. 'Let's get you back to where you belong.'

I watched him lead Honey back through the door, nodded goodbye to him, and headed outside.

The sky was a little clearer today, the canopy of grey and black broken here and there with patches of pale-blue emptiness, and as I stepped out through the hotel door, I even had to shield my eyes for a moment as the sun broke briefly from behind a bank of dark clouds. It didn't last long though, and as I paused on the steps to light a cigarette, the sun clouded over again, the temperature dropped, and a mist of rain began to fall.

I heard the sound of a car approaching then, and when I looked up I saw a taxi crossing the car park. It pulled up in front of the hotel, the rear door opened, and Grungy Man got out. He paid the driver, waved away the change, and headed up the steps towards the door. His head was bowed down against the rain, and he seemed to be lost in thought, so he didn't actually notice me until he was almost at the door. I was watching him closely though, and when he did finally look up and see me, I saw the brief falter in his step and the quick flash of surprise in his eyes. It only lasted a moment, and he recovered from it pretty well – casually nodding his head at me and mumbling 'All right?' before carrying on through the door – but by then it was too late. I'd seen the unguarded look in his eyes, and I knew he hadn't wanted me to see it. So now all I had to do was work out what the hell that meant.

The misty rain was thickening now. It wasn't getting any heavier, or falling any harder, there just seemed to be more of it. It was the kind of rain that clings to your skin and seeps down into your bones, and I'd had just about enough of being cold and wet over the last few days, so I called across to the taxi driver, who'd got out of his car to get something out of the boot, and I asked him if he could take me to the village.

'Yes, mate,' he said. 'No problem.'

I put out my cigarette and crossed over to the car. It was

141

a silver Skoda Octavia, reasonably new, with a plastic TAXI sign on the roof and the words ISLAND CABS printed on the door. The driver held the rear door open for me, and I thanked him and got in the back. He was a drab and paunchy middle-aged man, with thinning red hair and a somewhat sickly pallor. As he opened the door and slid into the driver's seat, I glanced at his private-hire licence displayed on the back of the seat. The head-and-shoulders photograph of him on the licence was a good ten years out of date, showing him when he still had a full head of hair and still had a trace of hope in his eyes.

'Where you going, mate?' he said, looking at me in the rear-view mirror.

His name, according to the licence, was Eric Atherton.

'Is there a café in the village?' I asked him. 'Or a McDonald's or something?'

'There's a place called Tony's,' he said, fastening his seat belt. 'They do all-day breakfasts and stuff. Or there's a Greggs at the top end of the High Street.'

'Tony's sounds good.'

'Right.'

He put the car into gear, turned on the wipers, and we drove off into the rain.

'I was going to walk,' I said to him, leaning forward conversationally. 'But it's not really walking weather, is it?'

'Not really,' he answered.

I waited for him to go on, but surprisingly, for a taxi driver, he didn't seem interested in talking about the weather. In fact, from the way he was totally blanking me, staring sullenly straight ahead, I got the the impression that he didn't want to talk about anything at all. *Just my luck*, I thought. *The only time I've ever wanted a talkative taxi driver, and I get the only one in the world who's got nothing to say.*

'It must be good for you, though,' I said, trying again. 'The rain, I mean . . . you must get plenty of fares when the weather's like this.'

'Yeah.'

'I suppose you're a lot busier in the summer . . . ?'

He grunted.

'Mind you,' I went on, 'I was quite surprised at how busy the hotel is at this time of the year. I mean, it's not *packed* or anything, but it's a lot busier than I thought it'd be. There were even some Americans staying there.' I shook my head. 'Amazing really. I was talking to them yesterday. They're from Dallas. Can you believe that?'

Another grunt.

'Actually, I think you probably met them, didn't you?'

'Who?'

'The Americans from the hotel. Didn't you drive them to Hey yesterday?'

'I drive a lot of people to Hey,' he said, trying to sound uninterested, but I saw him glance at me in the mirror, and I could see the sudden wariness in his eyes.

'There were three of them,' I said, as if I was trying to jog his memory. 'Mum, dad . . . a teenage girl. A *really* nice family, you know? He's a photographer, I think . . . I'm not sure about his wife . . .' I looked at Atherton, smiling inanely. 'You *must* remember them . . . Texan accents—'

'Yeah, yeah,' he said, trying to sound bored now. 'I think I remember them . . . but, like I said, I drive people around all day—'

'It's a shame about the girl, don't you think?'

'What?' he snapped, staring at me in the mirror.

'You know,' I said, looking straight at him. I tapped my ear. 'I mean, she copes with it really well . . .'

He frowned. 'What are you *talking* about?'

'Well, she's deaf, isn't she?' I frowned back at him. 'You must have realised . . . didn't you see her using sign language?'

'Deaf . . . ?' he muttered, utterly confused now. 'Oh, right, yeah . . . yeah, of course . . .' As he looked away from me and turned his wayward attention back to the road, I could see the growing annoyance in his eyes, and I guessed that he was already going over in his head what he was going to say to whoever it was who'd told him – or maybe threatened him, or paid him – to lie about the Swalenskis.

You could have fucking told me.

Told you what?

That she was deaf.

Who?

The girl.

What girl?

The American girl.

Deaf? What the fuck are you talking about? She wasn't deaf . . .

And I realised too, as Atherton dropped me off outside a poky little café in the High Street, and I glanced over my

144

shoulder as I went inside and saw him talking animatedly to someone on his mobile . . . I realised that whoever he was talking to was going to be asking him, *Who the fuck told you she was deaf?* And Atherton would say, *Some fare I just picked up from the hotel . . .*

And whoever he was talking to would quickly figure out who he meant, and what that meant, and then a decision would have to be made about what to do. Which didn't make me feel all that comfortable, but sometimes the only way to find out what's going on is to keep poking around until something happens. And from the look on Atherton's face as he drove off up the High Street, glaring at me through the café window, I was pretty sure now that I wasn't going to have to wait too long for something to happen.

12

By the time I'd finished my all-day breakfast, bought some cigarettes, and walked up through the village to the country park, it was getting on for three o'clock. The rain had just about stopped, but the air was still cold and damp, and the distant sea looked slow and heavy beneath lumbering slate-grey skies. The country park was deserted. Seagulls were squabbling around a litter bin, wheeling and squawking in the wind, and scraps of plastic and torn carrier bags were flapping noisily in the branches of wind-stunted trees. The grass was wet, the ground slick with mud.

When I reached the bottom of the field, I stopped and looked out over the beach. The light was poor, fogged with a shifting grey haze, and although I could just make out the Point in the distance, I couldn't see anything with any real clarity. There seemed to be something going on near the pillbox, movement of some kind . . . but it was too far away, and too shrouded in mist, to see what was causing the movement. I kept watching for a while, and at one point I thought I saw the shape of a boat just off the shore, but it was only visible for a fraction of a second before blurring back into the gloom, and in truth it could have been anything – a buoy, a wave, a sandbank . . .

Or it could just as easily have been nothing.

Just another illusion.

Or delusion . . .

'Yeah,' I muttered to myself as I started down the steps to the beach. 'Delusion . . . that's more like it. Maybe it's *all* a fucking delusion . . . the sea, the beach . . . life, death, everything. It's all just one big fucking delusion.'

For some reason, this struck me as being incredibly funny, and while I don't know if I was actually laughing out loud as I carried on down the steps, I was definitely laughing inside my head, and when I finally sensed that I wasn't alone, and I looked up and saw a teenage boy watching me from the foot of the steps, I could tell from the way he was looking at me – with a mixture of freakshow curiosity and mild disgust – that I must have been, at the very least, smiling to myself like a lunatic.

'I *knew* there was something wrong with you,' he said, curling his lip.

It was the boy from The Swan, the younger of the two brothers. He was wearing a padded nylon coat over his grubby white tracksuit, Nike basketball boots, and a flame-print beanie hat.

'It's Lyle, isn't it?' I said, descending the last few steps.

He shook his head. 'Lyle's my brother. I'm Kyle.'

'I bet you get that all the time.'

'Get what?'

He had a mobile in one hand and a paperback book in the other. I glanced around, remembering the long-haired biker I'd seen sitting here the day before . . . he'd had a mobile in his hand too. Coincidence? I didn't think so.

'What are you doing here, Kyle?' I said.

147

He gave me his curled lip again. 'What are *you* doing here?'

'I'm wondering why people keep asking me what I'm doing here, that's what *I'm* doing.'

'Yeah?'

I nodded. 'Yesterday it was the hairy biker, today it's you . . .' I smiled at him. 'Who's on sentry duty tomorrow? Your brother?'

Kyle shook his head. 'I don't know what you're talking about.'

'Of course you don't.' I lit a cigarette, glancing at the book in his hand. 'What are you reading?'

He looked briefly at the cover of the book. 'It's what's-his-name,' he said. 'You know, *Angels and Demons*?'

'Any good?'

'You tell me,' he said, grinning. 'You're the fucking book expert.'

I smiled at him for a moment, and then I began walking off along the beach. 'You can call them now,' I said over my shoulder. 'Tell them I'll be there in about ten minutes.'

Kyle started to say something, opening his mouth and half-raising his hand, but either he changed his mind or he couldn't decide what to say, and I left him standing there with his mouth hanging open and a dimly troubled look in his eyes.

I still had no idea what had happened to the Swalenskis, but I was reasonably sure that when they'd set off from the hotel yesterday morning they'd been heading for the beach, and that Bryan would have been looking for a good spot to take pictures of seabirds, which I imagined would have to be a fairly quiet location, probably on the east of the island, possibly near the Point. I knew that Chelsey had never made it back to the hotel, and I was pretty sure that her parents hadn't either, which meant that if there was anything to find, any clues as to what had happened to them, the beach was the place to look.

So I took my time getting to the pillbox, just ambling along, keeping my head down and my eyes open, stopping every now and then to kick over a piece of driftwood or take a closer look at something in the shingle. I knew that I was being watched now. I'd guessed right that something was going on up at the pillbox, and that Kyle – and the hairy biker before him – were acting as lookouts, ringing ahead to let whoever was up there know that someone was coming, and as I made my way along the beach I could see now that there were three or four figures hanging around the pillbox, keeping a close eye on me, watching what I was doing.

I didn't try to disguise it.

Because whoever they were, and whatever they were up to, they were there . . . at the pillbox, and that in itself was enough to convince me that they had *some*thing to do with Chelsey's death. And I wanted them to know it. I wanted them to know that I had faith in myself, that I didn't doubt what I'd seen . . . and if they thought I wasn't worth worrying about because I was just a drunken fuck-up, I wanted them to know that they might want to think again.

So I let them watch me as I searched the beach, looking for evidence, looking for proof, and a couple of times I even let them think I'd found something. All I had to do was bend down and pick up a pebble, study it for a while, then carefully put it in my pocket, and that was enough to get them thinking.

Of course, I wasn't unaware of the possibility that all this was just another facet of a greater delusion, and that maybe the figures up at the pillbox weren't watching me at all, and that they weren't doing anything sinister either, and that even if they *were* watching me, all I was to them was a man on the beach, picking up pebbles and putting them in his pocket.

But, for the most part, I *did* have faith in myself and what I was doing, and although I couldn't eradicate all thoughts of delusion from my mind, I could at least take some comfort from the fact that if I really *was* delusional, I probably wouldn't be aware of it. And I could feel the cold metal of the key in my pocket too, the key to the pillbox . . . I could feel it, I could hear the pebbles rattling against it. *It* was real. The pillbox was real. The dead body of Chelsey Swalenski had been real.

I was a few hundred yards from the pillbox now, close enough to see that the figures up ahead were all men, and that there were four of them, but it was still too hazy to make out any more detail. I stopped for a moment and looked around. The tide was out, the mudflats stretching way out into the distance. The vast spread of slick brown ooze shimmered eerily in the misty grey light, giving off a dull, almost metallic, gleam. The flats looked harmless enough, but I remembered my father's countless warnings to keep away from them, especially those around the Point.

'One foot in the wrong place, John,' he'd say, 'and you'll sink down into the depths before you know what's happening.'

I could see a few flocks of waders patrolling the distant shoreline, and I wondered if they were the kinds of birds that would have interested Bryan Swalenski. And, if so, where would he have photographed them from? From here, from the open beach? Or would he have wanted to be higher up the beach, where the gorse and grasses would give him some cover? I guessed it depended to a certain extent on whether the tide was in or out at the time, and although I knew that it was in when I'd found Chelsey's body, I had no way of knowing what time it was when Bryan was taking pictures. But then again, I thought, maybe he was more likely to have been walking along the higher ground, in between the saltmarshes and the beach, because from there he'd be able to see both the birds on the shore-line *and* the birds that frequented the saltmarshes and the creek. I thought about that for a while, and eventually I came to the conclusion that since the chances of me finding anything were so remote anyway, it didn't really matter whether I carried on along the open beach or cut up to the higher ground.

I lit a cigarette, pulled a coin out of my pocket, and flipped it into the air.

Heads, open beach.

Tails, higher ground.

It came down tails.

*

I didn't find anything – no clues, no evidence – I didn't even see many birds, just some stubby little brown things flitting around in the gorse and two swans drifting along the creek. Apart from that, nothing. The whole place seemed oddly lifeless. Even the air seemed unnaturally still, and as I neared the pillbox I realised that the beach was bathed in silence.

I wondered if it had anything to do with the four men watching me. They were standing in a ragged line in front of the pillbox. I recognised two of them – Lyle Keane, Kyle's older brother, and the hairy biker from the caravan park – but I'd never seen the others before. One of them was another biker – boots, filthy jeans, black leather jacket – but he was quite a bit older than the guy from the caravan park, in his mid- to late thirties at least. He had a crooked mouth, ashen skin, and his long greying hair was tied back in a ponytail. Crudely lettered tattoos on the fingers of each hand spelled out *CUNT* and *FUCK*.

The fourth man seemed relatively clean-cut in comparison to the others. Medium height, medium build, with neatly combed light-brown hair and a clean-shaven face, he looked – at first glance – quite unremarkable. I guessed he was in his mid-twenties, but he had a peculiar sense of agelessness about him, and I wouldn't have been surprised to learn that he was five years older or five years younger than I thought. He had no tattoos, no jewellery, no piercings. He was dressed almost conservatively in dark-grey chinos, cheap trainers, and a reasonably new black windcheater jacket. And although he was probably just a bit too plain to qualify as handsome, there was certainly

152

nothing overtly unpleasant about him . . . until, that is, you looked into his eyes. His eyes were the coldest things I'd ever seen – cold, empty, void of all emotion. They were soul-sucking eyes, the eyes of a dead-hearted man.

I stopped in front of the four men, a few yards away from them, and lit a cigarette. They stared at me for a while, not saying anything, and while they were busy showing me how tough they were, I took the opportunity to gaze over at the pillbox and see what I could see. Which, as it turned out, wasn't very much. The door was closed, and from where I was standing all I could see through the gun slit was a narrow slab of darkness. There was nothing on the ground around the pillbox, no clues as to what the men might be doing here, and the pillbox itself looked exactly the same as the last time I'd seen it.

'Are you looking for something?' I heard one of the men say, and when I turned my attention back to them I saw that it was the biker with the ponytail who'd spoken. He had a strong London accent, guttural and coarse, like wet gravel pouring from a bucket.

'I'm always looking for something,' I said, smiling at him. 'Aren't you?'

He didn't react, he just stared at me.

'Actually,' I said, moving towards him, 'I'm looking for a body. A girl's body.' I heard Lyle Keane make a dumb little snorting sound, the stifled giggle of an idiot child. I ignored him, keeping my eyes on the ponytailed biker as I stopped in front of him. 'Do you know anything about a dead girl?' I said to him.

Again, he said nothing, just carried on staring at me.

I held his gaze for a moment, then looked at the dead-hearted man. He was standing a few paces back from Ponytail, just to the right of him. 'How about you?' I said. 'Do you know anything about a dead teenage girl?'

Dead-Heart smiled. 'That's some kind of question you're asking.'

His voice was soft and easy.

I said, 'Are you going to answer it?'

'Well, now,' he said, stroking his chin, 'let's see. Do I know anything about a dead teenage girl? Hmmm . . .' He narrowed his eyes, pretending to think. 'Does she have a name, this girl?'

'Chelsey Swalenski.'

'Swalenski? What's that, Polish?'

'American,' I said, staring at him. 'She was staying at Victoria Hall with her parents, Bryan and Ruth. They're from Dallas.'

'Right,' he said, nodding. 'Are they dead, too?'

'You tell me.'

He smiled again. 'Well, Mr Craine . . . it is Craine, isn't it? Or would you prefer Chandler? Or maybe it's easier if I just call you John. Is that all right with you, John?' He looked at me, waiting for a reply. When I didn't say anything, he just shrugged and carried on. 'Well, anyway . . . what was the name again? Salenski . . . ?'

'Swalenski.'

'Swalenski, right . . . Swalenski . . .' He shook his head. 'Nope, I can't say it rings any bells.' He looked at me. 'How exactly did she die, this girl?'

'Someone broke her neck,' I said, instinctively moving

154

towards him. Ponytail put out his arm, blocking my way. I stared at him. He stared back, daring me to make a move. I thought about it for a moment, then stepped back and looked at Dead-Heart again. 'Someone broke her neck,' I repeated. 'Then dumped her body in the pillbox.'

'The pillbox?' Dead-Heart said, glancing over his shoulder. 'What, *this* pillbox?' He looked back at me. 'When did this happen?'

'Yesterday, sometime in the afternoon, early evening.'

'Really?'

'Yeah, really.'

He frowned. 'You're absolutely sure?'

'I was here,' I said simply. 'I saw her body. She was lying in the pillbox with a broken neck.'

'That must have been quite a shock.'

'Yeah.'

'Did you call the police?'

I lit another cigarette.

'Nasty habit,' Dead-Heart said, watching me. 'Did you know that cigarettes are more addictive than heroin? Worse for your health, too.' He smiled. 'So what happened when the police got here, John?'

'I think you probably know the answer to that.'

'Did they seal off the crime scene? Did they call in the murder squad? Did they zip up the body in a big black bag and cart it off to the mortuary?'

I gave him a long hard look, trying to see beyond the emptiness of his eyes, but there was nothing to see. He just stood there looking back at me, mildly amused at most.

'I'm going to find out what happened to her,' I said quietly, still staring at him.

He laughed, a thin breathy sound. 'Do you want some advice, John? Do you know what I think you should do?' He put his hand in his pocket and started moving towards me. 'I think you should go back to the hotel, buy yourself a nice bottle of whisky, and get yourself good and drunk.' Ponytail stepped to one side, and Dead-Heart stopped in front of me. 'Here you go,' he said, tucking a £50 note into my coat pocket. 'The whisky's on me. Now, if you don't mind, I've got things to do.'

'I'm guessing it's drugs,' I said.

He sighed. 'What?'

I glanced around at the others. 'I mean, it's a bit obvious, isn't it? The four of you on a deserted beach, another one keeping watch . . . a fishing boat just offshore . . .' I turned back to Dead-Heart. 'You might as well be wearing T-shirts with *DRUG SMUGGLERS* printed on the front.'

Dead-Heart just smiled at me. 'Boon was right about you. You really *have* got it bad, haven't you? If I were you, John – God forbid – I'd book myself into rehab or something. You know, before the fantasies get any worse.'

'You know Sergeant Boon, do you?'

'I know lots of people.'

'What I don't understand,' I said, gazing around again, 'is what you use the pillbox for. Temporary storage, maybe?' I looked back at him. 'Is that it? The drugs come in off the boat and you keep them in the pillbox until you're ready to move them on? Is that how it works?'

'I give up,' Dead-Heart said, shaking his head. 'Really . . . I can't be fucked with this any more.'

'Do you mind if I take a look?' I said, moving off towards the pillbox.

I heard him sigh again, then mutter something to someone, and I sensed Ponytail following me as I headed over to the pillbox, and at the same time I saw Lyle Keane and the other biker stepping in front of me, barring my way and blocking my view through the gun slit. I looked at them for a moment, sizing them up, but I already knew there was no point in trying to get past them. I glanced over my shoulder. Ponytail had stopped a few paces behind me. I looked over at Dead-Heart.

'Is this where I get my neck broken?' I said to him.

He shrugged. 'Neck, spine, legs . . . who knows? Maybe we'll just break your fucking heart.'

'I doubt it,' I said, smiling at him.

'What you need to do now, John,' he said quietly, 'is turn round and walk away. Do you understand?'

'Yeah,' I said, looking away from him. 'I understand.' I started edging over to my left, away from Kyle and the biker, trying to get a look at the back of the pillbox. They mirrored my movement, stepping to their right, once again blocking my way.

'I'm a patient man, John,' I heard Dead-Heart say. 'But you're really starting to get on my nerves now. Are you listening to me?'

'Yeah,' I said, 'yeah, I'm listening.'

But I wasn't. Not any more. I'd stopped listening to him the moment I'd spotted a flash of black in the gorse bushes over to my left. It was about six feet away from me, half-buried in the sand behind a tangle of gorse – a small patch of matt black plastic. *It could be anything*, I told myself, quickly looking away from it. *The lid of a plastic box, a child's toy ... anything at all.* But it didn't *look* like anything at all – it looked like the back of a mobile phone. And Cal had been pretty sure that Chelsey's phone was on the island somewhere . . . and if it *was* her phone . . .

There wasn't time to think about it. I could see Dead-Heart looking at Ponytail now, giving him the nod, and I guessed that meant my time was just about up. If I wanted to get hold of the phone, I had to do something right now.

'All right, all right,' I said to Dead-Heart, holding up my hands and shuffling meekly away from the pillbox to my left. 'I'm going, OK . . . I'm going.'

Dead-Heart flicked a look at Ponytail, telling him to wait, then turned his attention back to me. 'Go on then,' he said quietly.

I took another half-step to my left and turned to the younger biker. 'Does Robyn know about Chelsey?' I said to him.

'What?'

'Robyn Mayo . . . does she know what you did to Chelsey?'

'What the *fuck*?' he snarled, moving angrily towards me. 'What do you fucking know about Rob—?'

'We're closer than you think,' I said, smiling at him. 'I mean, me and Robyn . . .' I held up my hand, fingers crossed. 'We're like that.'

He was running at me now – his eyes wild, his jaw tight,

158

his fist clenched – and I just had time to back-pedal a little further to my left so that when he hit me – a swinging punch to the side of my head – I was already reeling back towards the gorse bushes. I rode the punch as best I could, and although everything went black for a moment as I staggered back and dropped to the ground, I was conscious enough to make sure that I fell where I wanted to fall – face down into the tangle of gorse bushes, on top of the mobile phone. And as I lay there in the sand, moaning and groaning – which I didn't have to fake – I just managed to fumble around, find the phone, and slip it inside my shirt before the biker caught up with me and slammed his boot into my back. I rolled away and tried to get up, but he kicked me again, this time catching me full in the belly. My lungs emptied, and as I doubled over, wheezing and choking, struggling for breath, another shuddering kick slammed into my head, sending me sprawling backwards into the sand.

I was pretty sure I'd had it now.

The blow hadn't quite knocked me out, but I barely knew where I was. My head was spinning, my ears ringing, and everything around me had turned to fog – a thick whirling cloud of blurred skies and tilting sands that changed direction every time I tried to get up . . .

I couldn't get up.

The biker was standing over me now – a blurred black shadow looming out of the fog – and as he raised his boot to stomp on my head, everything seemed to slow down . . . and for a timeless moment I was acutely aware of the tiniest detail – scuff marks on the heel of his boot, scratched leather, the dulled tarnish of a metal buckle . . .

And I felt no fear.

Just a slight disappointment that it was going to end like this – getting stomped to death by a biker on a beach.

Ah, well . . .

The boot was descending now, a great distorted black thing coming down through the clouds . . .

I closed my eyes and smiled, thinking of God in a black leather jacket.

It's all right, John, a voice in my heart said. *I'm here.*

'Hey, Stace,' I said happily. 'You're just in time—'

'Stevie!'

It was another voice, a dead-hearted voice, calling out from the fog.

'That's enough.'

I opened my eyes. The giant boot had stopped.

'Not now, OK?'

I blinked. The boot had gone.

'Just leave him.'

The blurred black shadow wavered for a moment, muttering curses under its breath, and then it moved away, still cursing, and faded into the fog . . .

13

I don't remember all that much about getting back to the hotel. I have a vague recollection of being dragged to my feet, and someone – probably Dead-Heart – telling me to 'fuck off out of it before I change my mind', and then all I really remember is stumbling along the beach in the rapidly fading light, semi-consciously confused as to where I was and why I wasn't dead.

Don't worry about that now, the comforting voice in my heart said. *Just concentrate on what you're doing.*

'What *am* I doing?'

Walking, moving, staying alive.

I smiled. 'I missed you, Stace.'

I missed you, too.

'Where did you go?'

Nowhere.

'How was it?'

Pretty quiet.

I laughed. 'It's good to have you back.'

Even if I don't exist?

'Who says you don't?'

We both do.

'Yeah, well . . .' I grinned. 'Existence is overrated anyway.'

*

I didn't look at the mobile phone until I was safely back in my hotel room, and even then it was quite some time before I felt well enough to start examining it. I was still quite shaken up – dizzy, nauseous, disorientated – and now that the adrenalin was beginning to wear off, I was really starting to feel the effects of the kicking I'd taken. My head wasn't too bad – just a dull throbbing behind my eyes – but my belly was hurting like hell, and there was a deep gnawing pain in my back that stabbed right through me every time I moved.

I found some painkillers in my bag, poured myself a tumbler of whisky, and sat down gingerly on the edge of the bed. I washed down the pills with a long slow drink, then lit a cigarette, and drank some more.

'Fuck,' I said, rubbing at the small of my back.

I still didn't understand why they hadn't killed me.

I told you, John . . . don't worry about it.

'I'm not *worried* about it. I just don't understand it. If they killed Chelsey—'

Maybe they didn't.

I reached into my shirt and pulled out the mobile phone. It was a smartphone, and it looked almost new. I stared at the dull black screen, and a blurred grey face stared back at me. The face in the screen was a mess – bruised, bloody, dusted with sand – and as I gazed into its haunted eyes, my vision began to blur again, making the eyes shimmer like dull black stars, and nausea welled up in my stomach.

I put down the phone, hobbled into the bathroom, and threw up.

*

After I'd showered and put on some clean clothes, I felt a little bit better. Not great, not by a long way, but good enough. As I emptied the pockets of my dirty clothes, transferring the contents to my new clothes, it struck me that maybe I shouldn't be carrying the key to the pillbox around with me. If Boon realised that it was missing, and that I might have taken it . . .

I gazed around the bathroom for a while, looking for somewhere to hide the key, and then – unable to find anywhere suitable – I went back into the other room and crossed over to the corner nearest the bed. The carpet here wasn't fixed properly to the floor. I crouched down, peeled it back, slipped the key underneath, then flattened the carpet back down again.

Hardly foolproof, but it would do for now.

I lit a cigarette, picked up Chelsey's mobile phone, and took it over to the bed. I thought it might take me a while to get the hang of it, but once I'd worked out how to turn it on and unlock the screen, the rest of it was surprisingly straightforward. And besides, all I was really interested in – for now, at least – was the camera function. Partly because the stored images would tell me if it really *was* Chelsey's phone or not, but more importantly, if it was Chelsey's phone, there was a chance that some of those stored images might shed some light on what had happened to her.

I touched the camera icon on the screen.

The camera function came on, showing a close-up view of my knees.

I pressed another icon in the bottom right-hand corner of the screen and a series of thumbnail images appeared, displayed in a grid. At the top of the grid it said, *Camera Shots (163)*. There were ten images on the opening screen, two lines of five, and I didn't have to look any further to know that this *was* Chelsey's phone. If the picture of her parents on the beach together wasn't enough, the one above it – which clearly showed Chelsey taking a picture of herself – put the question beyond doubt.

I stared at the picture. Like most self-portraits taken with a mobile phone, she'd misjudged the positioning of her face, and at least a third of it was missing from the shot. The rest of it though, despite being wobbly and slightly out of focus, a little bit blurred, a touch distorted . . . well, there was something almost perfect about it. It wasn't a manufactured image, it wasn't slick, it had no pretence . . . it was just a carefree snapshot that captured the essence of the moment – Chelsey on the beach, happy, smiling, her head cocked playfully to one side, her light-brown hair blowing in the wind . . .

I touched the screen, enlarging the picture.

Her eyes were bright and open to the world.

Her smile was heartbreaking.

I examined the background, trying to work out where the picture was taken, but all I could see was a blur of grey shingle fading into a slightly paler blur of grey sky. I touched the *Menu* icon, selected *More*, and brought up the *Details* box, which told me that the photo was taken on 30 October at 14.28.

Saturday afternoon.

Yesterday afternoon.

It seemed like a lifetime ago.

I went back to the main screen again and started going through the other photographs. At first glance they didn't look particularly interesting, just random snapshots of the sea and the beach, and a couple of blurred close-ups that looked as if they'd been taken in error . . . but then, when I studied one of these blurred shots again, I realised that I was looking at a hand. It was a large hand, scarred and dirty . . . and it was reaching out towards the camera.

'Shit,' I said.

The word *FUCK* was crudely tattooed on the fingers of the outstretched hand.

I spent the next hour or so examining all the photographs that Chelsey had taken on the beach that day. By noting the time that each picture had been taken, and by studying the images over and over again – zooming in and out on every little detail – I eventually managed to piece together a fragmented outline of the events leading up to Chelsey's death. A lot of it was sheer guesswork, of course – filling in the gaps between each picture, imagining what had happened off-screen – and because most of the crucial photographs, the last eight pictures on the camera, had been taken in a hurry, they were so blurred and shaky that it was difficult to make out exactly what was going on. But even so . . .

Every picture, even if it is slightly blurred, tells some kind of story.

And this, I thought, was Chelsey's.

She'd left the hotel with her parents between 08.30 and 09.00 and they'd walked into the village, where, at 09.44,

Chelsey had taken a picture of her mum and dad posing together in the doorway of a quaint little antique shop called Hale and Hearty. They'd spent some time in the village, perhaps a couple of hours, then they'd headed off to the beach, stopping for a while in the country park, where Chelsey had snapped her father standing at the bottom of the field, facing out to sea, taking photographs with a telephoto lens. By 12.51 they'd left the park and were on the beach. They hadn't gone far though, and in the next picture, which showed Chelsey's dad hunkered down in a patch of gorse gazing out over the saltmarshes, the park was still clearly visible in the background. The following photo – the one that showed her parents together on the beach – was timed at 14.16, and although there was no photographic evidence of what had happened in the preceding eighty-five minutes, my guess was that the Swalenskis had either taken a packed lunch with them or bought something to eat from the village, and that they'd stopped somewhere on the beach for a leisurely snack of sandwiches and crisps, or bagels, or pies, or whatever a family from Texas would choose to eat when on holiday in the south-east of England.

Next came Chelsey's self-portrait, and after that, at 15.33, there was another photo of Chelsey, which must have been taken by one of her parents, probably her mother. It was a long shot of Chelsey standing beside a small thicket on the edge of the saltmarshes. In the background of this image I could see the pathway along the creek, and while I couldn't identify the exact location, I was fairly sure that at this point the Swalenskis were about halfway along the beach.

By 16.27 though – the time of the next picture – they were definitely within sight of the pillbox. It was clear that Chelsey had taken a lot of time over this shot, as it was easily the most accomplished of all the photographs, but as well as showing how proficient she could be when she wanted, it also showed how much she loved and cared for her father. The image was a head-and-shoulders shot of him stretched out in the sand, half-hidden behind some tall grasses, with his camera pointing out to sea. The focus on his face was perfect, revealing both the intensity of his concentration as he ignored the rain that was now pelting down, and the serenity of his patience as he waited for just the right moment to get the best picture. It was quite obvious that he not only had a passion for what he was doing, but that he was enormously skilled at it too. And, furthermore, that Chelsey was incredibly proud of him, both as a father and as an artist. Her mother was in the picture too, sitting cross-legged in the background with the hood of her waterproof coat pulled up, but because of the close-up focus on her father's face, her mother's image was blurred and hazy. The image of the pillbox beyond her was even more out of focus, which made it hard to tell exactly how distant it was, but it certainly wasn't much more than thirty yards away.

It was twenty-two minutes after she'd taken the picture of her dad that Chelsey took the first photograph of the fishing boat. There was no way of telling if she'd moved position or not by then, but if she had, I got the impression that she hadn't moved very far. The fishing boat was approaching the shore from the direction of the Point, and in this first photograph it was too far away, and the weather was too bad, to make out any detail. In the next picture, though, timed at 17.01, the boat was a lot closer. It was moored just offshore, which – with the high tide – wasn't all that far away, and Chelsey had used the zoom as well, so although the light was beginning to fade, and – as far as I could tell – the flash on the camera wasn't turned on, it was easy to see that the boat was a rusty old thing, maybe 20–25 feet in length, with the registration mark FS 821 painted on the side. I didn't know for sure if it was the same boat I'd been seeing over the last few days, but it looked very similar. There were two people on board. One of them was in the cabin – a brutish-looking man in a thick black coat and dark woollen hat who I'd never seen before – while the other one, wearing only a windcheater and chinos, was standing on the deck, looking out towards the beach.

Dead-Heart.

The light was noticeably lower in the next two images, both timed at 17.06, but the boat was still clearly visible, as were the three large packages stacked on the deck beside Dead-Heart and the other man. The packages were roughly cube-shaped, about a foot square, and tightly wrapped in black plastic sheeting.

Chelsey and her parents must have realised by now that the boat was bringing in drugs, and they must also have realised what a dangerous position that put them in. If the men on the boat were to see them . . .

'Don't let them see you,' I could imagine Chelsey's father whispering to her. 'Move over there, behind those gorse bushes . . . keep your head down. And put your phone away.'

And Chelsey does as she's told, moving carefully behind the gorse, keeping her head down, keeping out of sight . . . but she doesn't put her phone away. She just turns it to silent. She might be a little bit frightened, and she knows that her father is right to be cautious, but she's a teenage girl, she's adventurous . . . and it's not as if you come across drug smugglers every day, is it?

So she keeps hold of her phone, and at 17.11, when her father's not looking, she takes another picture. This one shows Dead-Heart in an inflatable dinghy, halfway between the fishing boat and the beach, and waiting for him on the beach is Ponytail.

Now Chelsey focuses on Dead-Heart, zooming in on his face, and just as she's about to snap him, he sees her. Click. The picture shows his ice-cold eyes staring directly at the camera.

And then, perhaps, Dead-Heart points up the beach and shouts, and Ponytail turns to see what he's pointing at, and he sees the three of them hiding away in the gorse, and perhaps he sees Bryan Swalenski's camera, with its telephoto lens . . . and now Bryan has to decide what to do. Ponytail is heading up the beach towards them, and it won't be long before the dinghy reaches the shore and the other man clambers out, and then he'll be coming after them too . . .

What does Bryan do?

He's not a physical man, and even if he was, he'd be no match for the big biker and the man from the dinghy. It's possible that *he* could outrun them, but what about his wife and daughter? So perhaps Bryan concludes that the best course of action is to try reasoning with the men from the boat, just tell them the truth – *look, I'm a wildlife photographer, OK? I'm on holiday here with my wife and daughter. We weren't spying on you or anything, we just happened to be here . . . and whatever it is you're up to, we don't care, it's none of our business, and you can rest assured we won't say a word to anyone about anything . . .*

And perhaps it's then that either Dead-Heart or Ponytail hits him, and he falls heavily to the ground, and as he's lying there looking up at them, Chelsey – incredibly – takes another picture, and we can see that Ponytail is already on the move. He's after Chelsey and her mother now. And it's impossible to tell if they're running away from him, or running towards Bryan, because in the last three photographs – the last three photographs that Chelsey will take – everything has descended into a blur of blind fear and panic.

A mother's petrified face . . .

A whirl of shingle, a desperate lunge . . .

The tattooed fingers of an outstretched hand.

14

'So what do you think happened to them?' Cal said.

It was almost seven thirty now, and I'd been on the phone to Cal for the best part of an hour. I'd told him everything – from the inexplicable disappearance of Chelsey's body, to my recent confrontation with Dead-Heart and the others – and now I'd just finished telling him all about the photographs I'd found on Chelsey's camera.

'Just a second, Cal,' I said, putting my phone down. I went over to the table and poured myself a drink, and while I was there I opened up the wrap of cocaine and quickly finished off what was left. I sniffed hard, wiped my nose, then took my drink back to the bed, lit a cigarette, and picked up the phone.

'Sorry, Cal,' I said. 'What were you saying?'

'I heard that,' he said.

'What?'

'I'm not stupid, John. I know what a snort of coke sounds like.'

'Well, you should, the amount *you* stuff up your nose.'

'That's different—'

'How is it different?'

He sighed. 'I'm just worried about you, that's all. I'm just . . . well, you know . . .'

'I'm fine, Cal,' I assured him. 'Really . . . I know what I'm doing.'

'Yeah?' I could hear the smile in his voice. 'So what exactly *are* you doing?'

'Fuck knows,' I said, taking a drink. 'I mean, I thought I was coming down here to get away from it all . . .'

'Why don't you come back then? Just pack your bags and fuck off out of there. I mean, there's nothing stopping you, is there? It's not as if you're working a case or anything.'

'I can't just leave, can I?'

'Why not?'

'Because . . .'

Because what? I asked myself. *Why can't you just leave? Cal's right, isn't he? You're not working a case, you're not beholden to anyone, you don't have to stay here . . . and so what if a young girl is dead, and probably her parents too . . . what are they to you? You don't know them. You don't owe them anything. They're just people . . . a mother, father, a daughter . . .*

'John?' Cal said.

'Yeah . . . ?'

'What do you think happened to them?'

My guess, and it *was* just a guess, was that after Bryan Swalenski had been punched to the ground, things had simply spiralled out of control. Chelsey and her mother were probably screaming and shouting, desperately trying to help Bryan, and perhaps one of them tried to call 999, and Dead-Heart and Ponytail had to stop them, and then

172

maybe there was a scuffle, a bit of grabbing and shoving, perhaps another punch or two, and it's possible that one of the punches was too hard, or that one of the Swalenskis just fell heavily and smashed their head on a rock or something . . . and once one of them was dead, or seriously injured, there were only two options left for Dead-Heart and Ponytail: either face the charges and go down for life . . . or kill the other two.

'Right,' said Cal. 'So you think they're all dead?'

'Yeah, I do.'

'What happened to the parents' bodies then? I mean, why weren't they in the pillbox too?'

'I don't think they *meant* to put Chelsey's body in the pillbox. I think their plan was to load the bodies onto the boat and take them somewhere to get rid of them, either out at sea, or maybe in the mudflats out by the Point . . . I think they were probably in the process of loading the bodies when I turned up.'

'And they would have known you were coming because the guy you saw on the steps would have warned them.'

'Yeah, but they didn't have enough time to get all the bodies on the boat before I arrived, so they just dumped Chelsey's body in the pillbox, assuming that I wouldn't go anywhere near it, and then all they had to do was wait for me to leave again and they could come back and finish the job.' I tapped ash from my cigarette. 'They were probably out at sea somewhere getting rid of the parents' bodies at the same time that I was finding Chelsey's.'

'You don't think they stayed on the beach then?'

'I don't know . . . I suppose it's possible. I mean, it was

pretty dark by then, and the weather was really bad. It wouldn't have been all that difficult to keep out of sight.'

'It might explain what happened to Chelsey's body,' Cal said. 'If they were still there, or even if just one of them was still there, they could have moved the body while you were waiting for the police.'

'There were no footprints though, no sign that anyone had been near the pillbox.'

'Footprints can be covered up.'

'Yeah . . .'

'I can't think of any other explanation, John. Bodies don't just disappear, do they? And the police didn't have time to do anything, so unless . . .'

'Unless what?'

'You were drunk, right?'

'Yeah.'

'How drunk?'

'Not enough to see imaginary bodies.'

'Had you taken anything else?'

'A bit of speed.'

'A bit?'

'A couple of lines.'

'And that's it?'

'Yep.'

'Anything else I should know about?'

'Like what?'

'Hallucinations, voices in your head . . . anything like that?'

I laughed. 'Are you seriously suggesting that I might be insane?'

174

'No, I'm *asking* you if you might be.'

'Do you think I'd admit it if I was?'

'Well, yeah,' he said, laughing. 'Because if you *were* insane, you probably wouldn't think there's anything wrong in admitting it.'

I smiled. 'I'm not going mad, Cal.'

'You sure?'

'I'm as sane as you.'

He laughed again. 'All right . . . so if we assume that you weren't imagining things, that has to mean that between the time you saw Chelsey's body and the time the police showed up, someone moved the body. Right?'

'Yeah.'

'And the chances are that whoever did it, they'll have got rid of the body by now, so you're probably not going to find it.'

'Probably not, no.'

'So you don't actually have any proof that anyone was killed?'

'I've got the photographs.'

'Do they show anyone being killed?'

'No . . .' I said, looking down at Chelsey's phone as it beeped.

'What was that?' Cal said.

'Chelsey's phone . . . the battery's low.'

'Is that the first warning?'

'No, it's been flashing low for a couple of hours now. Listen, Cal—'

'Turn it off,' Cal said quickly.

'What?'

'The phone, turn it off.'

'Why? It's only a low battery. My phone keeps going for ages on a low battery—'

'That's because *your* phone's a piece of shit, John. The battery on a phone like Chelsey's runs out really quickly, especially if the GPS and Wi-Fi are turned on. So turn it off now, OK? Before the battery dies completely. Then later on there should be enough power left to turn it back on again and send the photographs to me. All right?'

'Yeah, yeah . . . I'm doing it, I'm turning it off . . . OK, it's off now.'

'Were there any video clips on the phone?'

'Not any recent ones, just some stuff that Chelsey filmed when they were in Scotland.'

'Right, so all we've really got, evidence-wise, is a bunch of blurry photographs and . . .' He paused, thinking about it. 'There *isn't* anything else, is there?'

'Nope.'

'And you don't think it's worth going to the local police?'

'Not if Boon and Gorman are anything to go by, and they probably make up about 50% of the local force anyway. And if Boon and Dead-Heart are connected, which they are, then I'm pretty sure that Boon has some kind of involvement in the drug-smuggling operation, even if all he does is turn a blind eye to it and keep his mouth shut.'

'Does that mean he'd know what they did to the Swalenskis?'

'Not necessarily . . . well, not at first, anyway. But if he *is* involved with the smuggling, they've got him over a barrel, haven't they? If he doesn't do what they tell him, they just remind him that he's a cop, and that if they go down for anything, he's going down with them, and everyone knows what happens to cops in prison.'

'Right . . . but what about the old guy who runs the hotel, and the taxi driver? I mean, why are *they* telling lies? What have they got to gain by helping to cover up three murders?'

'Nothing, probably. But they might have something to lose if they *don't* help.'

'Like what?'

'I don't know . . . it could be anything. Hale's a small place, Cal. It's hard to stand up to people when you live in a small place.'

'You don't think they're involved then?'

'Only in so far as they've been told to go along with a story, and that's what they're doing. I doubt if they actually *know* anything.'

'What about this other guy, the one you asked me to find out about? Oh, shit . . . I haven't told you about him yet, have I? Sorry, I completely forgot—'

'You mean Grungy Man?'

'Yeah, I did what you asked, hacked into the hotel reservation system, and you were right. There *is* only one man staying there who matches your description. He's in room number two. According to the booking details, his name's Mark Allen, he's twenty-eight years old, and he lives in Harwich. The only problem is, I did some more checking, and according to *me*, he doesn't exist.'

'It's a false name?'

'False name, date of birth, home address, telephone number . . . false everything. Whoever he is, John, he's not Mark Allen.'

'Who the fuck is he then? And what's he doing here?'

I was talking to myself as much as to Cal, and I wasn't really looking to him for an answer anyway, so when he started telling me about face-recognition programs, and how he hoped to be incorporating one into his automated search system soon, and that when he did he wouldn't need a real name to instigate a search, he'd just need a picture . . . well, I kind of stopped listening for a while. I went over and stood by the window, not really thinking about anything, just gazing out into the darkness . . .

'John?'

I put the phone to my ear. 'Yeah?'

'You're not listening to me, are you?'

'Yeah, I am. It's all very interesting—'

'What is?'

'What you just said . . . face recognition, new software . . .'

Cal sighed. 'Look, I have to go in a minute. The doctor's coming to see me for a final check-up to make sure I'm OK to go home. If everything's all right, I should be out of here by Tuesday.'

'That's great.'

'Yeah, but look . . . I know you don't want to go to the local police with any of this—'

'It's not that I don't *want* to, Cal, it's just that there's no point.'

'OK, but what about Hey CID? I mean—'

'No,' I said simply. 'Absolutely not.'

'Mick Bishop's not the only officer there—'

'Bishop *is* Hey CID. He runs the whole fucking place. You know that, Cal.'

'Yeah, I suppose . . .'

'It was Bishop's men who put you in hospital, remember?'

'I know—'

'I don't want *any*thing to do with that fucker.'

'Fair enough. I was just thinking out loud, really . . .' He paused for a moment. Then, 'There is another option, you know.'

'Yeah?'

'In a couple of days' time, back in the States, someone's going to realise that the Swalenskis haven't come home. Family, friends, work colleagues . . . they'll start asking questions. And someone will eventually get in touch with the Dallas police, and then *they'll* start asking questions . . . so, you know . . .'

'I could just leave it to them, is that what you're saying?'

'Why not?'

'Because,' I said.

'That's it? Just *because*?'

'It's all I've got, Cal.'

I wasn't even sure what I meant, but it seemed to work for me. I was doing what I was doing *because*.

There wasn't anything else.

It was all I had.

'I have to go, John,' Cal said. 'The doctor's here. Don't do anything with Chelsey's phone until I've called you back, OK?'

'Yeah, no problem.'
'Gotta go.'

It couldn't have been much more than ten minutes later when I heard a knock at my door. I was out on the balcony, smoking a cigarette and mulling over my conversation with Cal, and at first I wasn't sure what the tapping sound was. I stepped back into the room, paused to listen, and a moment later I heard it again – a light *tap-tap* at the door.

'Hello?'

A male voice.

I didn't recognise it.

I went over to the door, looked through the spyhole, and saw the face of a man who didn't exist.

15

When I opened the door to the man who called himself Mark Allen, he smiled at me and said, 'Hey, sorry to bother you, but I was just wondering if you've got any skins?'

'Skins?'

'Yeah,' he smiled again. 'You know, Rizlas, cigarette papers . . . ? I just realised I've run out, and the nearest shop is all the way down the village, so if you've got any to spare . . . ?'

I looked at him for a moment, wondering what he was really after, but whatever it was, he was pretty good at keeping it hidden. My gut feeling told me that he probably didn't mean me any harm, but I was well aware that the cemeteries are littered with people who'd mistakenly trusted their gut feelings, and with that in mind I was tempted to just close the door on him, and I very nearly did. But in the end, curiosity got the better of caution, and I stepped to one side and ushered him in.

'Yeah,' I said, 'I think I might have a packet of Rizlas somewhere.'

'Cheers,' he said, following me inside. 'There's nothing worse than running out of papers, is there?'

'There's a cigarette machine in the lobby,' I said, keeping

my back to him as I picked up Chelsey's phone from the bed. 'It probably doesn't have tobacco—'

'No, I'm all right for cigarettes,' he explained. 'It's just the papers I need, if you know what I mean.'

I went over to my holdall, crouched down, slipped the phone in a side pocket and began rummaging around in the bag. 'Do you want to sit down?' I asked, indicating a chair by the window.

'Thanks,' he said, going over to the chair. 'I'm not keeping you from anything, am I?'

I shook my head, still rummaging. 'Won't be a minute . . . I'm pretty sure they're in here somewhere.' I glanced at him, smiling. 'You haven't been going round knocking on everyone's door asking for Rizlas, have you?'

'No,' he said, laughing quietly. 'I kind of assumed that most of the other guests wouldn't have much use for them.'

'But *I* would?'

'Well . . .' He smiled. 'You've got that look, you know?'

'Yeah? What look's that?'

'Hey,' he said, holding up his hands. 'No offence or anything. I didn't mean—'

'It's all right,' I said, smiling at him again. 'I know what you mean.'

He grinned. 'I know you do.'

I saw him glance over at the table then, and I realised that he'd seen the empty wrap of cocaine I'd left there. 'Here you go,' I said, standing up and passing him a packet of Rizlas.

'Thanks,' he said, taking the packet. 'Do you fancy a quick smoke?'

182

I shrugged. 'Why not?'

He held out his hand. 'I'm Mark, by the way. Mark Allen.'

'John Chandler,' I said, shaking his hand.

As I went over and sat at the table by the wall, I wondered if he knew that Chandler wasn't my real name, just as I knew that Mark Allen wasn't his . . . and for a moment or two I let myself think that maybe he had his own version of Cal too, and that perhaps he'd been on the phone to *his* Cal for the last hour or so, and his Cal had told him that John Chandler didn't exist . . .

I lit a cigarette and poured myself a drink. 'Do you want one?' I asked Allen. 'I've only got whisky—'

'No, I'm all right, thanks,' he said, without looking up from the joint he was rolling. I studied him as he took a little bag from his pocket and began sprinkling grass into the joint. He had dark, thoughtful eyes, longish black hair, and a somewhat half-hearted-looking goatee beard. He was wearing his ripped jeans and Converse trainers, with a black waistcoat over a long-sleeved Timberland T-shirt. He had a small diamond stud in his right ear, leather bracelets on his wrist, and a plain silver band on his ring finger. I noticed that he wasn't putting a huge amount of grass in the joint. Which either meant that it was really strong stuff, or that – for some reason – he didn't want either of us to get too stoned.

He coughed, covering his mouth. 'Sorry,' he said, clearing his throat. 'Fucking chest cold . . . can't seem to get rid of it.'

'Maybe you should have picked somewhere a bit warmer

183

for a holiday. I mean, the weather down here isn't exactly ideal for getting rid of a cold, is it?'

'You can say that again.' He lit the joint, coughing on the smoke. 'Mind you, the shitty weather is actually one of the reasons I'm here.'

'What do you mean?'

'I'm a writer,' he said, taking another toke on the joint. 'Well, I *will* be a writer when my first book comes out, that's if I ever finish the fucking thing.' He looked at me. 'That's what I'm doing here . . . trying to finish the book.' He shrugged. 'That was the idea anyway – you know, lock myself away somewhere, somewhere with no distractions, so I can knuckle down and finish the manuscript before my publishers change their minds.' He got up and passed me the joint. 'Trouble is,' he went on, 'even in a shithole like this, where there's nothing to do and it's raining all the time, I can still find *some*thing to distract me – TV, the pub, a bit of puff . . .' He sat down again, grinning. 'I mean, all I need is a couple of spliffs and I can quite happily stare out of the window all day.'

I nodded, taking a puff on the joint. 'So you're a writer?'

'That's the plan, yeah. The book's supposed to come out some time next year, and then hopefully, if it does OK, they'll sign me up for another one.'

'What kind of stuff do you write?'

'Science fiction.'

'Right,' I said, nodding. 'Right . . .'

The grass had already gone to my head, giving me that nice little buzz you get from the good stuff, and as I reached across the table to tap ash into a saucer, I realised that the pain in my back had almost gone.

'Do you like science fiction?' Allen asked me.

I shook my head. 'Not really . . .'

'Why not?'

I shrugged. 'I don't know . . . I just never really got into it, I suppose.'

'So what kind of stuff *do* you like?'

'All sorts really . . .' I got up and passed him the joint. 'You know, as long as I like it, I'll read pretty much anything—'

'Except science fiction.'

I laughed. 'Yeah, sorry.'

'Hey, no problem,' he said, smiling. 'It'd be a pretty boring world if we all liked the same thing.'

I nodded. 'Do you write full-time? I mean, is that how you make your living?'

'Well, yes and no, really. I used to work in a call centre, but I packed it in about six months ago to concentrate on the book. I haven't made any money out of it yet, but my wife's got a reasonably well-paid job, so we live off her money, and I stay at home and try to write a bestseller while I'm looking after the kids.'

'You've got kids?'

'A baby girl and a five-year-old boy, Molly and Daniel.'

I nodded, sipping whisky, and I wondered how much of what he was telling me was true. He was a good liar, I had to give him that. And good liars will often use elements of the truth to make their lies more believable. So while I was 100% sure that he wasn't a writer, despite his convincing performance, I wasn't quite so sure that he was lying about his wife and kids. In fact, from the look in his eyes when he mentioned them – a momentary glimpse of longing – I'd be willing to bet that they were as real as it gets. Not that it made much difference.

Either way, I still didn't know who he was.

'What's the book called?' I asked him.

'*Cat Black*,' he said.

'*Cat Black*?'

He smiled. 'It makes sense when you read it.'

'Well, good luck, anyway,' I said. 'I'll keep my eyes open for it.' I smiled at him. 'You never know, I might even read it.'

He laughed. 'I'll send you a copy if you want . . . 10% discount.'

'Only 10%? I can get it for nothing from the library.'

He stood up, smiling, and passed me the joint again. There wasn't much of it left, but I had a couple of puffs anyway, savouring the hot burn of the smoke in my throat.

'So . . .' Allen said, rubbing his eyes. 'What about you, John? What are you doing here? You're not writing a book as well, are you?'

'That'd be really weird, wouldn't it?' I said. 'The two of us staying here, both trying to finish our books . . .'

'Yeah,' Allen smiled. 'What are the chances . . . ?'

'I tell you what would be even weirder,' I said, stubbing out the joint. 'If I *was* a writer, and I *was* staying here, trying to finish my book, and the book I was writing was about an author who's staying in a shitty old hotel on an island, trying to finish his book, and he meets another author in the same hotel who's also trying to finish *his* book . . .'

'Yeah,' said Allen, 'and then one of them finds out that the other one's book is a masterpiece, so he murders him—'

'Right, and he steals his book, planning to pass it off as his own—'

'But then he realises that it's not finished, and he can't finish it because it's a masterpiece, and he's not good enough to finish a masterpiece—'

'Hold on,' I said, laughing. 'I've lost track of who's who now. Are these two authors the ones in the novel—?'

'Which novel?'

'The one I'd be writing if I *was* a writer . . . and I *was* staying here, trying to finish my book—'

'Which you're not.'

'No . . .'

Allen grinned. 'So?'

'So what?'

He laughed. 'What *are* you doing here?'

'Oh, right . . . yeah . . . what am I doing here? Good question.' I lit a cigarette and blew out a stream of smoke. 'The answer's pretty boring really . . . I'm just taking a break, I suppose.' I sighed. 'I was actually meant to be going to Cancún for two weeks with my girlfriend, we've had it booked for months, but we split up about three weeks ago, and I'd already booked the time off work, so basically I had two weeks off with nowhere to go.'

'Why didn't you go to Cancún anyway?'

I smiled. 'I wanted to, but so did my girlfriend, and there was no way we were going together. So we tossed for it.'

'And she won?'

'Yep.'

'But still . . . I mean, surely you could have gone somewhere better than this?'

I shrugged. 'Yeah, I thought about it. I looked at all kinds of places – Spain, Ibiza, Italy, Greece . . . but everywhere seemed so fucking sunny and happy, you know? And I suddenly realised that I just wasn't in the mood for sunny days and smiling faces . . .'

'So you came here?'

'Yeah,' I said, grinning. 'Pretty pathetic, eh?'

'*Very* pathetic.'

'Thanks.'

He smiled. '*De nada.*'

'I used to come here when I was a kid,' I told him. 'With my mum and dad, you know, on Sunday afternoons . . . we'd drive down in the car, go for a walk on the beach . . .' I sipped whisky. 'I haven't been down here for years, and I just thought . . . well, you know, it's a nice quiet place, especially at this time of year, and it might be just what I need. A couple of weeks on my own, just walking on the beach, soaking up the memories, emptying my head, sorting myself out . . .'

'And is it working?' Allen asked quietly.

I shook my head, smiling. 'I should have gone to Ibiza.'

He laughed. 'At least you're not at work though.'

'That's true.'

'What kind of work do you do, if you don't mind me asking?'

'Insurance,' I said. 'I'm a fraud investigator for an insurance company in Hey.'

'Really?'

'Yeah.'

'You're an *investigator*?'

'Well, yeah, but I only deal with fraudulent insurance claims. I mean, I don't skulk around in a dirty raincoat or carry a gun or anything.'

'I bet you're working on a case right now, aren't you?' he said playfully. 'All that stuff about Cancún and your girlfriend . . . that's all just a cover story, and what you're *really* doing down here is investigating some kind of maritime insurance scam—'

'Or a fraudulent author scam,' I said, looking at him.

He only hesitated for a fraction of a second, but it was enough to confirm what I already knew.

'Yeah, all right,' he grinned, quickly recovering his composure. 'It's a fair cop.' He held out his hands, wrists up, ready to be handcuffed. 'You got me bang to rights, guv'nor.'

I laughed, and for a moment or two we both just sat there, smiling quietly at each other, and I think we both knew that we'd reached a point where we either had to stop playing games and tell each other the truth, or we both had to back off for a while and give ourselves time to consider our next move. I was quite happy to let him make the decision, and so I just carried on sitting there in the silence, waiting to see what he did.

Eventually, after maybe twenty seconds, he took a breath,

glanced at his watch, and said, 'Well, I'd better get going, John . . . things to do, you know?'

'More distractions?' I said.

'Something like that.' He got to his feet and passed me the packet of Rizlas. 'Thanks for these.'

'It's all right,' I said. 'You can keep them.'

'You sure?'

I nodded. 'I've got some more somewhere.'

'Thanks,' he said, putting them in his pocket. 'If you need them back, or if you need anything else . . . I'm in room two, just down the corridor.'

'OK,' I said, getting up to see him out.

'By the way,' he said casually, 'what the hell happened to your face?' He grinned. 'Did you get attacked by a gang of fraudulent authors?'

'No,' I said, smiling. 'It was smugglers.'

He laughed. 'There's a lot of them about.'

'I know.'

He paused at the door and turned to me, as if he'd suddenly just remembered something. 'Are you going to the Halloween thing at The Swan tonight?'

'What Halloween thing?'

He shrugged. 'I think it's just a band playing really. I mean, I don't think there's anything particularly Halloweeny about it, but it might be all right, you know . . .'

'What kind of band?'

'Just a local blues band . . . they're from Hey, I think. The Blue Hearts?'

'Yeah, I know them. I've seen them play a couple of times. They're not bad.'

Allen glanced at his watch. 'Well, if you fancy it . . . I'll see you there. The band's due on around ten.'

'OK,' I said. 'Maybe see you later then.'

'Yeah.'

He smiled once more, nodded goodbye, then opened the door and left.

16

It was almost nine thirty when I left my room and headed off down the corridor. I was feeling a bit numbed and woozy from the whisky and dope, but I'd had a good snort of speed just before I left, and I could already feel it doing its job – lifting me up, driving me on, filling me with some kind of purpose.

I'm not saying anything, John, I heard Stacy say.

I smiled. 'You don't have to.'

I'm not sure about that.

'It's all right,' I told her. 'I know what I'm doing.'

Yeah, of course you do.

Arthur Finch was at the reception desk when I entered the lobby, and I could see the wary look in his eyes as he watched me approaching. I wasn't entirely sure if what I was about to do was a good idea or not – not just from Arthur's point of view, but from mine as well – and I also had no way of knowing what the consequences might be, but sometimes reasoning can only take you so far, and in the end you have to put it to one side and just go with your feelings.

And this was one of those times.

'Evening, Arthur,' I said, smiling at him.

He nodded at me. 'Is everything all right?'

'Fine thanks. Are you busy?'

He shrugged. 'Not particularly.'

'I wondered if I could have a quiet word.'

He hesitated. 'Well . . . yes, I suppose so . . . what is it you wanted to talk about?'

'Do you think we could go somewhere a bit more private?'

I'd imagined Arthur's rooms to be the same as all the other hotel rooms, but as he led me reluctantly – and somewhat nervously – through the door marked PRIVATE and then down a short hallway to another door, opening it up and ushering me inside, I quickly realised that I was wrong. The room he showed me into was a large, high-ceilinged place, comfortably furnished with a clutter of armchairs and settees and tables of various sizes, with a thick old carpet on the floor, ornaments and pictures all over the place, and an impressive bay window that looked out over the car park. Logs were burning in an open fire, and the lighting was low, the rich red walls flickering warmly in the firelight. A faint smell of pipe smoke lingered in the air.

As soon as I stepped through the door, Arthur's lurcher, Honey, came lolloping out through a doorway at the far end of the room, followed almost immediately by the other two dogs. As all three of them trotted up to me, wagging their tails, and I bent down and said hello to them, I could sense Arthur's anxiety beginning to fade.

'I think they like you,' he said.

'Are they related?' I asked him, stroking their heads.

'These two are the last of a litter Honey had six months ago. The big bruiser's called Finn, the other one's Beulah.'

They were both slightly bigger than their mother, with broader heads and thicker bodies, and they both had a mixture of Honey's golden colouring and random patches of black and tan.

'We think the father was a rottweiler,' Arthur said. 'But only Honey knows for sure.'

I straightened up and smiled at him. 'What happened to the rest of the litter?'

'We gave them away.' He looked down at his dogs. 'Beulah's going soon, aren't you, girl?' He looked back at me. 'A couple from Hey are taking her when they get back from their holiday, which just leaves Finn. I'd love to keep him, but there just isn't enough room here for two big dogs.' He looked at me. 'You wouldn't be interested in taking him, I suppose?'

A picture of Bridget's dog, Walter, flashed into my mind. Walter was a big old greyhound, as tall as Finn but not so heavy, and he'd been a fixture in the house I shared with Bridget for years . . . and as I looked down at Finn now, I could see Walter quite clearly, sitting in the hallway at home, waiting at the foot of the stairs with his chewed rubber bone in his mouth . . .

He'd been the love of Bridget's life.

'Finn's a wonderful dog,' Arthur said. 'House-trained, happy, full of life . . . he just needs a loving home—'

'I don't think so,' I said. 'I mean, I'd like to have him, I really would . . . but I'm not sure it'd work.'

'Well, if you change your mind . . . or if you know

anyone else who might want him, you know where we are.'

I nodded.

'Excuse me a moment,' Arthur said. 'Ellen,' he called out softly. 'Are you there?'

After a moment, the elderly woman I'd seen at the reception desk appeared from another door on the other side of the room. 'Yes, dear?'

Arthur smiled at her. 'Could you keep an eye on reception for a few minutes, please?'

'Of course,' she said, glancing at me.

'This is Mr Chandler,' Arthur said to her.

'Pleased to meet you,' I said.

She smiled and nodded, then went out through the door.

I looked at Arthur. 'Your wife?'

'No, just a close friend. My wife died a long time ago. Ellen has a flower shop in the High Street, she helps out at the hotel now and then.'

'Right,' I said.

'Shall we make ourselves comfortable?' he suggested, indicating a pair of armchairs either side of the fire.

We sat down, and the three dogs joined us, stretching out in front of the fire.

Arthur took a pipe from his pocket and began filling it with tobacco. 'You can smoke if you like,' he told me.

I lit a cigarette.

He said, 'So, what's on your mind, John?'

'Well, first of all,' I told him, 'I think you probably know by now that Chandler isn't my real name . . .' I looked at him, but he said nothing, just carried on fiddling with his pipe. 'My real name's John Craine,' I went on. 'The reason I gave a false name when I checked in was—'

'I know who you are,' he said quietly. 'And I understand why you used a different name.'

'You do?'

He nodded. 'I read the newspapers, John. I watch TV.' He looked up at me. 'I might be old, but I'm not senile.'

'Well, I just wanted to apologise—'

'There's no need,' he said. 'It's none of my business what you call yourself.'

'Maybe not,' I said. 'But I'd still like to apologise.'

'For what?'

I shrugged. 'Deceiving you, I suppose.'

'But you didn't.'

I shook my head in exasperation. 'Do you always do this?'

'Do what?'

'Make everything *really* difficult.'

He smiled, a twinkle of genuine amusement in his eyes. 'I'm sorry, John. I didn't mean to—'

'Apology accepted,' I said, cutting him off. 'You see? That's all you've got to do. You say sorry, I say OK, and that's it. Nice and easy.'

He nodded, still smiling, and went back to stuffing his pipe. 'I'm assuming that's not all you wanted to talk to me about.'

'No . . . no, it's not.'

He put the pipe in his mouth, held a lighter to it, then puffed away for a few seconds, blowing out smoke from the side of his mouth, and when he was finally satisfied that he'd got it going, he took it out of his mouth, sat back in his chair, and looked at me. 'All right,' he said, 'let's hear it.'

I told him then how I'd found Chelsey's body in the pillbox, and how – by the time the police had arrived – the body had gone. I also told him, without going into any details, what I thought had happened to Chelsey and her parents, and who I thought was responsible, and that it was fairly obvious that a number of other people were involved in trying to cover it all up.

Arthur didn't say anything while I was telling him this, he just sat there quietly, smoking his pipe, listening carefully, occasionally muttering something to one of his dogs.

'The thing is,' I continued, 'I know that someone must have told you to say that the Swalenskis checked out, and you must have arranged to have their room cleared out, and I know for a fact that you changed their check-out date on the hotel computer—'

'How do you—?'

'Please,' I said, holding up my hand. 'Just let me finish, OK?'

He looked at me for a moment, then nodded.

'My guess is that you didn't know what had happened to the Swalenskis, you didn't know *why* you were told to lie about them, you just did as you were told. And I'm sure you had your reasons . . .' I shrugged. 'Maybe they threatened you, or maybe you think you owe them something . . . I don't know. But all my instincts tell me that you're a fundamentally decent man, and that if it was at all possible, you wouldn't have anything to do with these people, whoever they are. I could be wrong, of course. I mean, for all I know, you could be a fundamentally *evil* man . . .' I smiled. 'In which case, I'm probably making a huge mistake . . .' I looked at him. '*Am* I making a mistake?'

He smiled sadly. 'We all make mistakes, John.'

'That's true.'

He shook his head. 'I can't . . . I can't help you, I'm afraid. I'm sorry, but I just—'

'I'm not after a confession,' I said. 'That's not what I'm here for.'

He frowned at me. 'I don't understand . . .'

'It's up to you what you do, Arthur. I'm just telling you how things are.' I looked at him. 'The way it stands at the moment, I know that Chelsey was killed, and I'm pretty sure that her parents were too, but I can't prove it, and there's a good chance that I never will be able to prove it. But I'm not going to stop trying. If I do find anything conclusive, I'll probably pass it on to the police, but for now I'm happy to keep them out of it. So, as far as you're concerned, in the short term at least, you don't have anything to worry about. But eventually – and this is the thing, Arthur, *this* is what you have to understand – eventually, one way or another, the police are going to start asking questions. It might be Hey CID, it might be police from America . . . but whoever it is, it's going to happen. And when it does . . . well, it's only taken *me* a day or so to get this far, and I'm just a washed-up private investigator. How long do you think it's going to take for a full-scale police investigation to find out what's going on?'

Arthur didn't say anything, he just nodded, but I could

tell from the downcast look on his face that the reality of the situation was beginning to sink in. I kept quiet for a while, giving him time to think, and as I sat there in the silence, listening contentedly to the crackle of burning logs, Finn got to his feet, stretched his back, then came over and sat down next to me, resting his head in my lap. I gave his ears a gentle scratch, smiling to myself as he thumped his tail on the floor, and I couldn't help thinking of Walter again. This time I pictured him not in my house but in the pet shop in Hey that Bridget co-owned. It was the day that Bridget had taken me upstairs to the flat above the shop, and Walter had been curled up in a cushion-strewn dog basket on the landing, and when I'd said hello to him he'd looked up at me and thumped his tail a couple of times, but he'd been too warm and comfortable to make any effort to move . . . and I'd thought that was fair enough. And then I'd followed Bridget into the flat, and she'd shown me the front room, and after that we'd gone into the bedroom . . .

She was pale and beautiful and she smelled of straw . . .

'I really don't know what to do,' Arthur said quietly. 'If I could tell you—'

'You don't have to tell me anything,' I said.

He just looked at me.

I stood up. 'Like I said, it's up to you what you do. I don't have any answers, I'm afraid.'

'Perhaps there aren't any.'

I nodded. 'That's how it is sometimes.'

He sighed heavily, then wearily got to his feet, and it was quite noticeable how much he'd changed in the last ten minutes. It was as if he'd suddenly become a tired old man, struggling to get out of his chair, his head bowed down, his shoulders sagging . . .

'Do you need a hand?' I asked him.

He shook his head. 'I'm fine, thank you.'

'I can see myself out,' I told him. 'There's no need for you—'

'No, really . . . I'm fine.' He smiled at me. 'I'd better go and relieve Ellen anyway. She worries if she has to use the computer.'

I walked with him across the room.

'It's really nice in here,' I said, looking around. 'Very . . .'

'Cosy?'

I smiled. 'Have you been here long?'

He nodded. 'Thirty-odd years now. I bought the hotel in August '79.'

'Really? I didn't realise you owned it.'

'I don't any more. I had to sell up about ten years ago. I just manage the place now. Of course, things were very different thirty years ago—'

'Do you know who that is?' I said, interrupting him as we passed the bay window.

'Sorry?'

Two men had just left the hotel together and were walking across the car park. One of them was Mark Allen, the other was Dead-Heart.

'That's Mr Allen,' Arthur said, looking out of the window. 'He's a guest—'

'No, I meant the other one. Do you know him?'

'Oh, yes . . .' Arthur said warily. 'I know him. I wish I didn't . . .'

'What's his name?'

'Garrow . . . Ian Garrow. He lives on a houseboat down by the boatyards.'

The two men had reached the end of the car park now, and I was expecting to see them turn left, towards the village, towards The Swan, but they didn't. They turned right. And as I watched them heading up the road, I wondered where they were going, and what they were doing together . . .

I looked at my watch.

It was just gone ten o'clock.

I looked at Arthur. 'Do they know each other, Allen and Garrow? Are they friends or anything?'

'Friends?' he said, shaking his head with a wry smile. 'No . . . no, they're not friends. They might know each other, but they're not friends.'

'What makes you say that?'

He looked at me. 'Ian Garrow doesn't have friends.'

I thought about going after Allen and Garrow when I left the hotel, but by the time I'd got to the end of the car park the street was empty and they were nowhere to be seen, and as I had no idea where they'd gone, there wasn't much point in trying to follow them. So, after thinking about it for a couple of seconds, I pulled up my collar and headed off towards The Swan.

It was a bitterly cold night, made even worse by the icy wind that was whipping in from the sea, but at least it wasn't raining for once. Occasional fireworks were fizzing and popping in the starless night sky, and as another rocket whizzed up into the darkness and erupted in a starburst of colour, I wondered idly if these were early Bonfire Night celebrations or just more evidence that Halloween's takeover bid was now almost complete. In a few years' time, I thought, the only people celebrating Guy Fawkes Night will be doddery old fuckers who like burning things.

Yeah, Stacy said. *Like you.*

'I'm not doddery,' I said, smiling.

No?

'I'm just old and sour.'

Although it was too late now for the very young trick-or-treaters to be out and about, there were still plenty of older ones roaming the streets. Gangs of teenagers, some of them dressed up as ghouls, monsters, axe murderers, others just wearing scary masks, or balaclavas and sunglasses. And while most of them were just enjoying themselves – having a laugh, dressing up, getting a bit drunk – there were others whose intentions weren't quite so harmless. To them, Halloween was just a licence to fuck people up. I saw a bunch of them throwing eggs at an old woman's house, another group chasing some Goths down a backstreet, and as I neared The Swan, a car pulled up at the side of the road next to a couple of young girls dressed up as sexy vampires, and when the men in the car honked the horn and beckoned the girls over, and the girls tottered across the pavement, giggling drunkenly, I saw the man in the driver's seat lean out of the window and sneeringly shove his hand between one of the girl's legs. She screamed, the man cackled, and as the car drove off, tyres squealing, both girls started sobbing.

Happy Halloween.

My phone rang just as I was going into The Swan, and as I stopped outside to answer it, the deafening sound of the Blue Hearts' opening song erupted from inside the pub:

I'M A HOG FOR YOU, BABY!
I CAN'T GET ENOUGH OF YOUR LOVE!

I stuck my finger in my ear and yelled into the phone, '*CAL! IS THAT YOU?*'

'John?'

'*CAN YOU HEAR ME?*'

'What the *fuck's* going on?'

'*HOLD ON!*'

I moved further away from the pub, heading back out onto the street, where the music wasn't quite so loud.

'Can you hear me now?' I said into the phone.

'Yeah, that's better. Where are you? And what's that fucking awful noise?'

'It's a band called the Blue Hearts. They're playing in a local pub—'

'The Blue Hearts from Hey?'

'Yeah.'

'Christ, are they still going? They were all nearly dead when I last saw them, and that was a good ten years ago.'

'Yeah, I know. I saw them with Stacy a couple of times

203

and they'd been around for years even then. They still sound all right though.'

'You think so?'

I laughed. Cal wasn't a great lover of blues music.

'Anyway,' I said, 'how did it go with the Doc? Did you get the all-clear?'

'Yeah, I'm going home on Tuesday.'

'That's great, Cal.'

'Yeah, I can't wait, to be honest. This place is doing my head in.'

I lit a cigarette.

Cal said, 'So what are you doing at a Blue Hearts gig? You're not actually out and about enjoying yourself, are you?'

I quickly told him about Mark Allen's visit, and his affectedly casual mention of the gig.

Cal said, 'So you think Allen wants you to be there?'

'Why else would he tell me about it?'

'What do you think he's doing? I mean, *why* does he want you there?'

'I don't know . . . but there's only one way to find out, isn't there?'

'Yeah, I suppose . . . but just be careful, OK?'

'I'm always—'

'Yeah, yeah, I know . . . you're always careful.'

I smiled.

'Anyway,' he went on, 'I just wanted . . . remind you about . . .'

'Cal?' I said into the phone. 'You're breaking up. I can't hear you.'

'. . . you were . . .'

'Cal?'

The line went dead then, and when I checked the screen of my mobile I saw that there was no reception. I ended the call, waited a few seconds to see if the signal came back, and when it didn't, I put the phone in my pocket and headed off into The Swan.

The Blue Hearts were playing 'Little Queenie' when I went inside. The pub was crowded, the air hot and sweaty, and the music was so loud that I could feel the floor shaking. I stood at the back of the bar and watched the band for a while, and it was surprising how little they'd changed. They were a classic three-piece blues band – guitar, bass, drums – with the guitarist doing most of the singing and occasionally playing the harmonica. While there was no doubt that all three of them looked their age – and they must have been well into their fifties by now – they didn't seem to have lost any of their energy or passion, and as I stood there watching them, they didn't sound any different to how they'd sounded all those years ago . . .

Yeah, said Stacy, *and they were too loud then.*

I smiled. 'You remember going to see them?'

How could I forget? I couldn't hear anything for three days afterwards.

'We'd only just met, hadn't we?'

I think it was our third date. You asked me if I wanted to go and see 'a nice little blues band'—

'Yeah, and you said that you'd love to.'

I was lying. I can't stand blues bands.

'You should have said, Stace. I wouldn't have minded.'

I know. Her voice held a smile. *But I was dizzy with love, John. I didn't care what we did. I would have said yes if you'd invited me to a Duran Duran gig.*

In my heart, I gave her a look of disbelief.

All right, she said, laughing, *maybe not Duran Duran . . .*

I smiled. 'No one loves anyone *that* much.'

As her quiet laughter faded from my heart, the sound of the Blue Hearts' rock 'n' roll faded back into my head. *Meanwhile,* the singer sang, *I was still thinking . . .*

I wiped a sweaty tear from my eye and went to get a drink.

17

The Swan was so packed full of people, the whole place a seething mass of bodies and booze, that it was hard to find somewhere to stand, let alone sit, but after fighting my way through the crowds for a while, I finally managed to squeeze myself into an emptyish spot near the far wall that offered me a reasonably good view of most of the pub. It had taken me so long to get served at the bar that I'd got myself two drinks – two pints of Stella with a large Scotch in each – to save me the bother of having to queue up again in another ten minutes. I put one of the pints on the floor, placing it carefully between my feet, then straightened up, took a long thirsty swallow from the other, and started looking around.

Apart from a few girls who'd taken the opportunity to dress up – or dress down – provocatively for the occasion, there wasn't a great deal of Halloween spirit on show. There were one or two pumpkin candles dotted around, and someone had made an effort to draw a skull and crossbones on a chalkboard behind the bar, but their heart clearly hadn't been in it – the skull looked like it was smiling, the eye sockets had eyes, and the crossbones weren't even finished. But as Mark Allen had said, it probably wasn't meant to be a particularly Halloweeny thing anyway, it was just a band playing in a pub, and it just happened to be Halloween.

I drank some more and carried on looking around.

By the time I'd finished my first pint and started on the second, I'd scanned every inch of the pub – the bar, the tables, the function room – and I hadn't seen any sign of Mark Allen. Unless he was outside in the smoking area, or in the corridor, or the toilets, I was as sure as I could be that he wasn't there.

And neither was Ian Garrow.

But just about everyone else was.

The Keane brothers, Lyle and Kyle, were hanging around by the door, guzzling down Budweisers with a bunch of kids who looked just like them – pale and skinny, bad skin, tracksuits, trainers, big coats. The rag-sucking kid was with them again, leaning against the wall, sucking drunkenly on his rag, his dim eyes barely open. Lyle looked pretty drunk too, and from the way he kept staring at me – his mean little eyes full of hatred – I guessed that he was probably even drunk enough to try something. When I raised my glass to him and gave him a smile, he grabbed his crotch and gave me the finger.

He's just a boy, John, Stacy reminded me.

'I know.'

I turned my attention to a group of people sitting around a table by the window. I didn't recognise all of them, but there was no mistaking Ponytail and Stevie, the biker who'd kicked the shit out of me, and Robyn, who was sitting beside him, staring at nothing, and I was fairly sure that one of the others was the brutish-looking man from the fishing boat. He had the battered face of a retired boxer – hard scarred skin, thickened brow, badly-fixed broken nose – and although he was sitting with the others, he didn't seem to be engaging with them all that much. He was basically just sitting there, drinking his beer, keeping himself to himself. Every now and then though, I'd see him glance over in my direction, and I knew that he wasn't the only one who had his eye on me. While none of the others were quite so obvious about it as Lyle, I knew that they were all watching me too, and when I saw Stevie lean over and say something to Robyn, and Robyn slowly raised her head and looked blearily in my direction, I guessed that they were talking about me as well.

Robyn had obviously made an effort to look good for the night. Her hair was loose and fashionably shaggy, her face almost doll-like – black eyes, red lips, pale skin – and she was dressed quite simply in a plain black T-shirt and jeans. But no matter how good she looked – and she *did* look good – nothing could hide the fact that she was quite clearly whacked out of her head. And when she looked over at me, I don't think she had any idea what she was supposed to be doing.

I saw her mumble something to Stevie – *who am I looking at?*

Him, Stevie told her impatiently, nodding in my direction. *The one in the black suit, leaning against the wall . . . the guy with the beat-up face.*

Robyn looked over at me again, stifling a yawn. *What about him?* she said to Stevie.

He says he knows you.

He knows me?

Yeah . . . how the fuck does he know you?

Who?

I just fucking told *you, the guy in the suit . . . ah, forget it.*

As Stevie shook his head and started talking to Ponytail, and Robyn went back to staring at nothing, I tried to work out how I felt about her. She was my half-sister, we were family, and whether I liked it or not, that instinctively stirred in me an irrational sense of protection and care. But on the other hand . . . well, I didn't *know* her at all, did I? And her mother had obviously decided not to tell her about me, so Robyn didn't know me either . . . she didn't even know who I was. So what was the *point* in having any feelings for her? What purpose did it serve? Was it simply a vestige of animal self-interest, the genetic remains of something that had crawled into my ancestors' chromosomes a hundred thousand years ago . . . or was it, I wondered, just another useless fucking emotion?

I looked at Robyn . . . wrecked and hopeless.

And I saw myself in her.

And I realised how lucky we both were to live in a place and time that has no evolutionary parameters, where nothing is unsuitable, where nothing cares what you are, or what you do, or whether or not you deserve to survive. We *all* survive in this world – the weak, the useless, the ruined, the broken . . .

The unfit fit.

I took another long drink and carried on looking around.

I hadn't been surprised to see the likes of Lyle Keane and the bikers in the bar – in fact, I would have been more surprised if they hadn't been there – but there was another familiar face in The Swan that night who I definitely hadn't been expecting to see, and that was Linda, the woman from the hotel. I don't really know *why* I was surprised to see her – she was young, she was local, she probably enjoyed a night out as much as anyone else . . . why *shouldn't* she be here? But I think there was just something about her – an air of austerity, a sense of purpose – that, to my mind, seemed out of place amid all the noise and revelry. Like Robyn, she'd gone through the motions of dolling herself up for the night – make-up, styled hair, short flowery dress over skinny blue jeans – and if you didn't look *too* closely, she gave the impression that she was enjoying herself – drinking with friends, chatting, smiling, laughing. But I *was* looking closely, and the closer I looked, the more obvious it became that it was all just a show.

She was sitting at a corner table with two hippyish women and a dark-skinned man, all of whom were about the same age as her, and when I'd first seen them they'd all been watching the band, the women tapping their feet to the music, the man coolly nodding his head . . . and Linda, too, for the most part, seemed happy enough just sitting there watching and listening to the Blue Hearts. But every now and then she'd sit back and look around, and while she tried to make it seem casual, as if she was merely gazing curiously around the bar, my guess was that she was looking for someone. And as the night went on, she began looking round more and more often, and when she wasn't scanning the room, she always had one eye on the door.

She was looking for someone.

Someone who was supposed to be here by now . . .

But they weren't.

And that was beginning to worry Linda. But she didn't want anyone to know it. And as I looked over at her again now, I saw one of the hippyish women glance at her just as her eyes flicked anxiously at the door again, and the woman frowned, seeing the tension in Linda's face, and she put a concerned hand on her arm and said something to her . . .

Are you all right, Linda?

And Linda was suddenly all smiles again. *Yeah, yeah, I'm fine . . .*

Are you waiting for someone?

Sorry?

The woman glanced at the door, then turned back to Linda. *I just thought—*

Do you want another one? Linda said, picking up her friend's glass. *Same again?*

I watched her as she got to her feet and began heading for the bar, and then – when she was out of sight of her friends – I saw her leave the empty glass on a table and go through the door that led out to the smoking area at the back.

I finished my drink, gave it a minute, then followed her outside.

The smoking area was as crowded as the pub, if not more so, and it took me a while to spot Linda among all the other bodies milling around the small paved yard, all of them clutching their drinks and frantically smoking their cigarettes. Linda was right at the back of the yard, standing in the corner with a mobile phone held to her ear. She

212

wasn't smoking. After I'd lit a cigarette and watched her for a while, I realised that she wasn't talking either. She was calling someone, getting no answer . . . redialling, listening again, still getting no answer . . .

Shit, I saw her say.

She looked up at the sky for a moment, thinking things through, then went back to her phone and started thumbing the keys . . . sending a text.

I smoked my cigarette, watching her, wondering who she was trying to contact . . . and why she seemed so worried.

She's probably just waiting for her boyfriend, Stacy said.

'Yeah,' I agreed.

And maybe they're going through a bad patch or something, and she's worried that he's seeing someone else . . .

'Yeah, maybe.'

You don't sound very convinced.

I shrugged. 'Something doesn't feel right . . .'

What do you mean?

'I've no idea.'

Linda had finished the text now and she was trying the phone number again. She put the phone to her ear, listened for a second, then gave up. I saw her shake her head, sigh heavily, glance at her watch . . . and then she started threading her way through the crowd of smokers, heading back into the pub. Lost in her thoughts, her mind elsewhere, she didn't see me leaning against the wall by the door, and if I hadn't said anything to her, she would have walked straight past me.

'Hey, Linda,' I said.

She looked at me, her eyes blank, and I thought she didn't recognise me.

'It's John,' I reminded her, smiling. 'From the hotel . . . ?'

She glanced through the door, then looked back at me. 'Did you want something?'

'No . . . no, I was just saying hello, that's all.'

'Yeah . . .' she said absently, giving me a cursory nod. 'Look . . . I have to go . . . I'll, uh . . . sorry, I have to go.'

And, with that, she was gone.

I stayed outside for a while, smoking another cigarette and wondering if I was wasting my time here, but I knew that if I went back to the hotel I'd just drink myself to sleep, and although I probably *was* wasting my time here, at least I was doing *some*thing.

And besides, I told myself, what's time for if *not* to waste?

In hindsight, it might have been better if I had gone back to the hotel and drunk myself to sleep . . . but then what good is hindsight anyway? If we knew in advance what the consequences of our actions were going to be, we'd never do anything at all.

Robyn was just coming out of the Ladies' toilets as I headed along the corridor on my way back to the bar. She stopped briefly in the doorway, turning away from me to wipe something from her face, and I almost took the opportunity to turn round and go back outside before she saw me, but by the time I'd slowed down and thought about it, she'd already glanced over her shoulder and spotted me.

'Well, well,' she said, smiling broadly at me. 'Look who it is . . .'

I went up to her and smiled back. 'You missed a bit.'

'Eh?'

I ran my finger over my upper lip, letting her know that she still had traces of white powder under her nose.

'Oh, right,' she said, wiping her lip with the back of her hand. 'Has it gone now?'

I nodded.

She smiled again. 'Thanks.'

Her eyes were wild, darting all over the place, and her skin was stretched tight.

'What's your name?' she asked me.

'John.'

'Right, John,' she said, glancing quickly up the corridor. 'We need to talk . . . come here.' She reached out and grabbed my hand, took another quick look behind her, then opened the door to the Ladies' and dragged me inside.

'Hey, hold on,' I said. 'What are you—?'

Grinning quite manically now, she clamped her hand over my mouth and half-pulled, half-shoved me across the tiled floor towards one of the cubicles. Without stopping, she raised a foot and kicked the cubicle door open, and the next thing I knew she'd pushed me inside, squeezed in after me, and was locking the bolt on the door.

'What are you doing?' I said. 'I can't—'

'Sit down,' she said, turning to face me.

'This is ridic—'

'*Sit.*' she said firmly, putting her hands on my shoulders and pushing me down onto the toilet.

She wasn't particularly strong, and I could easily have resisted her . . . it wouldn't have been any trouble at all to stay on my feet, shove her out of the way, unlock the door and get out of there. But it's not every day that you get forced into a Ladies' toilet by your half-sister, and I suppose I just wanted to find out what the hell she was doing. So I let her push me down, and then I just sat there, looking up at her, waiting to see what she did.

'Stevie says you've been talking about me,' she said, staring right into my eyes.

'Really?'

'Yeah, really . . .' She grinned. 'He seems to have got it into his head that you've been fucking me.'

'*What?*'

'I told him you hadn't—'

'Yeah, sorry,' I told her, suddenly feeling incredibly awkward. 'What it was—'

'It's all right, John,' she said, leaning down and putting her finger to my lips. 'I mean, I don't *mind* if you want to fuck me, but you can't go mouthing off to Stevie about it. He'll kill us both if he finds out—'

'No, no,' I muttered, shaking my head and starting to get up. 'No, you don't understand—'

'What's to understand?' she said, smiling as she put her hand between my legs.

I quickly sat down again. 'No, look,' I stammered, 'listen to me, this isn't—'

'What's the matter, John?' she said, stepping back and pouting at me. 'Don't you *want* some of this?'

She'd whipped off her T-shirt and put her hands on her

216

hips before I knew what was happening, and for a night-marish moment I found myself sitting on a toilet, unable to move, staring up in disbelief at the half-naked figure of my half-sister.

I was so shocked, so mortified with embarrassment and confusion, that I couldn't do anything for a few seconds – couldn't move, couldn't speak . . . I couldn't even breathe – but then the outside door slammed open and a gaggle of girls came bursting into the toilets, all of them shrieking and laughing, and the sudden influx of sound released me from my paralysis. And then all I remember is scrambling to my feet and reaching for the door, desper-ately trying to avoid any contact with Robyn – which was virtually impossible in such a confined space, especially as Robyn was doing everything she could to make sure that I couldn't get out without manhandling her – but somehow, eventually, I managed to unlock the door and force my way out . . . and then, with the sound of Robyn's laughter ringing in my ears, together with a cackle of whoops and yells from the other girls who'd just come in, I got out of there as fast as I could.

All I was looking for when I went into the Men's toilets was a place of sanctuary, a bolt-hole, a cave . . . a fucking great hole in the ground. Anywhere would do. As long as no one could see me, and Robyn wasn't there, I really didn't care. I just needed a minute or two to sort my head out, to start breathing again, to let my heart slow down . . . to give my skin a chance to stop crawling. And as the Men's toilets were right next door to the Ladies', making them the first thing I saw when I bolted out into the corridor, I didn't even think about it. I just shoved open the door and scurried inside.

'Fuck,' I said as I headed for a cubicle. 'Fuck, fuck, *fuck* . . .'

'Hey,' a voice said from behind me, sounding offended. 'There's no need—'

'Fuck off,' I said, without looking round.

There were only three cubicles. One of them was engaged, another one had a broken lock, but the one at the far end was vacant and unbroken. I went inside, shut the door and locked it, then sat down on the toilet and lit a cigarette. A cold shiver prickled my skin, shaking me from head to toe.

'Shit,' I whispered, taking a long hard drag on the cigarette. 'Fuck . . .'

I blew out my cheeks.

Took a couple of deep breaths.

Ran my fingers through my hair.

And started to feel just a tiny bit better. I even felt the beginnings of a smile as I imagined what I'd say when Cal next asked me if I'd met up with Robyn yet . . . but the smile only lasted a moment, and as I remembered the cold reality of Robyn's coke-crazed abandon, I despised myself for even considering it something to smile about. She was only eighteen, for God's sake. She was just a kid. And whether we knew each other or not, whether my feelings for her were irrational or not, she *was* my half-sister, my little sister, my kid sister, and *this* was how she spent her nights – stoned out of her head with her shit-kicking boyfriend, dragging total strangers into toilet cubicles, acting like a slut . . .

I *wanted* it to be none of my business.

Nothing to do with me.

But it was.

I was her brother.

And a brother looks after his sister, no matter what.

He forgives her everything.

I shouldn't have run away from her, I thought. *I should have explained who I was and why I'd said what I'd said to Stevie . . . I should have—*

'. . . helped you, Robyn . . .'

I froze, holding my breath and listening hard, trying to work out if the muffled whisper I'd just heard was real or not. It *sounded* real . . . it sounded like a voice I knew, a woman's voice, hushed and urgent, very nearby . . . but my head was full of voices too, real and imagined, and unless I was in a much worse state than I'd thought – unless I was so fucked-up that I wasn't where I thought I was – I was alone in a toilet cubicle . . . *alone* in a toilet cubicle . . . so the voice *had* to have come from inside my head.

Didn't it?

I closed my eyes and listened . . .

I could hear the familiar echoed sounds of a Men's toilet: hand-dryers roaring, men farting, pissing loudly, laughing and spitting, hawking up phlegm . . . I could hear the muffled rock 'n' roll thump of the Blue Hearts, still playing, the music rising and falling as the toilet door opened and closed . . .

'. . . where's Garrow? . . .'

It *was* a real voice.

It *was* very nearby.

I looked around the cubicle. It was as grim and primitive as every other Men's toilet cubicle I'd ever been in: a scabby white shithole, reeking of gas and piss, the walls scrawled with the dirt of men's minds – a felt-tipped penis ejaculating from its monster eye, two giant black gooseberries slung from its neck . . . crude vaginas, telephone numbers, sick messages, angry obscuration, imbecilic threats and taunts . . .

'. . . I can't help you if you don't help me . . .'

It *was* real . . . the voice . . . it was coming from a nasty little peephole in the Contiboard wall on my right. It was the kind of hole that you often see in toilet walls – crudely gouged out by some sick little man, then usually blocked up with screwed-up wads of toilet paper . . . but this one wasn't blocked up. This one was open. A rough-edged hole in the wall, no more than half an inch wide, a dirty little tunnel that burrowed through into the Ladies' toilets next door. That's where the voice was coming from.

'. . . I don't *know* where he is . . .'

'. . . what about Stevie? . . .'

Voices.

Not just *a* voice, but voices. Two women, both whispering. I was fairly sure that the first voice belonged to Linda, and the second voice was definitely Robyn's.

I leaned forward and carefully put my ear to the wall.

'. . . he's not telling me anything . . .'

'. . . I need to *know*, Robyn . . . if you can't . . .'

The whispers kept cutting in and out with the rise and

fall of all the background noise – the music, other voices, hand-dryers, toilets flushing – and all I could really hear were disjointed fragments of the conversation.

'. . . all right, I'll do my best . . .'

' . . . the whole thing . . . by Tuesday . . .'

As a hand-dryer started roaring again, momentarily drowning out the whispered voices, I sat up and tried to work out what was going on. I didn't get very far though. All that really came to me was – Linda and Robyn? Linda and *Robyn*? Which wasn't a great deal of help. I leaned forward again, listened at the hole for a moment, and then – hearing nothing – I swallowed my instinctive sense of embarrassment and disgust and put my eye to the peephole.

From what I could see – which wasn't a lot – Robyn was sitting on the toilet, and Linda was standing in front of her. It was definitely Linda – I recognised the pattern of her dress – and from the way she was standing, and the way she was moving her hands, I got the impression that she was getting impatient with Robyn. Impatient, but not angry. It was an impatience curbed with concern . . . and perhaps even fear.

'. . . if you see him . . .'

'. . . yeah . . .'

'. . . call me . . .'

'. . . yeah, look . . . gotta go . . .'

They were getting ready to leave.

I stood up, dropped my cigarette into the toilet, flushed it, and turned to open the door. I didn't know what I was going to do next, if anything. I was still trying to digest what I'd just seen and heard. I had no idea if I was going to do anything about it, maybe confront Linda, or Robyn, or both of them, or if I was just going to carry on watching and waiting . . .

I didn't know.

And I never got the chance to find out.

As I unlocked the cubicle door, sliding back the grubby brass bolt, the door suddenly slammed back into my face, and as I staggered backwards into the cistern, with my head spinning and blood streaming out of my nose, Lyle Keane appeared in the doorway, his eyes raged with alcohol, a six-inch knife in his hand.

18

Lyle should have taken his time. If he'd waited for me to get to my feet, all he would have had to do was step forward and stab me at his leisure. I couldn't have done anything to stop him, not in the cramped confines of the cubicle. I would have been trapped, defenceless, an easy target . . . and even if I had been able to get out of the cubicle, I still wouldn't have got very far, because Lyle wasn't alone. Behind him, I could see three more tracksuit boys, all of them hyped up and spoiling for blood. But Lyle was too drunk, and too stupid, to bide his time. Instead, as I lay there half-sprawled/half-sitting on the toilet, with my back against the wall and my legs in the air, he came lunging in after me with the knife raised recklessly over his head, and all I had to do was lean back, brace myself against the wall and hammer a two-footed kick into his chest. I caught him pretty hard, and although I don't think it hurt him too much, it was enough to send him staggering back out of the cubicle, struggling for air, which gave me a few precious seconds to get to my feet and prepare myself for his next move.

I knew that the odds were still firmly stacked against me, and I didn't really hold out much hope for myself, but as someone once told me – *no one wants to die, no matter*

how much pain they're in or how pitiful their lives are . . .
we'll all do anything to live another moment or two. And
that's all I was doing really, just trying to stay alive for
another brief moment or two.

Lyle had totally lost it now. I'd humiliated him, made
him look weak in front of his friends, and as he came at
me with the knife again there was so much despair in his
eyes, so much ruin and hatred, that I almost felt sorry for
him. But that didn't stop me from slamming the cubicle
door into his head as he came charging through the
doorway, and I didn't think twice about cracking the door
into his head again as he dropped to the floor, and then
once again as he fell to his knees . . . and once more, for
luck, as he dropped the knife and slumped face down on
the piss-soaked floor.

Feeling sorry didn't come into it.

I quickly stooped down, grabbed the knife, then stood
up and faced the others. As they stood there in front of
me, staring hard, I thought for a moment that I might just
make it. The odds still weren't all that good. There were
three of them, only one of me, and they were all pretty
mean-looking, and it didn't look as if they were going to
back down . . . but at least I had the knife now, and they
were all empty-handed. But then one of them, with a snide
little grin, reached into his trackpants and pulled out a
knife, and almost immediately the other two followed suit,
and now my only advantage was gone. I glanced around
the toilets, not really expecting to see anyone else, and even
if I had seen anyone, I doubted very much if they'd be
willing to help me. But there was no one around anyway,

the place was deserted, and I guessed that when Lyle and his tracksuit boys had come in they'd told everyone to fuck off, and they'd probably left someone outside too, guarding the door, to make sure no one came in.

I looked back at the tracksuit boys.

'You're on your own, fuckhead,' the first one said.

'So it seems.'

Grinning at me, he raised his arm and levelled his knife at my head. 'You ready for this?'

Shit, I thought, steadying myself. Then, *Ah, fuck it . . .*

'Come on, then,' I said, smiling at him. 'What are you waiting for?'

They weren't as dumb as Lyle, and as they spread themselves out in a ragged semicircle and began inching cautiously towards me, it was pretty obvious that they knew what they were doing. And as I quickly weighed up my options, I realised that none of them looked too good. Making a run for it was out of the question, and if I stood my ground and took them on, I didn't stand a chance. But if I took the only other option – locking myself in the cubicle – all that would do was hold them off until they kicked the door in, which would probably give me an extra couple of seconds at most . . .

They were only a few steps away from me now – their eyes staring, their muscles tensed, ready to strike . . .

I started edging back into the cubicle.

Another few seconds was better than nothing . . .

A hand grabbed hold of my ankle, and I looked down to see Lyle's bloodied face grinning up at me as he wrapped both arms round my legs, clinging onto me, stopping me from moving . . . I tried kicking out to break his hold, but he wouldn't let go. And now the first tracksuit kid was lunging at me, going for my face with his knife, and even as I managed to grab his hand and deflect the blade, I could see the other two kids coming at me. I jabbed my knife at one of them, momentarily forcing him back, but that gave the other one the chance he was waiting for, and as he swung his knife at me, aiming for my belly, I knew there was nothing I could do.

I saw the grin on his face . . .

White teeth.

A flash of silver . . .

I braced myself . . .

Suddenly the kid jerked back, a tattooed hand on his neck, and I heard a dull thump. The other kid staggered back, holding his head, and when a deadly soft voice said, 'What the fuck are you doing, Jase?' I saw a flash of fear in the first kid's eyes, and almost immediately he dropped his knife and backed away from me. And then Ian Garrow stepped into view from my right, smiling calmly, and I realised that the tattooed hand belonged to Ponytail, who was now standing behind Garrow, staring at the tracksuit kids as they headed sheepishly for the door.

'You all right, John?' Garrow asked.

'Uh, yeah . . . I think so.'

He glanced down at Lyle, who still had hold of my legs.

Lyle grinned anxiously at him. 'What?' he muttered. 'We were only—'

Garrow kicked him hard in the head – once, twice – and Lyle slumped back down to the floor.

226

'Fucking retard,' Garrow said, shaking his head. He glanced over his shoulder, watching the tracksuit kids leave, then he turned back to me, smiling again. 'Sorry about this, John. Are you sure you're OK?'

'Yeah . . .' I said, bewildered. 'Yeah . . . I'm fine.'

Garrow shrugged. 'They're just kids, you know . . . they spend all night drinking, take a few pills, get a bit over-excited . . .' He smiled again. 'It's the parents I blame. There's just no discipline these days, is there?'

I nodded, not sure what to say. I didn't have a *clue* what was going on here. As I reached into my pocket for a much-needed cigarette, Garrow confounded me further by taking out a lighter and offering me a light.

'Thanks,' I mumbled.

'Listen,' he said, 'about yesterday . . . you know, at the pillbox? I just wanted to apologise, OK? Stevie shouldn't have reacted like that.' Garrow grinned. 'He just can't help himself sometimes. He's a bit insecure, you know? Not that that makes it all right, of course . . . but anyway, like I said . . .' He shrugged again. 'I think we *all* probably got off on the wrong foot a bit, didn't we?'

I just stared at him, totally bemused.

'I'm Ian, by the way,' he went on, offering me his hand.

I shook it. His hand was surprisingly cold and limp.

He smiled. 'Let me buy you a drink, John, all right? Bury the hatchet and all that . . .'

Bury the hatchet? I thought.

'Come on,' he said, gently taking my arm. 'I know the landlord here. He keeps some really nice Scotch for special occasions. We'll share a couple of glasses together. How does that sound?' Without waiting for me to answer, he glanced down at Lyle Keane's still motionless body, then turned to Ponytail and said, 'Clear that up, Lloyd.'

I was still trying to work out what Garrow's game was as I left the toilets with him and we headed back to the bar. Why all the sudden pleasantries? Why the apology? And why had he saved me from the tracksuit kids? It didn't make sense. But nothing about tonight had made any sense so far, and as Garrow led me over to a table at the back of the bar, signalling to the barman as we went, I knew that the only way I was going to find out anything was by playing along with the game.

So I sat down, and Garrow sat down opposite me, and within a few moments the barman had brought over two hefty measures of whisky in crystal tumblers and set them down on the table. Garrow didn't thank him, didn't even look at him, but the barman still gave him a servile smile, as if Garrow was some kind of royalty.

'Cheers, then,' Garrow said to me, picking up one of the glasses.

I picked up the other glass, touched it to Garrow's, and took a long drink. It *was* good whisky – smooth and smoky, with a slight peaty aftertaste . . . all of which was wasted on me. I would have been just as happy with the straight-forward bite of Teacher's or Bell's. But what the hell? It was whisky, it was fine. It was free.

I drank some more.

It did the trick.

Garrow watched me, amused. 'Is that better?'

I nodded. 'Better than nothing.'

'So tell me,' he said casually, leaning back in his chair. 'What the fuck did you do to Lyle Keane to piss him off so much?'

I've never really understood the difference between a psychopath and a sociopath – and to be perfectly honest, I've never really cared – but I've met enough of them over the years to know that they really *can* be almost hypnotically charming, and although we all like to think that we're far too astute to be taken in by any kind of emotional fakery, the simple truth is that unless the deception is blindingly obvious, most of us won't have a clue that we're being deceived until it's too late . . . and even then, we'll still find it hard to believe. Of course, it always helps if you don't trust anyone in the first place, which I don't, and I also had the advantage of knowing – or, at least, guessing – that Garrow *was* a psychopath/sociopath, and that as such he was perfectly capable of coming across as an engaging, charming, likeable man – which he did. But even though I knew it was all just a sham, and that behind the mask there was nothing remotely engaging or likeable, he still managed to make me feel curiously at ease. And as we sat there together that night, talking and drinking, I had to keep reminding myself that we *weren't* just sitting there, talking and drinking, that Garrow was either after something or up to something, and that if I wanted to find out what it was, I'd have to keep my wits about me.

But it was really difficult. Partly, I think, because everything was beginning to catch up with me now – the drink and the drugs, the shock and confusion of the last few hours, the ever-constant murmur of the black place – and my wits simply weren't up to much any more. But it was also really hard to stay on my toes because Garrow really *was* good company. He didn't just talk to me, he *engaged* me, asking me questions about my work, my life, my opinions, and although I was very cautious at first – keeping my answers as simple as possible, not really telling him anything – he was such a good listener, and his interest in me seemed so genuine, that I soon found myself opening up to him. I don't think I told him anything he didn't already know, and I was still more or less aware that everything about him – every word, every gesture, every facial expression – was fake, but somehow it just didn't seem to matter any more. And by the time Garrow had brought the conversation back to our encounter on the beach again, I'd almost forgotten what a dead-hearted bastard he really was . . .

Almost.

'Can I be honest with you, John?' he said, leaning forward and lowering his voice. 'I mean, *really* honest?'

'Yeah, of course.'

The pub had quietened down a bit now. The Blue Hearts had finished playing about twenty minutes earlier, and the bar was beginning to empty out. Not everyone was leaving though, and although it was pretty late – sometime around midnight – there was no sign that the pub was getting ready to close.

'This is strictly between you and me, OK?' Garrow said.

'No problem.'

He smiled. 'Do you want another drink?'

I shook my head. I'd already had three, and I still had another full glass in front of me, and over the last few minutes I'd begun to feel slightly nauseous, so I thought I'd better ease up for a while.

'You sure?' Garrow said.

'Yeah, I'm fine.'

He glanced around to make sure no one was listening, then he leaned forward again and spoke quietly. 'You were right about the drugs, OK? At the beach, yesterday . . . that's what we were doing. The stuff usually comes in at night, or really early in the morning, but there's been a few problems over the last couple of days and we've had to take some shipments during the day.' He shook his head. 'It's been a pain in the fucking arse, to tell you the truth . . . everyone gets really edgy, you know?'

'Yeah, I can imagine.'

He sipped his drink. 'I mean, that's partly why we gave you such a hard time, you know, because we were all so fucking pissed off.'

'Right . . .'

'Mind you,' he added, smiling. 'We probably would have given you a hard time anyway, come to think of it.'

'Yeah? Why's that?'

'Why do you think? I mean, there we were, unloading a boat full of dope, and along comes a private investigator asking all sorts of questions . . . what do you think we're going to do? Make you a cup of fucking tea?'

I grinned. 'How did you know I was a private investigator anyway?'

He shrugged. 'Contacts, you know . . .'

'Boon?'

Garrow just smiled.

I said, 'Does he know?'

'Know what?'

'About the drugs.'

'He knows that stuff comes in, booze, cigarettes . . . everyone knows. It's no big deal. I mean, it's been going on round here for centuries . . . everyone just takes it for granted.' He shrugged again. 'And besides, there's fuck all else to keep the island going.'

'So the police don't do anything about it?'

'Not as long as they get their cut.'

'And they don't have a problem with drugs coming in?'

Garrow looked at me. 'Do you?'

I shook my head. 'I couldn't give a shit.'

He smiled. 'Neither do the police. As long as it's not too obvious, and we don't get involved with anything too heavy, they're quite happy to let us get on with it.'

'What does "too heavy" mean?'

'We don't deal in smack, we don't deal with people we don't know, and we don't deal too big. It's mostly just grass, dope, a bit of blow now and then . . . that's all.'

'Nothing nasty.'

'That's right.'

'All nice and soft.'

His mask slipped for just a moment then, and I saw a flash of irritation in his eyes. But that's all it was, an almost imperceptible flash.

'Are you sure you don't want another drink?' he said, smiling again.

I looked at him. 'Why are you telling me all this?'

'Why?'

'Yeah, what's in it for you?'

He grinned. 'What's in it for me?'

I smiled.

He stared at me. 'There was no dead girl, John.'

'What?'

'In the pillbox . . . on Saturday. I was there. We'd just finished unloading some dope when Stevie called to warn us that you were coming.' Garrow leaned forward, looking me in the eye. 'Nothing happened, John. There was no girl, no one got killed. There was no one there apart from us. And all we did was unload the boat and stash the gear, and then we fucked off out of there as quick as we could. That's the God's honest truth, John.'

It was all very convincing, and if I didn't know that he was lying I probably would have believed him. He'd told me the truth about the drug smuggling, hadn't he? He'd confided in me, put his trust in me . . . he'd shown me how open and honest he was. So why *shouldn't* I believe him now?

'Look,' he said softly, 'I'm not trying to tell you what to do or anything, and I know how confusing it must be . . . I mean, if *I* thought I'd seen a body, I'd probably feel exactly the same as you. So I understand what you're going through, John. I really do. But all I'm saying is—'

'You want me to stop poking around, is that it?'

He grinned. 'You can poke around as much as you want. It's up to you if you want to waste your time. But things could get really awkward around here if you start getting outsiders involved . . . do you know what I mean?'

I nodded. 'It'd be kind of awkward for me anyway . . . you know, if I went to the police in Hey and tried telling them that I'd found a dead girl, but then her body had suddenly vanished.' I smiled. 'I've got my reputation to consider for a start. I mean, who the hell's going to hire a mentally unstable private investigator?'

Garrow laughed. 'A lunatic might.'

'True,' I said. 'I suppose I could always specialise. Investigations for the insane . . .'

'It's probably not the most reliable of markets.'

I nodded, grinning, and started to get to my feet.

'Where are you going?' Garrow said.

'I need a cigarette.'

'Sit down,' he said. 'You can smoke in here.'

I looked around and was surprised to see that there weren't that many people left in the bar now, and that some of them were smoking, including the barman. As I sat back down and lit a cigarette, Garrow looked over at a table by the door where Stevie and Robyn were enjoying a joint with a few others.

'Hey!' Garrow called out to them. 'Any chance of having some of that over here?'

It was around then, I think – just after Stevie and Robyn had come over and joined us, and I'd had a few puffs on the joint – that I first started feeling a bit strange. Initially I just thought it was the nausea I'd felt earlier, but although there was *some*thing going on in my stomach, and there was something about it that reminded me of being sick, it wasn't really a nauseous feeling. It was more of a numbness, a tingling numbness . . . like pins and needles, only inside me. It wasn't an unpleasant feeling, just totally unfamiliar, and although I felt quite panicky for a while – as you do when you feel something that you've never felt before – I soon realised, as the tingling numbness began to spread through my body, that there was nothing to worry about. It was a warm feeling, a good feeling, calming and smooth . . . like a slow infusion of honey. It wasn't going to hurt me. There was nothing to worry about . . .

'Are you all right, John?' I heard Garrow say.

And I realised that my eyes were closed. I opened them, blinking away a cloud of tiny stars, and I looked round the table. Lloyd had joined us, Lloyd the Ponytail . . . and the man from the boat, the Brute . . . and I could see Robyn watching me, hiding her smile from Stevie . . . and Stevie rolling another joint . . .

Skunk, I thought. *That's probably what it is. Skunk. We're smoking skunk . . . and this is what it does to you . . .*

'John?' Garrow said again.

'Yeah?'

'How are you feeling?'

'Wonderful,' I muttered. 'Never fucking better.'

He stared at me for a second or two, his face utterly blank, and when I looked back at him, gazing deep into his eyes, I saw nothing at all. There was a void where his eyes should have been. And for a non-existent moment we were one and the same: nothing and nothing.

He blinked once, then smiled at me and said, 'I got you another drink.'

As I took a deep breath and let it out slowly, I could

feel the air in my lungs, I could *feel* the oxygen filtering into my blood . . . I could feel every cell in my body. And every single one of them felt good.

I felt good.

Perfect.

Warm and weightless . . .

I didn't feel anything.

I lit a cigarette and reached for the tumbler of whisky.

19

I don't know how long I sat there with Garrow and the others in the end, drinking and smoking the night away, because at some point I totally lost track of the time. And it wasn't just that my watch was broken – which I assumed had happened during my encounter with Lyle and his boys – so I didn't actually know what time it was, but I also didn't seem to have any concept of time at all. One moment everything would feel really slow, almost without time, and then suddenly I'd realise that ten minutes must have passed in the blink of an eye.

If I hadn't been so out of it, it probably would have been really unnerving.

But, as it was, I barely even noticed it.

In fact, I wasn't really aware of anything after a while . . . not in a strictly coherent sense anyway. I mean, I knew what I was doing, and on one level I was acutely aware of everything around me – the people, the bar, the background music . . . I could hear every voice, see every expression, I could determine the nuance of every little gesture – but it was all so isolated, so disconnected, that no matter how clear each individual moment was, that's all they were – moments – and when your existence consists of a series of unconnected, and therefore meaningless, moments, it's kind of hard to make much sense of anything.

And it's also really difficult to remember.

So although I *know* that I stayed there for some time with Garrow and the others, I have no recollection of talking to any of them, and if I did, I can't recall what we talked about . . . and while I get the feeling that I was there for about an hour or so, it could just as easily have been twenty minutes, or two hours . . . and I certainly don't know how much I drank, or how much dope I smoked . . .

All I can really remember, oddly enough, is suddenly realising that my bladder was achingly full and that I hadn't emptied it for God knows how long, and even then I almost decided that it didn't matter. I'd reached that stage of intoxication where physical pain takes on a distance, a remoteness, and rather than actually feeling it, you just kind of know that it's there. And it's really not a problem to put up with it. And that's how it was with my bladder. It just seemed a lot easier to sit there and ignore the faint throbbing ache than to get up and walk all the way to the toilets, especially as I wasn't even sure that I could stand up, let alone walk across the room. But then it occurred to me that although *I* could easily put up with a full bladder, maybe my bladder couldn't, and as soon as I started thinking about that, and how embarrassing it would be, I suddenly began to feel the pain and I realised that I really *did* have to go.

It wasn't as difficult as I'd imagined – getting to my feet, mumbling the word 'toilet', stumbling just a little as I left the table and headed for the door to the corridor – in fact, I didn't feel anywhere near as drunk or stoned as I'd thought I was. That's not to say that I didn't feel incredibly strange, because I did, but it wasn't an alcohol- or cannabis-induced strangeness, I was pretty sure of that. It was something else . . . an alien feeling, something that made me feel heavy and weightless at the same time, as if I was both floating *and* drowning . . . because the air was liquid . . . and the floor was too far away . . . The world was becoming elastic.

And as I went into the toilets, it started getting worse. The walls, the ceiling, the sinks . . . everything was distorting, bending, shifting . . . the planes, the angles, the colours . . . the shapes of things melting and reforming in the sterile white light . . . and even when I stood still and closed my eyes, trying to shut out the weirdness, it still didn't stop. My inner darkness was ablaze with colours – reds and yellows and electric blues, bars of bright white light, black flashes, fluorescent stars . . .

'Shit,' someone said . . . a giant's voice, deep and slow and without a point of origin . . . distended, disguised, everywhere . . .

'Fuck.'

I opened my eyes.

Everything was suddenly back to normal again. The walls were just walls, the sinks were just sinks . . . everything was just how it should be.

I started laughing, but it sounded too weird, so I stopped.

I lit a cigarette, went over to a urinal, and emptied my bladder.

*

When I went back into the bar, everyone had gone. Not just Garrow and the others, but everyone. The entire pub was empty. There was no music playing, no voices, no nothing . . . just a deserted room, clouded with smoke, and heavy with silence. I stood there for a moment, just looking around, and for a second or two I couldn't remember where I'd just come from or how long I'd been gone . . . and I began to think that I must have fallen asleep somewhere, or maybe I'd passed out, or maybe—

'You all right, mate?'

I looked over at the sound of the voice and saw the barman coming out of a door marked STAFF, wiping his hands on a cloth.

'We're closed,' he said.

'Since when?'

'Five minutes ago.'

'That was quick.'

He shrugged, wiping his hands again.

I said, 'Don't you check the toilets before you close?'

'Yeah, I was just going to.'

I looked at him, and for a fraction of a second his face began to melt. I blinked, and the melting stopped. 'What time is it?' I asked him.

He grinned. 'Time to go home.'

They say that your whole life flashes before your eyes when you're dying, and while I can't be sure if that's true or not, I believe that you see your own death when you're born. That's why babies scream – that and the bare-faced liberty of it all. I mean, who asked you? That's what I want to

*know. Before you were born . . . who the fuck asked you
if you wanted a life? Before you were born . . . it's hard to
imagine, isn't it? No space, no time, no existence . . . it's
hard to accept. No nothing. Imagine that . . . the emptiness
and the utter silence, the cold and the dark and the never
knowing . . . think of it . . . and then take it away. And
what are you left with? Less than nothing. And that's what
you were before you were born. You were timeless and
spaceless and everythingless. Nothing to nothing to nothing.
And I think that perhaps you were happy enough with that.
But now it's gone. Stolen. And even death can't give it back
to you, because the stain of life is indelible.*

Who asked you?

No one.

*And that's got to be some kind of fucking liberty, don't
you think?*

. . . don't you think . . . ?

. . . don't you think . . . ?

. . . don't you think . . . ?

I wasn't sure if the echoes I was hearing were in my mind
or in the mist of the icy night air, and as I carried on
walking along the empty streets, heading back to the hotel,
I knew that I was struggling to be sure of anything. Was I
talking out loud? Was I hearing voices? Was I talking to
myself? Was I in my head or somewhere outside of it? I
didn't know . . . but at least I *knew* that I didn't know.

Or, at least, I thought I did.

And that was the trouble . . .

It's always the trouble.

You are whatever you are. You feel whatever you feel, sense whatever you sense. Your state of mind *is* your state of mind. And that's all you have. You can't step to one side and see yourself as you really are, it's just not possible, because what you really are won't let you. A drunk can only see through drunken eyes, a lunatic can only think lunatic thoughts . . . and a drug-addled mind can only have a drug-addled self-awareness. So although some distant part of me *knew* that I'd been drugged, and that my mind and body were out of control, I still couldn't deal with it rationally *because* my mind was out of control.

It was all I could do to just keep going.

I wanted to stop. I wanted to lie down and close my eyes and wait for it all to go away – this boundless nightmare of circling lights and rippling roads, shimmering buildings and tilting walls, the frightening roar of the blood in my veins, the monstrous moan of the wind – I wanted it all to stop. But I knew that it wouldn't, and that I had to keep going. And when I heard a crash of footsteps thundering towards me, and I heard the echoed swell of a thousand laughing voices, and I looked up and saw a writhing mass of horror-show heads and screaming mouths bearing down on me like some awful slavering beast, I didn't *want* to be petrified . . . I didn't *want* to cower away from the beast like a terrified child, flattening myself against a wall, hiding my head in my hands . . . and I didn't want to flinch with fear when one of the beast's many laughing heads snapped towards me like a rabid snake and screamed '*YOU CUNT!*' into my face . . .

But I couldn't help it.

I had to stop then.

As the gang of drunken boys in their Halloween masks carried on down the street, laughing and spitting, shouting and whooping, I lowered myself slowly to the ground, and then I just sat there, shaking and trembling, trying to think.

I lit a cigarette.

And tried to think . . .

I needed to find my self, my knowing self, the part of me that knew that Garrow or one of the others must have slipped something into my drink or put something in one of the joints, the part of me that knew – and had known all along – that I *wasn't* just stoned on skunk, or some other form of really strong cannabis. But although I knew that this knowing self was in there somewhere, I still couldn't get to it. It was too far away, too weak . . . it was too deeply buried in the madness. And as I sat there smoking, staring into the night, the only voice I could hear in my head was the voice I'd heard before, the voice that talked of birth and death and screaming babies . . .

And I knew that voice was full of shit.

I put out my cigarette, rubbed my eyes, and got to my feet.

A light rain had begun to fall, shimmering silver in the mist. I saw a million shining jewels . . .

I shook my head and got going.

That's how it was all the way back to the hotel – the truth coming and going, the tide of reality ebbing and flowing – but although the outside world hadn't stopped playing its tricks on me as I crossed the car park and headed for the muted lights of the lobby, my inner world was beginning to make a bit more sense. It still wasn't up to much in terms of rational thinking, and as I opened the hotel door and went inside, and the ceiling of the lobby dipped down towards me, I was still having to focus all my attention on the more immediate tasks of staying on my feet and not being terrified. But once I'd done that, and the ceiling had returned to where it was supposed to be, I began to feel – to *think* – that I'd almost made it. All I had to do now was cross the lobby . . . ignoring the disconcerting tilt of the floor . . . then open the door and go through into the corridor . . . trying to ignore the disembodied voices – *hey, are you OK? . . . you all right, buddy? . . . you need any help? . . . take it easy, OK?* – and the remembered smile of a gum-chewing teenage girl . . . *what was she listening to on her iPod?* . . . forget about it, you're nearly there now . . . just keep going, keep moving . . . one step, another step . . . we're nearly there . . . just a few more seconds and we can go inside and shut the door, shut out the world . . . we can drink and drink until the darkness comes and there's nothing more to fear, no more monsters, no more voices, no more madness . . . just a timeless void of nothingness until we wake again . . .

And then everything will be OK.

I fumbled in my pocket, found the keycard, and was just about to swipe it when I realised that the door wasn't shut properly.

'Fuck,' I whispered, looking around.

The corridor was empty.

I stayed still and listened hard.

Nothing.

I looked at the door. It was pulled to, resting on the latch . . . and I wondered for a moment if I'd left it like that. I closed my eyes, trying to remember, trying to picture myself opening the door, walking out, pulling the door shut behind me . . . *had* I pulled it shut behind me? I couldn't remember. It was too long ago . . . a thousand years, at least.

'Fuck it,' I said, opening my eyes.

I really didn't need this, not now. Whatever it was . . . I *really* could have done without it.

I took a deep breath, let it out slowly, and nudged open the door. Nothing happened. I waited for a minute, another minute, standing as still as I could, listening intently, staring through the half-open door at the silent darkness inside . . .

Nothing moved, nothing made a sound.

I took another breath, went inside, and turned on the light.

The room had been totally ransacked. There was stuff strewn all over the floor – clothes, bed sheets, empty drawers, whisky bottles – my holdall had been emptied out, cupboards opened . . . the whole place had been turned upside down.

I moved carefully across the room, looking around at the mess, trying to think what it meant, and who could have done it . . . and why? What were they looking for? And, more importantly, had they found it? I stopped and looked down at the upended holdall at my feet.

Chelsey's phone . . .

'Shit.'

I'd put the phone in my bag when Mark Allen was here . . .

I knelt down and went through the holdall, just in case, but there was nothing in it. No phone . . . and no drugs either.

'Fuck,' I said, looking around again, scanning the floor . . . but I knew it was a waste of time.

I straightened up and lit a cigarette.

And I thought about Mark Allen.

He could have seen me putting Chelsey's phone in the holdall. He could have told me about the Blue Hearts gig at The Swan to get me out of my room, and while I was out he could have broken in and taken the phone . . . and that's why he hadn't shown up at the gig. He'd been too busy ransacking my fucking room . . .

I felt a slight breeze then, a draught of cold air, and as I turned to see where it was coming from, I saw one of the balcony doors swinging open. I froze for a moment, my heart beating hard, but after a while I realised that there was no one there . . . it was only the wind. I breathed out, and went over to the doors, wondering why Allen would have opened them . . .

It didn't make sense.

But then, as I took hold of the door and went to close it, and I glanced out into the darkness, I realised – with a sudden sickening horror – that Mark Allen hadn't ransacked my room. Not unless I was seeing things again . . . and I wished to God that I was, but as my head started spinning and I forced myself to step out onto the balcony to get a closer look, I knew that I wasn't imagining things. The beach itself was bathed in darkness, but in the light from my room I could clearly see the metal stake, about five feet long, that had been fixed into the sand just beyond the balcony . . . and there was no doubt at all that the severed head impaled on the stake was the severed head of Mark Allen.

I barely had time to feel anything. A moment's stunned sickness, a split second of utter emptiness . . . and then I heard, or felt, a presence behind me. I turned instinctively, too numbed to know what I was doing . . . and there, right in front of me, was the greasepainted face of a clown.

It's not real, I thought, staring at its grinning red gash of a mouth, its diabolic eyes . . . and then a bomb went off in my head, and as my legs buckled and I dropped like a sack to the floor, I just had time to think, *Shit, it is real*, and then the clown leaned over and hit me again.

There was no pain then, just a drifting darkness, a hollow black noise, and the vaguest awareness of strong hands prising my jaws open, forcing a bottle into my mouth, pouring some kind of liquid down my throat . . .

And then the world shut down.

20

Everything hurt when I woke up – my head, my eyes, my heart . . . everything felt sick and dirty and abused. My mouth was bone dry, my belly was racked with cramps, and I smelled so bad, so sour and stale, that the taste of my own breath made me retch.

I was cold, freezing. The sheets were damp with sweat.

Sheets . . . ?

I was in bed.

How did I get into bed?

I couldn't remember . . . I couldn't remember anything. My head was full of mush.

I couldn't open my eyes.

I just lay there, shivering and groaning, trying to remember . . . trying to think . . . trying to find something, anything . . .

Nothing . . . there was *nothing* . . .

Open your eyes.

'I can't . . .'

Open them.

I took a deep breath, swallowing down a gulp of sickness, and slowly opened my eyes. The grey light of day was skulking in through the curtained windows, giving everything a flat and empty look, like a picture in an old

magazine. The clock radio on the bedside table said 13.31.
I looked around, taking in as much as I could without
moving my head – my clothes piled neatly on the floor,
my holdall, the carpet, the walls, the table . . . everything
nice and tidy, everything in its place . . .

Why does that feel wrong?

I forced myself to move my head, raising it just enough
to see the rest of the room. Nothing *looked* wrong . . .
everything seemed just as it should be . . . but it just didn't
feel right. And as my gaze fell on the curtained balcony
doors, I felt something stirring in the back of my mind, a
distant memory of something awful . . . something staring
back at me . . . something . . .

I couldn't get hold of it.

My stomach lurched, gripped by a sudden pain. I
stumbled out of bed, stooped naked to the bathroom, and
spent the next five minutes being violently sick.

An hour or so later, after I'd showered and dressed, taken
some painkillers, drunk a lot of coffee and smoked a few
cigarettes, I didn't really feel much better. But at least I
didn't feel any worse, and I was fairly sure that I'd done
all the throwing up I was going to do. And, more importantly, my head wasn't quite so mushy any more. I still
couldn't remember anything very clearly, but as I sat at the
table, drinking more coffee and smoking another cigarette,
things were starting to come back to me, and although they
didn't make any sense at first – monsters, knives, half-naked
girls . . . painted faces, lunatic voices – it wasn't too long
before I had at least some of the night pieced together. I

remembered being in The Swan, I remembered all the craziness with Robyn and Linda, and the fight with Lyle and the tracksuit boys . . . and then Garrow and Lloyd . . . and feeling drugged . . . and then . . .

Then it all got a bit vague.

There was some kind of monster . . .

A snake?

And someone called me a cunt . . .

And then . . . ?

I gazed slowly around the room. I could see it now . . . the way the room had looked when I'd got back last night – or this morning, whenever it was – I could *see* it: stuff strewn all over the floor . . . clothes, bed sheets, empty drawers, whisky bottles . . . my holdall emptied out, cupboards opened . . . the whole place ransacked . . .

And now it was *un*ransacked.

Nice and tidy, everything in its place . . .

I got up and crossed the room, looking around at the *lack* of mess, trying to think what it meant, and who could have done it . . . and why? I stopped and looked down at the holdall at my feet. Last night it had been emptied out, thrown on the floor . . . but now it was all zipped up, neatly positioned against the wall.

I knelt down and opened it. Nothing seemed to have been touched. I rummaged around, checking all the pockets . . . and, as far as I could tell, the only thing missing was Chelsey's phone. Everything else was still there . . . including my drugs.

'Fuck,' I said, shaking my head, totally confused.

I closed my eyes and tried to concentrate, digging deep,

trying to remember the last thing I did, the last thing that happened, the last thing . . .

A bomb.

Someone hit me.

That was it. Someone hit me . . .

A clown . . .

A *clown*?

Jesus *Christ* . . .

Did that *really* happen?

A fucking *clown*?

It happened . . . I *knew* it. I could *feel* it – the bomb going off in my head, falling to the floor, drifting into darkness . . . and then something else . . .

A taste of something . . .

Something awful.

And then, quite suddenly, I remembered Mark Allen.

I straightened up, turned slowly towards the balcony, and stared numbly at the curtained doors. I remembered it all now – feeling a slight breeze, a draught of cold air, turning to see where it was coming from, realising that one of the balcony doors was open . . . then glancing out into the darkness and seeing Mark Allen's severed head, impaled on a metal stake . . .

I swallowed hard.

I didn't want to go over there now and open the curtains. I didn't want to see that terrible thing again. But I knew that I had to, if only to prove to myself that I wasn't losing my mind.

I went over to the doors, paused for a moment, then opened the curtains and looked out through the glass.

There was nothing there. No metal stake, no severed head, just a rain-darkened balcony and, beyond that, the empty grey gloom of the beach.

I sat down on the bed and went over everything again – from talking to Mark Allen in my room, and later on seeing him leave the hotel with Garrow . . . to as much as I could remember about being in The Swan and coming back to my room afterwards. It had been a long night, with a lot of drinking, a lot of madness, and a lot of stuff that still didn't seem real. I was quite sure now that most of the unreality was a result of someone spiking my drink, or putting something in one of the joints, but whether or not that accounted for *every*thing . . . that's what I couldn't work out.

Had my room *really* been ransacked?

Had I *really* seen Mark Allen's head on a spike?

Had I *really* been attacked by a clown?

Or had I just imagined it all?

There wasn't much evidence either way. My memory was too hazy to rely on, and about the only thing I knew for certain was that Chelsey's phone was no longer in my bag. So, unless I hadn't put it in there in the first place, or I'd never even *had* it in the first place – neither of which I was willing to accept – that had to mean that someone had been in my room.

My mobile rang then.

I took it out of my pocket and looked at the caller display. It was Cal. I really wasn't up to talking to him just yet, so I thumbed the DECLINE button, and then quickly checked the 3 MISSED CALLS message on my phone. They were all from Cal – one at 00.23, one at 10.55, and the last one at 12.16.

I'd call him back later.

I went over to the corner of the room and lifted the loose carpet, half-expecting the key to the pillbox to be gone. But it was still there. I put it in my pocket and went into the bathroom. There was an extendable shaving mirror mounted on the wall. I pulled it out and angled it so I could see the back of my head, and when I carefully brushed back my hair, I could clearly see an egg-sized lump just behind my ear. Someone had definitely hit me, I thought, going back into the other room, and whoever it was, clown or no clown, they'd probably given me something to *keep* me knocked out, and that's what the vague memory of the bottle being forced into my mouth was all about. They'd knocked me out, given me something to make sure I didn't wake up, and then they'd cleaned up my room, put everything back in its place, and they'd even undressed me and put me into bed . . .

But why?

I put out my cigarette, lit another, and thought about it . . .

At 14.43, I still hadn't come up with any answers. Nothing made sense. Nothing added up. I glanced over at the whisky bottle on the table. It was half-full. Last night it had been on the floor, empty. I got up, went over to the table, uncapped the bottle and sniffed it. It smelled like whisky. Nothing else. It smelled like the promise of thoughtless comfort . . .

I put the cap back on.

I went into the bathroom, took some more painkillers, and drank two glasses of water. My face in the mirror was the face of a tired and beaten-up man. I drank another glass of water, ran my fingers through my hair, and went out onto the balcony.

A quiet rain was falling, as grey as ever, and the skies were heavy and low. The beach was empty, the tide coming in, and way out in the distance a container ship was just about visible on the horizon.

I lit a cigarette and gazed down at the sand, trying to remember where the metal stake had been fixed. There was no sign that anything had ever been there – no marks in the sand, no footprints, nothing. But the sand was wet, sodden with rain, and it was quite possible that whatever signs had been there had long since been washed away. I carried on looking, searching the area just in front of the balcony, and after a while I spotted something. I leaned forward, stretching out over the railing, and stared down at a small patch of dry sand just to the left of the right-hand balcony post. The ground there was sheltered from the rain by the post, and at the edge of the strip of dryness, I could just make out a small dark spot. I knew that it was probably nothing – just a drop of dried oil or something – but I clambered over the balcony and squatted down for a closer look anyway, just to make sure.

Close up, it was still hard to tell what it was. I was pretty sure that it was a drop of something, some kind of liquid, and that although it had dried in the sand, it didn't look as if it had been there all that long. It wasn't black enough to be oil, but it was dark . . . a browny darkness, tinged with red.

Was it blood?

Possibly . . .

Could it be mine? I'd taken a few whacks in the head recently, some of which had bled quite a bit, and I'd spent a fair amount of time out on the balcony . . .

It could quite easily be mine.

But if someone *had* been out here last night, playing gruesome Halloween tricks with Mark Allen's head . . .

It could be his blood.

I took out my mobile and snapped a close-up picture of the spot, then I stood up and moved back a few paces and took another photo. After that, I climbed back over the balcony and went inside, found an envelope in one of the drawers, picked up a clean teaspoon, then I went back out and carefully dug out the dried spot and spooned it, sand and all, into the envelope.

As I sealed the envelope, put it in my pocket, and began heaving myself back over the balcony again, I caught a glimpse of myself in a full-length mirror on the back wall of my room, and it was such a pitiful sight that – cliché or not – I really *didn't* know whether to laugh or cry. The figure in the mirror was just *so* pathetic – a forty-year-old man with the face of a beaten-up street drunk, dressed in a cheap black suit, wearing no shoes or socks, struggling to climb over a balcony with a burning cigarette hanging from his lips, his bloodshot eyes squinting to keep out the smoke . . . I mean, what the fuck does he think he's doing? Digging up sand with a teaspoon, putting it into an envelope

. . . like some kind of *CSI*-obsessed lunatic who's convinced that he really *is* Gil Grissom . . .

I started laughing then . . .

The laugh turned into a hacking cough . . .

And I lost my balance, slipped off the railing, and landed on my back.

And that's where I was – lying on my back on the balcony, smiling stupidly at the sky – when I heard someone knocking at the door.

There was something about the sound of the knocking that made me think of Mark Allen, and as I made my way over to the door and put my eye to the peephole, I wasn't quite sure how I'd feel if I saw him standing in the corridor. Obviously I'd be pleased that he wasn't dead, but on the other hand . . .

It didn't matter.

It wasn't Mark Allen.

How could it be? Mark Allen was dead.

It was Linda. She was wearing an apron and she had her cleaning trolley with her, but I got the feeling that she wasn't here to clean my room. I opened the door, ready to ask her in, but she didn't even give me a chance to speak, she just barged right past me and marched into the room.

'Hold on,' I started to say. 'What are you—?'

'Shut the door,' she snapped.

'What?'

She stared at me. 'Shut the fucking door.'

I could tell from the look in her eyes that she wasn't in the mood for arguing, so I turned round and shut the door, paused for a moment to steady myself, then turned back to face her.

'Do you want to sit down?' I asked, smiling.

'No,' she said icily. 'I don't want to sit down. I want you to tell me what the fuck you think you're doing.'

21

As Linda stood there glowering at me, waiting for me to tell her what the fuck I thought I was doing, my first reaction was to angrily ask her what the fuck she thought *she* was doing, but even as the thought formed in my mind, I realised that I was too tired and too confused to summon up any anger, so instead I just went over to the table, sat down, and lit a cigarette.

'I know who you are,' Linda snapped. 'I know—'

'Sit down, for Christ's sake,' I said wearily, looking at her. 'Please? Just sit down, OK?'

She glared at me for a moment, then went over to the chair by the window and sat down.

'Thank you,' I said.

A hard rain was just beginning to fall, the heavy drops streaming down the window, and out over the sea the island skies were a solid mass of dark rolling clouds.

'You're John Craine, aren't you?' Linda said, her voice a little calmer now.

'Yes.'

'You're a private investigator.'

'I am.'

'Do you mind telling me what you're doing here?'

I smiled at her. 'Do you mind telling me what *you're*

doing here? I mean, no offence or anything, but I don't usually get interrogated by hotel employees—'

'Are you still involved with DCI Bishop?' she said, ignoring my question.

'*What?*'

'You heard me.'

'What's Mick Bishop got to do with anything? And how the fuck do you know him anyway?'

'Are you working for him?'

'Christ, no,' I said. 'Why the hell would I be working for Bishop?'

'For the same reason that everyone else does,' Linda said simply. 'Because he's got something on you, or you need the money, or you don't want to get locked up, or beaten up, or worse . . .' She looked at me. 'We know all about Bishop, John. We know how many people he's got in his pocket, all the bent cops and politicians, the pimps, the dealers, the buyers . . . we know that nothing gets past him.'

'Who's "we"?' I asked her.

She looked at me for a few seconds, weighing things up in her mind, and it was quite obvious that she didn't *want* to tell me the truth, but she also knew that she wasn't going to get anything out of me if she didn't. And so, with a heavy sigh, she reluctantly began to explain herself.

Her name, she told me, was Linda Ransom, and she was a customs officer with HM Revenue and Customs. She'd been working undercover at the hotel for almost a year as part of a major HMRC investigation into a network of drug-smuggling operations based in the south-east of England.

'I can't go into any more detail than that,' she said, looking at me. 'But you *have* to understand how big this investigation is. It's been running for over three years now, and we're getting very close to making some significant arrests. Not just here, but in Harwich, London, Amsterdam, Morocco . . . it's a global operation, John. We've invested huge amounts of time, manpower and money, and we simply can't afford to run the risk of *any*thing being compromised. Do you understand?'

'Why should I believe you?' I asked.

'*What?*' she said angrily.

I shrugged. 'It's a fair enough question. I mean, how do I know that you're telling me the truth? You could be feeding me a pile of shit, for all I know.'

She looked disdainfully at me. 'And why would I do that?'

'That's not my concern, is it?'

She sighed. 'You're an investigator . . . you must know what *undercover* means, for Christ's sake. It means you don't go round carrying your official fucking ID in your fucking pocket just in case—'

'Again,' I said, 'that's not my problem, is it? My problem is simply knowing whether to believe you or not.'

She glared at me. 'I could just have you arrested, you know.'

'For what?'

She glanced over at my holdall. 'Possession of a Class A drug, for a start.'

260

I smiled. 'So you *were* searching my bag the other day.'

She shrugged. 'It's part of my job.'

'I'm still not convinced.'

She stared at me. 'One phone call, that's all it would take. I could have you arrested and taken away in less than ten minutes. Would *that* be enough to convince you?'

'Yeah, it would,' I said, holding her gaze. 'But if you *are* who you say you are, and if you were going to arrest me, you wouldn't be sitting here talking to me now. So it's not going to happen, is it?'

'Don't be too fucking sure,' she muttered.

I just smiled at her, not saying anything, and she lapsed into a thoughtful silence for a while.

Although it was only just gone three o'clock, the sky was so dark now, and the rain so heavy, that there was very little light coming in through the window. I considered getting up to turn on the light, but the cloistered dimness of the room was actually quite comforting, especially for my still-throbbing eyes, and I decided to leave things just as they were. If Linda Ransom didn't like it, she knew where the light switch was.

As I glanced back at her, wondering idly if she really *was* called Linda Ransom, she looked at me and said, 'A man called Mark Allen came to see you yesterday, didn't he?'

'Yeah . . .' I replied hesitantly.

'He told you that he was a writer, that he was trying to finish a book . . .'

I said nothing, just sat there, waiting for her to go on.

'His name's not Mark Allen,' she told me. 'It's Mark

261

Ballard. And he's not a writer, he's an undercover customs officer too. The reason he came to see you was to find out what you're doing here.'

I looked at her, trying to keep the image of the severed head from my mind. 'That still doesn't *prove* anything,' I said, my voice a little shaky. 'All it tells me is that you know a man called Mark Allen, or Mark Ballard, you know that he came to see me, you know what he told me—'

'I know all about the Anna Gerrish case too,' she said.

I froze, staring at her.

She smiled ruefully. 'All that crap about Anton Viner . . . Bishop bullshitting the press conference . . . yeah, right . . .' She was nodding confidently now, knowing full well that she'd got my attention. 'And do you know what else I know?' she said. 'I know that an SO13 officer called Les Gillard was shot in the knee a few weeks ago, and although it was kept *very* quiet, I have it on good authority that this shooting took place within spitting distance of an office in Hey registered to John Craine Investigations.' She smiled at me again. 'Now, I'm not saying that this *proves* anything . . .'

'Yeah, all right,' I sighed. 'You've made your point.'

'You believe me now?'

I shrugged. 'Yeah, I suppose . . .'

The truth was, I'd pretty much believed her from the start anyway, and all I'd been doing for the last five minutes was giving myself time to work out what it meant, and how much I should tell her, while at the same time trying to squeeze as much information from her as I could. I'd had no idea what she might tell me, but when she'd mentioned Bishop and Gillard, that was the last thing I'd been expecting. And if I *had* needed proof that she was who she said she was, the fact that she knew *any*thing about Bishop and Gillard would have been more than enough to convince me. Her suspicions about the Gerrish case though, and her veiled suggestion that I had something to do with Les Gillard's shooting . . . well, that was something else. That was actually quite disconcerting. Because if she knew the whole story . . . well, I just had to hope that she didn't.

'Does Bishop know you're here?' she asked me.

I looked at her.

She sighed. 'Look, I just need to know if you're in touch with him or not, OK? Because if you are, if you're working with him in any capacity whatsoever . . . well, that's going to be a major problem.'

I knew exactly what she meant, and she was right – Mick Bishop had been a dirty cop for more than thirty years, and it was highly unlikely that he wouldn't be aware of all the major drug-smuggling operations in the south-east . . . in fact, it was highly unlikely that he wouldn't actually be part of them. What Linda didn't know though, what she *couldn't* know, was that in the last few weeks the primary – if not the *only* – motivation behind Bishop's corruption had been removed.

The only people who knew about that were Mick Bishop and me.

But while he no longer had any reason to carry on being corrupt, I was fairly sure that he'd find it almost impossible to change his ways. Thirty years of dirty work is hard to leave behind. So I thought long and hard about Mick

Bishop. I went back to the conversation we'd had just a week ago, when he'd suggested that I leave town for a while, and I tried to remember if it was at all possible that he'd somehow planted the idea of Hale Island in my mind . . . but nothing came to me. Nothing at all. Hale Island had been my idea, mine and no one else's.

And that's what I told Linda Ransom.

'So,' she said, when I'd finished, 'you're not actually working for *any*one at the moment?'

'No, like I said—'

'You're just trying to get away from it all.'

'That's right.'

'Waiting for things to blow over.'

'Yeah.'

'And are they?'

'Are they what?'

'Blowing over.'

I shrugged. 'As far as I know . . .'

She nodded. 'And all this business with the American girl—'

'Chelsey,' I said. 'Her name's Chelsey Swalenski.'

'Right . . . so what happened with her then?'

I looked at Linda, wondering how much she knew – about Chelsey, about the Swalenskis, about anything – and I wondered again how much I should tell her. I lit a cigarette, smoked it thoughtfully for a while, and decided to tell her everything . . . up to a point.

And that's what I did.

*

'And that's why you've been nosing around, is it?' she said, when I'd reached my point. 'That's why you've been stirring things up, asking all kinds of awkward questions . . . because you think you saw the body of this girl in the pillbox—'

'I don't *think* I saw it,' I corrected her. 'I *know* I saw it. And for the last time, *this girl* has got a fucking name, OK? Her name is Chelsey Swalenski.'

'Yeah, all right, I'm sorry . . . but look, John—'

'Don't you care about her?'

'Of *course* I do . . . but unless you have any proof that Chelsey or her parents have been harmed in any way, there's really not much I can do about it.' She looked at me. '*Do* you have any proof?'

I thought of the photographs on Chelsey's missing camera, the altered check-out date on the hotel computer . . . and I realised that that was it. Apart from a belly full of bad feelings and a head full of stuff that might or might not have happened, I had nothing. No proof. No evidence. Nothing worth a damn.

I looked at Linda. 'If I could prove to you, right now, that Chelsey was dead, that she was murdered, and that she was killed by the people you're investigating . . . what would you do?'

'*Can* you prove it?'

I smiled at her. 'You answer my question, and I'll answer yours.'

She didn't smile back, she just sat there, as stern as ever, thinking things through, and after a while she said, 'Why should I tell you anything?'

265

'Why not?'

'Because anything I tell you might jeopardise our investigation, that's why not.'

I nodded. 'OK, but what if I know something that might *help* your investigation?'

'Do you?'

'Maybe . . . but if you don't help me—'

'I'm not making any *deals* with you.'

'I'm not asking for one. All I want to know is what you'd do if I provided you with proof that Chelsey Swalenski was murdered. You tell me that, and I'll tell you what else I know.'

She shook her head, not happy at all, and I thought for a moment that she was going to start warning me about the consequences of withholding information, or that maybe she'd even threaten me with arrest again . . . although, as a customs officer, rather than a police officer, I wasn't even sure that she had the power of arrest. Not that it mattered, because eventually, after looking really pissed off for a while, she shook her head once more, sighed heavily, and began to answer my question.

'All right, listen,' she said, 'I don't know why I'm doing this, but I'm going to be as honest with you as I possibly can, OK?' She looked at me. 'If you could convince me today that Chelsey was murdered, I give you my word that once this investigation is over I'll pass on every scrap of evidence you have to the police. Not the local police, because they can't be trusted, and not Hey CID either, because they're even worse . . . but there *are* good forces out there, with honest officers, and I know who they are, and although I can't promise you the earth, I *can* promise you a clean, thorough and exhaustive investigation. If Chelsey has been murdered, if her parents have been murdered, you'll get your investigation.'

'Right,' I said. 'But not until *your* investigation is over.'

'Look,' she sighed, 'if the police get involved now . . . well, just imagine it. The whole island will turn into a circus. There'll be CID all over the place, forensics, uniforms, the media . . . and everyone we're after will stop what they're doing and get rid of any evidence, and all the work we've done over the last three years will be wasted.' She shook her head. 'I'm not going to let that happen.'

'That's ridiculous,' I said. 'I mean, do you *really* think that taking down a few drug dealers is more important than catching the killer of a fourteen-year-old girl?'

'No, of course not—'

'Well, that's what it sounds like to me.'

'You just don't *get* it, do you?' she said angrily. 'First of all, we're not just talking about "a few drug dealers", as you put it. We're talking about serious players here – buyers, distributors, financiers—'

I laughed.

She glared at me.

I said, 'Come *on* . . . you're not trying to tell me that Garrow and his boys are *serious players*, are you? I mean, yeah, they might be seriously nasty, they might even be killers, but all they're doing drug-wise is bringing in a few bales of grass and a bit of blow now and then. It's hardly a fucking cartel, is it?'

She stared at me. 'Have you finished?'

'All I'm saying is—'

'You have *no* idea what you're talking about.'

'No?'

'Did I say anything about Garrow being a player?'

'Well, no . . . but—'

'Garrow's just a hired hand. Almost everyone on Hale is a hired hand. They all just do what they're told. But if you want to get to the people at the top, you have to start with the people at the bottom. So, yes, we know all about Garrow's little team . . . and, incidentally, they actually bring in a lot more than you think. A *lot* more. But, as I was trying to tell you, that's not what we're after. We're after the big stuff, the big money, the big names, and if we can take *them* out . . . well, who knows how many ruined lives we'll be saving.'

'You think so?'

'Yeah, I do. Don't you?'

'Not really. I mean, as soon as you put away one big name, someone else will take their place, and nothing will change.'

'So what do you suggest we do?' she sneered. 'Just give up?'

I shrugged and lit a cigarette, unwilling to get into the argument.

'Anyway,' Linda said, 'getting back to the point . . . the other reason for delaying any police investigation is that we have to consider the safety of our sources. It's taken us a long time to build up a good relationship with our informants, and if the police were to come down here asking lots of questions, there's no telling what might come out, and as you said yourself, there's some seriously nasty individuals involved in all this, and if they were to find out that one of their own has been passing on information . . .'

She didn't have to finish the sentence, I knew what she meant. And I also knew now that my growing suspicion that Robyn was Linda's informant – a suspicion that my conscious self had been doing its best to play down – was almost certainly true.

And that changed things.

I wasn't sure how . . .

It just did.

I reached for the whisky bottle, then stopped, remembering that it might have been spiked. I thought about risking it, imagining the taste . . . the raw bite of whisky in my throat . . . and then the warming glow . . . the sedative heat, working its way into my blood, my heart . . . taking away all the pain . . .

I stubbed out my cigarette and turned to Linda.

'What have you got on Robyn?' I asked her.

'Sorry?'

'Robyn Mayo . . . why's she working for you?'

Linda's surprise only showed for a moment, a brief look of puzzlement in her eyes, and then almost immediately she regained her composure. 'I'm not even going there,' she said coldly. 'Whatever you think—'

'I think you need to be more careful,' I told her. 'If *I* know she's your informant, which I do – and it didn't take me long to find out, without even trying – what makes you think that nobody else knows?'

'No,' Linda said, shaking her head. 'No, that's not . . .'

She paused, looking at me, and I could see a hint of self-doubt in her eyes. '*Does* anyone else know?'

'I've no idea.'

'How did you find out?'

I told her.

She listened.

The rain kept falling.

Ten minutes later, the rain was still coming down, I was still feeling like shit, and Linda Ransom was still just sitting there, thinking about what I'd just told her. I hadn't planned on telling her that Robyn was my half-sister, but I'd realised as I was explaining things that if I hadn't told Linda the truth, she may well have assumed that my concern for Robyn was based on other reasons, and I didn't want her thinking that there was anything like that between us, so I'd given Linda a very brief summary of my father's history with Serina Mayo, and I'd also explained that Robyn still didn't know who I was, and that I'd like it to stay that way for now. Linda had told me that while she couldn't promise anything, she could see no reason why anyone else had to know.

As Linda carried on thinking, I went into the bathroom and took some more painkillers, washing them down with a glass of water. I refilled the glass and drank some more, wishing it was whisky, wishing . . .

What?

Wishing I'd never come here? Wishing I had some control over the things inside me? Wishing, as ever, that Stacy was here . . . that our child was here . . . wishing for some kind of life?

270

I was wasting my time.

I went back out, went back over to the table, and sat down.

'Are you all right?' Linda asked.

I lit a cigarette. 'Wonderful, thanks.'

She looked at me for a moment, trying to work me out, and then – with a somewhat resigned shake of her head – she put it from her mind and got back to the business in hand. 'All right, listen,' she said. 'This is all going to be over in a couple of days, OK? Three days at most. I can't tell you any more than that. The logistics of an investigation this size are so complex that it'd take me about a week to explain everything—'

'And you don't trust me anyway.'

'Right,' she said, almost smiling. 'Anyway, once it's all over, you won't have to worry about Robyn. We look after our informants. No one's going to know what she's done. And besides, with a bit of luck, there won't be anyone left to worry about because they'll all be locked up.'

'With a bit of luck?' I said, unconvinced.

'You know how it is, John. Nothing's ever guaranteed.'

I looked at her. 'And you're not going to tell me how you got Robyn on your side?'

'I can't . . . I'm sorry.'

I nodded. 'How about telling me who's behind everything then? If Garrow's just a hired hand, like you say . . .'

She smiled. 'You know I'm not going to tell you that.'

'Yeah, well,' I said, grinning. 'It was worth a try.'

'Why do you want to know anyway?'

271

I shrugged. 'Just curious, I suppose.'

'Hale's not a good place to be curious.'

'So I've gathered.'

'If you want my advice—'

'I don't.'

She looked at me. 'All I'm saying is—'

'You want me to leave the island?'

'I'd feel a lot better if you did.'

'To be honest, I don't really care how you feel. I'm more concerned with the fact that a young girl has been murdered and no one seems to give a fuck.'

'Oh, come *on*, John.' Linda sighed. 'We've already been through this. Where's your proof? You haven't given me *any*thing, have you? How can I instigate a murder investigation when all I've got is the word of an alcoholic drug user who *claims* to have seen a dead girl in a pillbox but is unable to explain how her body seems to have vanished? I mean, seriously . . . if I went to the police with that, what do you think they'd do?'

'Not much, probably,' I agreed. 'But maybe if you left out the "alcoholic drug user" part . . .'

Linda laughed quietly. 'Sorry, I didn't mean it to sound so . . .'

'Accurate?'

She smiled.

I said, 'It's all just a ruse, you know.'

'What is?'

'This fucked-up personality thing. You see, when people think you're drunk or out of your head on something, they lower their guard, they don't take you seriously, and that

272

gives you an edge. And sometimes, as a private investigator, having that edge is all you need.'

Linda looked at me, not sure whether to believe me or not.

I grinned.

She smiled. 'Bullshit.'

'Yeah, but I had you going for a minute though, didn't I?'

She shook her head, still smiling, and I saw her glance at the whisky bottle on the table. When she turned back to me, and realised that I'd caught her looking at the bottle, she actually seemed a little awkward for a moment, which I thought was quite endearing.

'I think it's spiked,' I told her.

'What?'

'The whisky . . . I think somebody might have put something in it. That's why I haven't had any . . . in case you're wondering.'

'I wasn't.'

'That's OK, then.'

She frowned at me. 'What do you mean anyway? Who's put what in it? And why?'

It was my turn to feel a little awkward now, and as I remembered the events of the previous night – the voices, the visions, the severed head, the clown – it was very tempting to keep it all to myself, especially as Linda already seemed to have me tagged as a delusional alcoholic. I mean, if I started talking about severed heads and evil clowns, all that was going to do was convince her beyond question that she was right. So why bother?

I didn't know.

But I told her anyway.

And the rain kept falling.

'Show me,' she said grimly, getting up and heading over to the balcony doors. 'Show me where you think you saw it.'

I went over and opened the doors. It was almost fully dark now, and with the rain pouring down from the blackening sky, it was virtually impossible to see anything. I took out my penlight and turned it on.

'It was right there,' I told Linda, directing the torch at the spot where I'd seen the severed head. The beam barely showed in the darkness.

Linda gazed out into the night. 'And this morning it was gone?'

'I know it *sounds* crazy . . .'

She looked at me. 'Have you looked around?'

I nodded.

'Did you find anything?'

I took the envelope from my pocket and passed it to her. 'I think it might be blood. There was a single drop of something in the sand, just down there . . .' I indicated the place where I'd found it. As Linda looked down at the ground, I took out my mobile, navigated to the photo gallery, and showed her the pictures I'd taken of the possible blood spot.

She peered closely at the photos. 'Is that all there was? Just the one spot?'

'That's all I could find.'

'No footprints or anything?'

I shook my head. 'It rained during the night.'

She turned and gazed out into the darkness again.

I lit a cigarette. 'You were waiting for him at The Swan, weren't you?'

She nodded. 'He was supposed to meet me at ten.'

'And he didn't show up at all?'

She shook her head. 'I called him around ten thirty, but there was no answer. I left a message on his voicemail, asking him where he was, and I texted him as well, but he still didn't get back to me. I gave it another half an hour, then called him again, and this time his phone was dead. No ringing tone, no voicemail . . . nothing.' She sighed. 'I came back here to see if he was in his room . . . there was no sign of him. Arthur said he'd seen him leaving earlier with Garrow . . .'

'Yeah, I saw them too.'

Linda looked at me.

I said, 'It was just gone ten. I don't know where they were going, but they turned right after they'd left the hotel.'

'They turned *right*?'

'Yeah.'

She frowned. 'Garrow's houseboat is in the opposite direction . . . why would they have turned right? Where the fuck were they going?'

'Did you know that he was meeting with Garrow?'

'No . . . but the whole point of him being here was to get a bit closer to Garrow and the others, and the easiest way to do that was to score a bit of gear off them . . .' She paused, suddenly thinking of something. 'Maybe that's where they were going . . . to the caravan park to get some stuff off Stevie Haynes . . . yeah, that makes sense. If the opportunity arose for Mark to make a buy, he wouldn't have turned it down. And he wouldn't necessarily have had time to let me know. So the fact that he went off with Garrow isn't in itself unusual . . .' Her voice trailed off, and she stared quietly into the distance for a while, deep in thought. I joined her, lost in my own dark thoughts, and as we stood there together in the crashing silence of the rain, I slowly began to see how things might really be. The severed head, the clown, the ransacked/unransacked room . . . there *was* a way that it could all make some kind of sense. I thought about it some more.

The tide was coming in fast now, the rain-battered waves rolling up the beach, and way out in the distance I saw a flash of lightning, a faint white flicker on the horizon. I gazed down the beach at the black sheen of the sea. It was getting closer all the time, closer and higher. I'd never seen it so high before.

'How sure are you that you were drugged last night?' Linda asked.

I looked at her. 'As sure as I can be . . .'

'What does that mean, exactly?'

'My head was kind of scrambled,' I said. 'It still is . . . so I can't be absolutely sure about *any*thing.'

'But you're as sure as you can be?'

'Yes.'

She nodded. 'Any idea what they might have given you?'

'I think the stuff the clown gave me was probably GHB or roofies.'

'Rohypnol?'

'Something like that . . . I mean, I was out like a light

276

for a long time, and when I woke up I could hardly remember anything.'

'What about earlier on, in the pub? Do you think that was roofies too?'

'No . . . I don't think so. Whatever it was, it didn't make me feel sleepy . . .'

'How *did* it make you feel?'

'Just . . . I don't know. Just really weird, I suppose.'

'Were you hallucinating?'

'Not exactly . . . I was seeing and hearing some pretty strange stuff, but at the same time I *kind* of knew it wasn't real. It was like . . . I don't know. It's hard to explain.'

She looked at me. 'What else had you taken?'

'A bit of speed . . .'

'How much?'

'Just a line, before I went out.'

'Anything else?'

'A few drinks . . . well, *quite* a few, I suppose. And there was a fair bit of dope going round when I was in the pub . . .'

'Christ,' she muttered, looking away from me and shaking her head.

I didn't say anything. There was a part of me that felt I *ought* to say something – how *dare* you fucking judge me? – or at least make a *show* of being resentful or hurt, but the truth of the matter was, I didn't really care what she thought of me. And besides, she was probably right anyway.

'All right,' she said wearily. 'So let me just get this straight . . . last night, when you saw Mark's head, or rather when

277

you *think* you saw it, you were standing out here on the balcony—'

'No, I was at the doors. The doors were open, I went to close them, and that's when I saw it.'

She looked at me. 'You were totally *wrecked*, John. Speed, dope, whisky . . . maybe something else . . . it was late, you were tired . . .'

'I saw it. It was there.'

She sighed. 'And then the clown hit you.'

'I turned round first. I sensed someone was behind me, and when I turned round—'

'So how long were you standing there looking at the head? I mean, how much time was there between seeing the head and seeing the clown?'

'Not long . . . maybe a couple of seconds.'

'Right. So you actually only saw the head for a second or two?'

'Yeah . . .'

'And then you turned round, saw this clown, and he hit you?'

'Yes.'

'Where did he hit you?'

I angled my head and showed her the bump.

'Shit . . .' she whispered, looking at it.

'Is that real enough for you?' I said.

'What did he hit you with?'

'I don't know.'

She looked at me, slightly confused now, not knowing what to believe. 'Was he wearing a mask? You know, a clown mask? Or was his face actually painted?'

I thought about it, trying to remember . . . that grinning red mouth, those diabolic eyes . . . *it's not real . . . it is real . . .*

'John?' Linda said.

I shook my head. 'I can't remember. I've got a vague feeling that it *seemed* like a painted face . . . but it could just as easily have been a mask, I suppose. I don't know . . .'

'He didn't say anything?'

'No.'

'Did you see what he was wearing?'

'No.'

'I mean, was he *dressed* like a clown?'

'I don't know . . . I only saw his face.'

She sighed again. 'And when you woke up this morning, there was no sign at *all* that the place had been ransacked?'

I hadn't told her about Chelsey's phone yet, and as I looked at her now, I still couldn't decide if there was any point in telling her. What difference would it make? Even if she *did* believe me . . .

If it doesn't make any difference, I thought, *why not just tell her anyway?*

So I did.

And the rain fell for ever.

'You realise that none of this makes any sense, don't you?' Linda said.

'Maybe that's the whole point.'

She looked at me, waiting for an explanation.

'It all goes back to Chelsey,' I said. 'I mean, if you can just accept for a moment that everything I've told you is true, that Chelsey and her parents stumbled across Garrow and the others when they were bringing in a shipment of drugs, and then something happened, some kind of confrontation, and Chelsey ended up getting killed . . . maybe on purpose, maybe accidentally—'

'Yes, but—'

'No, let me finish,' I said. 'If you accept all that, and if you accept that I *did* see her body in the pillbox, and that somehow it was removed while I was waiting for the police to arrive . . .' I looked at Linda. 'Then everything else *does* make sense.'

She frowned. 'I'm sorry, I don't see how.'

'You said it yourself,' I explained. 'I take drugs, I drink a lot . . . maybe I'm not as mentally stable as I could be—'

'I never said that.'

'You didn't have to,' I said, smiling at her. 'The thing is, if everyone *thinks* I'm so messed up that I can't be trusted, and then stuff starts happening to me, stuff that's so weird that even *I* begin to doubt myself . . .'

'No one's going to believe you,' Linda said.

'Right. No one's going to believe that I saw Chelsey's body, no one's going to believe that I saw incriminating photographs on her mobile . . . no one's going to believe a word I say. And on top of all that, I'm going to start thinking that I'm losing my mind . . .' I looked at Linda. 'Of course, it's also quite possible that I *am* losing my mind, in which case . . .'

'There's no reason to believe you.'

I smiled. 'Exactly.'

Linda leaned on the railing and looked out over the

beach. She didn't say anything for a while, she just stood there, thinking quietly . . . and, once again, I took the opportunity to mull things over too. There were a lot of holes in my theory, a lot of things that didn't add up, but that didn't concern me too much. There's always stuff that doesn't add up, and it doesn't necessarily mean anything. Sometimes the holes are eventually filled in, sometimes they're not.

And if they're not . . . ?

Well, the world's full of holes, isn't it?

'All right, look,' Linda said, turning to me. 'I'm going to have to think about this some more. I'll make some phone calls, talk to some people, see what I can find out about Mark . . .' She shook her head. 'That's the thing I really can't believe about all this, John. I mean, if it *is* true, if you really did see what you thought you saw . . . well, I just don't get it. Why would anyone go to such lengths just to fuck with your mind? It doesn't make sense.'

'No,' I agreed. 'But when does cutting off someone's head *ever* make sense?'

She shook her head again. 'Anyway, I'm going to look into it, all right?' She glanced at the envelope I'd given her. 'I'll get this to forensics, and I'll give them the whisky too, see what they can find. Although, actually . . .' She looked out at the rain-soaked beach again. 'The tides are unusually high at the moment, and if it carries on raining like this as well, the causeway could be flooded for days. And if that happens . . .' She sighed once more. 'Shit.'

I guessed she'd just realised that if the Stand was flooded and no one could get on or off the island, not only would

281

she be unable to send anything to forensics, but more importantly for her, the logistics of the drug-smuggling investigation might be affected.

'I have to go,' she said, turning from the balcony. 'I'll be in touch as soon as I can . . .' She looked at me. 'I don't suppose you're going to do the sensible thing and go back to Hey, are you?'

'I can't, can I?' I said, smiling at her. 'Not if the Stand's flooded.'

She wasn't in the mood for smiling any more. 'What's your mobile number?' she said.

I gave it to her, and she keyed it into her phone as she went back into the room. She stopped by the table, wrote something on the hotel notepad, then ripped off the sheet and passed it to me. 'That's my number,' she said. 'If anything happens, call me . . . and I mean *any*thing, OK?'

'Yeah.'

She took a pair of latex gloves from her pocket, picked up the half-empty whisky bottle, and started heading for the door.

'Do you want me to get you another bottle?' she said.

'Uh, yeah,' I said, surprised. 'That'd be good.'

'I'll bring one up in a minute.' She turned and looked at me. 'Look, John, I know I can't *tell* you what to do, but please . . . keep out of it from now on, all right? Just leave everything to me. Can you do that?'

'Do I still get the whisky if I say no?'

'I'm not joking, John—'

'Neither am I.'

'God,' she sighed, shaking her head. 'Why can't you just—?'

'All right,' I said, smiling. 'I'll do what you want, OK? I'll keep out of it.'

'Seriously?'

'Yeah.'

'Promise?'

I nodded. 'I promise.'

She looked into my eyes for a few moments, searching for the truth, and I just held her gaze and looked back at her. She was very good at not giving anything away, and as I stood there staring into her eyes, with my hands behind my back, there was no way of telling whether she believed me or not.

Not that it mattered.

'I'll be in touch,' she said eventually, giving me a final piercing look.

I nodded.

She turned round, opened the door, and went out.

I waited a few seconds, listening as she wheeled her cleaning trolley away, then I brought my hands from behind my back and childishly uncrossed my fingers.

22

My mobile rang again while I was waiting for Linda to bring me a fresh bottle of whisky, and even after I'd checked the screen and seen that it was Cal, I still didn't want to answer it. I didn't want to speak to anyone. All I wanted was a drink. I *needed* a drink, and I needed it badly. And as I paced around the room, smoking a cigarette I didn't want and glancing anxiously at the clock every few seconds, waiting for Linda to bring me what I needed, I knew that I was sinking down into addiction again, and that the deeper I sank, the harder it was going to be to drag myself out of it.

I *knew* that.

And I fully intended to deal with it . . .

But not right now.

Right now, I *really* needed a fucking drink.

'Hey, Cal,' I said, reluctantly answering my phone. 'Listen, can I call you back? I'm just—'

'Fucking *hell*, John,' he said angrily.

'What?'

'I've called you about a million times . . . where the fuck have you *been*? I was getting really worried—'

'Yeah, sorry,' I told him. 'I was going to call you earlier, but something came up.'

'Jesus, John,' he said. 'You could have at least texted me

or something, you know . . . I mean, for all I knew, you could have been dead.'

'Sorry, Cal,' I said, as I heard a knock at the door. 'Look, just give me *one* second, OK? There's someone at the door. All right?'

He sighed. 'Yeah, OK . . .'

I went over to the door, looked through the peephole, and saw Linda heading back along the corridor towards reception. I opened the door, about to call out after her, but then I saw that she'd left the bottle of whisky on the floor. I picked it up, went back inside, uncapped the bottle and took a long slow drink, letting the heat of the whisky soak down into the pit of my belly . . .

Ah, God . . .

What else do you need?

I found a glass, poured myself a couple of inches, then went back over to the bed, lit a fresh cigarette, and picked up the phone.

'Cal?'

'Fuck, John. What's going on?'

'That was Linda.'

'Who's Linda?'

By the time I'd finished bringing Cal up to date with everything, it was almost six thirty. The rain was showing no sign of easing up, and the lightning I'd seen earlier, flickering on the horizon, was gradually moving in from the sea. There was thunder in the air too, and although it was hard to hear anything over the persistent crash of rain, I could feel the skies beginning to shake and rumble.

285

Cal had a lot of questions.

And a lot of concerns.

I *wanted* to answer them all – partly because I felt guilty about not getting in touch with him sooner, and I wanted to make amends for keeping him in the dark, but mainly because Cal was the closest thing I had to a genuine friend, and I just didn't *want* to hurt him in any way – but the simple fact was that I'd been talking non-stop for over three hours now, going over and over the same old stuff, and I'd just about had enough. I was all talked out. I needed some time on my own, time to think . . . time to *not* think.

And I had to get out of this room.

I had to go somewhere . . .

Do something.

I had to go somewhere.

'Listen, Cal,' I said. 'I'm really sorry, but I have to go.'

'Where are you going?'

'I want to make sure that Robyn's OK.'

'Why shouldn't she be?'

'Because if it *was* Garrow or one of his boys who cut off Mark Ballard's head, that might mean they knew he was working for customs, and if they're sadistic enough to cut off a man's head, they're not going to be averse to torturing him first to find out what he knows, are they? I mean, I'm not saying that they did, just that it's possible. And if they did torture him . . .'

'He might have told them about Robyn.'

'Yeah, and if they know she's a grass, she's in big trouble.'

'Right,' Cal said. 'Are you going to talk to her?'

'No. I'm just—'

'I don't think you should talk to her, John. Not yet.'

'I'm not *going* to talk to her, Cal. I'm just going to check that she's all right. She won't even know I'm there, all right?'

'Well, yeah, I suppose so . . . but listen—'

'I have to go.'

'I know, but just give me a few minutes, OK? This might be important.'

'What?'

'I've been doing some poking around . . . I haven't *just* been sitting here worrying myself sick about you, you know. I've been busy.'

'What have you found out?'

'Well, I *think* I might know who's pulling the strings down there. I mean, I don't know for sure, but everything points to a guy called Tait . . . Ivan Tait. Have you heard of him?'

'The name's familiar.'

'He used to be the MP for Hey East, lost his seat in 2005.'

'Oh, yeah . . .' I said, remembering now. 'Wasn't he mixed up in some kind of scandal or something?'

'He's mixed up in a lot of things. There were rumours that his son, Jamie, had something to do with a gypsy kid who went missing from the island about ten years ago, but even back then Tait had a lot of influence – lots of connections, lots of money – and nothing was ever proved. His son's not around any more, he moved to Florida soon after the kid went missing, but Tait still lives on Hale. He's got a big house on the west of the island . . . a *really* big house.

Must be worth at least three or four million. And that's not all he owns. I mean, this guy's *seriously* loaded, John.'

'Having lots of money isn't a crime,' I pointed out.

'It is if it's drug money.'

'How do you know it's drug money?'

'Because it's laundered, for a start. At least, some of it is. There's no question that Tait makes a lot of money from his various legitimate businesses – his shipping company alone netted him over four million last year – and since he left politics in 2005 he's been branching out into all kinds of different areas – property, storage, machinery, haulage . . . and it's all perfectly legal. But if you dig a little deeper, which I have, you'll find that a lot of these companies have subsidiaries, and the subsidiaries themselves have subsidiaries, and so on, and so on . . . and even when you take a really close look at these smaller corporations, it's almost impossible to link them back to Tait. His name doesn't appear on any paperwork. He doesn't own them, he's not a director . . . he's not even a shareholder—'

'But they're his.'

'Right. And it's through them that he owns most of the island.'

'What do you mean?'

'He fucking *owns* it, John. I mean, not the island itself, obviously . . . well, not as far as I know, anyway. But virtually everything *on* the island – every property, every business, every scrap of land . . . it's all owned by a handful of companies, and those companies themselves are owned by other companies, and so on, and so on . . .'

'OK,' I said. 'But again, that's not actually illegal, is it?'

'Not in itself, no . . . although, come to think of it, it might be. But the point is, if Tait owns everything on the island, it not only gives him complete control over the place, which is a pretty handy thing to have if you're bringing in drugs, but it also provides him with everything he needs to launder the profits.'

'Through the companies, you mean?'

'Through the businesses that the companies own. I mean, take your hotel, for example—'

'He owns the hotel?'

'I told you, John – he owns everything. The hotel, shops, residential properties, taxi companies, restaurants . . . all he has to do is feed the drug money through all these little businesses, and that's it. Clean cash.'

'Can you find out if he owns a place called Hale Organics?'

'Yeah, just a second.'

I heard him tapping his keyboard.

'And while you're at it, check the caravan park.'

'OK.'

Tap tap tap.

I said, 'Can you prove any of this, Cal?'

'Nope.'

Tap tap.

'Could anyone prove it?'

'Probably not. Hold on . . .' *Tap tap tap.* 'OK, Hale Organics . . . is owned by a company called JTL Catering. That's one of Tait's. And the caravan park . . . yeah, that's registered to SX Leisure, which is actually a subsidiary of JTL.'

289

'Is there anything else that links Tait to drugs?'

'Half a dozen offshore bank accounts.'

'That doesn't prove anything.'

'Regular trips to Holland, South America, West Africa—'

'Ditto.'

'All right, how about he just smells dirty?'

I smiled. 'That'll do it for me.'

'Look, I know it's all circumstantial, John, but when you add everything together—'

'Do the police or customs know about him?'

'I'd be surprised if they didn't. There was a report in the *Guardian* a couple of months ago that mentioned his shipping company in relation to a people-trafficking operation that customs busted in Harwich, and his name's come up a few times in a long-running investigation into a possible arms-for-drugs network in the Middle East . . . but it's all just supposition so far. And Tait's a very respectable man, John. Highly successful, very wealthy, with friends in all the right places . . . and he's a philanthropist too. Last year he gave half a million of his own money to a local children's hospice.'

'What a fucker.'

'I know,' Cal said, laughing. 'That's exactly what I thought. Anyone who gives half a mill to a bunch of dying kids has got to be guilty of something.'

'I doubt if a jury would see it that way.'

'Probably not.'

'And people like Tait never get to face a jury anyway. No matter what they fucking do.'

'I know . . . but that's not why I told you about him anyway. You know that, don't you?'

'Yeah . . .' I said, thinking about it. 'Yeah, I do.'

'The more you know . . .'

'The safer you go?'

He laughed. 'Is that a saying?'

'It is now.'

'Yeah, well . . . you know what I mean, don't you?'

'Yeah. Thanks, Cal.'

'No problem. Just watch how you go, all right?'

'Yeah. I'll try to call you later on if I can. But don't worry if I don't, OK?'

'You can always text me.'

'Fuck that.'

He laughed again. 'I'll tell you what, if I haven't heard from you by the time I leave here tomorrow morning, I'll jump in a taxi and come and get you. How's that?'

'Better make it a boat,' I said, glancing out at the rain.

'What?'

'Nothing . . . I've got to go, Cal. See you later, OK?'

'Yeah. Go safely, Nunc.'

'You too.'

I thought about walking over to Robyn's house, but the rain was so heavy that I decided to ask Arthur Finch to call me a taxi. I'd taken the last of the amphetamine sulphate before leaving my room, washing it down with a few hefty shots of whisky, and as I hung around the lobby waiting for the taxi to turn up, I could feel the combination of speed and alcohol working its way into my system, lifting me up and calming me down, giving me just enough balance to think.

I thought about Ivan Tait, and what – if anything – he meant to me. I knew that Cal was probably right about him, he probably *was* the man at the top, and I remembered Linda Ransom telling me that 'if you want to get to the people at the top, you have to start with the people at the bottom,' and that the HMRC investigation was 'after the big stuff, the big money, the big names,' and it was probably safe to assume that one of the big names she was talking about was Tait. But what did that mean to me? What did it mean to Chelsey Swalenski, to her father, to her mother . . . ?

Ivan Tait hadn't killed them, had he?

Maybe he *did* ruin lives, as Linda had suggested. Maybe he *was* up to his eyes in drugs and guns and people trafficking, and maybe the world *would* be a better place without him . . . although, personally, I somehow doubted it. But that wasn't the point.

The point was . . .

Fuck it.

I didn't know what the point was.

All I knew . . .

I glanced over at the reception desk, watching Arthur as he bumbled around, fiddling with bits of paper, tapping occasionally at the computer keyboard . . . and I wondered what I would do if I were him. What would I do if I'd bought this place in 1979, and then I'd had to sell out to Ivan Tait ten years ago, probably because the hotel wasn't making any money? What would I do if I was an old man and I knew that the hotel still wasn't making any money, and that the only reason it was still open for business, and still

292

providing me with a home and a living, was that Tait was using it to launder his illegal earnings . . . ?

Would I do anything about it?

And if Tait's people had told me to change the check-out date of the Swalenskis' reservation, and to keep my mouth shut about it . . . would I have stood up to them? Would I have said, 'No, this is wrong, I'm not going to do it . . .'?

Of course I wouldn't.

Arthur saw me looking at him then. He smiled, a little self-consciously, I thought, and as I nodded back at him, I saw him glance over at the door.

'Your taxi's here, John,' he called over.

I nodded again, looked over at the slouching taxi driver who'd just come in, and then followed him outside to his car.

23

'Can you wait for me, please?' I asked the taxi driver when we pulled up outside Robyn's house. 'I might want to go somewhere else.'

He grunted something, which I assumed meant OK, and I got out and went over to the house. The curtains were closed in the front room, but the lights were on, and I could see the faint flicker of a TV, so I guessed that someone was in. I knocked on the door and waited. After a few moments, I saw Serina peeping out through the curtains. I raised my hand to give her a wave, but by then she'd already gone, and the next thing I knew she was unlocking the bolts, removing the safety chain and opening the front door.

'Hello, John,' she said, glancing up and down the street. 'Are you all right?'

'Yeah . . . is Robyn in?'

Serina looked at me. 'I haven't told her about you—'

'Yeah, I know.'

'I was going to, but—'

'It's all right,' I said. 'I wanted to see her about something else.'

'What do you mean?'

'Sorry,' I said. 'It's a bit complicated . . . I just need to see her.'

'Is she in trouble?'

I hesitated, not knowing what to say.

'What's she done now?' Serina sighed.

'She hasn't done anything, as far as I know . . . look, I'm sorry, I know this probably doesn't make any sense—'

'Fucking right, it doesn't.'

'I'll explain everything later, OK? I promise. But right now, I really need to see her.'

'She's not in,' Serina said coldly.

'Do you know where she is?'

Serina shrugged. 'Fuck knows . . . she could be anywhere.'

'When did she go out?'

'Couple of hours ago.'

'Was she with Stevie?'

'No . . . but I think he called her before she went out.'

'Could you try calling her?'

'Why? I mean, what's so important—?'

'Please,' I said. 'Just call her . . .'

Serina sighed again, then grudgingly pulled a mobile from her pocket. 'What do you want me to say?'

'I don't know . . . just ask her where she is.'

'She won't tell me.'

'What's her number?' I said, taking out my phone.

'It's all right,' Serina said, thumbing keys on her phone. 'I'll do it.'

I tried to catch a glimpse of the number she called, but she only pressed a couple of keys, so I guessed it was on speed dial. If I hadn't lied to Cal about not talking to Robyn, I realised, I could have got her number from him . . . or I could have just asked him for it anyway. I shook my head, annoyed with myself for not thinking things through.

'No answer,' Serina said quietly, clicking off the call.

'Voicemail?'

'She doesn't use it . . .' She looked at me, her eyes worried. 'Why isn't she answering? She *always* answers her phone.'

'It could be anything,' I said, trying to reassure her. 'She's busy, she didn't hear it, she doesn't want to talk to you . . .' I smiled. 'I mean, you know what kids are like.'

'She's not a kid.'

'No, I didn't mean—'

'I wish she fucking was.'

'Look,' I started to say. 'I'm sure there's nothing to—'

'Hey, mate!' the taxi driver called out. 'You going to be much longer?'

'Just a minute,' I told him.

'It's just I got other fares waiting—'

'Just a fucking *minute*, all right?'

'All right, all right,' he muttered, shaking his head and holding up his hands. 'I was only fucking saying . . . I mean, shit, there's no fucking need for that . . .'

I turned back to Serina. 'Any idea where Robyn might have gone?'

'The Swan, maybe . . . or there's a couple of places in town . . . or she might be at Stevie's . . .' She stared at me. 'You think she's in trouble, don't you?'

'I don't know,' I said honestly. 'Listen, I'll have a look round, see if I can find her . . . do you want me to call you if I do?'

Serina nodded. 'I'll keep trying her phone . . . and I'll text you her number, OK?'

'Yeah, thanks.' I smiled at her. 'And don't worry, OK?'

She looked sadly at me. 'When someone tells me not to worry, that's when I know it's time to start worrying.'

I tried The Swan first, but Robyn wasn't there, and when I asked the barman if he'd seen her recently, he told me that he didn't know anyone called Robyn.

'Yeah, you do,' I told him. 'Robyn Mayo. She was in here last night with Stevie. And later on she was drinking with Garrow and me—'

'I don't know what you're talking about,' he said.

I stared at him. 'You served us, remember? You brought us two glasses of your *special* whisky, and you made sure that I got the right one, and you had this really simpering look on your face, like you wanted Garrow to give you a pat on the head or something, but he didn't even look at you, did he?'

'Fuck you,' the barman said quietly, staring back at me.

I held his gaze for a moment, tempted to say something else, but in the end I thought better of it. He wasn't going to help me, that was obvious. There was no point wasting any more time with him. I turned away and looked round the bar, checking to see if there was anyone else worth talking to, but I didn't see anyone I recognised. I saw a lot of people drinking though . . . people drinking beer, people drinking wine, people drinking whisky . . . and as I stood there watching them, I had an overwhelming desire to *be* them. And just for a moment, there was nothing in the world I wanted more than a chilled pint of Stella and a large Scotch or two . . . and I very nearly turned back to the bar, but then I remembered the barman, and I realised that I'd have to make an effort to be nice to him – or maybe even apologise – before he'd serve me, and although I actually considered it for a second or two – and I knew that I *could* do it if I really had to, I could grovel, smile, apologise, I could demean myself – but I wasn't quite that desperate yet.

Not yet.

I closed my eyes for a second . . .

Took a couple of deep breaths . . .

And headed for the door.

I'd told the taxi driver to wait for me when I'd gone into The Swan, and although he'd made it quite obvious that he didn't want to – grumbling and moaning like a sulky little kid – I was fairly sure that he'd still be there when I left the pub, mainly because I hadn't paid him yet. So I was kind of surprised to find that his car was gone, and for a moment or two I just assumed that he'd moved it for some reason, parked somewhere else, or maybe he'd seen me coming out and was just turning the car round . . . but as the rain slapped down into the dimly lit car park, and a flash of lightning lit up the night, it soon became obvious that he'd gone.

'Fucker,' I muttered, edging back into the shelter of the doorway.

I wondered if he'd had a call from someone . . .

Or maybe he'd called someone, asking for advice. *I got Craine in my car, what do you want me to do?* Or maybe . . .

I shook my head. It wasn't worth thinking about.

I lit a cigarette, took out my phone, and checked to see if Serina had texted me Robyn's number yet. She had. I called the number. It rang . . . and rang . . . a crash of thunder rolled across the sky . . .

No answer.

'Shit.'

I thought about calling Linda . . .

Have you seen Robyn? I'm really worried about her . . .

You promised you'd keep out of it, John.

Yeah, I know, but I had my fingers crossed . . .

I didn't call Linda.

I thought about what Serina had said when I'd asked her where Robyn might be. *The Swan, maybe*, she'd said. *Or there's a couple of places in town . . . or she might be at Stevie's . . .*

I thought about calling another taxi . . .

There wasn't any point.

I looked up at the pouring rain, wondering where the hell it all came from, and as another bolt of lightning cracked open the night, followed almost immediately by a shuddering boom of thunder, I thought about going back into the pub, just for a quick one . . . maybe two at the most . . . just until the storm died down a bit . . .

I shook my head.

Spat angrily on the ground.

And as I walked off into the rain, I really wasn't sure how much more of myself I could stand.

Stacy's voice came back to me as I was scurrying along the empty streets towards the caravan park.

Don't be too hard on yourself, John, she said.

'I'm not,' I told her. 'I'm just being honest.'

You're doing the right thing—

'Only just.'

You didn't go back into the pub.

'I nearly did.'

But you didn't, did you?

'Not this time, no. But I thought about it . . . I mean, I actually *thought* about going back in there for a couple of drinks instead of trying to find Robyn.'

But you didn't.

I shook my head. 'I shouldn't even have gone there. If I'd had any fucking sense I would have gone straight to the caravan park in the first place.'

Why?

'Because if Robyn was in The Swan she would have answered her phone, wouldn't she?'

I suppose so . . .

'And if she *is* in trouble, if Garrow's lot know she's a grass, they're not going to do anything to her in The Swan, are they? They're going to take her somewhere quiet, somewhere private—'

Stevie's place. His caravan.

'Yeah.'

But you don't know *for sure that she's there, do you?*

'No.'

She could be anywhere.

'Yeah, but I don't really know where *anywhere* is, do I?'

*

There were no lights showing in the caravan park, no sign that any of the caravans or trailers were occupied, and as I made my way down a sodden gravel track that ran through the middle of the park, the only sound I could hear was the relentless roar of the rain. There was still a faint echo of thunder in the air, but that was more of a feeling than a sound, and the lightning seemed to have drifted back out to sea, the distant flashes shimmering in the dark like a broken neon light on the horizon.

I was absolutely soaked to the skin now, but oddly enough it felt OK. I didn't feel particularly cold, and now that I couldn't get any wetter, the rain didn't actually bother me any more. In fact, I almost felt part of it, at one with it . . .

Me and the rain.

Christ . . .

Although there were no lights anywhere, and the night was a deep moonless black, I resisted the temptation to use my penlight. If there *was* anyone here – which I was beginning to doubt – I didn't want them to see me coming, and even the discreet beam of my penlight would show up like a laser on a night like this. So I kept it in my pocket, and I kept my eyes wide open, and after a while they adjusted to the dark well enough to let me see where I was going. Not that I really *knew* where I was going. All I could remember about Stevie's caravan was that it was dirty and white, and situated somewhere down at the lower end of the park. But as I carried on down the track, sloshing my way through the puddled gravel, I realised that almost all of the caravans were either dirty or white, or dirty *and* white, and most of those that weren't were either cream or beige, which in the darkness made them *look* dirty and white. It also struck me that, for all I knew, Stevie might just have been staying in the caravan the other day . . . he might not actually live there at all.

In which case . . .

I was fucked.

But I was here now. I was nearing the lower end of the park, and it was becoming increasingly obvious that it wasn't just the lower end in a geographical sense, it was the lower end all round. The track was now more mud than gravel, the caravans and trailers were noticeably more shabby, and although the whole park was draped with an air of seediness and neglect, the atmosphere down here was markedly worse. There were bonfire remains, oil drums overflowing with litter, empty gas canisters . . . one of the caravans was just a burned-out shell, a few rain-warped boards hanging from a blackened steel skeleton . . . and there was a faint smell of waste everywhere, the cloying stink of human shit.

And in the midst of all this, there was a light.

A dim yellowed light, in the window of a caravan, about twenty yards away from me, just to the left of the track. A dirty white caravan.

I stepped off the path, crouched down beside a ramshackle trailer, and stared through the rain at the caravan. There wasn't a lot to see. The front of the caravan was facing away from me, and the window at the back was quite small. The light was showing through an old and yellowed venetian blind, the blind lowered but the slats not fully closed. There was no sign of any movement at first, but after a few minutes a blurred shadow moved across the blind. The shadowed figure paused for a moment, turned, then went back to wherever it had come from.

I waited . . .

Two minutes, three minutes . . .

No more movement.

I straightened up, glanced around, then headed slowly towards the light. I moved cautiously, keeping in close to the caravans on the left-hand side of the track, and I never took my eyes off the window. It was impossible to move quietly through the thick, clinging mud, but whatever noise I made was easily drowned out by the clattering roar of the rain, so as long as no one *saw* me coming, it didn't really matter if I kept losing my footing and slipping over in the mud . . . which I did. And by the time I finally got to the caravan, I was so caked in sludge, so indistinguishable from everything else, that even if someone had looked out of the window they probably wouldn't have seen me anyway.

I crept up to the window, keeping in close to the side of the caravan, and stopped beside it. I put my ear to the wall and listened. I could hear a voice . . . faint and muffled . . . a man's voice. He was talking to someone. I closed my eyes, listening as hard as I could . . . but I couldn't make out what he was saying. The tone of his voice was friendly enough, perhaps even intimate, but there was something about it that didn't feel right . . . something that didn't ring true. A misplaced emphasis here, a hint of impatience there . . . I could have been wrong, but I was fairly sure that whatever he was saying, he didn't mean it.

I heard another voice then, a female voice, and although it was a lot fainter than the man's voice – and a lot weaker too – I knew straight away that it was Robyn's. And she didn't sound good. She sounded frail, anxious . . . maybe even a little frightened.

I edged closer to the window. It was at head height, the slats of the blind more closed than open, and from where I was standing, I couldn't really see through them at all. But there was a narrow gap in the blind where one of the slats had come loose, and it didn't take me long to find that if I crouched down a little and angled my head to one side, I could see through this gap into the caravan. It still wasn't much of a view – it was a bit like looking through a very narrow letter box – but it was enough.

Stevie was standing with his back to me, so I couldn't see his face, but there was no doubt it was him – the long greasy hair, the filthy jeans, the tattoos. He was shirtless, his bare back decorated with a winged skull, the Grim Reaper riding a motorbike, and two naked women. Robyn was sitting on a grubby little bed in front of him. Her knees were scrunched up to her chest, her arms wrapped tightly around them, and it was obvious that she was suffering – shaking, sweating, her skin deathly pale, her eyes wide open. She was pleading with Stevie for something, and it wasn't hard to guess what she wanted.

I watched as Stevie moved towards her, talking quietly as he went . . . he stopped in front of her and reached out his hand. Robyn flinched, backing away. Stevie waited, holding out his hand. Robyn looked up at him. Stevie reached out again and stroked her sweat-soaked hair. Robyn tried to smile, but she was hurting too much. She grabbed hold of Stevie's hand and started begging him – *please, Stevie, please . . . I really need it, you've got to help me, I'm fucking dying . . . please . . . I'll do anything, you know I will . . .* She let go of his hand and reached for his zip.

Stevie batted her hand away.

Robyn started crying.

I closed my eyes then, not sure I could watch any more . . .

But I knew that I had to.

When I opened my eyes again, Robyn was still sitting on the bed, frantically rubbing her arms, but Stevie was nowhere to be seen, and just for a moment I thought – *shit, he's seen me, he's coming out* – but before I even had a chance to start panicking, he suddenly reappeared again, walking back in from somewhere to the left of the window and going over to Robyn. She couldn't take her eyes off him now, she was staring at him as if he was the only thing in the world, and when he stopped in front of her and held out his hand, showing her the syringe he was carrying, her eyes almost popped out of her head.

As she whipped the leather belt off her jeans and started wrapping it tightly around her upper arm, Stevie just stood there, watching her, enjoying her fumbling desperation, and when she was ready, and she reached out for the syringe, he snatched it away from her, grinning, holding it up in the air, making her beg for it . . .

No! Stevie . . . please don't, Stevie . . . please, give it to me . . .

And then, tired of that, he just tossed the syringe on the bed – as if he was throwing scraps to a pig – and watched in disdain as Robyn scrabbled around for it, found it, dropped it, found it again . . .

I wanted to close my eyes again then. I didn't want to see my half-sister shooting up – sobbing and shaking as she searched for a vein, her hand trembling as she jabbed the needle into her skin . . . I didn't want to see the almost instantaneous roll of her eyes as she shot the heroin into her arm . . . but I made myself watch every squalid little moment.

And it really got to me.

It was by no means the worst thing I'd ever seen – not by a long way – and I'd seen junkies shooting up before, so it wasn't as if I didn't know what to expect . . . and I'd known all along that Robyn was a junky, and I was perfectly aware of what that meant . . . I mean, I wasn't *surprised* to see her sitting on a dirty bed sticking a fucking needle in her arm . . .

But it still really got to me.

I hated it.

I hated everything about it – the grubbiness, the despair, the squalor, the waste . . . and Stevie, the bastard, just fucking standing there, scratching his balls and watching her as she slumped back against the wall, her eyes flickering, her head nodding limply . . .

I nearly made a move then.

Robyn didn't look right at all. She wasn't moving, her

eyes were closed, her mouth hanging open . . . it wasn't right. I wasn't even sure she was still breathing.

I had to do something.

But just as I was about to move, I saw Stevie go over to the bed, and I forced myself to wait . . . just give it a second, see what he does. I watched him as he leaned over the bed and placed two fingers on Robyn's neck, searching for a pulse . . . and after a few heart-stopping moments I saw him nod to himself, seemingly satisfied, and then he removed his fingers from her neck and gently slapped her face. She didn't react at first. Her head just lolled to one side. But then he gave her another slap, a little harder, and this time – thank God – her eyes fluttered open.

I breathed out.

She still looked really bad – barely conscious, struggling to keep her eyes open – but at least she was alive.

Stevie was talking to her now, holding her chin in his hands, making her look at him, making her listen . . . I couldn't hear what he was saying. I saw Robyn's lips moving, mumbling something as she tried to focus on Stevie's face, and I saw her trying to nod her head at him, but she couldn't even manage that, and as her head rolled to one side and her eyelids drooped, Stevie took hold of her shoulders and lowered her down to the bed. He stood there for a moment or two, just looking down at her, his face totally blank, and then he turned round and headed off to his left. I quickly moved back from the window, holding my breath again as he passed by and moved out of sight again.

I waited . . .

The ground at my feet was waterlogged now, the rain

slapping down noisily into the fetid ooze. The muddy streams and ever-growing pools all around me were crusted with a dirty grey froth and streaked with the slick sheen of petrol. I smiled ruefully to myself, remembering Stacy's voice. *Go somewhere nice*, she'd told me, *and try to forget about everything. You never know . . . you might even enjoy it.*

And as I raised my head and gazed up into the silvered blackness, letting the cold rain sting my skin, I wondered why I *couldn't* just forget about everything . . . forget about Stacy, about my father, about Robyn . . . about Chelsey . . . and Mark . . . why couldn't I just let it all go? I mean, whatever I did, whatever I was doing . . . none of it would make any difference, would it? Not in the long run. Nothing ever makes any difference. Who did this, who did that, why, where, when, how . . . ?

Who fucking cares? In a hundred years' time we'll all be dead anyway – me, Robyn, Stevie . . . whoever killed Chelsey – and nothing that any of us do now will mean a fucking thing. So what's the point? Why *not* just go somewhere nice and try to forget about everything? You never know, you might even enjoy it . . .

John?

'What?'

He's coming back.

'Who?'

Stevie . . . come on, *John, snap out of it, for Christ's sake. Look!*

I rubbed my eyes and shook my head, trying to clear the weight of the black place from my mind, and as I turned back to the window again, I was just in time to see Stevie coming back dressed in a long, black, hooded raincoat. He glanced briefly at Robyn, who was still dead to the world, then he scooped up a set of keys and a mobile from a fold-away table, dropped them in his pocket, and headed for the door.

I moved away from the window and started edging around the side of the caravan. It was slow going, the thick mud clinging to my feet at every step, and just as the light in the caravan went out, and I felt the door slamming shut – the thin walls of the caravan shuddering with the impact – my right foot sank down into the ooze almost up to the knee, stopping me in my tracks, and I thought for a moment that I wasn't going to make it. I pulled hard, straining my leg, and at first I couldn't get any purchase . . . but I tried again, pulling harder, and again . . . and just as Stevie appeared, putting up the hood of his raincoat and stooping through the rain, my foot flew out with an audible *gloop* and I scrambled out of sight behind the caravan.

I waited a few seconds, just in case Stevie had heard anything, and then I cautiously inched my head round the corner, hoping to see him walking up the track, heading away from the caravan, away from Robyn, away from me . . .

But he wasn't there.

I couldn't see him anywhere.

Shit . . .

I glanced instinctively over my shoulder, half-expecting to see him looming up behind me, but just as I was turning my head, bracing myself for the worst, a flicker of light caught my eye . . . not behind me, but straight ahead, directly opposite the caravan, on the other side of the track. It was only a very brief glint of light, and by the time I'd turned back and refocused my attention it had already gone. But I didn't need it any more. I could see Stevie now – or, at least, I could see the shape of him . . . his tall, black, hooded figure outlined dimly against the paler darkness of the trailer in front of him. It was a long, low-roofed trailer, and I guessed that it had once been rented out as a holiday home, but no one in their right mind would want to stay in it now. The walls were buckled, the windows green with algae, and the roof was almost covered in a thick spread of spindly weeds and yellowed grasses.

Stevie was standing at the door of the trailer, and as he raised his arm, reaching towards the door, I thought for a second that he was going inside. But he didn't. Instead, he just took hold of something halfway up the door, leaned forward and looked closely at it for a moment, gave it a couple of tugs . . . and that seemed to be it. He stood there for a little while longer, not doing much, just looking around, maybe thinking something through, and then – after another quick check of what I was now guessing was a padlock – he turned round and began walking away. And this time, to my relief, he *did* head up the track, away from the caravan, away from Robyn, away from me . . .

I waited, watching him go, his hooded darkness reminding me of the Grim Reaper tattooed on his back. I watched him slouching up the track, fading away into the murk of night, and when he was out of sight, I waited some more . . . and I found myself wondering about the trailer, and why it was padlocked . . . why bother padlocking the door of a place that looked as if it would fall apart at the slightest touch anyway? It didn't make sense. And I wondered what might be inside . . . something valuable, something secret . . . something . . . nothing?

And then, as the black thoughts began drifting back into my mind – *who cares what's in the trailer or why it's padlocked? who fucking cares? what difference does it make . . . ?* – I straightened up, ran my fingers through my soaking wet hair, and started trudging round to the front of the caravan.

311

24

The caravan door was locked, but when I took out my penlight, shielding the beam, and had a closer look, I found that the lock wasn't a problem. It was nothing, just a very cheap and basic latch mechanism, and even if I couldn't pick it – and I was fairly sure that I could – the door itself was so flimsy that a couple of good kicks would do the trick. I snapped the thin metal pocket-clip from my penlight, took out my wallet, removed a credit card, and got to work on the lock.

It didn't take long.

When the lock clicked open, and the caravan door swung free, I paused for a moment, suddenly realising that I had no idea what I was going to do once I was inside. I had no plan . . . I hadn't thought anything through . . . I hadn't given any rational thought to *any*thing.

I thought about that for a moment, quickly realising that there wasn't much I could do about it now, then I took a breath and opened the door.

It was pitch-black inside. I turned my penlight back on and looked around. Robyn hadn't moved, she was still lying on the bed, her eyes closed, and when I went over and crouched down beside her, she gave no sign that she was aware of my presence. I shone the penlight into her face, studying her closely, trying to work out what kind of condition she was in. Her breathing was reasonably steady, neither too fast nor too slow, and although she was quite pale there was no obvious discolouration to her lips or her skin, no sign of any blueing. I took hold of her wrist and checked her pulse . . . and again, as far as I could tell, it seemed steady enough.

I let go of her wrist, sat back, and lit a cigarette.

I was fairly sure that she hadn't overdosed, that she'd probably just had a heavier hit of heroin than she was used to . . . or maybe the stuff Stevie had given her was purer than normal. Either way, I didn't *think* she was in any real danger. But what did I know? I wasn't an expert. I wasn't a fucking doctor, was I? I didn't even know for sure what she'd taken. The only sensible thing to do, I told myself, was to call for an ambulance. Get her to a hospital, get her checked out . . .

I looked at her, trying to think . . . trying to work out the consequences of calling an ambulance – what would it mean? what might happen? was there any way it could do more harm than good?

'Jesus *Christ*,' I said angrily, shaking my head. 'What does it fucking matter? Just *do* it.'

I took out my mobile and dialled 999.

Nothing happened.

No signal.

'Shit.'

I got up and walked around the caravan, staring at the reception bars on the screen of my mobile, hoping in vain to find a signal . . . but, of course, I didn't. I looked around, searching for a landline, but I knew I was wasting my time. I went over to the door, stepped out into the rain, and wasted another few minutes wandering around, pointlessly waving my mobile about – as if holding it up a few feet higher was really going to make any difference – and then I gave up and went back inside again.

As I closed the door behind me and crossed over to the bed, a faint voice murmured in the darkness.

'Stevie . . . ?'

I shone the penlight towards the bed and saw that Robyn was awake . . . or, at least, vaguely awake. She was slumped against the wall, leaning sideways, her half-open eyes squinting at the torchlight.

'Wassat . . . ?' she muttered weakly, raising a hand to shield her eyes. 'Stevie . . . ? 'S'at you?'

'Hey, Robyn,' I said quietly, lowering the penlight. 'Stevie's not here at the moment—'

'Who's that?'

'John Craine,' I said. 'We met in The Swan the other night, remember?'

'Where's Stevie?'

'Are you OK?' I asked her, slowly moving closer. 'How do you feel?'

'Who the fuck are you?' she said, looking confusedly around the room. 'What's going on . . . ? Where's Stevie?'

'He'll be back in a minute.'

'Who're you?'

'John Craine.'

'Who?'

I sighed. 'Listen to me, Robyn, OK? Just listen—'

314

'Shit,' she groaned. 'I'm fucked.'

'Yeah, I know . . . Robyn?' As her eyes closed and she started slumping to one side, I reached across the bed, caught hold of her shoulders, and pulled her back up. 'Robyn?' I said sharply, giving her a gentle shake. 'Wake up . . . hey, *Robyn*.' Her eyes fluttered open again, and she gazed blankly at me. Her pupils were tiny. 'You need to stay awake,' I told her, sitting down on the edge of the bed. 'Do you understand?'

She frowned at me. 'Where's—?'

'Look at me,' I said firmly. 'Don't look away, look at *me* . . . all right, good . . . now, what's my name?'

She shook her head. 'I don't know . . .'

'Yes, you do. Concentrate, think about it . . . look at me. My name's John, OK?'

'John?'

'Yeah—'

'Where's Stevie? I want—'

'Forget about Stevie, he's not here.' I took hold of her hand. 'What's my name?'

'John.'

I smiled. 'Good . . . now, listen to me, OK? Are you listening?'

She nodded.

'What's my name?'

She sighed. 'John.'

I smiled again. 'All right . . . how are you feeling now?'

'Sick . . . fucked . . . why's it so fucking *dark* in here?'

'You're going to be fine,' I said, giving her hand a quick squeeze. 'Trust me, all right?'

315

'I can't *see* anything.'

'Hold on,' I said, reaching down to the floor and picking up a candle stub in a saucer. I took out my lighter, lit the candle, and put it back on the floor. The flame flickered in the draughty air, casting candlelight shadows across the walls. 'Is that better?' I asked Robyn, putting the penlight in my pocket.

She nodded.

'Right,' I said. 'Do you think you can stand up?'

'Why?'

'You'll feel better.'

'I'm too fucking tired . . .'

'I know,' I said, getting to my feet without letting go of her hand. 'But you just need to stand up for a minute or two, all right?' I gently pulled her towards me. 'Come on, up you get.'

'I can't . . .'

'Yes, you can. Come on . . .'

I tugged on her hand again, pulling a little harder this time. Although she resisted for a second, she quickly realised that she'd have to make an effort if she wanted to stay where she was, and in her state – high as a kite, sick as a dog – making an effort was the last thing she wanted to do. So she just gave in to me.

'All right, all right . . .' she muttered, shuffling forward. 'Just let me . . . hold on . . . let go a second, all right?'

Her coordination wasn't up to much, and as I let go of her hand, she flopped limply to one side, then kind of half-rolled, half-crawled across the bed, before finally swinging her legs round and sitting up unsteadily on the edge of the bed.

316

'All right?' I asked her.

'Do I *look* all right?'

I smiled and held out my hands.

She looked up at me. 'Can't I just stay here?'

I shook my head.

She sighed heavily, wiped sweat from her forehead, then reached up and took my hands. 'Don't *pull* me up, OK? Just . . . I don't know. Just help me.'

'OK.' I looked at her. 'Ready?'

She nodded, took a breath, tightened her grip on my hands, and pushed herself up off the bed. She almost fell straight away, but as her legs buckled and she toppled over to one side, I reached down and grabbed her round the waist just in time. She leaned in to me as I helped her straighten up, putting her hands on my shoulders to steady herself, and after a moment or two she regained her balance.

We just stood there for a while then – her hands on my shoulders, my hands on her waist – and as she concentrated on getting her breath back, I studied her face in the flickering light. She looked a little better now. Her skin wasn't quite so pale, and her eyes – though still very sleepy – were a little more human.

'It's John, right?' she said, turning those eyes on me.

'Yeah. John Craine.'

'Have you got a cigarette, John?'

I took out my packet, lit one, and gave it to her.

'Thanks,' she said, taking a puff and blowing out smoke. 'So what now, John Craine?'

'We walk.'

'Where to?'

'Nowhere.'

For the next twenty minutes or so, I just walked with Robyn around the caravan, talking to her all the time. There wasn't a lot to actually walk around, just the main living space – which was a cramped and cluttered mess anyway – and a smaller area behind a narrow partition that I guessed was meant to serve as a kitchen. It had a sink, a crappy little cooker, a few cupboards . . . but mostly it was just piled up with all kinds of crap – boxes, crates, bottles, coats, boots, piles of magazines . . . bits of this, bits of that. At the back of the kitchen area, a folding door led through into a tiny cubicle that housed a sickly-smelling chemical toilet.

It was a wretched place – cold, dirty, clammy, dull – and everything about it reeked of a deeply depressing baseness. It was everywhere, in the air, in the very essence of things, and by the time I'd walked round the caravan for the umpteenth time, I'd seen enough to know what kind of life Stevie lived. I'd seen the dirt, the squalor, the grime . . . I'd seen his stacks of smuggled cigarettes, his soft-porn biker magazines, his hard-core fuck magazines, his *Combat Handguns* magazines . . . I'd seen his shotgun, leaning against the wall in the kitchen, and his crates of booze – beer, whisky, brandy, cider – stacked up in the toilet . . . and I'd seen all his drug paraphernalia scattered haphazardly on a rickety wooden table by the wall – scales, spoons, plastic bags, foil, pipes, syringes . . . all kinds of shit. There were lots of empty wraps on the table, and some that still had a few scraps of coke or speed left in them, but there was no sign of any heroin. There was a battered old steel safe on the floor under the table, though, and from the way that Robyn kept glancing longingly at it, I guessed that was where Stevie kept his stash.

'Does he use much?' I asked Robyn as we left the kitchen area again.

'Uh?'

'Stevie . . . does he use the stuff or just sell it?'

'Where is he?' she said. 'Where's he gone?'

'I don't know. Does he shoot up?'

She shook her head. 'He likes his meth . . . speed . . . he likes the dirty stuff.' She looked at me. 'When's he coming back?'

'I don't know. Keep walking.'

She hadn't been very steady on her feet when we'd first started walking, and I'd had to help her quite a lot – keeping my arm round her shoulders, supporting her when she stumbled – but after a while she'd begun to move with a bit more confidence, and now – as we started yet another shuffling circuit of the caravan – she was walking without any help from me at all. I was still talking to her though – just jabbering away, mostly about nothing – making sure she didn't start nodding off again.

'How long have you known him?'

'Who?'

'Stevie.'

'I don't know . . . fucking for ever.'

I checked my mobile again, still no signal.

'What's my name?'

'John.'

'John what?'

'I don't know . . .'

'Yes, you do.'

'Give me a cigarette.'

'John what?'

'Just give me a fucking cigarette.'

I gave her a cigarette, lit one myself. My head was aching . . . the clatter of rain on the roof of the caravan was drumming in my ears . . . my mouth was dry. I needed a drink.

'Craine,' Robyn said, blowing out smoke. 'John Craine.'

'Do you remember me?'

'No . . . yeah, you were in the pub. Stevie said you were . . .'

'I was what?'

'Can't remember.'

We passed by the window again . . . I looked out again, looking for Stevie . . .

'Where's my phone?' Robyn said, stopping suddenly and digging in her pockets.

'I don't know.'

'I want to call him, see where he is—'

'No, you don't.'

'Have you got my phone?'

'No.'

'Where the fuck is it?'

'I don't know.'

'Give it to me.'

'I haven't got your phone, Robyn. Here . . .' I reached into my pocket and passed her mine. 'Help yourself.'

She looked at me, took the phone, and looked at the screen. 'There's no signal.'

I shrugged.

She gave it back to me.

I said, 'How are you feeling now?'

'Fucking awful.'

'You swear too much.'

'Fuck off.'

I smiled at her.

After a moment's hesitation, she smiled back.

'You look good when you smile,' I told her.

'Yeah?' she said, sniffing self-consciously. She wiped her nose, at the same time wiping the smile from her face. 'What do you care what I look like?'

'I was just saying—'

'And what the fuck are you doing here anyway?'

'Looking after you,' I said. 'Trying to help—'

'I don't need any fucking help.'

I looked at her. 'Does Stevie know about you and Linda?'

She froze. 'What?'

'If he knows that you've been talking to her—'

'Who the fuck's Linda?'

'It's all right, Robyn,' I said quietly, looking into her eyes. 'I know all about it. That's why I'm here. You don't have to pretend—'

'I'm not—'

'Listen to me,' I said firmly, taking her by the shoulders. 'This is important—'

'I don't have to —'

'Just fucking *listen*, all right?'

She glared at me, anger showing in her eyes, but she didn't say anything.

'Look,' I said calmly. 'I know what's going on, OK? I know all about the drugs coming in, I know who's involved, I know about the customs investigation, and I *know* that you're Linda's informant.'

Robyn said nothing, just carried on staring at me. She was doing her best to look defiant, but I could already see a real sense of fear creeping into her eyes.

'It's OK,' I assured her. 'I mean, you don't have to worry about me. I'm not with customs, I'm not with Garrow or Tait, I'm not with anyone. I'm just . . .'

'What?' she said quietly. 'You're just what?'

I sighed. 'Why don't we sit down?'

She looked at me for a moment, went to say something, then changed her mind and just nodded. As she went over and sat down on the edge of the bed, I glanced out of the window again, but all I could see was a wall of black rain.

'I won't be a minute,' I said to Robyn, heading into the kitchen area. I crossed over to the toilet, slid back the folding door, and grabbed a bottle of Johnnie Walker Black Label from one of the wooden crates stacked against the wall. I cracked the seal and unscrewed the cap, found a relatively clean glass, gave it a quick wipe with my coat sleeve, and half-filled it with whisky. As I drank off a couple of inches and left the kitchen, I could already feel the alcohol taking hold of me.

I went over to a ratty old armchair, sat down and lit a cigarette.

'Don't I get a drink?' Robyn asked, looking at the glass in my hand.

'No.'

'Why not?'

'Heroin and whisky don't mix.'

She grinned. 'Wanna bet?'

'What's in the trailer across the track?' I said.

'What? Which trailer?'

'The one that's falling apart . . . directly opposite. It's got a jungle on the roof . . .'

'Oh, *that* one,' she said, nodding, then shaking her head. 'What's in it? I don't know . . . nothing, probably. Why?'

'Does Stevie use it for anything?'

She shrugged. 'I don't know . . .'

'What about anyone else?'

'Like who?'

'Garrow, Lloyd . . . any of them?'

She shook her head. 'Not that I'm aware of . . . but I'm not here all the time, you know. I just . . . well, you know . . .' She looked hesitantly at me. 'How come you know Linda Ransom?'

'I don't,' I said. 'Well, not really . . . we just kind of stumbled across each other, if you know what I mean.' I looked at Robyn. 'What about you? How come you know her?'

She stared at me. 'Why should I tell you anything?'

'Chelsey Swalenski,' I said.

Robyn frowned. 'What?'

'Two days ago, a fourteen-year-old girl called Chelsey Swalenski was killed on the beach. Someone broke her

323

neck. I think her parents were probably murdered too.' I paused for a moment, looking into Robyn's eyes, and I was almost certain that her bewilderment was genuine. She wasn't hiding anything. She didn't know anything about Chelsey. 'I think Garrow or Lloyd probably killed them,' I went on. 'They killed Chelsey, they killed her parents . . . and if they know you're a grass, I think they'll probably kill you too.'

Robyn stared at me for a moment, then tapped cigarette ash into a saucer and looked away. She sniffed, wiped her nose . . . picked absently at her fingernails, chewing on her lip . . . she took an anxious drag on her cigarette, and another, tapped ash into the saucer again . . . and then, without looking up at me, she said, 'I never wanted anything to do with them . . . Garrow, Lloyd . . . Tait . . .' She shook her head. 'And I *didn't* have anything to do with them . . . not at first, anyway. I mean, I knew that Stevie was mixed up with them, and I kind of guessed what was going on, but I didn't actually *know* anything. I'd see Garrow and Lloyd now and then when they came round here, and I met Ivan Tait when Stevie got me the job at the farm shop, but that was about it.' She looked at me, a hint of bitterness in her eyes. 'I didn't have anything to do with all this smuggling shit until I got caught with the coke.'

'What do you mean?' I said. 'What coke?'

She sighed. 'I was making a delivery for the farm shop, driving some stuff into Hey . . . this was about eighteen months ago, I suppose. I don't usually make the deliveries, I just work in the shop, you know . . . on the till, in the café sometimes . . . but the guy who usually does the driving was off sick or something, or maybe he was doing something else . . . I can't really remember. Anyway, I ended up driving the van into Hey.' She paused for a moment, rubbing her eyes, then went on. 'About halfway there, I got stopped. The police pulled me over, searched the van, and it turns out there's a couple of kilos of coke hidden away in the back with all the vegetables and shit.' She stubbed out her cigarette. 'So they nick me, take me off to the station at Hey, and the next thing I know I'm in this poky little room with a couple of guys from customs, and they're offering me a deal. I can either work for them as an informant, they tell me, in which case they'll drop all the charges and let me go, or I can go down for the two keys of coke.' She looked at me. 'They said they'd charge me, there and then, with intent to supply . . . *and* they'd make sure I didn't get bail, so I'd be locked up straight away . . .' She shook her head. 'I already had a couple of convictions for possession. If I'd gone down for intent, I would have done time. Five or six years, maybe even longer. I couldn't do that. I just couldn't . . . it would have killed me.' She gazed sadly around the caravan. 'Not that this is much better . . .'

'Did you know the coke was in the van?' I asked her.

She shook her head. 'I wouldn't have gone near it if I had.'

'Why do you think you got stopped?'

She looked at me. 'The cops told me it was a random vehicle check . . . they *said* they just got lucky.'

'You don't sound very convinced.'

She smiled sadly. 'Yeah, well . . . it didn't take them long to find what they were looking for. And when I got to the station, the customs guys were already there.'

'So you think they knew about the delivery?'

'Yeah, they knew.'

'How?'

She just shrugged.

I looked at her for a moment or two, trying to work out what it was that was troubling me about her story. I was fairly sure she was telling me the truth, but there was *some*thing about her account that didn't feel right, something that didn't add up . . . I just couldn't seem to pin it down.

And right now I didn't have time to dwell on it.

'I think it's best if you leave the island,' I said, getting up and going over to the window. 'At least for a while anyway. We need to get in touch with Linda and get you out of here as soon as possible. If Garrow knows about you—'

'How could he?' Robyn said. 'I mean, you keep *telling* me that Garrow knows, or Stevie knows, but why should I believe you? Why should I believe *any*thing you tell me?'

'Why would I lie to you?'

'Why wouldn't you?'

I looked at her. 'Does the name Mark Allen mean anything to you?'

She thought about it for a moment, then shook her head. 'I don't think so.'

'Mark Ballard?'

Another shake of her head. 'Who are they?'

'They're the same person,' I explained. 'Ballard's his real

326

name. He's an undercover customs officer, working with Linda. I think Garrow might have got to him.'

'What do you mean, *got to him*?'

'It's possible that Ballard has told Garrow about the customs investigation.'

'Why would he do that?'

Because he didn't want to die, I thought, looking out of the window. *He wanted to see his wife again, and his two little kids . . . he didn't want to die.* I leaned in closer to the rainswept window, peering through the gloom at the broken-down trailer across the track . . . and I suddenly remembered the strange feeling I'd experienced in the Swalenskis' hotel room that time when I was lying under the bed, listening to Mark Ballard as he wandered around the room . . . and I'd thought he was me, the echo of me. And now, as I gazed through the rain-blurred darkness at the dilapidated trailer, I began to sense that same strange echo again, only this time I didn't feel that he was me . . . I felt that I was him. I *was* Mark Ballard, Mark Allen, Grungy Man, and for a fleeting moment I was paralysed, petrified, screaming and sobbing . . . *please don't hurt me any more . . .*

A faint light blinked in the distant darkness.

I quickly turned towards it, staring up the track . . . but there was nothing there now, just blackness and rain and acres of mud. I waited, keeping my eyes on the spot where the light had been – or where I thought it had been – but I still didn't see anything. I watched for a bit longer, wondering if it could have been a flash of lightning, or if maybe I'd just imagined it . . . and then suddenly I just couldn't think about anything any more. I'd had enough.

My head was buzzing, the rain was drumming, my eyes were starting to hurt . . .

'Are you all right?' Robyn said.

I turned to her, rubbing my forehead. 'What?'

'Are you OK? You look a bit—'

'It's just a headache,' I said. *Just a migraine . . . oh, yeah, they can be real bad . . . your sister suffers from migraines, doesn't she, honey?*

'There's some aspirins somewhere,' Robyn said. 'Do you want me to get them for you?'

'No, thanks,' I said, smiling at her. 'I'll be all right.' I went back over to the armchair, picked up the glass of whisky and finished it off. I took out my mobile and checked the screen. Still no signal.

'It's the weather,' Robyn said. 'The reception's always shit when the weather's like this.'

I put my phone away. 'We need to get in touch with Linda and arrange for you to get off the island.'

Robyn shook her head. 'The Stand'll be flooded by now. No one's going to be leaving the island for the next day or so.'

'Where's the nearest landline?'

'You still haven't told me why you're doing all this.'

I looked at her. 'There isn't time—'

'Make time.'

I shook my head. 'You don't understand—'

'No,' she said calmly, '*you* don't understand. I want to know why you're doing this, and I'm not going to say another word until you tell me, OK?'

The candle on the floor had almost burned out now, the

328

orange-blue flame fluttering weakly in the darkness, but as I stared long and hard into Robyn's eyes, the clarity of her determination was clear enough to see. She meant what she said. And while I knew that this wasn't the right time to tell her the truth, I also knew that it wasn't a moment for lying either.

'What do you know about your father?' I said softly.

'My *father*? What's he got to do with anything?'

'Do you know who he was?'

'Yeah . . . yeah, I know who he was.' Her voice was cold. 'He was the selfish bastard who fucked my mum and then killed himself. But I don't see what—'

'Do you know his name?'

She glared at me, tight-lipped.

'His name was Jim,' I said, holding her gaze.

'So?'

'Jim Craine.'

Her mouth dropped open. 'Craine?'

I nodded. 'He was my father too.'

She didn't say anything for a while, she *couldn't* say anything . . . she just sat there, staring at me, visibly shocked and confused, trying to comprehend what I'd just told her, trying to digest what it meant . . . and it was clear that she was still doped up to the eyeballs and was finding it hard to think straight . . . but eventually, after blinking her eyes a couple of times and nervously licking her lips, she managed to find her voice.

'I don't get it . . .' she muttered, shaking her head. 'How can we have the same father? I mean . . . well, that would mean that we're, you know . . . that you're my . . .'

'Brother,' I said, smiling cautiously. 'Well, *half*-brother anyway . . .'

'Half-brother . . . ?'

'Yeah.'

'Shit . . .'

I grinned. 'I know.'

'Fucking *hell* . . .'

'You swear too much.'

She looked at me, still incredibly confused, but there was just a hint of something else in her eyes now, something that made me feel really good. And as we sat there looking at each other in the candlelit darkness, I saw the beginnings of a smile on her face, a smile from the heart, the smile of a little sister . . .

And then lights flashed again, a sweep of headlights in the window, and this time there was absolutely no doubt that they were real.

25

'Shit!' Robyn said as I turned to the lights in the window. 'Get down! Don't let them see you! Get *down*!'

As I lowered my head and stooped out of sight, the beam of the headlights flooded into the caravan and I saw Robyn stumbling across the room towards the window. I could hear the car now, a low rumbling growl, right outside the caravan.

'Fuck,' Robyn hissed, peeking out of the window.

'Who is it?'

'Tait . . . he's got Stevie and Mott with him.'

Who's Mott? I thought, as I heard the engine stop.

'Get in the kitchen,' Robyn said.

I looked at her. 'What?'

'Come *on*,' she snapped, heading over to the kitchen area. 'You have to hide, *quickly* . . . they'll be here any second.'

'What about you?' I said, following her.

'I'll be all right,' she said, looking around for a place for me to hide. 'You'll have to get in here,' she said, moving over to a pile of coats heaped on the floor beside the narrow partition. She stooped down and picked up an armful of coats. 'Lie down there,' she told me. 'I'll cover you up.'

I looked at her. 'What are you going to do?'

She grabbed me by the shoulder and shoved me down to the floor. 'Lie down,' she told me. 'Move right back against the wall and curl yourself up into a ball.'

I did as I was told. She threw the armful of coats over me, and then I felt her piling more on top.

'All right?' she said.

'Yeah.'

'Don't move, OK? Just stay there.'

Before I could say anything else, I heard her hurrying back into the other room, and a few moments later I heard the sound of the caravan door opening. Heavy footsteps thudded on the floor, the door slammed shut, and unseen voices filled the air.

. . . the state of my fucking shoes, Christ's sake. You know how much these cost? No, of course you fucking don't. Where are you going?

She's over here.

Wake her up then. And get a fucking move on. I want her at the shop before the roads get any worse. Shit, look at this mess . . . I've got a meeting in an hour. What's it going to look like when I turn up with shit all over my shoes? Fuck it.

A pause.

Then, *Mott, check in there.*

I held my breath, listening to Mott's footsteps as he padded into the kitchen area. He stopped by the partition, paused for a moment, then I heard him go over to the toilet and slide back the door. Another brief pause, then his footsteps came back again, passed me by, and I heard him say, *No, nothing.*

332

I didn't recognise his voice. But I knew Stevie's, and I could hear him now, shouting at Robyn.

Where is he?

Uhh?

Don't fuck me about, Rob. Just tell me where he is.

Who?

Craine.

Craine . . . ? I don't understand —

Last chance, Rob. Where is he?

Please, Stevie . . . I really don't know —

You lying fucking bitch.

Slap.

No! Stevie, don't —

Slap.

I was halfway to my feet and already looking for Stevie's shotgun when I heard Tait's voice – *Wait a second, Stevie . . . hold on* – and at the sound of his words I paused . . . edging back behind the partition . . . waiting . . . listening . . . ready to grab the shotgun and make a move if I heard another slap. I had no idea what kind of move I was going to make – especially if it turned out that the shotgun wasn't loaded – but I couldn't just lie there and do nothing while Stevie slapped Robyn around. So I waited, lowering myself back down to the floor, and I listened . . . but everything seemed to have gone quiet now. No slaps, no raised voices . . . just the sound of the rain, and a very faint muttering . . . Were they whispering?

Why would they be whispering?

Then I heard Tait's voice again: *So we're going to leave her here then?*

Yeah, Stevie replied. *She'll be all right now for a couple of hours.*

You sure?

Yeah.

All right, good. Where's that stuff I asked you for?

I'll go and get it.

I pulled the coats back over my head and lay perfectly still as Stevie's footsteps came into the kitchen area. I heard him stop, pick something up, and then – after a moment's hesitation – he left again.

All right? Tait said to him.

Yeah.

Right, let's go.

I could feel something nagging away at the back of my mind as I listened to them heading for the door, a feeling that something wasn't quite right . . . but I just couldn't get hold of it. I carried on listening – heavy footsteps, the door opening . . . then slamming shut . . .

I waited.

Silence.

The rain kept falling . . .

I heard the car start up, the engine revving . . . rumbling, growling . . . I heard it pulling away.

I waited.

A minute, two minutes . . .

The nagging feeling wouldn't go away . . .

Three minutes.

I crawled out from under the coats and slowly got to my feet. The lights were off, the caravan draped in darkness again. I stood there for a moment, listening, thinking, trying

334

to work out what it was that was bothering me . . . and I had a feeling now that it was something that Tait had said, something about . . . something . . .

No, it was no good.

It'd just have to wait.

I took out my penlight, turned it on, and went to check on Robyn.

I was about halfway across the caravan when the light came on, and as I froze, staring at the empty bed where Robyn should have been, a voice from behind me said, 'You really are a dumb fucker, aren't you?'

Everything fell into place all at once then, and by the time I'd turned round to face the voice, I already knew what had happened. They'd realised I was there, they'd taken Robyn, and they'd left Stevie behind to deal with me. And as I looked at him now – standing there with the shotgun levelled at my head – I knew that he was right: I really *was* a dumb fucker.

'How did you know?' I asked him.

He grinned. 'You call yourself a private detective?'

'Investigator, actually. Private investigator.'

'Is there a difference?'

'Not really.'

'Yeah, well . . . whatever you fucking call yourself, you're not very good at it, are you?'

'Obviously not,' I said, gazing down the barrels of the shotgun.

'If you want my advice,' he said, grinning again. 'I mean, I'm no Sherlock fucking Holmes or anything . . . but next time you're trying to hide somewhere, it's probably best if you don't leave muddy footprints all over the place.'

I looked down, gazing around at the trails of mud I'd left on the floor, pathetically trying to convince myself that I hadn't seen them before because the light hadn't been on . . . but that only made me feel even more pathetic. I mean, the footprints were everywhere . . . you'd have to be fucking blind to miss them. *Or blind drunk*, I thought. *Or just fucking shit at everything . . .*

I closed my eyes for a moment.

Of course, I realised now what it was that had been bothering me, and I knew that when Tait had been going on and on about *his* muddy shoes, I'd almost got the message . . . but what good was 'almost' to anyone? And what good was realising anything now? Now was too late . . .

Everything was always too fucking late.

I let out a breath, opened my eyes, and looked at Stevie.

'What's it like?' he said, grinning. 'I mean, being a useless piece of shit . . . how does it actually feel?'

I stared into his eyes. 'It has its advantages.'

'Yeah?'

I said nothing, just carried on staring at him.

He stared back at me for a moment, then blinked. 'Well, anyway—'

'It gives me an edge,' I said.

'What?'

I took a step towards him.

'Don't even think about it,' he said, tightening his grip on the shotgun. 'Any closer, and I'll blow your fucking head off.'

I took another step, then stopped. The shotgun was now about six inches from my head. I stared down the barrels at Stevie. 'The difference between you and me,' I said, 'is that I *know* I'm a useless piece of shit, but you . . . ? Well, you think your life's worth living, don't you? Am I right?'

'Just fucking . . . stay where you are, OK?'

'And maybe you're right,' I said, inching closer to him. 'Maybe your life *is* worth living . . . I mean, I can't see it myself, but what the fuck do I know?' I smiled at him. 'The point is, Stevie . . .' Another half-step forward. 'You *want* to live, don't you?'

'I'm fucking warning you,' he said, inching back towards the wall. 'You come any closer and I'll—'

'You'll what?' I said, taking one more step. His back was against the wall now – he couldn't move any further. The shotgun was no more than two inches from my head. I slowly leaned forward, resting my forehead against the barrels. 'Your hands are shaking, Stevie,' I said. 'What's the matter – too much speed? Yeah, I know what that's like . . . mind you . . .' I raised my hand and held it out, showing him how steady it was. 'I seem to be OK at the moment. You know why that is?'

He swallowed hard, not saying anything.

'It's because I don't fucking care,' I whispered, smiling at him. 'Do you understand? I don't care if you pull the trigger . . . I don't care if you blow my fucking brains out . . . I just don't . . . fucking . . . *care*.'

His hands were trembling so much now that I could feel the shotgun barrels shaking against my head, and I began to wonder how sensitive the trigger was . . . and as

I started thinking about that, I suddenly realised how familiar this all was – a gun barrel resting against my head . . . imagining how it would feel if the gun went off . . . hearing a voice that might have been mine, or it might have been my father's . . .

It won't feel like anything, John.

It won't feel like anything at all.

I grabbed hold of the shotgun and wrenched it to one side, and as Stevie tried to yank it back, I lunged forward and hammered my head into his face. Something went *crack* – his nose, I guessed – and as he let out a groan, still fumbling for the shotgun, I headbutted him again, even harder this time, giving it everything I'd got. As he slumped back against the wall, coughing up blood, I ripped the shotgun from his hands, swung it back, and smashed it into the side of his head. He went down hard, hitting the floor with a lifeless thump, and when I hit him again, clubbing the shotgun into the back of his skull, he barely even moved. He just lay there, blood bubbling from his mouth, a broken tooth embedded in his torn lower lip, a reddened sliver of bone showing through his greasy black hair . . .

He was still breathing.

I raised the shotgun again, lifting it high above my head . . .

You'll kill him, John.

'Not now, Stacy.'

If you hit him again, you'll kill him.

'I know . . .'

I know you know. I'm just saying, that's all.

'What?' I sighed. 'You're just saying what?'

338

You know what.

I tightened my grip on the gun, telling myself to just do it, don't listen to her . . . just fucking do it . . . but I knew it was already too late. The moment I'd hesitated, that was it. The killing mist had gone.

'Fuck it,' I breathed out, lowering the shotgun. 'Fuck everything.'

I went into the kitchen area, poured myself a glass of whisky, drank half of it down, and lit a cigarette. I was already regretting what I'd done to Stevie. Not for his sake – I didn't give a shit about him – and I certainly didn't feel any remorse about cracking his head open, I just wished I'd asked him some questions first. What's Tait going to do with Robyn? Why's he taking her to the shop? What happened to Mark Ballard? Where's Garrow? Who's Mott? Why did they leave you behind to deal with me . . . ?

. . . call yourself a private detective?

I drank more whisky.

. . . you're not very good at it, are you?

I put down the empty glass, went over to the rickety table against the wall, and emptied out all the half-empty wraps I could find. I thumbed a couple of snorts up my nose, and as the mixture of coke and speed whacked in with an eye-watering surge, I took a final shuddering drink from the whisky bottle, wiped the speed-snot from my nose, and went back to check on Stevie. He was still unconscious, and from the look of him I didn't think he'd be waking up soon . . . if ever. I crouched down beside him and went through his pockets. I took his keys, and an

339

almost full pack of cigarettes, then I grabbed the shotgun and headed for the door.

While I'd been walking Robyn around the caravan, I'd noticed a 20-litre petrol can standing by the wall near the door, and as I crossed the room now, I was suddenly gripped with an overwhelming desire to burn the caravan to the ground. Destroy it, obliterate it, cremate it . . . all of it – the drugs, the shit, the dirt, the stink . . . the grubby little bed, the crates of booze . . . the base desires, the sack of flesh that called itself Stevie Haynes . . . just burn the fucking lot.

I went over and picked up the can of petrol.

Hold on, John . . .

Shook it . . .

John?

It was almost full.

John, listen to me.

I unscrewed the cap and sniffed the fumes, imagining an infernal rage of fire and smoke, the fierce orange flames consuming everything . . .

John!

'It's all right, Stace,' I said, quietly putting down the can. 'It was just a thought, that's all.'

As I opened the caravan door and stepped out into the pouring rain, I paused for a moment and thought about Robyn. I remembered Tait telling Stevie to *get a fucking move on . . . I want her at the shop before the roads get any worse*, and although I had no way of knowing for sure, I was fairly confident that he had to be talking about the farm shop. And if he wasn't . . . ? Well, there was nothing

340

I could do about it. I just had to assume that she was at the farm shop, and hope I was right.

I glanced across at the rundown trailer. I hoped I was right about that too . . . but at the same time, I couldn't help hoping I was wrong.

I turned to my left and gazed out over the rainswept country park, imagining the beach beyond it . . . the beach, the pillbox, the pathway along the creek . . . and I remembered the misty grey morning a thousand years ago when I'd seen Robyn disappearing off the pathway and heading down to a little wooden bridge that spanned the creek, and I hadn't known where she was going then, but I knew now that she'd been on her way to the farm shop . . .

The farm shop . . .

I looked over at the trailer again, trying to make up my mind.

'What do you think, Stace?' I muttered. 'What should I do?'

You have to check the trailer first.

'Are you sure?'

No. But if you are *right about it, it probably means that Robyn's safe enough for now.*

'And if I'm wrong?'

Well, you won't know unless you check it, will you?

As I headed across to the trailer, stumbling through the fetid mud, I wondered idly why I'd changed my mind about burning down Stevie's caravan. It wasn't that I didn't *want* to, or that I was concerned about the consequences, and I was fairly sure that morality had nothing to do with

341

it – morality had fuck all to do with anything – and I knew that I hadn't changed my mind for Stacy's sake, because I knew deep down that Stacy didn't exist, that her voice was nothing more than the voice of my own stupid heart, and I knew that this time it *wasn't* my heart that had stopped me . . .

So why *had* I changed my mind?

The only answer I could think of was that burning the caravan down would have made me feel better, and I didn't want to feel better.

26

When I unlocked the door of the trailer and went inside, the first thing that struck me was the silence. I could still hear the rain outside, but it was nowhere near as loud and intrusive as it had been in the caravan. It sounded distant, muffled . . . almost comforting. And that didn't make sense. The trailer was falling apart, the roof was covered in weeds . . . the rain should have been pouring in, the whole place should have been soaked. But it wasn't. It felt bone dry, hushed, waterproof . . . it somehow felt cocooned . . .

And when I clicked on my penlight and shone it at the roof, then swept the beam all around the trailer, I realised why.

The whole place was crammed full of stuff, for a start – stacks of boxes, piles of crates, racks of clothes . . . all kinds of stuff – and I guessed that had a certain sound-proofing effect. But the main reason that the interior of the trailer was so surprisingly quiet and dry was that it had been customised. The walls, the floor, the ceiling – everything was lined with some kind of thick black waterproof sheeting. The sheets were fixed to solid wooden boards, the boards bolted together, and the gaps between them filled with sealant. There were no windows, and the only way in or out was through the door, which I now realised was a sheet of galvanised steel with just a thin veneer of faded old wood on the front. The spaces between the plywood boards and the outer walls of the trailer were packed with insulating foam.

So, in effect, the outside of the trailer was just a shell, a facade of neglect, while the inside had been fitted out as a reasonably secure waterproof storage unit.

It was by no means a professional job, and when I turned on the lights and looked more closely, it soon became obvious that very little care had gone into the work, and it wouldn't have surprised me if Stevie had done it all himself. It looked rough and unfinished, and while it *was* probably waterproof, it didn't strike me as being particularly secure . . . but then if the stuff being stored in here had anything to do with Ivan Tait – which I was guessing it did – it probably didn't need to be all that secure. I mean, if Cal was right about Tait virtually owning the whole island, no one who lived here was going to be stupid enough to steal from him, were they?

Not that it mattered anyway.

The only reason I was thinking about any of this was to take my mind off what I was doing here, and as I leaned the shotgun against the wall and headed slowly down to the far end of the trailer, I carried on trying to distract myself by concentrating on the piles of stuff all around me. A lot of it was drugs – unopened packs of cocaine and heroin, polythene bags filled with wraps, bricks of cannabis stacked up on pallets – but there was all kinds of other stuff too: boxes of booze, vast quantities of cigarettes and tobacco, mobile phones, MP3 players, games consoles,

DVDs, laptops, iPads, black-market pharmaceuticals – Viagra, sleeping pills, diet pills. There were also several long wooden crates with Russian lettering on the side that I'd be willing to bet contained guns . . .

But none of this really took my mind off anything.

And, besides, it wasn't a *mind* thing now anyway. It was much more visceral than that – a gut thing, a body thing – and as I approached the end of the trailer, I could already feel what had happened in here. I could sense it. I could feel it on my skin . . .

And then I stopped.

I could smell it now . . . the smell of death, hanging in the air. A faint odour of shit . . . piss . . . the rancid sweetness of meat and blood.

I swallowed hard.

At the very end of the trailer, against the far wall, a long metal table was bolted to the floor. It had obviously been cleaned – I could smell the disinfectant – but whoever had scrubbed it down hadn't done a very good job. Even from a distance I could see numerous reddish-brown stains ingrained in the pitted metal surface . . . and as I moved a little closer I saw more dried blood on the legs of the table. I stopped again, not wanting to go any nearer, and the longer I stood there, staring emptily at the table, the more blood I saw. It was everywhere – spattered across the walls, pooled on the floor, sprayed over a pile of white cardboard boxes.

There was no doubt that this was where Mark Ballard had been killed. There was a good chance he'd been tortured too. Tortured, killed . . . decapitated.

There was a toolbox on the floor under the table.

Beside the toolbox was a chainsaw.

I hoped Mark had died before it was used.

I hoped . . .

Nothing.

Hoping was pointless.

I sank down to the floor, leaned back against the wall, and let the tears come.

A person has only so many tears, and I used up most of mine a lifetime ago, so I didn't cry too long for Mark Ballard. I stayed where I was for quite some time though, just sitting there, thinking, going over and over everything I knew, and everything I didn't know . . . asking myself dozens of questions, trying to fill in some of the holes . . .

I sat there for a long time.

I had to believe that Stacy was right, that my heart was right – that because Mark Ballard *was* killed in here, that probably meant Robyn was safe enough for now. I *had* to believe it. If they were going to kill Robyn, why would they have taken her to the farm shop when they already had a killing place here? The trailer was already compromised . . . why double the risk of discovery by compromising the farm shop too? It didn't make sense, did it?

No, I remembered myself saying not so long ago. *But when does cutting off someone's head* ever *make sense?*

I couldn't afford to doubt myself. I just had to believe that Robyn was safe . . . for now . . . She was safe. I needed time. I had to think . . .

I sat there.

Time passed . . .

The rain kept falling . . . distant, muffled, almost comforting.

I carried on thinking.

Drifting . . .

Floating . . .

Thinking . . .

I don't remember taking the key to the pillbox out of my pocket, but at some point I realised that I was holding it in my hand, staring intently at it, and that somewhere in the depths of my mind there was some kind of belief that it *was* the key . . . the solution. The answer to everything.

It was still far from clear – like a vague shape stirring in the silt at the bottom of a deep black pond – but it was there . . . I could *feel* it. And all I had to do now was reach down into the murky depths, bring it up to the surface, and hope that it made some kind of sense.

I closed my eyes.

27

I'd thought it was going to be easy, getting from the caravan park to the beach. All I had to do was find the narrow pathway that I'd seen Robyn crossing a few days ago – the pathway that had led her up to the car park – and from there it was just a short walk down the field, and then down the steps, to the beach. The trouble was, I just couldn't find the pathway, and the longer I looked for it – trudging around in the stinking mud, stumbling blindly through the almost impenetrable darkness – the more lost and confused I became, and after a while I realised that I was going round and round in circles and I had absolutely no idea where I was, let alone where the pathway might be. So, in the end, I had to resort to sliding down into a flooded ditch and clambering back up the other side to get to the car park . . . and then, after I'd crossed the car park and made my way down the rain-sodden field, I found that the steps had been cut off by the tide, so I had to turn back again and start looking for another way down to the beach. And that meant more trudging around in the darkness – stumbling from ditch to ditch, wading through stagnant pools, sinking up to my knees in the fetid mud of the saltmarshes . . .

*

It was past midnight when I finally emerged onto the higher ground of the beach. I was covered in stinking black mud, my clothes were ripped, my hands were scratched and bleeding . . . I was completely exhausted. There was nothing I wanted more than to sink down to the ground, close my eyes, and just sit there in the rain . . . just for a moment or two, just until I got my breath back. But as I looked around at the liquid black night, I knew that I didn't have time to rest. The saltmarshes to my left were flooded, the glistening dark waters lapping up over the shingle, and the swelling sea to my right was still rising, surging inexorably up the beach, and it wouldn't be long before the rain-battered waves broached the higher ground and began flooding into the marshes.

I gazed up ahead for a moment, trying to see the pillbox, trying to gauge if it was still above water . . . but it was too dark to see anything. I looked down to my right. The waves were lapping ever closer . . . and I realised now that even if I got to the pillbox in time, before the high ground flooded, there'd be very little chance of getting back the same way.

I just had to hope that the time I'd spent sitting in the trailer, the time I'd spent dredging through the silt of my mind, hadn't been wasted, and that when I got to the pillbox I'd find what I was hoping to find. Because if I was wrong, if I didn't find it . . .

It wasn't worth thinking about.

I checked in my pocket, making sure that I still had the key.

And then I started to run.

*

349

I hadn't done any serious running for years, and I'd forgotten how exhilarating it can be – working your legs, pumping your arms, sucking down the cold night air . . . it was energising, liberating, it made me want to shout and fly. And just for a while, as I pounded along the shingle, racing against the incoming tide, I felt like a child again . . . running along the beach, alone but never alone . . . running towards the pillbox, excited about what I might find . . .

I was a good runner back then.

I could keep going all day.

I could run for ever when I was a child . . .

But I was forty years old now. I smoked too much, I drank too much, I did just about everything too much . . . and before I'd got halfway to the pillbox, I was already remembering how agonising running can be – killing your legs, bursting your heart, boiling the blood in your veins . . . it was excruciating, soul-sapping, it made me want to howl and cry. And just for a while, I was on the verge of giving up. I simply couldn't do it any more. I couldn't run another step. Everything hurt too much, every breath seared my lungs . . . I had to stop.

You can't stop.

'I can't . . . fucking breathe.'

You can't stop.

'But I can't—'

You can't stop.

I kept going.

The incoming waves were just beginning to lap around the base of the pillbox when I got there, and after I'd paused

350

for a minute or two to gulp down some air and get some feeling back into my legs, I stumbled over to the gun slit, took out my penlight and shone it through the gap. There was no doubt that it was damp inside, and in places there was a fair amount of standing water, but as I swept the beam of the torch around, I was relieved to see that large areas of the floor were still relatively dry.

But even as I moved away from the gun slit, I could feel the waves creeping up over my feet, and I knew there was no time to waste.

The sweat was really pouring off me now, and as I went round to the back of the pillbox – my lungs still burning, my heart still pounding – I could feel the heat draining out of my body, and by the time I stopped at the top of the steps that led down to the cast-iron door, I was chilled to the bone. Shivering and shaking, I shone my penlight down the steps. The door was locked shut. I glanced behind me for a moment, looking back over the beach – or, at least, where the beach would normally have been – but it was all underwater now. There was no shoreline, no sand, no shingle, no higher ground . . . it was all gone. And in its place was a single great swathe of ocean darkness.

There was nothing out there. No stars, no moon, no lights . . .

I was alone.

I was just a kid, a young boy . . .

Alone in the darkness.

I was drunk . . . a drunk boy . . . timeless, ageless . . .

I turned back to the steps and began making my way down. One step at a time, keeping my hand against the wall, shining the torch at my feet . . . I could smell it now . . . the dank air, the stench of urine . . . the remembered smell of the pillbox . . . and as I neared the bottom of the steps, a more recent memory flashed into my mind – Sergeant Boon, telling me to wait at the top of the steps while he went down into the pillbox. I remembered him taking the key from his coat pocket and unlocking the door, then stooping down and squeezing through the doorway . . . and then nothing had happened for a few moments. I'd seen his torchlight sweeping around inside, and I'd guessed that he was just double-checking, making absolutely sure that there *wasn't* a body in there, and only then had he popped his head round the doorway and called out to me to come down . . .

But maybe I'd guessed wrong, I thought now. Maybe Boon had already known that there wasn't a body in there, and what he'd actually been doing was checking on something else before calling me down . . .

I'd soon find out.

I'd reached the foot of the steps now. I took the key from my pocket, shone the penlight on the keyhole, and unlocked the door. It swung open, clanging heavily against the concrete wall, and I gazed through the doorway into the darkness. My heart was pounding now, and as I crouched down and raised the penlight, a rush of blood swirled through my head, and for a dizzying moment or two I was timeless and ageless again . . . I was just a kid, a young boy . . . alone in the illicit darkness . . . alone with the dirty words scrawled on the walls and the ripped-up remains of dirty pictures . . . scared, excited, shameful . . . drunk . . .

I was crying . . . sickened and sad . . . I was staring at Chelsey's empty blue eyes, her rigid white skin, her broken neck . . . she was dead . . . she was nothing . . . nothing at all . . .

I wiped rain and sweat from my face.

Waited for my head to clear . . .

And went into the pillbox.

There was nothing there. No body, no trace of a body, no sign that a body had ever been there . . . nothing at all. No memories either. No empty beer cans, no bottles, no smells, no torn-up porn magazines . . . there was just a damp concrete floor, a few scattered puddles, moss-stained walls, bits of patched-up brickwork here and there . . .

I moved over to the middle of the pillbox and looked down at the floor, shining the penlight at the spot where I'd seen Chelsey's body. There was nothing there . . . nothing at all.

Satisfied now? I remembered Boon saying.

I stamped lightly on the floor. It felt and sounded solid enough. I inched forward and tried again . . . and this time, when I brought my foot down, I heard and felt a hollow *whump*. I stamped again, just to make sure: once – *whump* – and again – *whump, whump*. I stepped back, shining the torch on the floor again. I still couldn't *see* anything, but I knew now that I was right. There was *something* down there . . .

There *had* to be.

It was the only thing that made sense.

I lowered myself to the ground – moving carefully this

time to avoid another rush of blood – and I got down on my hands and knees and began searching every inch of the floor. Even at such a close-up level, it still took quite a while to find what I was looking for, but I didn't panic, I just kept looking – slowly, carefully, inch by inch . . . feeling the floor with my hands – until eventually I found the trapdoor.

It was so well disguised, and fixed so flush to the ground, that even now I could barely see it. All I could really make out was a vague square-shaped outline in the concrete, the sides about four feet across, and perhaps a slight difference in the texture and colouring of the ground within the square. Whatever the door was made from – and at the moment it was impossible to tell – it looked so similar to the concrete floor that it was hard to believe that it *wasn't* concrete.

I sat back and stared at it, slowly sweeping the beam of the penlight around the square, trying to work out how it opened. There were no obvious gaps round the edges, nothing to get hold of, no handles.

I reached into my pocket for my cigarettes. My pocket was waterlogged, and so were the cigarettes.

'Fuck it,' I said, crumpling the sodden pack into a ball and dropping it on the floor. 'And fuck this too.'

I leaned forward and thumped the hidden door with the palm of my hand. *Whump!* It was so solid, so well made, that it hardly moved at all . . . but it moved just enough to rattle a small hinged flap on one side. I reached over and pulled back the flap with my fingernails. There was a handhold underneath, a hollowed-out groove. I got to my knees, took hold of the groove, and pulled.

The trapdoor opened with surprising ease. It was a lot lighter than I'd imagined, and it made virtually no noise at all. There was no creaking, no squeaking . . . just the soft groan of well-oiled hinges. I still took my time with it though – opening it just a few inches, then pausing, listening . . . then another few inches, another pause . . . and I kept going like that until there was enough of a gap to let me see inside. I adjusted my position so that I was kneeling right in front of the opening, and then – holding the trapdoor open with one hand – I cautiously leaned forward and shone the torch downwards.

The beam lit up the walls of a brick-lined shaft. It was roughly the same size as the trapdoor above it – about four feet by four feet – and it looked to be about twelve feet deep. Metal rungs were fixed into one of the walls, leading all the way down to the bottom, and although I couldn't actually make out what was down there, I was fairly confident now that I was on the right track.

I got to my feet and pulled the trapdoor all the way back. I could see now that the upper side of the door had been coated with a thick layer of painted plastic resin to give it the appearance of concrete, and the door itself was made from some kind of lightweight metal, possibly aluminium. It was reinforced on the underside with steel struts, and the edges were sealed with flexible silicone strips. Hinged stanchions on either side of the door folded out to prop it open. I sat down, lowered my legs into the shaft, and placed a foot on the first of the metal rungs. It was kind of awkward getting my other foot on the rung, but after a bit of stretching and swivelling round, I got there in the end. And then all I had to do was sort of lurch forward, holding onto the sides of the shaft, and I was ready to start climbing down. I paused for a moment, wondering if I should shut the trapdoor behind me or leave it propped open. After thinking about it for a couple of seconds, I decided to close it. It wouldn't keep out *all* of the water if the pillbox flooded, but it would keep out a lot more than it would if it was open. I reached up, released the stanchion, and lowered the door over my head as I began to climb down.

There had to be something down there – a room, a chamber, a cave – it was the only thing that made sense. Garrow and the others had to have somewhere to stash the stuff they were bringing in from the boat, and while the pillbox itself was obviously no good for long-term storage, it worked perfectly well as a cover, a starting point, a gateway to somewhere else. But the real clincher for me, the thing that had convinced me that the pillbox *had* to lead somewhere else, was the disappearance of Chelsey's body. I *knew* that I'd seen it. It *had* been there. I *knew* that no one could have removed it while I was waiting for the police. Bodies don't just disappear. And as Sherlock himself once said, when you've eliminated the impossible, whatever remains, however improbable, must be the truth.

There *had* to be a way of removing Chelsey's body from the pillbox, and the only way possible, however improbable, was down.

So when I reached the bottom of the shaft, when I stepped off the final rung and shone the penlight around, it was no

356

great surprise to see that I was standing in the bowels of an underground chamber. It was a roughly dome-shaped cavern, carved out of solid rock – about thirty feet long, fifteen wide, and ten to twelve feet high. It was hard to tell if it was entirely man-made or a natural cave that had been hollowed out and worked on over the years, but either way I was pretty sure that it had been here for a long, long time. It *felt* old – the air, the rock, the sheer solidity of the place . . . everything about it felt ancient. Even all the stuff that was stored in there had something of the past about it. It was the same old stuff I'd seen at the caravan park – drugs, cigarettes, tobacco, booze, guns, cameras, phones, laptops – and, of course, in some ways a lot of it had absolutely nothing to do with the past. I mean, there's nothing particularly *ancient* about an iPad or an Xbox, is there? But whatever the stuff actually was – however modern it might be – it was all essentially just smuggled goods, and in that sense it was no different to all the other contraband that had been stored down here over the years.

I wasn't really *thinking* about any of this, it was all just white noise in my head, an involuntary murmur of background thoughts as I stood there sweeping my torch around the bare stone walls, the dripping rock, the boxes and crates, the cases and cartons . . . I stepped to one side, raised my head, and shone the torch up the shaft. I could see it now . . . I could see how it had happened. I lowered my head and directed the torch at the ground, studying the area around my feet. I could see it . . .

The confrontation on the beach . . . Bryan Swalenski

getting punched to the ground ... Lloyd going after Chelsey and her mother . . . and then everything spirals out of control, and the Swalenskis are dead, and Garrow and the others have to get rid of the evidence, so they start loading the bodies onto the boat, but then they get a call from Stevie, someone's coming, and they don't have time to get Chelsey's body on the boat, so they just dump it in the pillbox, assuming that I won't go anywhere near it . . . but, of course, I do . . . I go right up to the pillbox, I sit on the roof, smoke a cigarette, I look through the gun slit, I see Chelsey's body . . .

Were Garrow and Lloyd in the pillbox at that point? I wondered. While I was looking through the slit, were they hiding away in the shadows somewhere? Or had they already opened up the trapdoor and taken refuge inside the shaft? Either way, I thought, it didn't really make any difference. Once I'd moved away from the pillbox, they'd simply opened the trapdoor and dropped Chelsey's body down the shaft.

I could see it now . . .

Her lifeless body tumbling down through the darkness, bouncing limply off the walls . . . then crashing to the ground with a sickening thud.

I could see it.

I knelt down and shone the penlight on the ground. There wasn't much to see – a slight scrape in the rock, a faint darkening around the scrape . . . possibly the remains of a bloodstain. I shone the torch around, looking for more blood, but I didn't really expect to find any. She was already dead when she hit the ground, her heart had already stopped

. . . even if she had been injured in the fall, she wouldn't have bled very much.

I straightened up, looking around. I was cold, wet . . . exhausted . . . and I couldn't stop thinking about Chelsey's body, tumbling down the shaft, all alone in the empty darkness . . . I just couldn't get it out of my mind.

It wasn't *right*.

I closed my eyes for a moment, letting my heart go cold, and then I headed across to the far side of the cavern and stopped in front of a buttressed opening in the wall. It was well over six feet high, and at least four feet across, and when I moved a little closer and shone the penlight into the darkness beyond, I saw what I was hoping to see: a timber-framed tunnel, stretching out into the distance . . .

I paused for a moment, steadying myself, and then I headed off into the gloom.

28

The roof of the tunnel was wired up with a series of glass-domed lights, each one about twenty yards apart, but even if I could have found a light switch – which I couldn't – it would have been too risky to turn them on. So I just trudged on through the darkness, following the slowly fading beam of my penlight. As I moved through the underground silence, it wasn't hard to imagine smugglers from the past trailing up and down through the same stilled darkness – bringing in their goods, outwitting the customs men – generation after generation, playing the same old games, following the same old trade. The tunnel had probably been dug out centuries ago, back when the farm shop was still a church – long before the pillbox ever existed – and I wondered if over the years the local clergy had been willing participants in the smuggling business, happily allowing the contraband of the day to be stored in their church, or if – like most of the islanders today – they'd had very little say in the matter.

Of course, there was always the possibility that I was wrong, and that the tunnel *didn't* lead to the farm shop. It had made perfect sense when I'd thought about it in the trailer – the drugs came in off the fishing boat, into the pillbox, down the shaft, then along the tunnel to the farm shop, and from there they were distributed by van or car to the mainland . . .

It had all made perfect sense.

But after plodding through the tunnel for five minutes or so, with no sign of it coming to an end, I was beginning to have my doubts. There were no points of reference down here, no clues as to which way I was going, and because everything looked almost identical – just one rock wall after another – it was really hard to judge distances. I *felt* as if I'd been walking for miles, and I kept trying to visualise the photocopied map that Arthur Finch had shown me, trying to picture it all – the pathway, the creek, the saltmarshes, the small black cross that marked the position of the farm shop – and from what I could remember, if the map was accurate, the shop couldn't be more than half a mile from the pillbox, if that. And even allowing for my confusion, I was sure I ought to be there by now.

But all I could see in the almost dead beam of my penlight was more of the same – more rock walls, more timber supports . . . more underground silence stretching out into the same old darkness . . .

But then, up ahead, the darkness suddenly changed.

It wasn't an empty darkness any more, it was solid. A wall of solid black rock . . . and within the wall, set back in the rock, a heavy wooden door. Scarred and ancient, studded with bolts, bound with great iron bands . . .

A door.

I'd reached the end of the tunnel.

*

I turned off the penlight and just stood there for a while, listening to the darkness, trying to ignore the boom of my heart and the distant roar in my head. I thought I could hear something, somewhere beyond the door, a low and intermittent humming. A boiler, perhaps . . . some kind of heating system. Plumbing, maybe . . . refrigeration. But that was all. There were no human sounds, no voices, no footsteps.

I listened for a while longer, then stepped up to the door and took hold of the solid iron handle. I waited another moment or two, then turned the handle and pulled. The door inched open, and I peered cautiously through the gap. The room on the other side was in darkness, but there was just enough light showing through the frame of a closed door in the far wall to let me see that it was a large stone-floored basement, stacked here and there with wooden trays marked *HALE ORGANICS*. Three massive refrigeration units stood against a wall, humming and rattling quietly to themselves, and the opposite wall was lined with metal shelving and storage cupboards.

I eased open the door, paused for a moment to listen again, then stepped through into the basement.

The air was chilled, and I could smell the familiar earthy tang of fresh fruit and vegetables. I looked around, sweeping the penlight over the walls, the floor, but there wasn't much more to see. I clicked off the torch to save the batteries and gazed over at the door in the far wall. It was at the top of a short flight of wooden steps. Light was showing through the gaps between the door and the frame, and as I moved quietly towards it, I began to hear the murmur of voices. I tiptoed across to the steps and paused again, listening hard. The voices were low, but not whispered. Just the muffled sound of men talking. I heard the scrape of a chair . . . someone coughing, clearing their throat . . . a dull clink of glass on glass . . . more voices. I strained to catch what they were saying, but the sound was still too muffled. All I could tell was that there were at least two of them, possibly three.

I moved slowly up the steps. One at a time, keeping to the edges where the wood was more solid, letting my weight down gently . . . one cautious step at a time . . .

There was a small platform at the top of the steps, bounded with wooden railings. I lowered myself to the platform, sat down, and shuffled across to the door. It was an old panelled door, badly hung, with uneven gaps at both the top and the bottom. There was no lock, just a loose-fitting handle . . . but next to the handle, where I guessed the lock used to be, or where at one time it was supposed to be, there was a lock-sized hole in the door. A three-inch square, crudely hacked out with a chisel, it was almost dead level with my eyes. All I had to do was shuffle a little closer, lean my head slightly to one side, and I was looking through into the dimly lit room beyond the door.

It was a smallish room, much smaller than the basement, with whitewashed brick walls, bare floorboards, and steps at the back leading up to another door. To my right, flames were crackling in an open furnace. In front of the furnace, three men were sitting at a wooden table. One of them was Lloyd, another was the brute from the fishing boat, and although I'd never seen the third man before, there was no doubt in my mind who he was. Sitting at the head of the table, a brandy glass in one hand and a small cigar in the other, it was obvious both from his demeanour and that of the other two towards him that he was Ivan Tait. Dressed in wealthily casual clothes – a cashmere cardigan over an open-necked Tattersall shirt – he had a thickish mop of white-blond hair, a naturally tanned complexion, perfect white teeth, and the grizzled good looks of a well-aged man of means. He was probably in his early sixties, maybe a little older, but there was nothing remotely elderly about him. He was just what he was: rich, powerful, hard-headed, ruthless.

I could hear him talking now, and when he said to the Brute, 'Where were you?' and the Brute replied, 'On the boat,' I recognised the voice. The Brute from the boat was Mott, the man who'd been with Tait and Stevie in the caravan.

'Did you see what happened?' Tait asked him.

'Yeah, it was just like Lloyd said. He was just trying to get the camera off him, and he went a bit crazy, so Lloyd cracked him one. And then he saw the girl and the mother running off and he went after them.'

'I was only trying to stop them,' Lloyd added. 'I wouldn't have—'

'Shut up,' Tait told him, still looking at Mott. 'You saw what Garrow did?'

Mott nodded. 'The man with the camera was still on the ground. Garrow went up to him, leaned down and said something, and then he just picked up a big lump of driftwood and hammered it down on the poor bastard's head.' Mott took a swig from a bottle of beer, shaking his head at the memory. 'I couldn't fucking believe it.'

'Did he say anything about it afterwards?' Tait asked, looking from Mott to Lloyd. 'Did he say *why* he did it?'

'Not really,' Lloyd said.

'Didn't you *ask* him, for fuck's sake?'

Lloyd shrugged. 'He said he just felt like it.'

'That's it? He just *felt* like it?'

'Yeah.'

Tait sighed. 'All right . . . so you get the girl and the woman, and you drag them back over to Garrow . . .'

'If I'd known what he'd done to the guy, I would have kept them away.'

'Right, but you didn't.'

'Well, no—'

'And when they saw what he'd done, they just lost it. Is that right?'

'Yeah, they were hys*ter*ical, you know – screaming and howling and everything. I mean, the guy was a fucking mess, his head smashed in, blood and stuff all over the place . . . and Garrow was just standing there with the bloodied lump of wood in his hand, smiling. And the woman just went for him . . . I mean she really fucking *went* for him.' Lloyd shook his head. 'I couldn't keep hold of her. She was like a wild animal.'

'And Garrow put her down too.'

Lloyd nodded. 'Like I said, she ran at him, screaming and spitting like a crazy woman, and he just stood there, cool as you like, and at the last moment, just before she reached him, he swung the lump of wood at her head. She was dead before she hit the ground. Garrow still hit her again though, just to make sure.'

Tait leaned across the table and stubbed out his cigar in an aluminium ashtray. 'Why the fucking hell didn't you stop him?' he said to Lloyd.

'I couldn't, could I? I mean, what was I supposed to do? I had my hands full trying to keep hold of the girl . . . and I didn't know Garrow was going to whack the woman, did I? And even if I did, I couldn't have stopped him anyway.'

'You knew what he was going to do with the girl though, didn't you?'

'I tried to reason with him then. I *told* him it was stupid, there was no need for it—'

'But there was, wasn't there?' Tait said coldly. 'The girl had just witnessed him killing her parents. He had to get rid of her, didn't he?'

Lloyd looked puzzled, not sure why Tait was suddenly seeming to approve of Garrow's actions. 'That's not what he said,' Lloyd muttered. 'Garrow, I mean . . . he didn't say anything about her being a witness.'

'Really?'

'He told me that he wasn't going to hurt her. He promised. He just said that she was in shock, and that she needed help, and that he knew how to calm her down.'

Tait smiled. 'And you believed him?'

'I don't know . . . I mean, you know what he's like. He can be really . . .'

'Persuasive?'

'Yeah.'

'So you just gave her to him?'

Lloyd looked down. 'Yeah.'

'And he calmed her down.'

'Fucker just broke her neck.'

It was hard to tell what Lloyd was really thinking. He seemed genuinely upset about something, but whether it was remorse for what Garrow had done, or just annoyance at the fact that *he* was now having to answer for it, I wasn't really sure. Not that it mattered. And even if it *was* remorse . . . well, fuck him. Remorse is nothing, it means nothing. Remorse, guilt, shame . . . they're all the same: false emotions for false people. You don't feel them, you show them. And you only show them if you're caught doing something wrong and you want to be forgiven.

That's not emotion, it's manipulation.

Tait was talking again now.

'. . . yeah, I know all about that. It was me who had to sort it with Boon, and that's going to fucking cost me as well.' He shook his head, turning to Mott. 'Did you get rid of everything?'

Mott nodded. 'We took them out to the mudflats across from the Point.'

'All of them?'

'We had to go back for the girl later that night, but yeah . . . they're all out there, they're gone. I mean, nothing ever comes out of the flats.'

'What about Ballard?'

'Yeah, he's down there too. You don't have to worry about—'

'Don't fucking tell *me* what I have to worry about.'

'I didn't mean—'

'What do you think's going to happen when Ballard doesn't report in? You think customs are just going to *forget* about him? And the Americans too . . . I mean, we're not talking about some homeless junky or fucked-up crack whore who no one gives a shit about, this is an entire *family*, for Christ's sake. Father, mother, daughter . . . they're going to have relatives, neighbours, work colleagues, friends. And when they don't show up when and where they're supposed to, someone's going to call the police. And eventually the police will find out that they were here, and they'll come looking for them.' Tait stared at Mott. 'So pretty soon the whole fucking island's going to be swarming with customs and police. You think that's nothing to worry about?'

'Well, no . . . but you know people, don't you? I mean, you've got contacts—'

'You don't get it, do you?'

'What?'

Tait sighed. 'It's not a question of *whether* I can sort it out or not, it's a question of cost. Time, money, energy . . . I mean, I've got a fucking business to run. I've got deals lined up, places to go, things to do . . . I don't have *time* for this shit.' He angrily shook his head. 'Fucking Garrow . . . I mean, Christ, why did he have to do that to Ballard? What was he fucking *thinking*?'

'At least he got him to talk,' Lloyd said.

Tait glared at him. 'What?'

Lloyd shrugged. 'I'm just trying to look at the positives.

I mean, if Garrow hadn't found out about Ballard, if he hadn't got him to talk, we wouldn't have found out about Ransom and the girl, would we? We wouldn't have known that customs were on to us.'

'What do you think I am?' Tait said.

Lloyd frowned. 'I don't—'

'You think I'm stupid?'

'No . . .'

'You think I don't *know* what customs are doing? Of *course* I fucking know. I know exactly what they're doing. I know more about their investigation than Ransom *or* Ballard. I've known about it for the last three years. It was all under control, there *wasn't* anything to worry about. It was all going to plan until Garrow started killing people and cutting their fucking heads off. I mean, shit . . . why would he *do* that? What's the fucking *point*?'

'I don't think he meant to kill him.'

'Oh, I *see*,' Tait said sarcastically. 'It was just an accident, was it? He just *accidentally* took off his head with a fucking chainsaw—'

'Well, no . . . I mean, he didn't mean to kill him at first, he just wanted to get him to talk . . . but then . . . I don't know . . . I suppose he got a bit carried away.' Lloyd shrugged again. 'The thing with the head . . . Garrow only thought of that afterwards. He just thought it'd be a good idea, you know . . .'

'A good idea?'

'A good way to fuck with Craine's head.'

'And you went *along* with that?'

'No . . . well, yeah, but only—'

'I don't want to know,' Tait said, holding up his hands. 'Really, I can't listen to this shit any more. It's fucking pathetic.' He glared at Lloyd and Mott. 'Both of you should have known better. You should have come to me straight away—'

'We didn't want to bother you—' Mott started to say.

'Where's Garrow now?' Tait said.

'I don't know. I haven't seen him for a while.'

Tait looked at Lloyd.

Lloyd shook his head. 'I went to his houseboat a few hours ago, but he wasn't there.'

'Are the phones still out?' Tait asked, topping up his brandy glass.

Lloyd pulled a mobile from his pocket and checked the screen. 'Yeah, still nothing.'

'What time is it?'

'One fifteen.'

Tait looked at Mott. 'How long before the tide turns?'

Mott shrugged. 'It's hard to tell in this weather . . . it should be going out now, but it's probably going to be another hour or so.'

'Can you get the boat out?'

'What, now?'

'In a couple of hours.'

Mott thought about it. 'Well, I suppose . . .'

'I don't want you to *suppose*,' Tait said impatiently. 'I want to *know* if you can get the boat out in a couple of hours.

'Yeah,' Mott said. 'Yeah, of course.'

'Good.' He lit a cigar. 'All right, listen . . .'

I'd been concentrating so hard on listening to them – trying to understand what it all meant, and hoping all the time that one of them would say something about Robyn, so I'd know where she was and if she was still OK or not – that I hadn't given any thought to anything else. And it was only then that I remembered that my mobile had a voice recorder, and as I fumbled the phone out of my pocket and started searching through the menu, I was cursing myself for being such a fucking idiot. How many times over the last few days had I bemoaned the fact that I didn't have any proof of anything? And now, at last, when I'm finally in a position to get all the proof I need, I forget to do anything about it.

Call yourself a private detective?
You're not very good at it, are you?

I found the voice-recorder function, turned it on, and held the phone as near to the hole in the door as I could. I'd never used the function before – I use a specialised digital recorder when I'm working – so I didn't know if it would pick up the voices from here, or how much recording time it had, and I realised that I'd probably already missed most of the important stuff anyway, but I thought it was still worth a try.

Tait was talking to Lloyd again now.

'. . . and while Mott's getting the boat out, I want you to find Garrow, all right? I don't care how you do it, how many people you use . . . whatever it takes, just find him. And don't let him know there's anything wrong, OK? Just tell him that I need to see him, it's really important . . . whatever. Have you got that?'

'Yeah.'

'If he asks you what's going on, why I need to see him, just act dumb. You don't know anything about it. You got a call from me, I said I needed to see him, that it was really urgent, and that's it. That's all you know.'

'OK.'

'You'd best take one of the Range Rovers.'

'Right.'

Tait looked at his watch. 'And don't worry if you pass Boon's Land Rover coming this way when you're driving back. I'm expecting him.'

'Boon?'

'He's bringing Linda Ransom out here.'

'What for?'

Tait smiled. 'She's been working undercover too long, living a double life . . . she was lonely, confused, she got too close to the people she was supposed to be investigating, and in the end she went too far, becoming sexually entangled with both the leader of the drug-smuggling gang, Ian Garrow, *and* his second-in-command, Stevie Haynes, who was also the boyfriend of her informant, Robyn Mayo. And when Garrow found out about Linda and Stevie, it drove him over the edge, and he lost control of his mind, slaying a family of American tourists, and killing and mutilating one of Linda's colleagues.' Tait puffed on his cigar, grinning at Lloyd and Mott. 'How does that sound so far?'

They didn't answer, they just looked confused.

'Fuck's *sake*,' Tait sighed, exasperated, 'it's not *difficult*. We get Garrow out here, we tell him we're taking Ransom and Robyn out on the boat to get rid of them, OK?'

Mott nodded uncertainly.

Tait went on. 'You put Ransom and Robyn in the hold, take the boat a couple of miles out to sea, then you give Garrow a knife or a fucking axe or something and you get him to go down and do whatever he wants to the girls. And when's he's done with them, you kill him. Shoot him in the head, then wipe the gun and leave it in his hand. Then all you've got to do is leave everything as it is – the boat, the bodies – then get in the inflatable and fuck off.'

'Right . . .' said Lloyd, scratching his head. 'So we just leave the boat to drift . . .'

'Yeah . . . actually, it might be an idea to leave a key of coke in the hold too. Just to make it look good.'

'And what happens when the boat's eventually found?'

Tait shrugged. 'There'll be a murder investigation. The police will start looking into everything, trying to work out who the bodies are, what happened, who killed who, and why . . . and meanwhile we start spreading the story about Ransom and Garrow, maybe plant some kind of evidence to support it, get Stevie to confirm that he was fucking Ransom . . . I mean, we don't have to make it all watertight or anything. As long as it's reasonably believable, I can persuade the right people to buy into it.' He put out his cigar. 'Is there anything that links Garrow to the Americans?'

'What do you mean?'

'Anything we could leave with his body that would connect him to them.'

Lloyd frowned. 'Like what?'

'I don't fucking know, do I? I wasn't there when he killed them. That's why I'm asking you.'

'Oh, right,' Lloyd said. 'Yeah, I see what you mean. Well, I can't really think of anything . . . apart from the phone—'

'Whose phone?'

'The girl had a mobile. She was taking pictures of the boat, and she took one of me when I hit the guy, and maybe a few more—'

'And where's the phone now?'

'Craine had it.'

'*What?*'

'Craine had it.'

'How the fuck did *he* get it?'

'I don't know, but it's all right, we got it back.'

'When?'

'Sunday night.'

'And where is it now?'

'Garrow got rid of it, chucked it in the sea.'

Tait sighed. 'And what if Craine told someone about the pictures? Did you think of that?'

'Well, no . . .'

'He could have downloaded them, copied them, emailed them . . . I mean, Jesus *Christ*, what's the *matter* with you?'

Lloyd lowered his eyes.

'All right,' Tait said quietly. 'Don't worry about it now. Just go and find Garrow.'

Lloyd stood up. 'What about Craine? Do you want me to find him too?'

Tait shook his head. 'Just get Garrow.'

I watched Lloyd leave, slouching out through the door

at the back of the room and then I glanced at the screen of my mobile. The voice recorder had stopped, run out of time, I guessed. I slipped the phone into my pocket.

'Are you all right with this?' Tait said to Mott.

'Yeah.'

'I'll buy you another boat.'

'OK.'

'The police will want to talk to you when they find out the boat's yours. Just tell them that Garrow stole it.'

Mott shrugged. 'It's not registered in my name anyway.'

'No? So who owns it then?'

'My old man.'

'I thought he was dead?'

'He is.'

Tait smiled. 'You realise we're going to have to close everything down now, don't you? I mean, we can't bring in stuff through the island any more.'

Mott looked at him. 'I got the feeling that you were going to close it all down anyway.'

Tait nodded slowly. 'I'll probably still run most of the cash through here, but I've been wanting to move everything else to Harwich for a long time. It's just a matter of getting the infrastructure sorted out. Once that's ready . . . well, I'm going to need someone I can trust to run things on the ground.'

'Yeah?'

'You'd probably have to move.'

'To Harwich?'

Tait nodded. 'What do you think?'

'Do I get a new house as well as a new boat?'

'I don't see why not.'

'All right, I'll think about it.'

'Don't take too long.'

Mott got to his feet. 'I'd better get going.'

'How long do you think you'll be?'

'Hour and a half, maybe.'

'Right.'

Mott went out, and as Tait just sat there, thoughtfully sipping his brandy and puffing away on his cigar, I knew that if I was going to do anything, I had to do it now. Robyn was here somewhere, presumably locked away in a room, maybe tied up, or doped up, and right now the only thing between me and her was Tait. Boon would be arriving with Linda sometime soon, and I guessed that he wouldn't come on his own, so if I wanted to get Robyn out of here, I had to act now.

I didn't like the idea of not helping Linda, and I wished now that I'd brought Stevie's shotgun with me. I'd thought about it before leaving the trailer, but in the end I'd decided that it was too much of a risk. If someone had seen me stumbling around the caravan park in the middle of the night with a shotgun . . .

I should have taken the risk, I thought now. *If I had the shotgun, I could probably get Robyn and Linda out of here . . .*

But I didn't have it.

I was pretty sure that I could still deal with Tait though, and as I quietly got to my feet, wincing at the creak of pain in my knees, I was already running things through in my mind – open the door, move quickly over to the table, grab the brandy bottle, smash it, grab Tait, hold the broken bottle to his face, get him to tell me where Robyn is . . .

I put my hand to the door, took a breath, and was about to push it open when I heard a noise from the room – a door opening, then footsteps and voices coming in . . .

Get over there . . . watch her, will you?

Evening, Geoff. Thanks for coming.

I didn't have much fucking choice, did I?

I crouched back down to the hole in the door and saw Boon crossing the room towards the table. He didn't look very happy. Behind him, Gorman was standing beside Linda, holding her arm. Her hands were cuffed, her face was blank. Another man was leaning against the steps, smoking a cigarette, idly gazing around. He was heavy, thickset, his head shaved . . . I didn't recognise him.

'I don't like this, Ivan,' Boon said, shaking Tait's hand. 'I really don't like it at all.'

Tait smiled. 'I'm not paying you to *like* it, Geoff. I'm paying you to do it. But if you want out now, no problem. I'm sure Phil wouldn't mind taking over—'

'I'm not saying I want out, I'm just saying—'

'Is it still raining out there?'

'What . . . ? Yeah, yeah, it's pissing down . . .'

I looked over at Linda. She was a bit of a mess – rain-soaked, dishevelled, her hair all over the place – but I couldn't see anything physically wrong with her. No cuts or bruises. She wasn't struggling or anything, she was just standing there, staring straight ahead, tight-lipped and seemingly emotionless.

377

I straightened up again and slowly backed away from the door, rapidly trying to reassess my options. There didn't seem to be a lot to choose from. I could either get the hell out of there and go looking for help, or I could do something myself. The first option was hardly worth thinking about – the island was cut off, there was no mobile reception, and there was no one I could trust to help anyway. But Tait wasn't the only thing between me and Robyn now, there were four of them, and even if I *could* get to the table and arm myself with a broken brandy bottle before one of them got to me, which I doubted, I couldn't see myself getting much further with just a broken bottle.

I needed something else.

I needed a gun.

I slipped off my shoes and started scurrying around the basement, trying to find one of the long wooden crates with the Russian lettering I'd seen in the trailer. I was fairly sure I'd seen a couple in the cavern at the other end of the tunnel, but I didn't want to have to go all the way back there if I didn't have to. After I'd spent a few minutes looking round the basement though, I realised I was going to have to go back. There was nothing in the basement apart from fruit and vegetables – no drugs, no contraband, no guns.

'Shit,' I whispered, slipping my shoes back on.

I went over and glanced through the hole in the door again. They were all still there, just standing around, drinking brandy, smoking, talking . . .

I tiptoed back down the wooden steps and crossed over to the heavy wooden door that led through into the tunnel.

I was lost in thought as I pushed it open, trying to picture all the boxes and stuff in the cavern, trying to remember where I'd seen the long wooden crates, and as I hurried through the doorway, I didn't even see the figure standing in front of me until I'd almost run into him.

'Ah, there you are,' he said breezily.

I froze, looking up suddenly at Garrow's smiling face.

I don't know where he hit me, or how, I just remember his hand shooting out towards my head, a flash of blinding white pain, and then nothing.

29

I have a very vague – and quite possibly imagined – recollection of drifting awake for a few moments and seeing lights passing by overhead, and then I think I realised it wasn't the lights that were moving, it was me . . . and that, for some unfathomable reason, I was lying on my back. And it's possible that I thought I was on some kind of trolley, being pushed along some kind of corridor, perhaps a hospital corridor, but it's also possible that this only occurred to me later.

I remember trying to move my head, and realising that I had no idea how to actually do it, and I think I might have groaned . . . and then a grubby white cloud came down from nowhere and settled its weight on my face, and I breathed in a pungently sweet smell of chemicals, and dropped down into the darkness again.

The next time I began drifting awake, I could feel the familiar sensation of movement again, but this time it felt very different. It somehow felt further away from me, not directly connected to me . . . as if I was *in*, rather than *on*, the thing that was moving. I lay still, keeping my eyes closed, and listened.

An engine was chugging away somewhere . . . a steady

puttering sound. Boards were groaning, creaking . . . I could hear the gentle lap of waves. I could smell petrol, oil . . . the sea. I was lying on a wooden floor, on my side, my head resting on something that smelled faintly of tar.

My head hurt like hell, my mouth and my throat were incredibly dry, and I felt sicker than I'd felt in a long time. I didn't really doubt that I was in the hold of the fishing boat, but I'd made so many stupid mistakes recently that I wouldn't have been surprised if I was making another, no matter how certain I was. So I didn't move, I just kept perfectly still, and very cautiously opened my eyes.

Darkness . . . absolute darkness.

I listened.

Nothing . . . the chugging engine, the creaking boards, the lapping sea . . .

I carried on listening.

After a while, I heard a small movement nearby – a quiet scuffing sound. Another few moments of silence, another faint scuff of movement . . . and then someone sniffed – a moist, snotty, tearful sniff – followed by a long weary sigh, another quick sniff, and then I heard the mutter of a familiar voice.

'Shit . . . what a fucking mess . . .'

'Robyn?' I said quietly.

The pale light of a torch came on, about six feet away from me, lighting up the cramped confines of the hold, and I looked across and saw Robyn and Linda sitting on the floor next to each other, both leaning back against the wall.

'John!' Robyn said, her face lighting up. 'Thank *God* . . . I thought you were in a fucking coma.'

I smiled at her. 'You swear too much.'

She laughed, getting to her feet and coming over to me.

I glanced at Linda. 'Are you OK?'

She nodded.

I nodded back and turned to Robyn as she squatted down beside me. 'Hey, bruv,' she said, ruffling my hair. 'How's it going?'

A wonderful sense of warmth surged through me then, a rush of tenderness the like of which I hadn't felt for a very long time, and as I felt it spreading into my head and tingling at the backs of my eyes, it was suddenly all too much.

A sweet chemical nausea rose up in my throat, and there was nothing I could do but lean over and retch it all up on the floor.

'Sorry about that,' I said, sitting up and wiping my mouth. 'I never did like boats.'

'At least you're not dead,' Robyn said. 'Tait told me that Stevie was going to whack you with enough skag to kill a fucking horse . . .'

'I talked him out of it.'

'Really?'

I nodded.

She grinned. 'It would have been just my fucking luck, wouldn't it? I find out that I've got a long-lost big brother, and then ten minutes later I find out that he's dead.'

'Half-brother,' I corrected her.

'Half's good enough for me.'

I smiled. 'How are you doing anyway? I mean, you know . . .'

'Yeah, I'm all right. They gave me another hit when we got to the shop to keep me quiet . . . I'm fucking floating.' She looked around, smiling sadly. 'Good job, really. I just hope they do whatever they're going to do with us before it wears off and I start crawling up the walls.'

I looked over at Linda. 'How long have we been on the move?'

'Not long . . . five, ten minutes.'

'Are you all right?' I asked her again.

She sighed. 'Yeah, I'm fine. Just really pissed off, I suppose . . . I mean, I knew that Boon and Gorman were in Tait's pocket, but I thought he was just paying them to look the other way and keep their mouths shut. I didn't think the bastards actually *worked* for him.' She shook her head in disgust. 'They fucking arrested me . . . they came round to my flat with some big fucking bruiser and they *arrested* me . . . they put me in *cuffs*, for Christ's sake—'

'Yeah, all right,' I said, slightly irritated. 'We're all pissed off, OK? We've all had a hard time. But feeling sorry for yourself isn't going to get us out of this, is it?'

Linda glared at me. 'If it wasn't for you—'

'Yeah, I know,' I said wearily. 'If it wasn't for me, none of this would have happened, would it? No one would have died, we wouldn't be here . . . everything would be just fucking wonderful.'

'I didn't mean it like that,' Linda said quietly. 'I just meant—'

'Why didn't you tell me about the tunnel?' I asked her. 'You must have known it was there. You must have known how they'd hidden Chelsey's body—'

'Look, I'm sorry, OK? But if I'd told you everything, it might have compromised our investigation. I couldn't let that happen.'

'It wouldn't have made any difference,' I said.

'What do you mean?'

I sighed. 'Tait knows about everything anyway. He always has. You, Robyn, Mark, the entire operation . . . he's known about it all along.'

Linda shook her head. 'That's not possible . . . how could he know?'

'Money,' I said simply. 'Everyone has their price.'

'Yes, but—'

'And I wouldn't be surprised if it was Tait who set up Robyn as your informant in the first place.'

Linda shook her head. 'That's ridiculous.'

'Yeah, well, it doesn't matter anyway, does it? Not now.' I looked around the hold. 'All that matters now is working out how we're going to get out of here.'

'Where do you think they're taking us?' Robyn said.

I looked at her. 'I don't suppose you've got a cigarette, have you?'

She shook her head. 'They took everything off us – cigarettes, lighters, phones . . .'

I went through my pockets, hoping they might have missed something, but Robyn was right. They'd taken everything.

'All right, listen,' I said. 'We haven't got much time . . .'

I quickly ran through what Mott and Lloyd were planning to do with us. While I was talking, I got to my feet and looked around the hold. It was fairly cramped, just about big enough to walk around without stooping, and it didn't take long to realise that there was very little in there. A pile of folded tarpaulin sheets, some sacking, a box full of old engine parts, a coil of dusty nylon rope hanging from a nail in the wall . . . and that was about it.

When I'd finished explaining our situation to Linda and Robyn, neither of them said anything for a while, they both just sat there in the semi-darkness, quietly digesting what I'd told them. While I waited for them to say something, I went over to the far end of the hold and looked up at a wooden hatch in the ceiling. I knew it would be locked from the outside, but I reached up and gave it a shove anyway.

It was locked.

'Where's the coke?' Robyn said.

'What?'

'You said they were going to leave a key of coke in the hold to make things look better.' She gazed around. 'There's no coke down here.'

'Christ, Robyn,' Linda said. 'Is that all you can think about?'

'I wasn't thinking of it like *that*,' Robyn said. 'I was just wondering if it meant anything, that's all. You know . . . maybe it means they've changed their plan.'

'Oh, right,' Linda muttered. 'Sorry . . . I'm just . . .' She shook her head, annoyed with herself, and looked at me. 'What do you think, John? Did it sound to you like the cocaine was an integral part of the plan?'

'Not really,' I said, sitting down next to Robyn. 'It was more as if Tait was just thinking out loud. He probably just decided that we weren't worth wasting a kilo of coke over.' I shrugged, looking at Robyn. 'I don't think it means anything.'

'Yeah,' Robyn said, 'you're probably right—'

'But they *do* have to change their plans though, don't they?' Linda said suddenly, looking at me. 'You weren't supposed to be here, were you? Tait thought you were dead.'

'So?'

'Well, he set it all up to make it look as if there was something going on between Garrow, Robyn, and me . . . that's right, isn't it?'

'Yeah, but—'

'Garrow kills us, then they kill Garrow and make it look like suicide, and it all makes some kind of sense. That's how it was *supposed* to be . . . but now they're going to have to account for you.'

'Right . . .' I said doubtfully. 'And what difference does that make?'

'What difference?'

'Yeah . . . I mean, as far as I can tell, it just means that Garrow has to kill me as well as you and Robyn. Which doesn't really help us all that much.'

'But their story won't make sense any more, will it? Not with you on the boat. How are they going to explain that?'

'I'm sure they'll think of something.'

Robyn said, 'It doesn't matter though, does it? Whatever story they come up with, we're still going to end up dead.'

I paused for a moment, listening to the sound of the boat's engine. I thought I'd heard it change, a slight lowering

386

in tone, as if the boat was slowing down . . . but after listening for a while, it seemed to be chugging away quite steadily, so I guessed I must have been mistaken. 'Do you know who's actually on the boat?' I asked Linda. 'Is it just the three of them?'

'I only actually saw Lloyd and Garrow,' she said, 'but I could hear Mott in the cabin, and I *think* I heard him talking to the big bald guy who was with Boon.'

'Yeah,' Robyn agreed. 'He's definitely up there. I saw him when they were putting us down here.'

'The big guy, you mean?'

'Yeah.'

'Right, so there's four of them, and at least one of them's got a gun.'

Linda said, 'I suppose we have to assume that Garrow doesn't suspect anything.'

I thought about that for a while, then shook my head. 'I can't see how he'd know what they're planning. He couldn't have overheard anything, not from where he was, and even if he'd come into the basement while I was listening at the door, and I'm pretty sure he didn't, he still wouldn't have been able to hear anything. So unless one of them's told him, or he's somehow worked it out himself, I really don't see how he could know.'

'And if he did,' Robyn added. 'He probably wouldn't be up there, would he?'

We all just sat there for a while then, thinking quietly in the now-flickering light of the torch, and although I tried to concentrate on the only thing that mattered – working out how to stay alive – my mind kept drifting away . . .

and after a while I realised that I couldn't seem to think about anything. I was too tired. I hadn't eaten for God-knows how long. My head hurt. I needed a cigarette. I needed a drink . . .

'Why don't we just jump him?' Linda said.

I looked blearily at her. 'What?'

'Garrow . . . when he comes down here, why don't we just jump him? You know, get him before he gets us. There's three of us, only one of him. I know he'll probably have a knife, but they won't give him a gun, will they? And there's got to be something down here we can arm ourselves with . . .' She got up, went over to the box of old engine parts, got down on her knees, and started rummaging through it. 'They left this shitty old torch in here, didn't they? There might be something else in here, a chisel or a file or something. I mean, I know there's a good chance that he'll still get one or two of us, but it's worth a try, isn't it?' She pulled a rusty old cogwheel from the box, hefting it in her hand. 'If we all just go for him as soon as he shows himself—'

'There's no point,' I said.

She glared at me. 'We can't just give up, for Christ's sake.'

'I'm not giving up. I'm just saying—'

'What?' she snapped. 'You're just saying what?'

I sighed. 'We jump Garrow, yeah?'

'Right.'

'Knock him out, beat the shit out of him?'

She shrugged. 'Whatever it takes.'

'Then what?'

She looked at me, and I could see the realisation dawning in her eyes. Even if we could take out Garrow, it still wouldn't solve anything, not while the other three were still up there, one of them with a gun.

Linda didn't say anything, she just dropped the cogwheel back in the box, and then her shoulders slumped and she sank down dejectedly to the floor. As I gazed over at her, trying to think of something to say, my mind started drifting again, and I found myself thinking of Bryan and Ruth Swalenski . . . *we took them out to the mudflats across from the Point . . . and Chelsey . . . we had to go back for the girl later that night . . . and Mark Ballard . . . yeah, he's down there too . . .*

They'd all been down here, I thought, down in this lifeless black place . . .

'What if you told him?' I heard Robyn say.

I looked at her. 'Sorry?'

'When Garrow comes down, *tell* him that they're going to kill him . . . tell him everything you heard, the whole story. I mean, if he *knows* that once he's finished with us, they're going to kill him and frame him for everything . . . well, he'll try to do something about it, won't he?'

I nodded, thinking about it, trying to work out what Garrow would do. I looked over at Linda. 'What do you think?'

'Yeah . . .' she said cautiously. 'Yeah, it *might* work . . . but what's he going to do?'

'Well, if *I* was him,' Robyn said. 'And *I* found out that they were setting me up, I know what I'd do. I'd whack the fuckers.'

I smiled at her. 'You've got a lovely way with words.'

She grinned, a little embarrassed. 'You know what I mean.'

'But where's that going to leave us?' Linda said. 'Even if Garrow *does* get rid of the other three, he's not going to just let us go, is he? He's a killer, he's fucking crazy—'

'And he'll have a gun,' I added.

'It's still better odds though, isn't it?' Robyn said. 'If Garrow takes care of the other three, all we have to worry about—'

'No, hold on,' I said, suddenly thinking of something. 'He's not going to believe me, is he? As soon as I start telling him that he's being set up, that they're going to kill him, he's just going to think that I'm making it all up . . . he's not going to take my word for it, is he? Why should he?'

'There must be *some* way to convince him,' Linda said. 'Something Tait said . . . something that proves you're telling the truth—'

'Who searched you?' I asked her.

'What?'

I turned to Robyn. 'You said earlier that they took everything off us, emptied our pockets . . . who did it?'

'Does it *matter*?' Linda said.

I paused, listening to the engine again. It was definitely beginning to slow down now . . . and I could feel a change in the boat's direction. 'I haven't got time to explain,' I told Linda. 'Just tell me who searched you.'

'Gorman.'

I looked at Robyn.

'Mott,' she said.

'What did he do with the stuff he took from you?'

Robyn shrugged. 'I don't know . . .'

I turned back to Linda. 'What did Gorman do with your stuff?'

'I can't really remember,' she said. 'I think he just put it in his pockets . . . but I still don't see—'

'Listen,' Robyn said suddenly, looking upwards.

The engine was just idling now, puttering quietly as the boat began to drift, and in the relative silence we could hear the sound of footsteps creaking across the roof of the hold, moving towards the hatch.

'It's him . . .' Linda whispered. 'It's Garrow . . .'

The footsteps stopped.

We all stared at the hatch.

Another creak . . . a brief silence . . . then the rattle of a key in a lock . . .

As Linda started scrabbling around in the box of engine parts, I quickly stood up and helped Robyn to her feet. 'Just go over there,' I said calmly, indicating the wall furthest away from the hatch. I smiled. 'Go on . . . you'll be all right.'

She looked at me for a moment, glanced up at the hatch, then went over to the wall.

'Turn off the torch, Linda,' I said, heading over to the hatch.

'I'm not—'

'*Now.*'

Just as the hold plunged into darkness, the hatch inched open above my head and the blinding white light of a powerful torch flooded in through the gap. I stepped to one side, shielding my eyes from the light, and squinted up at the hatch.

'Hello, John,' I heard Garrow say. 'How's it going down there?'

'Listen, Garrow,' I said, angling my head, trying to see his face. 'There's something you need to know—'

'Well, I'm sure you're right, John. There's always something we need to know, isn't there? Or maybe not . . . maybe it's better if we don't know everything—'

'You have to listen to me—'

'Have you ever wondered how it would feel if you knew, with absolute certainty, when you were going to die?'

'Tait's setting you up,' I whispered, mindful that the others might be in earshot. 'He told Mott and Lloyd—'

'You've got two minutes, John. How does that feel?' The blade of a machete appeared through the gap, light dazzling off the steel as Garrow waved it around. 'Two minutes,' he repeated, 'before I cut your fucking head off. So if there's anything you want to do down there, any dark desires you've never satisfied, any mortal sins you want to confess . . . well, now's the time, John.'

'Mott and Lloyd are going to kill you.'

He hesitated for just a moment. 'Two minutes . . . make the most of it.'

The machete disappeared, the torchlight went out, and the hatch started to close.

'Check my phone!' I whispered loudly.

The hatch paused, then slowly inched open again. The torchlight didn't come on, but I could sense Garrow looking down at me through the darkness.

'Have you got my mobile?' I said.

No answer.

I rubbed the back of my aching neck. 'If you've got it, or you know where it is, listen to what's on the voice recorder. But don't let the others hear it, OK?'

Still no answer.

'Just listen to it. What have you got to lose? If I'm lying . . . well, it doesn't make any difference, does it? But if I'm not . . .'

I stared up into the silence, trying to gauge his reaction, but all I could see was a vague glimmer of soulless eyes against a backdrop of drifting darkness. The boat, I realised, was motionless now, just bobbing gently in the swell of the sea. And the rain had stopped too. The hatch gently closed, and I heard the lock being fastened.

Footsteps creaked . . . fading away . . .

Then silence.

Linda turned the torch back on.

I looked over at Robyn. 'All right?'

She nodded.

'What now?' Linda said.

'Have you found anything useful in that box yet?'

Nothing much happened in the next few minutes. Even without the chugging sound of the engine, it was still quite difficult to make out any sounds from above, and although we could hear footsteps, and the occasional mutter of muted voices, it was impossible to pin anything down. I kept trying to imagine Garrow sloping off on his own somewhere to listen to the voice recorder on my phone, but for some reason I just couldn't picture it. And, of course, I knew that whether or not I could picture it had no bearing whatsoever on the possibility of it actually happening – just as the act of sitting on a pillbox could never guarantee that bad things weren't going to happen to me . . . although, saying that, I remembered now that I *had* neglected to sit on the pillbox on the first day I'd been here, and there was no denying that bad things *had* happened . . .

My mind was drifting again.

I forced myself to stop thinking about Garrow. Whatever he was doing up there, whatever was going on, it was all out of my hands. Garrow either had my phone or he didn't. He was either listening to the voice recorder or he wasn't. And if the sound quality wasn't good enough, or the recorder had run out at the wrong time . . . if all Garrow got to hear was the sound of my breathing and an inaudible conversation in the background . . .

There was nothing I could do about it now.

'Is this any good?' Linda said, pulling a broken screw-driver from the box.

'Maybe,' I said, going over to take a look. 'Let me see.'

She passed me the screwdriver. It was a cheap old thing, about six inches long, with a snapped blade and a broken handle.

'Anything else?' I asked her.

'Just this,' she said, showing me a rusty piston rod.

'That's better.'

She looked up at me. 'How long do you think we've got?'

'I don't know . . . it depends what happens up there.'

Robyn came over. 'Maybe they'll all kill each other.'

I smiled. 'Yeah, maybe . . . but then how would we get out of here? We'd be locked in from the outside.'

'Shit,' she grinned, 'there's always *something*, isn't there?'

'Whatever happens up there,' Linda said. 'Somebody's going to be coming down here, aren't they? If it's not Garrow, it'll be one of the others. Or all of them. We need to decide what to do. Presumably they'll use the ladder—'

'What ladder?' I said, glancing over at the hatch.

'The ladder they used to get us down . . . oh, right, you didn't see it, did you? It's just an old wooden ladder, a bit like a stepladder . . . but not one of those foldy-out things, just a straightforward ladder, you know? The kind you lean against the wall . . . what are you smiling at? I don't know anything about fucking *ladders*, do I?'

'But it's not a foldy-out one?'

'No,' she said, grinning. 'It's the kind you lean against the wall.'

'So to get down here,' I said, moving over to the hatch, 'you have to prop the hatch open, slide the ladder down, and lean the top of it against the hatchway?'

'Well, yeah . . .' She looked up at the hatch. 'But I suppose if you've got a gun, you could just lean through the hatchway . . . you wouldn't actually have to climb down at all. You could just sit up there and pick us all off, one by one.'

'Garrow wouldn't do that,' Robyn said.

'Why not?'

'Because he's a nasty cunt, that's why. He likes cutting people, especially women. He might shoot John, just to get him out of the way, but he's not going to pass up the chance to come down here and—'

She stopped suddenly and we all looked up as the sound of a shot rang out somewhere above us. It wasn't very loud, not much more than a cold dull *crack*, and for a moment I thought it might be something else, but then I heard the clomp of running footsteps and a sudden clamour of guttural shouts, followed almost immediately by two more explosive *cracks* in quick succession, and then a sharp cry of pain . . .

'*Jesus Christ*,' I heard Linda mutter.

The heavy footsteps stopped, and for a moment it was quiet.

Hey! someone shouted. *What the fuck—?*

Another two gunshots – *crack!crack!* – and this time one of them splintered through the wooden hatch and thwacked into the top of the far wall.

'Fucking *hell*!' Robyn cried.

'Get *down*,' I told her, plucking a splinter from my cheek. 'Over there . . . against the wall. Cover your face.' As I wiped a trickle of blood from my cheek, I suddenly knew what I had to do. It was probably too late, I realised, and it probably wouldn't work anyway, but I could see it . . . I could *picture* it . . .

I went over to Linda. 'Where's that screwdriver?'

She passed it to me.

We both flinched as another shot rang out.

'And the piston rod,' I said, holding out my hand.

'What about—?'

'Please?'

She reluctantly passed me the heavy eight-inch steel rod. I quickly examined it. One end was a solid shaft, thick with rust, roughly an inch in diameter. The other end was similar, but with a narrower barrel, about half an inch across, jutting out from the shaft. I leaned down and punched the narrow end into the side of the cardboard box.

'What the hell are you *doing*?' Linda said.

I looked at the hole the piston rod had left in the cardboard – a slightly ragged half-inch circle – and decided it would do.

'The shooting's stopped,' Robyn said.

I listened. She was right . . . no shots. But then I heard footsteps . . . slow, deliberate steps . . . moving diagonally, across the boat . . . and a voice, too muffled to make out. Another voice . . . further away . . . a pleading tone. Then someone laughing . . .

'Come here, Robyn,' I said quietly.

She got up and came over to me.

'That's Garrow, isn't it?' she said, gazing upwards. 'He's fucking *enjoying* himself—'

'Never mind what he's doing,' I told her. 'I need your help.'

She looked at me, her eyes blinking rapidly.

'Listen to me, Robyn,' I said, taking hold of her shoulders. 'We *can* get out of here, OK? We can do it. But I need you to stay focused . . . all right?'

She nodded.

'OK,' I said, glancing over at Linda. She was still sitting by the box, staring up at the sound of footsteps crossing the deck. They sounded as if they were moving away from us.

'Linda?' I said quietly.

She looked at me. 'Yeah, I'm listening.'

'All right . . .' I took a breath. 'Garrow's going to be coming down here any minute, and when he does, I'm going to be lying on the floor beneath the hatch. I want him to think I'm dead, OK?' I glanced up at the splintered hole in the hatch. 'I want him to think that I was standing here, and I got hit by that stray bullet . . . it caught me just here.' I pointed at the centre of my forehead. 'All right?'

Linda said, 'Well, yeah, but—'

'Garrow thinks I'm dead, he lets the ladder down, starts climbing down, and then—'

A piercing scream cut me off, and we all looked up again. The scream faded to the muffled sound of desperate sobbing, and then – after a moment's terrible silence – we heard the awful dull hack of steel on flesh, followed immediately by another cry of pain, shorter and weaker this time, and then another thumping hack, and another . . . and then the solid thud of a body hitting the deck.

'*Jesus* . . .' Linda whispered.

'Take this,' I said to Robyn, handing her the piston rod. She just looked at me.

'Take it,' I said firmly, putting the rod into her hands. 'Come on, Robyn, we're running out of time.'

She was gazing up again now, listening to the sound of the body being dragged across the deck.

'Robyn!' I snapped.

'Yeah, yeah . . . sorry—'

'Just do what I tell you, OK? Don't ask any questions, don't think about it, just do it. Do you understand?'

398

She nodded.

'You're going to jab that piston rod into my head, narrow end first, so it looks like I've got a bullet wound in my head, OK?'

She looked at the piston rod. 'You want me to hit you with this?'

'Yeah, just jab it into my head. Hold it like this.' I arranged the rod in her hands for her. 'Now lift it up, bring it back over your shoulder a bit . . . that's it, then give it a good hard jab into my head.'

'How hard?'

'Hard enough to make a hole in my skin, but not hard enough to crack open my skull.'

She shook her head. 'I don't know—'

A heavy splash sounded outside – the sound of a body going into the sea, followed by the creak of footsteps coming over towards the hatch.

'Just do it, Robyn,' I said, leaning my head towards her. I braced my neck, gritted my teeth, and closed my eyes. 'Now!'

She didn't hesitate, thank God. She just did it.

The impact rocked my head back, stunning me for a moment, and the sudden bolt of pain was so excruciating that I felt it all the way down to my stomach.

'*God*, John!' Robyn cried, steadying me with her hand. 'Are you all right?'

'Yeah . . . just a bit dizzy . . .' I cautiously put my hand to my head and felt the wound. 'How does it look?' I asked Robyn. 'Is there a hole?'

'Yeah . . .'

'Is it deep?'

'Quite deep.'

'Does it look anything like a bullet wound?'

'I don't know . . . I've never seen one—'

'Is it bleeding much?'

'Quite a lot, yeah . . .'

The footsteps had reached the hatch now.

I pulled the broken screwdriver from my pocket, squeezed my eyes shut, and stuck the broken end of the handle into the hole in my head. The pain as I gouged it around was almost unbearable, and I had to stop after a second or two when another wave of dizziness started washing over me . . .

But at least I could feel the wound throbbing now, the blood oozing out, streaming down my face.

A key rattled in the lock . . .

I took the piston rod from Robyn, grabbed her by the hand and dragged her over to the hatch with me. 'You're hysterical, OK?' I whispered quickly as I lay down on the floor beneath the hatch. 'I'm dead . . . I've been shot in the head . . . you're distraught, your brother's been killed, you're out of your mind with grief. OK?'

Robyn nodded.

I smiled at her.

The hatch was opening . . .

I lay face down with my head turned to one side, giving Garrow a reasonably good view of my gunshot head. I had the piston rod under my body, the broken screwdriver hidden in my right hand, and my left arm was sticking out awkwardly by my side, twisted at an unnatural angle.

As Robyn crouched down beside me and began sobbing and howling, I steadied my breath, closed my eyes, and made myself dead.

'What's all the fucking noise about down there?' I heard Garrow say, and even with my eyes closed I could sense the beam of his torch sweeping the hold.

'You *killed* him, you fucking *bastard*!' Robyn sobbed. 'Look what you've *done* . . . you've fucking killed him!'

'Killed who?' Garrow said, faintly irritated. 'What the fuck are you talking about?'

I heard the hatch opening further.

'You . . . you shot him—'

'What's John doing down there?' he said, his voice tinged with a mild curiosity. 'What's happened to him?'

'I just *told* you, you fucking idiot . . .'

Easy, Robyn, I thought. *Don't push it.*

'He was just . . . just standing here,' she went on, still sounding genuinely distressed. 'And a shot came through the hatch . . . and then he just . . .'

Garrow was quiet for a moment, and I guessed he was looking for the bullet hole in the hatch. I hoped he didn't study it too closely and realise that the angle didn't fit with what Robyn was telling him.

'Get out of the way,' I heard him say. 'Let me see him.'

Robyn didn't reply, she just carried on crying.

'Move,' Garrow said coldly. 'Or I'll put a hole in your fucking head too. And stop fucking crying, for Christ's sake.'

I felt Robyn moving away from me.

I felt the light of the torch on my head.

I held my breath and kept perfectly still.

'Well, shit . . .' Garrow muttered to himself. 'Look at that . . .'

If he was going to shoot me, just to make sure that I really *was* dead, now was the time. And as I lay there in the silence, just waiting for the crack of the gun, I could feel every cell in my body screaming at me to move, get out of the way, don't just fucking lie there . . . move! And just for a moment I found myself feeling strangely – and somewhat inappropriately – disappointed. I mean, how come my instincts were telling me to do the worst thing possible? Why couldn't they do something useful, something that would actually *help* me, like telling me to relax, just take it easy, everything's going to be all right . . .

'Well . . . that's a bit of a shame, isn't it?' I heard Garrow say eventually. 'The more the merrier and all that, but I suppose he would have just got in the way, wouldn't he? He'd have just been a . . . what do you call it? Wallflower? Is that the right word?'

Gooseberry, I thought.

'Party-pooper? Stick-in-the-mud? No, that's not it . . .'

Someone tell him it's fucking gooseberry.

'Anyway . . .' Garrow said, and I could hear him getting hold of the ladder now. 'We can still have some fun together, can't we? Are you all right over there, *Mizz* Ransom?'

'Fuck off,' Linda told him.

He laughed. 'You sound just like Mark. He was full of it too . . . showing me how brave and heroic he was.'

I heard the heavy clunk of the ladder knocking against the hatchway.

'Mind you,' Garrow went on. 'He wasn't quite so tough when I started cutting his fingers off . . . squealing like a baby, he was. Crying for his mummy.'

Another clonk . . . then the sound of wood sliding on wood.

'God, you're sick,' Linda told him.

'Yeah, I *know*,' Garrow said chuckling to himself. 'It's terrible, isn't it?'

I could hear him guiding the ladder down now.

'If you don't move right now, Robyn,' he said. 'I *will* shoot you, OK?'

I heard Robyn moving back again.

'That's it,' Garrow said. 'A bit more . . . OK. Now sit down.'

She sat down.

The ladder started moving again.

I waited, listening.

I almost flinched when the foot of the ladder hit my right ankle, but I just managed to control myself.

'Oops,' I heard Garrow say. 'Mind your foot there, John.'

Then, *clunk*, and the ladder was down.

A brief silence, then a shuffle of movement as Garrow got onto the ladder, and then he slowly began climbing down. I tried to imagine how I'd come down the ladder if I were him, and I guessed he'd want to be facing Robyn and Linda, in case they tried to jump him, so he'd probably come down with his back to the ladder, facing outwards, steadying himself with one hand, the gun in the other, the torch under his arm . . .

Cautious . . . but precarious.

He was coming down warily, one step at a time, the wooden rungs of the ladder creaking softly with his weight . . . and I was counting his steps now . . . *one* . . . *two* . . . *three* . . . trying to guess where he was on the ladder, and how many rungs it had, and when I should make my move . . . not too soon . . . *four* . . . *five* . . . not too late . . . *six* . . . *seven* . . .

The creaking paused.

He was on the seventh step down.

I heard him say, 'Who wants it first then?'

I kicked back with my right foot, slamming it into the ladder, and as I felt it giving way, I twisted round and lashed out at it with my left foot. For a moment or two the base of the ladder juddered and wobbled across the floor, and I looked up and saw Garrow desperately trying to keep his balance, and then the top of the ladder slipped through the hatch and everything came crashing down. I grabbed hold of the piston rod and rolled out of the way just in time, and as I scrambled to my feet I saw that Garrow had landed heavily on his back just a few feet away. He looked dazed, winded, but he still had the gun in his hand. The torch had fallen from under his arm and was rolling across the floor, the light looping and strobing around the hold, and as I went over to Garrow and kicked the gun from his hand, I saw a monstrous shadow of myself looming across the wall.

As Garrow groaned and tried to get up, at the same time reaching for the bloodstained machete in his belt, the monstrous shadow stepped over him, raised the piston rod, and smashed it into his head.

I remember feeling totally empty then, void of all natural emotion, and as I began pounding the heavy steel bar into Garrow's already lifeless skull, hammering it down as hard as I could, over and over again, the only other thing I can recall with any real clarity is a feeling of detached curiosity as I gazed down at the bloodied pulp on the floor and wondered how a thing such as that could ever have been a life . . .

I don't know how many times I hit him, but by the time Linda and Robyn dragged me away, there was nothing left of Ian Garrow.

30

We found Mott in the cabin. He had a gaping wound in the back of his neck, no doubt from Garrow's machete, and he'd been shot in the head from close range. The big bald man had been killed near the stern of the boat. He'd been shot three times: once in the stomach, once in the chest, and once in the back of the head. As far as we could tell, Garrow hadn't used the gun on Lloyd, he'd killed him with the machete alone. There was no way of knowing for sure, as most of Lloyd's body was floating face down in the sea about twenty feet from the boat. The lower part of his left arm was missing, and his head was bobbing up and down against his shoulder, his neck almost sliced in half.

'You need to sit down,' Linda said to me. 'You don't look too good.' She turned to Robyn. 'See if you can find something to stop the bleeding from his head. Don't wash the wound or anything, just keep something pressed to it, a clean cloth—'

'Yeah, OK,' Robyn nodded.

'I'm going to call the coastguard on the radio,' Linda said. 'They'll get us back to the island, and then we can get John to the hospital—'

'What about all this?' I said, gazing around the boat.

'What about Tait and Boon . . . what about Garrow? What are we going to do about—?'

'I'm calling it all in, John. It's the only way.'

I could think of another way – get in the inflatable, set light to the boat, burn it, sink it . . . just leave the whole fucking mess at the bottom of the sea – but I was too tired to say anything. I couldn't even manage a shrug. I just watched Linda head over to the cabin, and then I let Robyn lead me over to a low wooden bench bolted to the deck at the side of the boat.

'You sit down there,' she told me, 'and I'll just go and find something to—'

'Just a minute,' I said, wandering off towards the stern.

'Where are you going? John . . . ? Fuck's *sake* . . .'

I went over to where the bald man was lying, crouched down beside him, and went through his pockets. I couldn't remember if I'd seen him smoking, but he looked like a smoker . . . and he was. I took a packet of Mayfair Superkings and a lighter from his trouser pocket, straightened up, and went back over to Robyn.

'There you go,' I said, passing her a cigarette and sitting down.

'Thanks,' she said, handing me a strip of cloth that she'd torn from her shirt. 'I'm not sure how clean it is . . . just hold it to your head and keep it pressed down.'

I lit her cigarette, and one for myself, and then we just sat there, smoking quietly, looking out into the distance. The sun was just beginning to rise, its low dawn light creeping up over the black horizon, dappling the sea with a glimmering sheen of crimson. The faint cries of unseen seabirds drifted in the air, and from somewhere on the boat I could hear the soft jangle of rigging blowing in the breeze.

'How's your head?' Robyn asked quietly.

'It hurts,' I said, looking at her. 'How's yours?'

'I don't know . . . I mean, it doesn't *hurt*, but . . . well, you know . . .'

'You need a hit?'

She sighed. 'I'm starting to rattle a bit, yeah.'

'How long before it really kicks in?'

'I'll probably be OK for a while . . .' She looked at me. 'What's going to happen when we get back to the island?'

'I don't know . . . probably not much. Not for a while, anyway. Whoever Linda's calling in – the police, customs – they're not going to be able to get here until the flooding goes down, and we can't get off the island either, so I suppose we're just going to have to wait.'

'What about Tait and Boon?'

'Well, knowing Tait, he's probably already heard that Linda's just called the coastguard, and it won't take him long to realise what's happened. He'll be busy covering his tracks by now. Boon too, probably. I don't think we have to worry about them.' I looked at Robyn. She was sweating now, her hands trembling. She was jiggling her foot up and down. 'Have you got some stuff at home?' I asked her.

'A little bit . . .'

'You can't go to Stevie's place.'

'I wasn't *going* to.'

'I doubt if he'll be there anyway.'

'Good. I never want to see that fucker again.'

'Will you be all right? What will you do?'

'I don't *know*, do I? I'll just . . . I don't know . . .'

She was crying now.

I put my hand on her arm. 'It's all right . . . we'll sort something out, OK?'

'It's *not* all right,' she said quietly, wiping her eyes. 'It's fucking pathetic . . . I *hate* it. I hate the fact that I'm sitting here with you, and we've been through all this terrible stuff, and we nearly died, and so many others *have* died . . . and all I can think about is sticking a fucking needle in my arm . . . it's *not* all right, is it?'

I squeezed her hand.

She looked at me. 'I'm sorry. I didn't mean to—'

'It doesn't matter,' I said gently. 'You're my sister, OK? That's all that matters. Whatever you do, whatever you *want* to do . . . you'll always be my sister.'

She smiled through her tears. 'Yeah . . .'

'And I'll always look after you, OK. No matter what.'

She sniffed, wiped her nose, and grinned. 'Does that mean that I have to look after you too?'

'I'm afraid so.'

We sat there smoking for a while, and then Linda came over to tell us that the coastguards were on their way.

'They won't be long,' she said. 'Twenty minutes, half an hour at the most. I just need to make another call before they get here, all right?'

We watched her go back to the cabin, and then Robyn said, 'Do you think she'll tell them what you did to Garrow?'

'I can't really see how she can avoid it.'

'Are you worried?'

'Not really . . . not at the moment, anyway. I expect when I'm charged I might start worrying a bit.'

'But it was self-defence . . .'

'I didn't exactly restrict myself to a "reasonable use of force" though, did I?'

She shrugged. 'It seemed reasonable enough to me.'

'Yeah, well . . . we'll just have to wait and see, I suppose.'

'Are you going back to Hey?'

'If I can, yeah.'

'Have you got someone to go back to?'

I looked at her. She was clearly in quite a bad way now – twitching, shaking, sweating – and although I didn't really feel like talking any more, I guessed she needed all the help she could get to keep her mind off everything else.

'Well, have you?' she said.

'Have I what?'

'Have you got someone *special* to go back to in Hey? A wife, girlfriend . . . ?'

'Uh, well . . .'

'I'm sorry,' she said, suddenly annoyed with herself. 'It's none of my fucking business, is it?'

'No . . . no, it's all right. I was just . . .'

'You don't have to tell me anything. Really. I was—'

'My wife died a long time ago,' I said.

'Shit, I'm sorry—'

'There's a nephew I'm very close to, he's called Cal . . . well, he's my nephew-in-*law*, actually. But apart from that . . .'

'No family?'

'My mother died a few years after my father . . . *our* father.'

'Any other sisters or brothers?'

'No.'

'What about a girlfriend?'

'Well, there *was* someone . . . not really a girlfriend, as such. But I'm not sure what's going on with us any more.'

'What's her name?'

'Bridget.'

'Is she nice?'

'Yeah, very nice.'

'So what's the problem?'

'Well, it's kind of a long story . . .'

'I don't mind. I like long stories.'

I sighed, looking at her again. She was shivering, trembling all over, sweating in the cold dawn air. I took off my coat and draped it over her shoulders. Then I put my arm around her, drew her close, and as we sat there together watching the sun come up, I told her all about Bridget Moran.

411

31

By late Tuesday evening, the flooding on the Stand had begun to recede and local radio reports were estimating that the causeway would re-open to traffic between eleven o'clock and midnight. I'd been to the doctor's and had my head stitched up, and then Robyn had taken me back to her place for something to eat. She'd called Serina from the hospital to let her know that we were OK, and I guessed she must have told her at least something about what had happened, because Serina started asking all kinds of questions about it as soon as we got to the house. After giving her a big hug, and telling her to shut up for a minute, Robyn disappeared upstairs and didn't come down for a good five minutes or so. When she did come down, she didn't look so sick any more, and it was fairly obvious – to both me *and* Serina – what she'd been doing.

While Serina went into the kitchen to make some coffee, I made Robyn promise again that she wouldn't go anywhere near Stevie, or anyone who had anything to do with him. 'If you get really desperate,' I told her, 'just call me, and I'll get you some stuff.'

'Thanks,' she said. 'But I should be OK. I've got enough to keep me going for a couple of days, and I can always get what I need in Hey or Harwich if I need to. But I'm kind of thinking that it might be a good time to try quitting anyway.'

'Really?'

'Yeah . . .'

I smiled at her. 'That sounds like a good idea . . .'

Serina came back in then. 'What sounds like a good idea?'

Robyn gave me a sisterly smile.

After we'd eaten, I felt so tired that I could barely keep my eyes open. Robyn said that I could crash in her bed for a while if I wanted to, but I really needed some time on my own now, so I asked Serina if she could drive me to the hotel, and half an hour later I was back in my room, lying fully clothed on the bed, staring up at the ceiling. I thought I might be too tired – and too wired – to sleep, but as soon as I closed my eyes, I was gone.

It was around eight o'clock in the evening when Linda rang.

'Sorry if I woke you up, John,' she said. 'But I just wanted to let you know what's happening.'

What was happening, apparently, was that she'd spoken to her bosses and told them everything that had happened, including the fact that the customs investigation seemed to have been compromised, and high-level discussions were now taking place between HMRC and SOCA, the Serious Organised Crime Agency, to decide how best to proceed.

'And they want to talk to you, John, OK?'

'Just talk to me?' I said.

'For now, yes.'

'Do I need to call my solicitor?'

413

'That's up to you. But at the moment, you're just a witness.'

'Right . . . so I'd just be helping them with their enquiries.'

She sighed. 'Just talk to them, all right?'

'When?'

'I told them you needed some rest, so they've agreed to leave it until the morning. We'll pick you up from the hotel at nine. Does that sound all right?'

'I suppose so.'

'Good . . . how are you feeling, anyway?'

'Tired.'

'Well, get some sleep now, and I'll see you tomorrow.'

I spent the next hour on the phone to Cal – telling him the whole story, assuring him that I was fine, that I'd be back soon, asking him what he knew about SOCA – and then, after I'd sat on the bed smoking cigarettes for a while, I did what I should have done days ago.

I called Bridget.

My heart was beating hard as I keyed in her number, and as I put the phone to my ear and listened to the ringing tone, I felt exactly the same way I'd felt a few weeks ago when I'd visited Bridget at her pet shop . . . when I'd opened the door and stepped inside, and I'd seen her at the counter, wrapping up bags of greeny-brown pellets for a plump old woman in a threadbare fur coat . . . and when the bell over the door had sounded, and Bridget had stopped what she was doing and looked over at me and smiled . . . and just for a second I'd felt sixteen years old again – stupid and pure, a blue-eyed animal, wanting and needing only this moment . . .

414

'Hello?'

'Hey, Bridget,' I said, 'it's me, John.'

'*John*!' she said. 'Thank *God* . . . where have you *been*? I've been trying to get in touch with you for *ages*.'

It was such a relief just to hear her voice, and it felt so good to know that she at least wanted to talk to me, that all I could do was sit there, smiling stupidly to myself.

'John?' she said. 'Are you still there?'

'Yeah . . .' I said, clearing my throat. 'Yeah, I'm here—'

'Where *are* you?'

'Hale Island.'

'Hale? What are you doing *there*?'

'It's kind of complicated—'

'Why haven't you called me?'

'Well, I was going to . . . but I didn't know, you know . . .'

'What?'

'Well, you left the hospital without saying anything, and I just thought that maybe . . .'

'I didn't know what I was doing, John. I'm really sorry. I wasn't thinking straight . . . I feel really bad about it now. But I just had to get away, you know . . . I was really fucked up about everything, and I just had to go . . . I wished I hadn't. I'm sorry . . .'

'It's OK,' I told her – and it was, of course, it really was. 'I totally understand. I mean, I thought it might be something like that . . . but then I thought that if you wanted to talk to me, you'd get in touch when you were ready. That's kind of why I didn't ring you . . .'

'Oh, God,' she sighed. 'I've been ready for ages . . . I've been *trying* to get in touch, but I lost your number—'

415

'I gave it to you at the hospital. I wrote it down, remember?'

'Yeah, I know, but I left in such a hurry . . . I must have left it behind or lost it or something. And I didn't realise that I didn't have it until I got to my sister's. I called the hospital, but they couldn't find it, and when I tried your home number, I just kept getting the machine. I tried your office number too, I even went down there . . . but it was all closed up, and no one knew where you were—'

'Are you back in Hey then?'

'Yeah, I've been back since Friday.'

'At the house?'

'Yeah . . .' She sighed again. 'I really miss you, John.'

'I miss you, too.'

'I don't like being here on my own . . . it's too empty.' I heard her swallowing back tears. 'And it's so quiet, you know . . . I keep thinking I can hear Walter, his collar jangling, or his footsteps on the floor . . . and then I remember that he's not here any more, and I can't stop crying all the time . . .'

'Yeah, I know,' I said softly.

'Sorry . . .'

'It's all right.'

'When are you coming back?'

I paused for just a moment, thinking about something. 'Listen,' I said, 'I haven't got a car at the moment, so why don't you come down here and pick me up?'

'What, now?'

'Well, not *right* now. The causeway's flooded at the moment, but it should be open by midnight.'

'And then we'll go back to the house?'

'Yeah . . . or if you want, we could stay the night here, and then go back in the morning. I'm staying at a hotel called Victoria Hall. It's a bit of a rundown old place, but it's right next to the beach—'

'Yeah, I know it. I've always wondered what it'd be like to stay there.'

'We'd have to leave quite early in the morning,' I said, remembering my nine o'clock appointment with HMRC and SOCA. *Fuck them*, I thought to myself. *If they really want to talk to me, they'll just have to come and find me.* 'So,' I said to Bridget, 'what do you think? How would you like to spend the night with me in a spooky old hotel?'

She laughed. 'I'd like it very much.'

'Good. And while you're here . . . well, there's something . . . someone . . . no, it's all right. We can talk about it when you get here.'

'Talk about what?'

'The thing I just thought of . . .'

'*What* thing?'

'The thing we can talk about when you get here.'

'Is it a good thing?'

'It might be.'

'Will I like it?'

I was beginning to wonder now. 'It's just something . . . I don't know. It's just an idea, OK? Maybe I shouldn't have mentioned it . . .'

'You can't *un*mention it now.'

'I know . . .'

'It doesn't matter, John. Whatever it is . . . don't worry

about it, all right? Right now, I just want to be with you. Is that OK?'

'Yeah,' I said, 'it's very OK.'

When I headed off to reception a little while later, I was just in time to see Arthur Finch leading his three dogs across the lobby towards the hotel doors. I called out to him, he stopped, and I went over and joined him.

'I was just on my way out, John,' he said. 'The dogs like a good run on the beach in the evening.'

I looked down at Finn, the larger of the two young dogs, and as he looked back at me – smiling his dog-smile, bright-eyed and happy, his long tail looping gently from side to side – it wasn't difficult to imagine him sprawled out on the carpet in my room, in Bridget's room . . . in *our* room. What *was* difficult to imagine was how Bridget would feel about him. She was still mourning Walter, she might not be ready to think about having another dog . . . it might be too soon for her, too confusing, too distressing. On the other hand . . .

I turned back to Arthur. 'Do you mind if I come with you?'

'Not at all,' he said. 'It'd be a pleasure.'

As we went through the doors and then headed round the back of the hotel towards the beach, I said, 'Would it be OK if I walked Finn for a while?'

Arthur smiled and passed me Finn's lead. 'Second thoughts?'

'Maybe,' I said, stroking Finn's hefty head.

Just maybe.

418

Author's Note

Like all forms of traditional storytelling, crime fiction is constantly evolving. As time moves on, and the world changes with it, the tradition gives birth to new ideas, new styles, new angles. Some of these sub-genres take root and flourish, sometimes becoming healthy enough to produce new ideas and styles of their own, while others burst briefly into bloom and then almost immediately die out again, like desert flowers after the rain. But that's the whole point of evolution: if it works, it survives; if it doesn't, it dies.

So, in theory at least, we're left with all the good stuff, the stuff that works. And whatever comes out of that good stuff, as long as it's good enough itself, will hopefully give rise to even more good stuff. And although after many generations a particular form of crime story may bear little superficial resemblance to its distant ancestor, they will both necessarily share the same fictional genes. The works of Kathy Reichs, for example, have little in common with the novels of Wilkie Collins, but the stories of both authors are founded on the same simple construct that essentially defines all crime fiction: a crime is committed, someone sets out to solve it. And basically that's it. That's what all crime fiction *is*.

But in the same way that all blues music is based on the same, very simple, three chord progression, yet is still very much alive and still constantly developing after more than a hundred years, so crime fiction too has never been held back by the apparent simplicity of its original premise. There are just so many different ways to take it. What kind of crime is committed? Who commits it, and why? Can we feel any sympathy for the criminal? Is there really such a thing as pure evil? Who is going to solve the crime? And why? What kind of person are they? How do they relate to the world? How do they relate to the criminal? What is the nature of crime? What is the nature of cruelty? Of hatred? Of goodness? And the list goes on and on . . . the possibilities endless.

Just like the blues.

For me, one of the key developments in crime fiction is the type of novel that focuses not so much on the crime itself, and the riddle-like mystery of whodunnit, but instead uses the crime, and the solution of the crime, as a framework for the portrayal of a character, or a series of characters, and their environment. The criminal act is still at the heart of this kind of novel, but it's not the be-all and end-all. It's the catalyst, the prime mover, the thread that keeps the narrative going, but the crime itself is no longer the defining element of the novel. Indeed, sometimes, by the time we get to the end of this kind of story, it almost doesn't matter who did it, or why, or whether they got away with it or not. What matters, what the book is *really* about, is the people, their journeys, their lives, their worlds.

Of course, this kind of crime fiction is by no means new, in fact it could be argued that some of the earliest detective tales – the Sherlock Holmes stories, for example – are as much about the detective himself as they are about the crime, but it is a distinct strand within the genre, and it has evolved over the years, refining and re-inventing itself to produce what I consider to be some of the best fiction ever created by some of the finest story-tellers: Raymond Chandler, Dashiell Hammett, John D MacDonald, Ross Macdonald, Lawrence Block, James Lee Burke . . . to name just a few.

These authors write stories about people and places, about moralities, emotions, human behaviour. The stories are of their time, and they reflect those times, but they're also essentially timeless. And while each author writes in their own very distinctive style, using different means, different approaches, different methods of storytelling, there are shared elements in all their work that seem to me to be links in an evolutionary chain: the private investigator, the loner, the outsider, the troubled soul searching for a purpose; an intense sense of place, and the intrinsic relationship between an individual and that place; an individual's faith in their own personal morality over the moralities and values of others; and the constant struggle to understand and come to terms with all the vagaries of life and death and everything in between.

Evolution is not just a linear process though. It doesn't simply move things forward in a chronological line, it works in all kinds of different ways. Sometimes it doesn't change things at all, because nothing needs to be changed. Sometimes it branches out, heading off in new directions. And sometimes it moves back, adapting and revitalising traditional ideas, before moving on again.

When I wrote my first John Craine novel, *A Dance of Ghosts*, I imagined it as having a place somewhere within this shifting evolutionary process. In particular, I wanted to go back to some of the traditional basics of crime fiction, combining elements of the classic American crime novel with more recent innovations in method and style. In short, I wanted to write the kind of crime novel that I fell in love with when I was young, and that I'm still in love with now. The private detective novel, the outsider with the troubled soul, the loner who plays by his own rules. I didn't want my detective to *be* Philip Marlowe, or Travis McGee, or Matt Scudder, but I wanted him to come from the same evolutionary line. And, as such, he had to have that intense sense of place that's so vital to this kind of story. He had to have his Los Angeles, his Fort Lauderdale, his New York. And he had to belong to it. Which is why I chose the fictional town of Hey in the real county of Essex as his place. Because I lived in Essex for a long time, and I know it. I know the towns and cities, and their underbellies, and I know the people who live on the fringes. I know what goes on in a place like Hey, and I know it has everything a crime novel needs.

Another point about evolution is that it has no awareness of what it's doing or where it's going. It's a blind process, it has no target or final purpose, it just does what it does. And although I have some ideas as to where John Craine might be heading after *Until the Darkness Comes* (I'm writing the next book right now), I'm quite sure that his life and his stories to come will be shaped as much by me as by the same blind process that shapes us all, and I think that's only fitting.

Kevin Brooks
January 2012

A Dance of Ghosts

Kevin Brooks

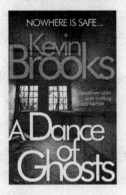

PI John Craine is struggling to cope with the weight of his past. Sixteen years ago his wife, Stacy, was brutally murdered. Craine found her body in their bed. And since then, to escape the pain and the unanswered questions, he has buried himself in work by day, and whisky by night.

But one phone call changes everything. The mother of missing young woman Anna Gerrish calls on his services, and Craine soon finds himself at the centre of a sinister web of corruption and lies that leads back into the murky waters of the past – and to the night that Craine has spent over a decade trying to forget. As he delves deeper and deeper into the case everything gets increasingly, terrifyingly, personal. And it's down to Craine to stop history from repeating itself.

arrow books

THE POWER OF READING

Visit the Random House website and get connected with information on all our books and authors

EXTRACTS from our recently published books and selected backlist titles

COMPETITIONS AND PRIZE DRAWS Win signed books, audiobooks and more

AUTHOR EVENTS Find out which of our authors are on tour and where you can meet them

LATEST NEWS on bestsellers, awards and new publications

MINISITES with exclusive special features dedicated to our authors and their titles

READING GROUPS Reading guides, special features and all the information you need for your reading group

LISTEN to extracts from the latest audiobook publications

WATCH video clips of interviews and readings with our authors

RANDOM HOUSE INFORMATION including advice for writers, job vacancies and all your general queries answered

Come home to Random House

www.randomhouse.co.uk